I0788163

NIKITA

THE DARK ANGEL CHRONICLES

INTERNATIONAL BESTSELLING AUTHOR

SERENIY RAYNE

AUTHOR NOTES

CONTENT WARNING

Content warnings are an important element to any novel. I don't ever want to harm a reader. So for this reason, I will list the warnings here.

- Primal hunting / chasing
- Biting and blood exchange
- Use of Thrall (mind control)
- Violence outside of harem
- Blood and gore
- Murder / Death
- Strong anti-patriarchy theme
- Real-life issues flipped to fit the world.

This is a paranormal why choose romance with poly elements. It's a journey of self-discovery and personal growth.

There are many situations included that are intended for MATURE audiences (18+)

Throughout this book, there are references/ instances that may trigger some individuals such as:

BDSM, thrall almost to the point of non-con, mate rejection, threats from outside of the harem, temporary death of a harem member, emotional damage, social issues in relation to wing color, aggression towards harem, death and torture, rough sex, biting, marking, mating, harem built through trials, unhealthy coping mechanisms, inability to produce offspring (male harem member), fangs, claws, and wings.

AUTHOR RAMBLINGS:

Dear Readers,

It's been a hell of a ride since I started back in 2019. As I continue on my author journey, it's been a path of growth and constant learning. I feel in the last year my craft has grown from the savage and aggressive in your face FMC's to the ones that have depth and problems like the rest of us. As silly as it sounds, I call them more realistic fantasy female main characters. I feel like my girls have become more relatable over time and their worlds are more immersive than before.

Since the fall, my life flipped upside down and a ten-year relationship / marriage ended. Along this journey, I found in my co-author probably one of the best friends I have had in a very long time. Cassandra and I spent a good part of last year working through personal problems and supporting each other through it all. No matter what our problems were, we could count on each other for the understanding and support we both needed.

No matter how daunting or dismal my day seemed, Cass, my Emotional Support Muppet was there with a comment, a meme or some song that struck a chord with us and our problems. There were dark days and then some even darker ones that made me question my life decisions. When those moments of doubt surfaced instead of reacting like I used to with rage and attacking what was hurting me. I went to my friend and talked through everything that was making me question myself. Much like Nikita goes to Aunt Sigrun or to Cyrus, Cass has become an integral part of my inner circle. I don't know what I would do without her.

I feel like Nikita is the fragment of myself I wish I can become. Much like me, she wallows in trust issues and has isolated herself from most of the world because of false perceptions that small-minded individuals have perpetuated. Like Nikita, we are loyal to a fault and will not allow an injustice to continue if it's within our power. If there's one thing I want people to take away from Nikita is that you are the only person who can limit you.

Last but not least, never let the terrorist, emotional or otherwise, win.

With love,

Serenity

READERS NOTES:

This is a continuation of the Dark Angel Chronicles, so previous characters mentioned in that four-book series will make appearances throughout the story. The characters of Aurora, Jayce, Klaus, Luna, Marco etc. come from the Aurora Marelup Saga as close family friends. You get to see one of the major interactions between Thana (Nikita's mother) and Aurora and her family in the bonus scene in the back of the Dark Angel Chronicles Omnibus. Neither series is required to be read to enjoy this book, it is suggested to read at least the Dark Angel Chronicles Omnibus.

This is a why choose romance with poly elements, meaning that everyone can love each other however feels right as long as all parties consent to it. This is a slow burn novel heavy on plot and major world building. There are at least two more books planned for this world that will happen, eventually.

If you find this book anywhere other than on a major retailers site, please email me at serenityrayneauthor@gmail.com with the link to the site.

Remember:

You control the narrative.

Those that seek to destroy you will eventually destroy themselves.

The true bullies in the world are the ones crowing the loudest, accusing others of what they themselves are doing.

Stay true to yourself.

Serenity Rayne

CHAPTER 1
NIKITA

The code green in the hospital didn't happen by accident. Something evil is lurking in the shadows, making the hair rise on the back of my neck. There's a second problem that's arising. I keep hearing a voice in my sleep. It's a male voice calling to me to save him and free him from his eternal torment.

"Sister, you seem deep in thought. Are you okay?" Damien asks as he rests a hand on my shoulder. He gives it a gentle squeeze, and I turn to face him.

"Yeah, this whole situation isn't sitting right with me. It's as if our response time is being tested." Staring out over the city skyline, I watch the sunset in the distance. The city lights slowly come to life as we watch day turn to night.

Damien comes to lean against the rail with his back facing the city so he can look at me. "Mom agrees that this is a setup. Dad and Gramps are also suspicious of how and why the bus was attacked." Damien unfurls his wings and flexes them several times, looking out across the cityscape.

A soft growl escapes my lips, thinking about how unfair the patriarchy is. The females have to hide their wings, yet the males who start all the fucking trouble can show theirs. Shaking my head, I head back towards the staircase and back into the hospital. Pissed off doesn't even describe how I'm feeling at the moment. The rage bubbles under the surface, and I feel as though my skin is crawling. As if something similar to my mother's beast is slithering under my flesh.

"Nikita?" My mom's voice stops me dead in my tracks, and I know she can feel the rage simmering under the surface.

"Yeah, mom?" She pulls me in for a hug, then pushes us into the darkness of one of the supply rooms nearby. The familiar whoosh of moving through the shadows comforts me. By the time we emerge, we're in dad's office in Club Dread. "I take it you wanted to talk away from everyone else?" Laughing, she finally gets a genuine smile out of me.

Mom touches her scrubs, and they turn into her black Reaper gown. "Yeah, the angelic side just doesn't get us. Don't get me wrong, I love my mates and children. But the angelic side does not know what we deal with." The bass thumps making my chest vibrate with every hit, distracting me for the moment. We exit dad's office and head out into the club. Mom knows that being around Dad and Gramps helps to settle my agitation.

Up on stage is my dad playing with his band. He's truly in his glory performing and part of me is jealous. I'm jealous of the freedom he has to do what he wants when he wants. Mom and I walk over to the bar, grab three Long Island iced teas, and head towards the stage. Dad's rock star mask drops briefly when he sees mom and me in the crowd. Waving the glass in the air, Dad steps forward and takes a long drink from the glass I offer him.

We stay up front and wait for dad to finish his set, then go to meet him backstage. Gramps is there waiting in the wings and hugs mom and me tightly. "What brings my two favorite girls here tonight?" Gramps holds me tightly to his side as Dad sweeps Mom off her feet and kisses her soundly.

One day I want a love like my mother and birth father have. Hell, her relationship with Christian and Gage is pretty awesome, too.

"Well Dad, the accident that happened tonight was no accident. To top it off, Nikita and I have been hearing whispers in the shadows." I look at Mom, shocked. I was unaware that she could hear the male, too. My eyebrows remain raised as I turn slowly to look at my present family.

Glancing up at my grandfather as he parses the information is interesting to watch. His eyes flicker to solid obsidian orbs, then slowly back to human brown. "The only thing I can think of is that perhaps I need to take the mantle of Death sooner than planned." He looks down at me and smiles.

"As true as that may be, I believe there are bigger fish to fry." I glance from my grandfather to my mother. "I will ascend sooner than later. But for now, we need to get a game plan together." Leaning back against the desk, I look between my elders and wait for their assessment.

Dad moves forward and wraps me in the tightest hug possible. He presses his lips to my temple, and I smile, hugging dad back just as tightly. "Daddy's little nightmare. You are my most precious creation; you are my life and love made flesh." He kisses my temple and sighs. "Your time is coming. Soon the invitation to the Mate Trials and then your ascension."

Pulling away from my father, I turn away as the rage bubbles deep in my chest. My wings burst free from my back as I turn to face my family with blackened eyes. "There is no power in Heaven or Hell that can make me go!" Engulfing myself in shadows, I leave the office only to manifest in the far corner of the club.

Fucking Mate Trials, why the actual fuck do stupid antiquated trials have to dictate the fate and paths of the females? Why do we have to hide our wings just cause the males can't control their dicks? There's a plethora of hot young men here tonight, and I need to find someone to scratch an itch. Someone to distract me from the impending doom of the trials that I know I cannot escape.

Focusing on my quarry, I make my move, heading towards the hot blonde I've set my sights on tonight. A whiskey sour manifests in my hand, and I offer it to the male and smile. "Hey, got ya a drink." He takes the offered drink and sips from it.

"Aren't you Cyrus's daughter?" The guy gets super stoked. His eyes light up and he's almost vibrating out of his skin.

"I am." Leaning against the wall, the male leans next to me.

"Wow! That's so cool..." He's a fan boy, my favorite kind of prey.

"It can be." A deep purr escapes my lips as I move to push him against the wall, my leg wedged between his.

We're about the same height, especially with me in heels. He's a dark Nephilim and could be easily controlled if I wished it. My eyes blacken, and I use my gift to compel him to be my willing blood bag for the evening. My gift will make him forget everything after I release him from my sway. I need to feed my dark gifts seem to be the most potent after I've fed. His eyes blacken to match mine and I know I have him. His hardened length presses against my hip as I hold him against the wall. My hands slide down his arms as I slide them over his head.

"Keep these here. Do not move them." My order slides like silk from between my lips and he obeys without question. No strings, no attachments. Just fuck'em and forget'em, then move on. It's how I've operated for the last five years. I don't have time for feelings. Though there's something below the surface, something I cannot put my finger on. No matter how good the sex is, no matter how long it lasts, it's never enough, nor does it feel right.

Leaning forward, I press my body flush against him, grinding myself against him, ready to move us to my place. The heat of his body ignites my desire, and I feel my gums ache. My lips press against his throat over his pulse. I feel his life force ebb and flow under my lips as his aura pulses and sings to me. I feel almost drunk, feeling the energy his life has. Just before I'm able to move us through the shadows, a large, warm hand on my shoulder stops me.

Turning my head slowly, I look over my shoulder, and who is standing there? Mother fucking Michael, the biggest wet blanket on the face of the planet. I swear he thinks he's my keeper.

"We should talk..." He tries to pull me from my prey, and I almost growl at him.

"About what!" I yell as I push away from the guy, breaking the thrall I have him under.

"What could an Archangel possibly find so interesting about me? I am going to ascend to the mantle of DEATH." My voice is hoarse from yelling, and thankfully my mom shows up and pulls Michael away. Oddly, he looks sad and hurt by what I said.

"Nikita!" My mother looks between us and shakes her head, actually looking disappointed in me.

As far as I know, I've always been my mother's favorite out of all her children, or at least I thought so. I'm not really sure about anything other than that every time I even get close to hooking up with somebody, Michael pops up out of nowhere and completely dashes any hopes of scratching the itch that's been building in my core for the last year and a half. The closer we come to the Mate Trials, the worse the urge to find whoever my mate is and ride that cock until I can't stand up is.

I stare at my mother and then look at the broken look on Michael's face, and it makes little sense to me. Why has he been following me around like a lost puppy dog for most of my life? As far as I understand, he is just an uncle or a close family friend who just has that creepy uncle vibe.

"Nikita, I think you owe Michael an apology," my mother says as she looks between the two of us.

Scoffing, I cross my arms under my chest and tilt my head to the side. "He's the one that keeps interrupting every time I try to hook up with somebody."

I look back and forth between them, and something is just not right. I can't parse out what little information I have in front of me because, honestly, I don't know what the fuck is going on at the moment. "Either somebody's gonna tell me what's happening, or I'm just gonna poof and go wherever the fuck I want, just to get away from everyone."

Staring between my mother and Michael, he steps forward, and a five-by-five card manifests between his index and thumb. Staring at the card, I feel horror deep in my chest. The dreaded invitation to the Mate Trials. This is the one thing I have been railing against for the last five years, and it will destroy my plans of flying around happily single for the next hundred years or so. Michael offers me the card, and the moment I take it, he vanishes in a ray of light.

Staring at the invitation itself, I see my name is on it with the cordial invitation to attend in two months. Locking my eyes on my mother, I feel nothing but anger. Then there's the disappointment at the fact that she's allowed this to happen. Anger at the fact that I'm being subjected to this ancient patriarchal subjugation of the female angels. "You know how I feel about this?" I say in a low tone to my mother.

"I do," she says and then shifts her fingernails to talons, then back again. "I also understand that before you could go any further with your Ascension, you need to harness the power of your mates. Whoever they may be." There's that flicker of chrome in Mom's eyes. I know she's hiding something from me. I know at that exact moment that she knows of at least one or two mates of mine, and she's hiding that information from me.

"Oh really now, let me guess," I say as I toss my hair to the side and look at my father and grandfather as they approach. "You already know who I'm going to be stuck with for the rest of eternity, don't you?" The growl is impossible to miss in my voice, and I watch my father and grandfather pale before me.

They know too. They're all in on it. How the Hell have I been this blind all this time to not see that they knew exactly who I was going to be saddled with? "So it is written, so it shall be done," is all I say is I throw my arms out to the side and vanish in a wisp of smoke.

CHAPTER 2
THANA

Where did I go wrong? It's the question I've been asking myself for the last several hours after watching Nikita's outburst with her dealing with Michael. I feel absolutely horrible that she's railing against everything as hard as she is. Part of it is because of my take no prisoners attitude all these years, and the other part is the fact that we gave her so much independence. She had so much power at such a young age that she never learned to temper what she had been given.

I know being saddled with an incredibly powerful mantle is nothing to scoff at. She is inheriting the mantle of death in less than six months. On top of the thought of going to the Mate Trials, it is probably more than she can handle. For me, watching Michael's heart break repeatedly over how his mate, my daughter, is handling things is killing me inside.

Raphael and the others assure me that things will change once she realizes who he is to her. But somewhere deep down, I don't think they're right. In the pit of my gut, it tells me that this is going to be one hell of a battle to get her to acknowledge the Archangel in her bond.

Now, I've already consulted all the oracles and every single piece of power I'm able to tap into to figure out who else is in her bond. I know Satan and Michael are both in her nest. We consider Satan more of an in-between entity. Not quite Dark Nephilim, not quite Light Nephilim; he's somewhere in the middle. He's kind of like a gray, mostly purified, but still with dark tendencies. The fact he's in the bond, I wouldn't say it's concerning, but it's different. A Prince of Hell, a fallen Archangel, is the mate to my daughter.

I still have a hard time dealing with that fact. Raphael and Christian are having the hardest time with it, and Metatron has pretty much just decided that it's an 'it is what it is' situation. How the hell he ended up the most Zen out of all of us is beyond me. But I'm thankful that he is.

Most nights lately, with Nikita's rebellion, I find myself more often bouncing between his and Raphael's bed. I'm trying to seek comfort from the light side of the bond because of all the ominous thoughts I keep having. I hope their angelic nature will wipe away all the darkness that keeps clouding my vision.

I can only hope for the best for my daughter, but in a way, I watch her struggle and fight against her dark nature. I don't honestly know what to do. In one sense, I don't want her to go to the Mate Trials and break Michael's heart further because I have a feeling there's a rejection on the horizon. But in the other sense, she needs to go through with this and, finally, be who she needs to be. Because whatever is coming, we need her at full strength. Luckily and unluckily for me, I have both daughters getting ready to go to the Mate Trials at the same time.

I also begged and pleaded with Metatron not to throw Seraphina in there, because, to be quite honest, I can't handle three of them going at once. It's bad enough they will divide my attention between my first two daughters. I don't need a third one thrown in there. This is the second Mate Trials for most of my sons, the third for Damien himself. Each time they come back, the two sons are named after my grandfather, Samuel, and Samael, who return, sad that they weren't chosen. But then you have Damien, who comes back, pours himself a pint, and kicks his feet back, celebrating that he's free again for another year.

It cracks me up how my sons take this differently. The lighter side of the bond is sad when they're not chosen. My Dark Nephilim sons could honestly care less. They're kind of happy about still keeping some semblance of freedom. I guess to be burdened with a mate of the light persuasion, it's a major drag for them.

There's a knocking at the door, and I look up to see Raphael still in his hot, professor, untouchable ways. He stands there looking there like a GQ model perfectly pressed. His muscular forearms ripple as he crosses his arms under his broad chest.

"What's got you in such a mood? You feel like a raging storm in my chest?" He walks over to me without hesitation, drops to his knees and parts my thighs, then wiggles himself in between to rest his head on my chest. Threading my fingers through his blonde hair. I start playing with its lengths, almost soothing myself by petting him.

"It's Nikita." And as soon as I say her name, he draws in a deep breath and lets it out slowly.

"Oh, is that all?" he says. And, to be perfectly honest, I'm sure it does not shock him that it is her vexing me. "What's wrong this time?"

I ponder his question, trying to figure out the best way to put it. "Michael gave her the invitation today."

He sits up suddenly, then back and rests on his heels. "Davina got hers four days ago. What took him so long?"

I can understand why he's questioning it. His own daughter was given hers before Nikita.

"I honestly think it is the fact that it's his mate." I'm not one hundred percent sure, but I believe that's the crux of the problem.

"I could definitely understand it, especially if she's as stubborn as you are." A forced laugh escapes Raphael's lips. It's not a joking matter, but I appreciate that he's trying to lighten the mood because of how dark the situation is.

"Yeah, but I fear what she's gonna do after she reveals her wings and sees who her mates are." Pinching the bridge of my nose, I squint my eyes closed tightly. The level of stress I'm under currently makes my chest hurt.

"Yeah, that's gonna be a Hell of a debacle, isn't it?" Raphael says just as Christian walks through the door.

"What did I miss?" he asks innocently.

"Nikita got her card today." Raphael puts it bluntly.

Christian pales at the news. "Oh, that's not good," is all he can say as he leans against the wall behind him, then stares between the two of us. "How did she take it?" He winces as he asks the question.

I finally release my nose and open my eyes, looking between the two of them. I know from my vision currently that my eyes are chrome. "She didn't take it very well, to be honest with you. I know she's going to rail against this one hundred percent, with no doubt." I fold my hands in my lap and stare at them for a moment.

"My biggest fear is that the minute she sees who's in her bond, she will take flight and disappear. Or she's just literally gonna disappear off the stage. Either option will not bode well." It's no secret within our family that we've been teaching all of our daughters to fly. But for them to fly in public, unlike every female before them that has not had the strength to lift themselves off the pedestal, could be detrimental to us.

"Granted, with two Archangels in my bond and one in Nikita's, we're more than likely safe. If we explain what was done, that it was the Valkyrie, and only the Valkyrie, that saw my daughter's wings during their training flights, we might not be in as much trouble as what could happen." Far too many things could go wrong in this picture to feel comfortable with it.

"I definitely understand what you're talking about. I've instructed my daughter not to take flight, no matter what happens. I forbid her from doing it," Christian says, looking down at his hands.

"Well, you and I both know there is no forbidding Nikita from doing anything. She does what she wants and is strong enough to get away with it," I say semi-sternly 'cause the only child we have strong enough to take on Nikita is her twin. Light cancels dark, so it would be an even match between them if they were to go at it head-to-head.

"As much as I was looking forward to this, I believe it may be more of a liability than a benefit at this point," Raphael says as he looks between Christian and me.

"Seraphina has some sway with Nikita. Do you want me to have her talk to her for us?" Metatron asks as he steps into the room and pulls me into a bone-crushing hug.

"If you think it will help, then please send her." I stare up into Metatron's eyes as they become golden orbs looking up toward the heavens.

"It's done. Why didn't you just ask her to do it?" The one question I had hoped he wouldn't ask.

Sighing, I rest my head on his chest and draw a fortifying breath. "Seraphina kinda blames me for her looking like Nikita. I'm not sure how that's my fault, but apparently, it is." Shrugging my shoulders, I look up at my big teddy bear.

He presses his lips to my forehead and stands there for several moments. I can tell he's pondering something. I just don't know what. "Seraphina wants to take the Hellcat out in exchange for talking to Nikita." Easy enough, if that's the only catch. I'm honestly in better shape than I thought previously.

Shortly after Metatron reaches out to Seraphina, she comes skipping into the room. Her hair, once almost perfectly white, is now a bubblegum pink. Arching a brow, I look at the change in her hair color, then up to her father, whose jaw has dropped in shock at what his daughter did.

Smiling, I can't help but let a soft giggle escape my lips. "And here we have the rebellion stage." I motion dramatically to my daughter, smiling.

Seraphina rolls her eyes and then sticks her hand out towards me. "I'll take the keys, mama."

Reluctantly, I dig in my pocket, pull out the keys to my Hellcat, and offer them to my daughter. "Don't worry, Mom. I'll take care of your favorite child." As she twirls the keys looking at me.

"Now, now I don't favor the car over you girls." That earns me a laugh from everyone with us.

Here Seraphina was trying to infer that it was Nikita, whereas the guys know it's the car. So to them, it was quite hysterical to hear me say something about the car regarding being the favorite child.

"Seriously, Mom, the car," Seraphina says, giving me that death glare that she's honestly perfecting.

"Well, would you rather I name one of your siblings? I mean, there's only ten of you." I stand there with my hands on my hips, leaning back against Metatron, who's trying not to laugh hysterically at our antics.

I watch Seraphina's eyes flicker between black and chrome, then a third color almost pops up. Which is kind of odd. When her eyes flicker back to black, I can almost swear that I see gold flecks burning in them. Staring, I move closer to my daughter and examine her eyes.

"Well, this is interesting," I say as I look between both of her eyes up close.

"Mom, you're freaking me out. What's going on?" Seraphina's voice wavers for several seconds, then steadies.

"I've never seen this, and there's nothing in my memory. Either for myself or my grandfather to tell me what this means."

"Mom, what are you talking about?" Seraphina grips my shoulders and gives me a light shake, trying to get the answer out of me.

"When you blacken your eyes, there are gold flecks in it. It's kind of cool, looks almost like a starburst." Arching a brow, Seraphina stares at me, completely puzzled.

"Like a starburst, really?" To dissuade her doubt, I grab my cell phone and snap a quick picture of her eye. I bring up the image and turn it around to face her. "That's weird."

"Not weird, sweetheart, unique," I say to her as I caress her cheek.

"Trust me when I say I think I have the freak angle and the family nailed down." I glance at my mates and then return my gaze to my daughter. "Well, you best be going. Try to catch your sister before she gets herself into anything, and let me know what you come up with." Seraphina nods as her eyes go back to normal.

"Don't worry. I'll be a good little spy and take care of business for you." Seraphina turns and leaves quickly. I just shake my head, looking at the boys.

"We said we wanted them strong and independent." Here we go. The fate of the known universe is now in Seraphina's hands. I'm kind of concerned about her sister going nuclear at the mate trials. Sending her in will hopefully solve all of our problems.

CHAPTER 3
NIKITA

THERE IS NO MISTAKING THE DEEP RUMBLE OF THE ENGINE OF MY mother's Hellcat coming down the road. I was dreading this, but it's quite unusual for Mom to drive here. Normally, she just manifests wherever she wants. Popping in, scaring the bejesus out of me. It's almost become a game between her and me, who can scare who the most in a week. Last week she was up on me by two. This week so far, I'm up by one. Live and learn, I guess.

I finish wiping the last coat of wax off of my Mustang and watch the nose of my mother's car round the corner. But the odd thing is, it's not Mom. From what I can sense, it's Seraphina, my almost doppelgänger. She parks the car and then exits. "Look what I've got for today."

I smile broadly and laugh. "Yeah? How did you get it from Mom? We all know how much our mother loves her damn car." Sometimes I swear she loves the car more than the rest of us. But that's a story for another day.

"Mom said that we should have a girl's day out."

"She did, did she?" Skeptically, I study my younger sister. The only concerning thing is Mom never lets that damn car out of her sight. Not once has she ever handed the keys over to Davina or me. Or any of my other brothers and sisters. Not once have any of us gotten to drive her car. It's quite puzzling. I stand here watching her for a few more minutes. I wonder what exactly my sister has promised Mom she would do.

"Well, yeah. She'd like for us to go and have a good day out. Sister time."

Tilting my head to the side, I drop the rag I was polishing my car with onto the ground. "Sister time? Do you honestly think I'll fall for that one? Mom's up to something," I say with a huff as I wave my hand past everything I used to wash and wax my car, and it manifests back where it belongs.

Seraphina looks down as she leans on the front fender of Mom's car. "She's worried about you."

I know the look that Seraphina is making. I know it all too well 'cause I see it on Mom's face periodically. It's usually when she feels like she's let someone down or is about to let someone down. Having the mantle of Destroyer has made it difficult for her to spend the amount of quality time she wants with each of us as we grew up so rapidly.

Unfortunately, because of our lineages, our growth rate was far more sped up than your standard Nephilim, but not as sped up as an Angel. Either way, we grew up a lot faster than she had hoped.

"What's eating you, Seraphina? You can tell me." She looks up at me, and her eyes are black with gold flecks. I can't help but do a double-take before moving close to inspect her eyes more.

"Does anyone know what this means?" I caress her cheeks, turning her head from side to side, looking deep into her eyes.

"They don't. Dad's gonna go see if any of the Angelic archives have any kind of explanation for it." She laughs, then smiles, looking up at me.

"I guess you're not the only one with the freak factor on ten. And that means Mom is not alone. Even more 'cause now it's you and me." Seraphina tries to lighten the mood, but I can tell just by the waver in her voice that everything is bothering her.

Stepping forward, I wrap my sister in my arms and hold her, crushing her to me. In a blink of an eye, I move her through the shadows. Quickly I extend my wings, unfurling them for the first time today, then wrap my younger sister up in them and croon to her. I moved the shadows in a pulsating manner around us. It sets our darkness at ease, being surrounded by the darkness.

"What's eating you, little one?" I say as I press my lips to her temple.

"Mom's afraid that if you end up with angelic mates at the Mate Trials, you're gonna up and vanish on us." The way Seraphina says it, I can tell it's also a worry and a concern for her.

I hug my sister tighter and rest my head against hers. "I promise I won't vanish." I kiss her temple again and stand there thinking about the implications of everything coming.

"Me, with angelic mates. Whose fucking bright idea was that?" I laugh, and Seraphina looks up at me.

"What's so funny? I thought this was something that you didn't wanna do." She tightens her grip around my waist, holding on to me, still clinging.

"You're right. This isn't something I want to do. I don't wanna go. But even after talking with Grandfather, it's for the best. If I'm supposed to take over the mantle of Death and Davina the mantle of Speaker, we need to build our nest." The fact of the matter is, as much as I rail against it, I need to do it. I have to do it because it's not just my life at stake. It's the fate of the known universe.

Grandfather is losing his powers because he's been doing the same job for so long. The minute I was born, the darkness aligned itself with me instead of him, fueling me instead of rejuvenating him. Every time he reaps a soul, he gets a little weaker. It's why Father, Mother, myself, and a couple of my other siblings have taken over doing his job for him.

"Aren't you scared?" Seraphina asks as she looks up at me.

I shake my head as I pull back, folding my wings to hang half open behind me. "There's nothing to be afraid of." I smile and relax a little more.

I look down at my right arm at the full-sleeve tattoo of the dragon Rex. "What does Mom's favorite movie say? Fear is the mind-killer." Seraphina laughs at the pop culture reference.

I can't tell you how many times the family has gathered around and watched the original Dune. Mom, of course, being the litera-ture buff she is, has one of the original publications and made us take turns reading it before we watched the movie. I miss those movie nights now that I think about it. "Let's go have a great day at Mom's expense," I say, smiling broadly at my sister as I draw my wings back into my body.

"Let's face it. If you're gonna be dumb, it's gonna be expensive." I head back to my Mustang, and Seraphina stares at me, tilting her head to the side, puzzled.

"What are you doing? I thought we were taking Mom's car." She motions back to the Hellcat. I laugh again. "Oh yeah, we're taking Mom's car straight to the racetrack." Seraphina's eyes flare wide open, staring at me and disbelief that I would take our mother's car to go race.

"Come on, sis, last one to the track buys dinner." With a wicked gleam in my eye, I jump into the driver's seat and fire up my Mustang. This new version of the 500 model is fast as anything. The predator motor they put inside is a work of art. The amount of ponies that go straight to the wheels. Almost 800 horse at my fingertips, and they wonder why I love driving everywhere. The car is black on black, and its sleek lines are sexier than the hottest male fitness model on this planet. I'd rather have a hundred of these GT500s than worry about trying to figure out where my mates are at all times.

Seraphina is off like a light before I even get the key in the ignition. Baby sister's learned, hasn't she? I fire up black sunshine and put the pedal to the floor, banging through the gears as one of Mom's favorite songs comes on. Sister Day begins with a friendly drag race. Wow, Mom's gonna be so proud.

We race through the local streets, zigging and zagging in and out of traffic to get to our destination. Baby sis forgot my GT500 has just shy of eight hundred horse while the Hellcat she's driving, even with all of Mom's modifications, only comes in around five hundred. Poor baby doesn't know what's gonna hit her. We arrive at the track, and the crowd goes wild, seeing Mom's car and thinking she will be racing tonight. It will surprise them when my little goody two-shoes sister emerges.

They've seen me and my GT500 here before. They know all too well what black sunshine can do on the track and how quickly we could tear things up. The announcer silences the crowd, and since I had already called ahead, he's well aware of the sisterly grudge match that's about to go on.

"Ladies and gentlemen, we have a rare treat tonight. Not only do we have the Destroyer's Harlot here on the track. But we also have Nikita's Black Sunshine. Though it may disappoint you, it's not the Destroyer driving tonight." The crowd boos and hisses, disappointed that Mom has not come out of retirement.

Seraphina and I pull up to the line, shut off our engines, and step out to wave at the crowd. The crowd goes wild, seeing the two of us standing there. And it isn't until Satan walks up to me to let me know he's working the tree tonight that I realize he's actually kind of cute. He's kind of got that swagger like Dad has that makes Mom swoon. But he's rather quiet, like Metatron. You never know what the man's thinking.

He orders us both to get back into our cars and inches us both up to be even at the line. The announcer sits there and announces what type of cars we're driving, what modifications have been done, and all that fun jazz because the crowd eats it up with a spoon.

Once we're lined up, Satan opens his wings and raises them high. They're an interesting mottled color. Some white and some black feathers spread throughout. There's still that black streak underneath the feathers closest to his body. The tops of his wings are as black as pitch, like mine. His primary flight feathers are also black. But they sprinkled the rest of the feathers with white.

Mom attempted to cleanse him completely to allow him to ascend, but his ascension only went so far. He wouldn't burn going into Heaven, but he's also not welcome. They have put a thousand years of penance before him. All because he was part of the coop that Lucifer had thrown. It was so bad that his personality split in half, dividing him between Satan and Lucifer. Apparently, Satan must have gotten more of the light left in him than Lucifer, who died at Mother's hands.

Revving the engine, I listen to my baby purr. She's just as thirsty for this race as I am. The minute Satan drops his wings, my foot mashes the gas pedal and I bang through gears. The song *'Die for Me'* plays in the background. All I hear is the roar of my engine.

Baby sis keeps up for a little while. I guess moms got nitrous in that thing. But as soon as I hit fifth gear, we are gone. All I see is baby sis in my rearview. The lights flash at the end of the quarter mile, and I'm declared the winner. It's not like it was really a fair race to begin with, but baby sis sometimes needs to be taught important lessons like this. Turning back around, heading back down the track, I lower my windows and wave at the crowd.

When I'm able to get into the back, away from everyone in the alley, I walk over and give my baby sister a big hug. She did her job tonight. She got me to realize the value of everything that's being done. Even though I don't like the idea of being forced to submit myself to this outdated patriarchal practice. Unfortunately, it's a necessary evil. If I wish to go forward, I must go through with the Mate Trials.

CHAPTER 4
NIKITA

~Two months later, June~

It is the day that I've been dreading. Mom, Dad, and Raphael are all running around like chickens with their heads cut off, trying to get Davina and me both ready for this debacle tonight. My sister, unlike myself, is excited, and she's looking forward to being up on that pedestal on display for all those heathens. Myself, I honestly don't give a fuck. I really don't want to go, and I've tried to find every way possible to get out of it.

Sadly, because Raphael is a healer, he knows all too well that there's absolutely nothing wrong with me. "Come on, Nikita, we gotta get going." My father says as he comes over and runs his hands down my bare arms.

"You look stunning in that blood-red gown." Rolling my eyes, I look at him like *well, that's because you bought it, and that's why you love it.*

"You know how much I hate wearing dresses?" I say to him through gritted teeth as I pull on the fabric that's on me. It feels like a death sentence, like a noose around my body instead of my neck.

"See, it's not that bad, Nikita. Come on, things could be a Hell of a lot worse." I raise an eyebrow at my dad as I look around.

Then there's Raphael, fawning over his perfect daughter. "As a male, you have a one in one hundred chance of possibly being chosen. As a female, you're guaranteed to be chosen whether or not you want to be." I throw the statistics in my father's face, and he nods solemnly along with me.

"Yeah, you guys do kind of get screwed, don't you?" He shrugs, hoping Mom didn't catch what he said.

"So who is it gonna be? You or Mom walking me up to the platform." I look between both of my parents. Arching a brow, I study both of them, waiting for a reply.

Dad just shakes his head no. "It's gotta be an Archangel." A low growl escapes my lips as I bare my elongated canines. I shiver with disdain because everybody is going to see me get walked up there. More than likely by somebody I don't want to have anywhere near me.

Next thing I know, large hands are covering my eyes. It can only be one person. "Little one, I'm the one that's escorting you up there. We know how much you hate other people," Metatron says, trying to sound friendly.

Turning, I force a smile as I look up at him. "I appreciate that." I look back at my mother as she pins the last curls in place for Davina, suddenly quite nauseous from the cuteness overload.

"Your sister is going first, and her father has decided to walk her up there himself," he says loudly, and I twirl my finger in the air as if I'm impressed by Raphael getting off his ass to walk with his daughter giving her away to the throngs of males. Bullshit like this makes my blood boil. Stupid angels and their rules.

"Come on, we're flying there as a family. Let's get going," Mom says as she spreads her wings wide. Rolling my eyes yet again, I choose darkness. Now with that being said, I vanish from Metatron's grip only to manifest by the tent at the back of the Mate Trials. *This is absolutely the last place I wanna be today. There is no way I want to be here at all,* I say to myself as I pace.

Aunt Jocelyn comes out of the tent and scoops me up into an enormous hug. "I know how you're feeling. It's not as bad as they make it out to be. Trust me," she says, flaring her eyes open and smiling.

"Easy for you to say. You wanted to be here. I don't." She nods her understanding and breathes in a slow, deep breath.

"I hope it won't be that bad for you," Joycelyn says as the joy she radiated earlier fades. "In the meantime, let me adjust your hair a bit and fix your makeup."

Nodding reluctantly, I allow her to fuss over me. It honestly helps me to calm down. I still don't want to take part in this farce.

Eventually, Mom and Davina make it to the tent while I drink my bourbon in the corner. Aunt Joycelyn squeals, seeing our perfect little angel arrive. Gag me with a fucking spoon. Princess Perfect is on deck.

Rolling my eyes, I touch Rex and have him manifest as a cat-sized dragon. Leaning my chair back on its back two legs, I rest Rex on my chest and pet him. Staring down at the dragon soothes me. I'm distracted to the point I don't notice Aunt Sigrun enter the tent to sit beside me.

"Nikita?" she whispers as she nudges my shoulder.

Cracking a smile, I turn to face her. "Hey, I'm glad you could make it." Forcing a laugh, I motion to my perfect sister, who has just arrived in the tent. "Must be nice to be the golden child. All the beauty and perfection in one body." I kiss Rex on the nose and he becomes the tattoo on my body again.

Sigrun leans forward and kisses my forehead. "You are the golden child. You are the closest anyone is to being a Fallen Angel without actually having to fall." She reaches up and into my hair and puts a single braid along my left temple.

"Yeah, I'm sure it quite thrilled the rest of Mom's mates having a borderline Fallen Angel as their child." There's a slight growl to my voice as the words leave my lips.

Aunt Sigrun laughs as she finishes up my braid, pulls one bead from her hair, and puts it at the end of my braid. "Well, you know what I say to that, right?"

She arches a brow, and a wicked smile crosses her lips. I lean forward and press my forehead to hers. "Fuck'em if they can't take a joke." We say in harmony and start laughing.

It's about this time that Dad and Gage make it into the tent and come and sit beside Sigrun and me. "Now, here's my favorite nightmare. I know if you had your choice, you would not be going through this debacle. But unfortunately, every female gets subjected to it at some point in their life."

Rolling my eyes, I chance a glance over at Gage, and he's nodding along with my father. "Yeah, I get it, but still, I wish we had some sort of choice in this matter. It's not like the females can say: Nope, not today, Satan."

Saying it how I did, Raphael looks up and over Davina at me. "I do not know where the humans got that phrase from. It's really inappropriate." Rolling my eyes, I stand up and roll my shoulders slightly.

"If you think about it, though. You say it to him almost daily. Anytime he asks you if there's something he can do to get out of work early. You say not today, Satan, not today. Pretty much easily predicted that no matter what he asks for, your answer is always not today." So, huffing out a laugh, I lean against my father's shoulder, staring at Raphael.

"So basically, the origin of the saying, not today, Satan came from you." I stare at him, my eyes blackening immediately. The Archangels seriously have no clue how much damage their mistreatment of anybody other than their own kind really does. In all seriousness, he does not know what the rest of us deal with.

He does not know that when I go to the Mate Ball with whoever gets stuck with me, or I get stuck with, we're gonna be stared at. We're gonna be laughed at and I'm possibly going into a rage. Mother's trying to stifle a laugh listening to the conversation between Raphael and Davina, and is getting ready to interject, but Metatron stops her before she even opens her mouth.

Today is not the day to try me, nor is it the day to test my patience. Because I've had enough of everything that's going on already, and we haven't even begun. Gabriel comes to the door and lifts the flap, motioning for Davina to follow him. Out of curiosity, I follow my sister out the door with Sigrun linked arm and arm with me. We watch him as they lead her off towards the stairs leading up to the pedestal. With each step she takes, I hear the death march that they always play at human funerals in my head.

Maybe it's just me being comical. Maybe it's because it's my personal dread of being transposed upon my sister. But either way you look at it, this will not end well. She will probably end up with a bazillion mates and not know which end is up anymore. She'll be pregnant within like five seconds of leaving this place and have like ten thousand babies within a month.

I know realistically it's not possible, but I mean, she is the perfect child, and everything always happens to her. As soon as she even attempts it, I wouldn't put it past her to pop out every grand-baby that mom's ever wanted in her entire life within the first five days of her being mated.

Dad must have picked up on my train of thought and just shakes his head. The way everybody is looking at each other, I think they already know who each of us is getting. It's gotta be a parent thing here. That or they all just have this meeting, and because Mom's the Destroyer, she can see who's bonded to who before they even know it. *I just really, really fucking hope that it's somebody actually worth my time and not gonna sit there and piss me off to no end.*

As my internal monologue keeps going off, my sister ascends the stairs, acting like a bride on her wedding day. I'm so over this shit already. I pace, and Raphael puts the blindfold on my sister when she gets to the top of the stairs. She spreads her perfect white opalescent wings as wide as they can go. I can't help but sigh and possibly growl slightly over the theatrics of all this crap. And then there's the shocker of all shockers. Sandalphon is one of her mates, and then Zadkiel, the Archangel that Mother rescued, is the other one.

I'm still sitting over here waiting for the other shoe to drop and see if there's a third mate that pops up out of nowhere, yet none comes. "I thought there's supposed to be a Dark Nephilim in each bond?"

Raphael somehow got out of walking his daughter up the ramp, and he's just sitting there staring at me. Then he blinks his eyes. "Well, I thought so, but apparently not this time."

"Oh, must be nice to be the exception." I know my tone's venomous, and he really doesn't deserve it from me, but I'm just so over this crap.

I know I keep saying it like a bazillion times, but I'm not gonna be done until I walk up there, have absolutely zero mates, and get to go home happy. But something in the pit of my stomach keeps telling me there's no way that can possibly happen. For me to ascend to the mantle of Death Eternal, I have to have at least one mate. So, unfortunately, I get at least one jerk to go home with. Hopefully, he's not a jerk, but if I get one of these light bastards, I swear I'm gonna scream.

Eventually, my sister comes back over with both of her mates, and she's all happy, and everybody is hugging and celebrating already. There are at least three other females to go before me, and I watch one by one that different Archangels and other regular angels are picked. I'm kind of hoping we run out of angels or people for tonight, and I get to go home and skip this whole thing tonight. But that is not my luck.

"Two more, then it's us, baby girl," Metatron says, smiling, still patting his brother on the back, celebrating that Davina has ended up with two Archangels.

Whoop Dee Doo. Isn't she special?

CHAPTER 5
NIKITA

I watch my overly jovial sister with her two perfect mates, hand in hand, and it makes me want to vomit. They make it to the bottom of the stairs. Then she smiles, bats her eyes, and climbs into their arms, and they take flight, heading off to who knows where.

"Come on, kiddo," Metatron says as he places his hand under my elbow and leads me towards the stairs.

"Interesting thing that's happening this year," he says as he motions towards the throng of males there.

"There are demons present. They're allowed to take part this year. Demons, Fallen, all the dark ones are present, and it's all because of you. It's an interesting turn of events, don't you think?" he whispers.

For once, I become very interested in what's happening. "They actually allowed the dark ones here?" I look excitedly at Metatron and then towards the marble stairs to my doom.

"Seeing that your mom's now the Destroyer, she's the one who said it would be fair for everyone to have a mate."

I nod my head along. It's probably one of the better things my mom's pulled off since she's taken that mantle.

I'm actually not concerned about going up the stairs now. They'll probably give me one of those light pains in the asses at some point, just to keep me in check. But the possibility of having a mate that's like I am? Now that's interesting. I walk up the stairs and hold on to Metatron, allowing my blood-red gown to flow behind me. I can't wait to be allowed to fly. I can't wait to have the freedom to do whatever I want whenever I want.

As for Grandfather's mantle, it's probably the most exciting part of this entire debacle. Becoming Death Eternal sounds like a most excellent adventure instead of the bogus journey I'm on. We reach the top of the platform, and I stand there looking out over everyone gathered. Angels, Archangels, and Dark Nephilim, as well as Fallen and demons, are all present. Oh, how times have changed. I guess they allowed the dark ones and the Fallen to come because of me. They know someone of my lineages cannot deal well with just having a Dark Nephilim in my nest. They knew somebody darker would have to be there. My little black heart swells with pride and happiness.

As I stand at the edge of the podium, looking down and over the throngs of males, I finally feel okay with this whole shenanigan. I walk back over to Metatron and turn around to face the crowd. "Do it," I say to him as he pulls out the blood-red blindfold that was picked out for me to match my dress.

As he covers my eyes, a sense of peace washes over me. Let's face it. I am the darkness and to be pushed into the darkness is nothing short of comforting. I stand here waiting for him to tell me to unfurl my wings. When the command comes. I spread my wings wide, unfurling them for the world to see. I allow the darkness to seep through every pore as I stand there, waiting.

Several moments pass, and I feel the rush of wind as if wings are beating around me. The first scent that invades my senses catches me off guard, and my heart fills with dread. I know that cologne. I know exactly who is on the pedestal with me. The wind shifts, and a second familiar scent comes to me. My heart clenches a little tighter, filled with the knowledge of who mate number two is.

The third scent that blows me is pure sulfur, brimstone, and blood. The sweet copper tang on the air tells me this is a creature of pure darkness. One that would almost rival my own.

 "You have three mates. I know one will be quite shocking to you. Maybe not as shocking as mate number two, but it may rank right up there. And the third, I would consider a dark horse in this race, one that, even with my infinite vision, I never saw coming," Metatron whispers as he reaches up and unties my blindfold.

I open my eyes, and all three males are before me. I just broke the most sacred covenant of all. I did not allow the Archangel to choose the first mate for me. Turning slowly, I look all three males directly in the eyes. Satan and the legendary Mordoc, the first ever recorded turned vampire in history. The Prince of Darkness himself. The first of the species, Hominis nocturnae. Seeing him in the bond makes my heart race a little faster. It's exciting for me that somebody will get me 100%. Someone whose darkness rivals my own.

And then there's Satan; he's lived on both sides of the line. Satan has been in the darkness, and he's been in the light. He also will understand me and all of my many facets. Last, there's Michael, who's played the part of uncle and friend over the last few years. I nod slowly, looking between the three of them, then back over to Metatron.

"I know because of you being an Archangel, you would more than likely choose Michael as my first mate." He nods soundly. "I hate to disappoint you." I stare directly at Michael and then turn my gaze to Satan. He makes the most sense to be the first mate. Having been both Archangel and Fallen, he will understand everything more than Michael ever could.

Michael's been there since close to when I took my first breath and now he is my mate. It's kind of still a little on the creepy side. I mean, he is gorgeous. He's powerful, and I'm pretty sure if Davina knew, she would be jealous. My eyes drift over to Mordoc, and I stare at his leather wings. They look like they should be attached to a dragon. It's appealing, black and blood red; the bone is evident in his wings with the thin, blood-red leather between them. Amazingly, the membrane itself is strong enough to hold him in the air when he takes flight.

"Nikita, you need to choose a first mate." Metatron reminds me again.

"I choose Satan. Because, for once, nobody is going to say not today Satan ever again." My eyes blaze to life and blacken immediately. Quickly, I close the distance between Satan and me and press my lips firmly to his. Reveling in the feel of his kiss, he tastes of sin and sweetness. It's an odd flavor combination but one worth having. We break away, and I look at the other two.

"We need to choose a nest. I obviously can't go back to my mother's."

Mordoc shrugs. "I have nothing up here."

Michael looks at me. "We can go to my condo."

And then Satan offers he still has possession of my father's apartment. Logically, Michael's house would have the most room. So I look at Michael. "We will use your home for tonight. But tomorrow, we will go look for a proper home for the four of us."

He agrees and then offers me his hand. "Let us help you fly." He winks at me and then I remember. I'm not supposed to use my wings. At least not yet, and that infuriates me. I allow Michael to pick me up, and I put my wings away. He leaps into the air, and we take flight, heading towards his home.

Once we are out of the line of sight of the Mate Trials, I disappear in a wisp of shadows, only to reemerge flying beside my mates. My black wings carry me through the air. Satan looks shocked, unaware that they have trained me all these years on how to fly just so I wouldn't be defenseless. Michael is kind enough to catch him and Mordoc up on the last seven years of my life. We eventually arrive at Michael's condo, and he lets us in. It's sparse and plain and extremely boring. There are going to be a lot of changes coming real soon.

Michael clears his throat and prepares to give us the grand tour around the inside of his condo. Honestly, I'd rather go home, but now that I have mates, that's impossible. I'm kind of stuck with where we're at currently. I'm trying not to be a royal bitch about this whole thing.

This is obviously a bachelor pad, and he was not prepared at all for any type of female to live here with him. I kinda wanna get mad. With as sheepish as he's acting and as much as Satan is trying to console him, I'm going to be more patient with this entire situation.

If my guess is right, he knew he had a mate all this time. Many times over the years, he's seen my wings and just said nothing to me. He kept telling me that someday I may get lucky and find my mate, yet he was there the entire time. The whole thing hurts as much as it aggravates me. I'm not sure if my emotions are more mixed up that he's in my nest or that he hid he was part of my nest and just didn't tell me for the last seven years.

Yeah, and then there's my sister. She's off living the good life. Oddly enough, with our uncle. I don't know how I feel about that one. I guess I got the better end of this. At least I'm not mated to our uncle. But in the other sense, if you think about it, Michael's been almost like another father, another caretaker all this time. *Oh dear God, do I have Daddy issues now?* This isn't good. I don't know how I'm gonna process all this without ending up with some sort of childhood trauma emerging.

The way the guys stop and look at me, I can tell they know something's going on in my head. "Okay, okay, okay, stop. I'll give."

They look at me, shocked, then tilt their heads to the side. I mean, seriously, are all three guys programmed exactly the same? A frustrated growl escapes my lips as I stare back at the three of them. I don't know what's more aggravating at this point, that they all seem to be cut from the same cloth or that now I get to wrangle three of them. I feel like I should be a zookeeper instead of their mate. The only possible bonus is I know Satan's preferences. The vampire God I am apparently mated to is not very picky, either. So the only stick in the mud in this house is Michael. *Oh, the fun we're gonna have with him.* I can only imagine the amount of stress, strain and upset he's gonna deal with when he walks in on Satan and my other mate going at it in the middle of the night. I can only imagine him walking in on the three of us, sharing an intimate moment. What is it gonna do to his sensitive sensibilities? I can only imagine what it will do to him the night I try to drag him in with the other two.

CHAPTER 6

MICHAEL

My heart breaks into a thousand pieces as I watch my mate open her eyes prematurely and look at the three of us. The abject horror on her face when she sees it's me in her bond, speaks volumes that don't need to be uttered out of her lips. I feel like I'm going to die watching how she stares at me. The tightness in my chest is stealing the breath from my lungs. If this is how dying feels, I pray, it ends quickly because I'm absolutely miserable. It's not the happy fondness of days gone by when we all used to just hang out. Literally, blow things up with the powers that we were given. Back when she was little the days were fun and short and carefree. Back when she looked up at me and ran to me, hugging me and loving me simply for me.

It's been Hell on me for the last seven, almost eight years, watching her grow and not being able to tell her she's mine. Just when I thought this was my time to shine and feel the love I had yearned for all these years... I don't know what I'm going to do now that I see that Satan, my once brother, is in the bond. And Mordoc, the first turned vampire ever recorded in history, is also here.

There's a supreme itching under my skin as I wait to see what she does. I already know what she's going to do. She's probably gonna claim Satan because he's the easiest one between the three of us. The biggest thing that points to him as the one she will claim is he's not me.

Mordoc is an unknown, and I've been literally seen as a family member since the day she was born. I don't know what I'm honestly gonna do at this point. I know I've been trying to protect her and keep her from making poor choices all these years. But I think that's driven a wedge between us, and any chance of having a relationship romantically has been flushed down the proverbial toilet.

My heart soars when Nikita climbs into my arms at the Mate Trials, allowing me to carry her for our first flight back to my apartment. I think we have finally broken through the barrier, and everything is going to be great. Then she disappears, exposing to the other mates in the bond that she can fly. Technically, this should not have happened. She should not have allowed herself to become that visible and vulnerable to the other two. But there are no secrets in the bond; there're no secrets between mates. For her to keep that secret from everybody would be beyond twelve ways of wrong.

We fly back to my apartment, and I feel naked before her. I've never once brought anybody back here, not even her father. Or not even my best friend, Raphael. Nobody has ever seen my apartment. Because as far as everybody knew, I only stayed in the Angelic Realm. But ever since Nikita was born, I've been here, staying close. Just in case anything happened, I could be there quicker. The hospital is only three blocks away. So that, by itself, should be a valid reason to have this condo.

I can see the turmoil on Nikita's face as she looks between the three of us and around the interior of my apartment. My imagination is running wild over what's going through her mind at this point. I know that I'm a major shocker, and it must be confusing as all Hell to her. When she tells us all to stop and wait, we freeze. It's terrifying the amount of power and control she already has over us, and it's all just because we saw her wings.

I mean, to be perfectly honest, she's had me wrapped around her little finger since the moment she was born, but that's a whole different subject altogether. I've always loved her, and my love has changed and grown over the last seven years. It went from protector and guardian to eventually seeing her as the woman she is. The gears shifted, and I started falling in love with her emotional and mental strength, intelligence, and sitting there and looking at everything as a battlefield and moving the chess pieces accordingly.

The warrior within me is pleased, but the man in me worries that my mate is going to get hurt one of these times when she goes to war. It's a battle that's gonna rage inside me from now until the end of time, but that's my cross to bear, not hers. We still wait on bated breath for her to decide to say whatever's on her mind. She takes several moments of walking around the interior of my condo before she stops and stands in front of us.

"I honestly haven't decided which of the three of you is going to be the first mate. I mean, by all rights and traditions, it should be Michael. But no offense," and she wins by saying it. "I'm still getting over the fact that you have been in my life since the moment I was born."

Nodding solemnly, I knew that was the crux of her problem with me. I bow my head low and submit to the fact that I'm not probably going to be the first mate. I hear her sigh softly, and her wings that were held up so proudly behind her slowly lowers. She's feeling the effects of the tether of the mate bond.

"I'm sorry, Michael," she says reluctantly, kicking at a fuzzy that somehow ended up on my floor.

"This is really tough for me." She looks between the three of us, then motions to the island in my kitchen and has us all sit down.

We quickly obey the wave of her hand and wait for her to continue. She opens up my fridge, reaches in there, and grabs out the bottles of juice I have in there. She grabs three glasses from my cupboard and pours the drinks, offering one to myself and Satan and one for herself. She looks at Mordoc and sees how his face is scrunched up in disgust, looking at the juice. She gives a single wink, and her wings hum. After several moments, she smiles and then pushes her hand out to her side, opening the small portal. *I did not know she could do that.* Through the portal, a minor demon walks through carrying a pitcher of sanguine fluid and offers it up to Nikita.

"Death," the demon says. Its voice is hollow and deep, making the hairs on the back of my neck stand up. "As requested, anything else, your Highness?" the demon says with a flourishing bow before backing away.

"No, that'll be all." As soon as the words are uttered, the demon backs through the portal, and Nikita closes it immediately.

She extends her hand, and the glass put in front of Mordoc slides to her, and she pours the scarlet fluid into it and offers it back to him. "I hope it's suitable for you. It's all that they really had right now."

A brilliant smile crosses the vampire's lips, and he lowers his head to her in deference. "You are an excellent mate, Nikita. I am blessed."

Nikita makes a disgusted sound. "Please don't say blessed. I've been shunned and mistreated since the moment anyone knew I was more darkness than light. Not by my family, of course; it's other mortals." Her voice has disdain and disgust, and I know this plight all too well.

We've been dealing with it ever since her mother came of age and had her turn at the Mate Trials. More and more dissension between the Light and Dark Nephilim has been happening since we discovered exactly how bad the interspecies problems were. It's not that the Archangels were blind to it, we would just hope that would pass, and it was just a person-to-person issue, not a white wings, black wings issue. *But apparently, we were wrong.*

Nikita stops, pours a bit of the sanguine fluid into her cranberry juice, and sips at it. "All right, guys, I know the Mated Ball is coming up in less than five weeks. Talk amongst yourselves, figure out who is gonna be the head mate, and we'll let it ride from there. I know in theory that to balance out the house's power, it should be Michael."

Satan and Mordoc nod, agreeing with her. Her jaw drops, shocked that the two darker mates actually agree with that stance.

"It's the way it's always been done," Satan says as he looks between me and Mordoc.

Mordoc laughs. "I don't want the responsibility of it. You want me to kill someone? Not a problem. You want me to raze a city, not a problem. Wrangle this circus not happening." He says, still laughing.

And there we have it. They have decided it. I'm going to be first mate. I don't even know the first thing about claiming a female. Let alone how to wrangle two Dark Nephilim. Well, technically, one Dark Nephilim and a demon in the nest. This is going to be crazy. I can only hope that Nikita's got a plan for all this.

She looks back at me and smiles. "I guess we're going to dinner then tomorrow night."

"Dinner?"

"Yes, dinner." She says with a force that shakes things in the interior of my house. Several cups fall from the shelf and a plate I don't remember buying also falls.

"I know you only as a guardian, Michael. I don't know you as the man, and if you expect to get any of my milkshake, well, you better start acting like the boyfriend or husband that you should be and not the babysitter you've always been," Nikita says before vanishing from behind the counter.

Who knows where that crazy girl of mine's gone? But I'm pretty sure it's gonna be an interesting night. Assuming the role of first mate, I decide to divvy out the rooms in my house to the other two guys. Bidding the others goodnight, I turn on my heel, head to my bedroom to shower, and hopefully sleep. I don't know if Nikita is returning here tonight. At least I know my place has been assured. The biggest hurdle is getting over how things have been done for the last seven years. At least it's a step in the right direction.

CHAPTER 7

NIKITA

I call my father's cell phone once I vanish from Michael's condo and head straight over to his club. I'm at a loss for what I should do right now. Part of me is haunted and tormented by the thought that the man that has always been there, the guardian I kind of looked up to, is now my mate. Definitely a kick in my crotch to think that I need to look at him differently than I have for the last seven years. *I mean, he is handsome, I'll give him that, and he's strong. Another bonus?*

But when I need him to follow me into the darkness, he's not able to. I get to do that alone. Well, not really alone, I can bring Satan and Mordoc with me, but that means I leave a mate behind. I completely understand where my mother was when she had to go to war in the rings. It makes sense now the stress, strain, and torments she dealt with because I can't think about leaving Michael behind.

Fuck, when the Hell did I start thinking of him like that? Damn this bond nonsense. I feel like I have a shackle around my throat with a heavy anchor hanging from the chain around my neck, stopping me almost to the point of clipping my wings. It's not how it's supposed to be, but it's how it feels to me. I've been free to do whatever I want for the last seven and a half years, and now I have to answer to three males. My life has officially gone to shit.

I feel the vibration in the shadows the moment my father manifests near me on the roof of his club. "How's my baby girl doing?" My father rushes over to me, and I immediately dive into his open arms.

I wrap my wings around his shoulders, and then he encapsulates me in his. I just sigh, holding on to him. "I'm beyond frustrated and aggravated and honestly am at a loss for what to do. It's common knowledge that you and Mom had a rough start. But I mean, Michael, seriously him. How the Hell did you guys keep that a secret from me for all this time? Why?" I ask him, more frustrated than angry. I feel my father draw in a big breath, then he rests his cheek on my head.

"I didn't want to keep it from you. I thought you should have known the minute you could comprehend what was happening. You two were always drawn to each other. Why, every time you were upset and if your mother and I couldn't comfort you, why you found solace in his arms? The mate bond has been strong between the two of you for the last six years. Well, technically, seven. No matter what happened or how upset you were, he was always the one to calm you down." My father pulls back and opens his wings to look down at me.

"I know what it's like to rail against the bond. Trust me, I did it, and it almost got me killed."

Nodding along, I listen to Dad recount the story of when he was abducted and almost bled out on the top of the pillar in the middle of the Shadow Realm. And how he had to be rescued by my mother, grandfather, and great-grandfather.

I listen to exactly what he's telling me, and I mean; I know he's right. Dad's always right. The other mates are a little questionable, but my parents are usually always usually 100% spot on. Gage, even though he fell, I feel like he's probably the most neutral out of all of them because he's lived on both sides of the color line, once as a Light Nephilim and now as a Fallen Dark Nephilim. Compared to other Dark Nephilim, he's much stronger than the others because he fell by choice. So it seems like since it was sacrificed, his powers were increased tenfold. He's just afraid to use them.

"But Dad, it's Michael. I mean, when I was younger, I had a massive crush on him, and Raphael quickly told me it wasn't proper for one so young to be so infatuated with a male so much older than her." Arching a brow I stare at my father.

He nods along. "I know he was an idiot. There is absolutely nothing wrong with the age difference. Let's face it, you're gonna live forever or damn close to it. There's no reason why a few thousand years between the two of you should make any kind of difference. Hell, look at your mom and Raphael. There's over a thousand years difference between them, and they make it work." I tilt my head side to side.

"Yeah, I never really thought about that."

"Exactly," my father says as he backs away, pulls his wings back, and then curls them back into his body.

"The only thing you've got to worry about doing, little one, is what is right for you, not what everybody else tells you." When Dad says that, everything seems to click into place.

"Well, I've got five weeks before the Mated Ball, so that means that there's no rush to claim anybody, right?" I watch my father visibly cringe and then nod.

"Yup," he says as he shivers slightly. "I really don't want to think about you and the other three if we can help it. Thanks, baby girl." The way he says it, I laugh and just can't help myself. I'm almost hysterically cackling.

"I got you, Dad. Last time, it's going to be mentioned."

"Thank fuck!" he says. "I don't think I can handle you talking about your sex life. To me, it's bad enough the conversation got this far."

"Oh, trust me, I know." He laughs when I sit there and wipe the imaginary sweat off my brow.

"Yeah, you're not the only one sweating out here, baby girl." As he laughs. "Are you gonna take the job here at the club or work at the hospital?"

"I didn't know the club was an option."

My father's eyes light up and then blacken immediately. "Of course, it's a fucking option. It's my fucking club. You can work here if you want. You don't have to be sentenced to the hospital just because Raphael thinks it's the best idea for you. Screw that he's not your father. I am." Dad finally takes a stance against their head mate, which is quite comical.

"All right, Dad, thanks for the options. I really appreciate it."

He smiles and nods. "Well, look at it this way. We're about maybe five miles from the hospital from here. So if something happens, it's only a matter of seconds for us to move through the shadows to get there. You know, to be perfectly honest, I think you'd be much happier working here than there. The whole idea of having Mom boss you around all day. I don't really see that as being much fun." He laughs and then looks around quickly.

"I mean, your mom bossing me around. Could be fun, but yeah, no." I laugh at Dad's looking around, making sure Mom's not gonna pop up behind him.

"Yeah, I get that, Dad. Honestly, I do. Yeah, you know I'll take up the job as a bartender. I enjoy mixing drinks anyway."

"Good, the job is yours," Dad says as he turns on his heel.

"Why don't you think about going home tonight? Back to where your mates are. Michael's condo has four bedrooms in it, so you're not being forced to stay in any one room if you don't want to," he says more for my comfort than anything else.

As I ponder his suggestion, it makes sense to me. I hug Dad and kiss him on the cheek before disappearing through the shadows again to manifest back in Michael's house. It's nearly four AM by the time I return, and all three guys are asleep in their respective rooms. I creep through the house slowly and notice each guy has left their bedroom door open as an invitation for me to join them.

I look in the room that should be Mordoc's but don't see him. It's really odd. Then I noticed his window is the one that faces the sunrise, and it makes perfect sense to me now. I look towards the closet, and it's a huge walk-in. He slid his bed in there and left the door ajar. Thankfully, the door opens out, so the sun comes through the window; it doesn't enter his closet. I draw the blinds on his window and then blacken the glass by touching it lightly, scorching it so that the sun cannot penetrate. Once I'm pleased with how the glass has been tempered, I walk out of the room.

Satan's room is the next one I come to, and he's curled up in a little ball, hugging his pillow to sleep. I can only imagine the nightmares that plague him when he's resting. All the years of being stuck on the inner ring of Hell. All the atrocities he's seen and done must haunt him something severe. I walk over gently, place my index finger on his temple, and soothe his mind, removing nightmares from his dreams. The minute I do, he uncurls his body, stretches out, and a soft smile graces his lips before returning to a deep slumber.

There are two doors at the end of the hallway. I know one's mine, and the other is Michael's. I walk past and pause in Michael's doorway. He's not asleep. He's sitting up with his legs crossed and his hands resting on his knees. His wings are bathed in a light white glow, and I have a feeling he's talking to someone in the Angelic Realm. I watch him for several moments and then lightly knock on the door. He opens his eyes, and they're brilliant glowing golden orbs. I feel like I'm lost in them.

I stare at him for several moments too long and then lower my gaze. "I'm home. I'm gonna go to bed for a while. I've got work tomorrow night at Dad's club. You're more than welcome to come to join me." I leave his doorway and go into the bedroom across the way. The black calla lilies that I love so much line the dresser. The salmon-colored roses that are my second favorite are on the windowsill. Pure white orchids, which have always been my birthday favorite, sit on the table next to the door to the bathroom.

"Do you like them?" I hear Michael's deep baritone voice behind me.

I give a soft nod. "I do. You know they're my favorite."

"I know. I just wanted to make sure you felt at home and welcome." The pauses in his sentence tell me he's uneasy and unsure of himself for once. The strongest Archangel, the one they send into battle in wars, is afraid, and I can sense it radiating off of him. It's something someone like me feeds off of.

"Thank you," I say as I turn slowly and kiss his cheek. The shock on his face is more than enough. I just turn, walk into the room, and lay down on the bed, fully dressed. Unfortunately, sleeping how I normally do is off the table. He comes in and hesitantly sits on the side of the bed.

"If you don't honestly want me here, you can tell me I won't be offended." I stay lying on my side. Just looking out at the bottom edge of the window. The sun's early rays are coming through as the sky is painted in hundreds of unique tones and colors, and it distracts me for a moment.

"It's not like I haven't fallen asleep on you before. You can stay," I say to him softly as I pull the sheet up in front of me like I always do, curling it close to my chest.

"Thank you," he says quietly, against the shell of my ear, before he kisses my cheek and lies on his side of the bed. He's curled away from me, giving me the option of whether or not I wish to curl up close to him. The pull is there; I'm drawn to him like a moth to the flame. Reluctantly, I roll over, curl my body around his, and wrap my arm over his rib cage, pressing my cheek against his shoulder. Within a matter of moments, sleep takes me.

CHAPTER 8
SATAN

since before the fall. I don't know what changed, but I can only
assume it has something to do with Nikita. I think she touched me
last night. Somewhere, somehow, and stopped the reoccurring
nightmares from happening. I didn't know that was within her
power, but if it is. I must show her how grateful I am for her doing
that for me. It's been damn near a thousand years since I've slept
peacefully—

actually longer than that. But who's counting?

I wander through the house, searching for her. I check Mordoc's
room, but she's not there. Next, I check Michael's room, but he's
not there. I make it to Nikita's room, and there she is, curled
around Michael's back with her head resting on his shoulder
blade, with her arm draped over his side. This has been a difficult
time for her, especially since he's been her protector and guardian
for most of her life. This must be a shock and a great difficulty
for her.

Part of me is beyond jealous that they've had all this time together, but in the other sense, the time that I've shared with her has been nothing short of as a friend and definitely not on the romantic side of it. He's had to maintain a platonic distance from her for her entire life. I've been able to joke with her, have fun with her, take her out for drinks, and hang out while maintaining a semblance of propriety. But never once in the time that we've been together or around each other have I ever had to keep a false separation between us. So in that sense, I believe I'm ahead of Michael in this game.

Mordoc has come up from the rings itself. I'm not sure which one, in particular, he was on. But I definitely know he was down there, and even last night, he was speaking about the whispers in the rings, that there's something else even bigger and badder that's about the surface. With all the recent attacks, like the one that happened, that probably sent almost two dozen people to the hospital. I'm wondering exactly what creature is rising from the abyss this time. I mean, they killed off all the big bads as far as I knew. So whatever comes now. It'll be something that we haven't seen before.

I make it downstairs and start preparing breakfast for everyone. Nikita was kind enough to ensure there's plenty of blood for Mordoc when he rises later. But for now, I'm gonna make waffles and eggs and bacon for myself, Michael and Nikita 'cause, after all, we all do have work today. It's always better to start the day off with a full stomach than to go to work hungry.

Halfway through cooking, lithe fingers thread up through my hair, and I can't help but sigh, knowing that it's Nikita touching me. "What are you making?" she asks as she rests her head on my shoulder, looking down at the pan in front of me, knowing full well she can see what I'm cooking.

"Well, I made breakfast for everyone. I know mate number three won't eat it. He's not gonna wake up till much later tonight. At least you, me and Michael can have a decent breakfast before we go start our day." She smiles and nods and then gives me a gentle kiss on my cheek before moving over to the refrigerator and pulling out the fresh juices. Michael, however, has a different approach to the morning. He makes it into the kitchen, slides it open and pulls out his coffee maker. I watch him as he grabs the pods and makes cups of coffee for everyone. If I had known that was in there, I would have started coffee long ago.

"Just living off juice is not gonna cut it." Nikita laughs as she sees Michael making the coffee.

He stops and stares at her for several moments. "I'll be honest. I'm not sure how you like your coffee." A sadness moves across his features, and wow, the big bad Archangel is at a loss for words.

Nikita attempts to be understanding. She nods at him, takes the cup, then reaches into the refrigerator to pull out the hazelnut creamer. She puts three sugars into her coffee and the hazelnut creamer and pours it until it's about cardboard colored, then shows Michael and me. "I like my coffee similar to how my mother does. Except I like mine a little darker."

Nikita smiles and then takes a seat at the table, and I put the first plate of bacon, eggs, and waffle down in front of her. I set Michael's down next and then my own. We eat in comfortable silence as we watch the food on our plates slowly disappear.

"So what's on everybody's plates for today?" I state plainly.

Nikita looks down briefly and then returns her gaze to meet mine. "I have to make a quick stop at the hospital. Double-check and make sure my mom and my other dad are all set for the day. Then from there, I've gotta go over to my birth father's club and make sure all the orders arrive on time like they were promised to be there. And I'm taking over there tonight as the lead bartender. And, um, I mean, that's pretty much all I've got planned for today," Nikita says, slightly fumbling with her words. I watch the corner of Michael's eye tick as he thinks about her being in that club.

I know that used to be her usual hunting grounds for finding guys to take to bed, so his protective streak blazes to life, concerned for the element she's willingly putting herself into. He still worries about whether she will fully bond with him. Especially with her utter disdain for always been treated. She also rails against the patriarchal tactics the Angels have held for thousands of years. I stare down at my coffee for several moments and then look over at Michael.

"Do you have plans for today?" I ask, snapping him out of the daze that he is in, staring at his mug. His eyes shine golden for several seconds, and then it passes.

"Well, I was gonna go house hunting. See if there's anything possibly suitable for the four of us to live in. Obviously, we need something with a dark basement because of Mordoc. Other than that, I'm not one hundred percent sure what to do."

Staring at Michael, I realize it's probably the first time in his existence that he's unsure of what his actual goals are. Being a natural leader, a general of the Angelic army, it must be difficult for him to not know whether he is the first mate in this nest.

Nikita studies the two of us for several moments and swirls her coffee in the bottom of her mug. "I'll decide tonight who's going to be first mate." She breathes in a deep breath, and I can hear her exhale slowly. "It's not a straightforward decision for me. I know it should have happened last night when my mates were revealed to me. I just can't bring myself to do it." The sadness in her tone bothers me and makes the hair on the back of my neck stand on edge. I've never in all of my existence wanted to destroy the thing that hurts her most so badly. Which unfortunately seems to be us.

"I understand," I whisper. "In a sense. I kinda want you to pick Michael to be the first mate," I stutter over my words as my nervousness hits an all-time high. "The temptation to be in control is too much for me, and I don't think with the atonement I need to achieve the temptation of power would be good for me," I say softly, regretfully, as I stare down at my coffee, hoping that somewhere within its darkness the answer will come to me and solves the turmoil within me.

Nikita reaches out and caresses my hand, gently holding onto it. "I understand completely, and I'm grateful that you've made your feelings and intentions known. I never thought of how it would affect you if I made you first mate." She gives my hand a gentle squeeze, and a look of sheer understanding crosses her face.

"Thank you for being honest with me," she says tenderly, then she turns to look at Michael and slides her hand over his thick forearm until she grips it, giving it a squeeze. "We need to talk," she whispers. It's not the dreaded 'we need to talk' that happens in relationships before a breakup. Their relationship started long before she came of age. It's gone through many phases, and I've watched most of them.

There's still a sadness in Michael's gaze since he's unsure of what may or may not happen now. He watches her carefully with a thoughtful expression. "Wherever you wish to go, whatever you wish to do. It will be done. I appreciate the fact that you wish to talk to me. It's all I can ever ask for," he says before he raises her hand and kisses the back of it. A small smile graces his lips before he vanishes in a wisp of golden glitter.

Nikita stares at her hand where Michael's hand once was for far too long. She watches as the last golden shimmer disappears from her light olive complexion. I was almost bathed in the golden light for a moment before it faded and vanished from sight. She sips a long draw from her coffee, then finally makes eye contact with me again.

"Do you believe I'm doing the right thing, Satan?"

Her question takes me back. I'm shocked that she would sit there and ask for my opinion. Being who I once was.

"I think it's a step in the right direction. It's too much temptation for me. And Mordoc cannot go out in the daylight with you if he's needed. So the second most logical choice would be Michael." A slow, solemn nod happens before she reaches out and takes my hand again.

"Thank you for being honest with me. It's just a bitter pill to swallow." She pauses between her words as I watch her mull them over before she speaks them. It's almost as if you can hear the gears turning in her head before the words escape her lips. "This will not be easy, and we have less than five weeks before the Mated Ball."

Thoughtfully, she looks down at her coffee, then finishes off the last of it before looking back up at me. "When Mordoc awakens, please tell him to meet me at the club tonight."

I nod and agree to her request, and she leans forward, stretching out over the counter and presses her lips gently to mine. Sending the tingle straight down to my groin.

It's been thousands of years since I've been kissed, and it is exquisite. I look back at her, and she's smiling with a light blush as she stares at me. "Settle down, big guy. We'll talk later." With that, she vanishes from sight. I know she said she was going to the hospital to see her mother and Raphael. So all I can do is be a good house husband until my shift comes up tonight, get Michael's house back in order, and do the dishes I've created. I can only hope that those two and this nest come together as they should.

CHAPTER 9
NIKITA

SATAN'S ACT OF SELFLESSNESS HAS DEFINITELY GIVEN ME A UNIQUE SPIN and perspective on this entire situation. Part of me wanted to take him as first mate. Mainly because he understands where I come from. He understands the darkness and the light. He understands that not everything is perfect, and that by itself would bring me a bit of comfort. A vampire would never understand what it's like to be out in the daytime and work with and deal with taking care of others. He mostly knows only death and destruction.

I take in a deep breath as I move through the shadows, heading to Raphael's office in the hospital. There's a closet in there that he keeps shut at all times. So that way, during the day, my mother or any other Dark Nephilim within the bond could manifest within his closet in the hospital without drawing attention to themselves. As I arrive in his closet, I hear him already discussing things with my mother. They're both concerned about who I'm taking as first mate. They saw who I was bonded to: Satan, Mordoc, and Michael. Two of them, then they expected the third not so much.

Mom is upset that there is going to be a vampire in the bond, a demon of sorts. Raphael keeps saying that everything happens for a reason and that she needs to be at peace with it. That with me rising to Death Eternal, it was meant to happen, and it's for the best for everyone. I knock on the closet door before opening it so I don't shock them as I step out. They were half expecting it to be my father and not me.

Raising a hand, silencing them before they get started. I shake my head slowly. "I've already heard enough, and with Satan's guidance, I have decided that Michael would be the first mate. Even though it's slightly uncomfortable to do so." Raphael smiles, then stands to embrace me. I return his hug, then sigh, looking up at him.

"I really wish you guys would have been honest with me that he was my mate. That I would have known who and what he is to me. Instead of thinking of him as a family member." I look down briefly before pushing away from Raphael to hug my mother.

"At least Mom had the whole not knowing who was hers. She had the surprise and the joy of people that she had hoped to be her mate in her bond. I instead end up with a man who I thought of more as an uncle than a romantic figure all by your doing." I say, staring right at Raphael.

"Every time I expressed even the slightest interest in him you told me he was my uncle and family, and that was it. You dismissed my feelings for him all this time." I enunciate my words, driving my point home. The crux of my problem is one Raphael himself created. There's no going back and correcting the damage he's done over these years. The only thing I can do now is hope for the best and try to move past everything I learned as gospel over the last seven years. And try to return to the initial feelings I had way back when.

Mother snuggles me tightly to her side, holding on to me. She understands where I'm at with this, and she threads her fingers through my long white hair, trying to soothe me. "I understand, sweetheart. We should have handled the Michael situation much better. We didn't need you forming the bond before it was safe. I guess the bond had already started to form, and that's why you had feelings for him." Mom's tone is mournful. I feel a shudder wrack her body as she thinks about it. Her sadness is clear, and I understand. She did what she thought was best for me to protect me. But in doing so, she made it difficult for me to have feelings for my mate.

Raphael lightly wraps his knuckles on the desk to turn my attention to him. "I am, however, slightly concerned about the vampire in your bond," he says as he looks at me. "Never once has a vampire ever risen to be part of an angelic bond. I'm not sure what effect it would have or if you can have children with him."

I ponder what he says and, come to think of it, I don't even know if Mordoc has a heartbeat. Whether blood flows through his veins because he lives or if he is actually undead, like the legend says. "I'm not sure that's even a valid concern," I say to Raphael as I ponder my next sentence. "If he is the undead like the legends day, it doesn't change the fact he's still my mate. He may not provide me with children, but that doesn't mean that he cannot provide me with love." It's a tough concept to wrap my head around, and yet it's one that I've already come to terms with.

"Unlike my mother, the need and drive to reproduce are unnecessary. Not all fairy tales have happy endings. To be honest, children are not the end-all be-all for me. I just want a happy life in my nest. Surrounded by those that I can love and trust and not have to worry about what's coming up behind me." They sit in relative silence for a few moments, listening to me, then Mother finally speaks.

"I understand, baby girl. But you have to understand where I'm coming from as well. He's only a concern because of what his food is and how we can best provide for him. Down in the rings, it's much easier to find him food. Up here, it's gonna be much more questionable." And that is where Mom's concern lies. In feeding him.

"It's kind of a concern for me, too. But I've already got it handled." I smile, step away from my mom, and look between her and Raphael. "That's easy enough to be solved," I say with as much authority behind it as possible.

"I've already opened a rift once before and called forth one of Mom's servants from the castle in the Shadow Realm. The one Butler to bring forth a pitcher of blood for my mate as needed. I will do so. That way, he does not need to hunt up here. I think about my bloodlust at the moment. How much do I enjoy a good glass after a long, strenuous day? But that, unfortunately, is something that comes with the whole darkness that's within me. I'm more Fallen than Angelic, and technically, I can't be Fallen because I never ascended to fall." I look between my mother and her mate.

My angelic father nods slowly. "As long as his food source is maintained, and he's not an issue here. Then it shouldn't be a problem," he states analytically as he looks over the reports on his desk.

"If you cannot obtain blood from the Shadow Realm for any reason, let me know, and I'll make sure I bring home some bags from here."

I look at Raphael, slightly shocked that he will steal blood from the hospital to support my mate. Maybe he's not as bad as I initially thought. I mean, he is an Angel. But maybe after being around my mom all this time, he finally understands the parameters in which the rest of us live. I just nod gently at him, acknowledging what he said.

"I greatly appreciate your offer. Thank you." With that, I just smile at him. Mom seems pleased with what we have come up with. I turn and leave, walking out of his office and through the hospital halls. Not even two steps out of his office, my outfit for the day switches to scrubs, and I blend in with everyone else. I make it past Aunt Jocelyn and smile at her, happy to see she's finally returned to work.

She embraces me briefly, and we catch up quickly on what's going on with her and her five children. Her children didn't grow as fast as mothers did. But they still grew faster than the average child. We set a date in the future to go to lunch together and converse about all that's changed. She gave me a hint about Michael that I didn't know. That he enjoys sweets. So I decide to make a quick detour to Klaus's and Jayce's bakery down in the city's heart. I figure I need to go try to show the big guy exactly how much I care. Hopefully, I can get over this mental block between us. Because until I claim him, I can't set the rest of the nest in order.

Arriving at Klaus and Jayce's bakery takes far less time than expected. As I walk through the doors, Jayce, as usual, is icing the newest cupcakes fresh out of the oven that Klaus had baked. I watch them work in harmony. Each one does their own job, ensuring everything within the bakery is in order. I giggle as the bell rings, walking through the door. "How're my two favorite uncles?" I practically sing as I approach the counter.

Jayce is positively beaming and glowing with happiness as he puts down the icing bag and races around the counter to sweep me up in the biggest hug ever. Giggling softly, I bury my face between his neck and shoulder, holding on tightly as he spins us in a circle. "There's my favorite dark angel." I laugh as he sits me down and smiles, looking me over.

"So, how was the Mate Trials?" Klaus practically sings from behind the counter.

"Well, I have three mates. One of them is Michael."

Klaus and Jayce clap positively, ecstatic over the news. "He is such a hunk."

"Oh my God, how did you end up with that one?" Jayce chimes in after Klaus.

"Apparently, he's always been my mate." I throw my hands up in the air and roll my eyes.

"Mom and Dad apparently thought it was okay to hide that fact from me," I say sarcastically as I look around at everything behind the glass in the bakery.

A slight growl escapes Klaus's lips, and then he laughs. "Parents, I swear." He rolls his eyes, trying to be funny and sarcastic as he looks at me. I know he's doing it more for my benefit, and they try to have a semblance of common ground with me. But I know he understands where my parents came from with it, and he will likely side with them.

"Yeah, well, it's still a little unnerving to me," I say honestly.

Jayce comes over and loops his arm with mine again. "Well, what exactly are you looking for?" he asks curiously as he motions back to the glass counter.

"I'm not sure," I say as I look at all the delectable treats behind the glass.

"Does Michael come here at all and shop for himself?" I look over at Klaus, and a knowing smile graces his lips.

"Pretty much all the Archangels come here, especially after discovering that this is where your mom gets all the good stuff from." He beams.

"Well, I'm glad Mom could increase your business like tenfold."

Klaus starts pulling out several different treats from behind the glass."Well, pretty much anything loaded with honey is a win when it comes to Michael. We literally have this one whole shelf just for things that he enjoys eating." Klaus motions to the third shelf down on the fourth counter.

"Well, why don't you give me two of everything? I'm going to go see him over at the precinct and bring him his snacks." Klaus gets to work boxing up two of the honey-laden treats.

Jayce comes over and pulls me to the side. "He's always spoken about you. That man has the patience of a saint waiting seven years for his mate to come of age. I honestly don't know how he did it." Jayce always loves to gossip, so whenever I need the truth out of anyone, he's usually the one I go to. He pulls me further and into the back of the bakery. Luna is standing there mixing different batters and working on the puff pastries she needs to replace behind the counter.

"Hey Luna," I say softly, not to frighten the poor little Omega. She smiles and waves at me.

"How's my favorite cousin?" She smiles broadly before running over and hugging me.

"I'm doing good. How about you?"

"Much better now that you're here." She grins. "I heard you finally got your mates." She squeals and starts bouncing up and down, and I can't help but laugh at her antics.

"Yep, not by choice, though." She tilts her head to the side and frowns.

"Really? Is it that bad?" Her question catches me off guard, and I stare down at the ground in front of me. Pondering the answer I should give her.

"Honestly, it's not. I mean, it could have been worse." I tilt my head to the side, pondering how much worse it could have been. I mean, seriously, if I ended up with my mom's friend Mark, I think I probably would have shot myself. But luckily, I didn't. He's such a wuss.

CHAPTER 10
MORDOC

Waking up in the closet in the Archangel's house was definitely a little uncomfortable. Though I found on a warmer a pitcher of blood waiting for me. My thoughtful mate left one of her feathers next to the pitcher and a glass. A nice fluted wine glass for me to enjoy my beverage. Sipping lightly at the blood provided to me. I can tell that she added a little red wine to it to keep it from congealing. Such a thoughtful mate I have.

I can tell it is a port wine because it adds an extra sweetness and robust body to the AB-positive blood she had brought me. I wonder exactly how she knew that was my favorite blood type to drink. Either way, the level of thoughtfulness that she has shown warms my little black heart. I knock back at least three glasses of blood before I even start feeling like the day is ready to begin. Opening the door cautiously, I notice that the room is bathed in darkness. A smile crosses my lips as I step out and flip on the light switch. It's now that I notice the windows have been blackened. Whatever Nikita did to them, they are black as pitch, and no light can get in.

I can still make out the world around me. But somehow, we are shielded from the sun. Yet again, more evidence of the fact that my mate is extremely thoughtful. I open the door to my bedroom that leads out into the hallway and note that it's also bathed in blackness. It's much easier now to move through the house. As I come to the end of the hall, I notice that this window has also been blacked out. I wonder how many more room windows in Michael's house my mate has destroyed just for my comfort. As I move through, exploring the entire house. Other than Michael's room, of course, Satan's windows are blacked out and destroyed according to angelic standards.

Moving towards the kitchen, I notice Satan sitting there calmly picking over his dinner. "Good morning," I say to him, and he looks up and offers me a smile.

"Did you find the breakfast that Nikita left for you?" Nodding, I hold up my glass that is half full and toast to him.

"Indeed, I did. It was most wondrous to wake up without having to look for a meal."

"I would believe so," Satan says as he pulls up his glass of red wine. I toast back at him, then we move together towards the table in the kitchen's corner. Sitting down, he pours more blood wine for me, topping off my glass.

"Where is our beautiful mate now?" I figure I'll question Satan since he is the only one awake in the house currently.

He runs his finger around the lip of the glass and then looks at me. "I know she's gonna try to work things out with Michael, so she's with him. The hospital, or she went to the bakery or her favorite coffee shop down the end of Newman, just before the enormous park down there."

Furrowing my brows, I stare at him, then look around the house and back at him. "I honestly do not know what you're talking about. Remember, I lived in the Shadow Realm, and we didn't have places like Newman, bakeries, or a hospital to deal with."

Recognition flares in his eyes as he stares at me. "Let's go take a flight, and we'll see if we can locate her. What do you say?"

Nodding my head, I flex my back, and my leather wings unfurl. He looks at me in wonder and then steps over slowly. "I've only seen wings like this on dragons," he says as he steps behind me to look at them. I flex my wings out to their full extension and wiggle the claws on the tips of the arc of my wings.

"It's interesting to have them. I don't molt like you do. But if I end up getting a cut in my leather, I fall, and it takes a very long time for it to heal. You lose a feather, there are other feathers to take its place. My leather gets caught or ripped, it takes longer for it to repair itself." I look down thoughtfully, hoping that my explanation makes sense to him.

He nods slowly, and then we head to the condo's roof. From there, we take to the skies, gliding over the city below us. We circle by the bakery. Which is long since closed. We head over to the hospital, and her car is not in the parking lot, nor was it at the house. We circle over to the precinct. Her car isn't there either. We spend the better part of the evening flying around, looking for our wayward mate.

We head over to a place he calls Club Dread and land on its roof. There's an entrance at the top; all he does is place his hand on it, and the door opens. Heading inside, the bass thump draws my attention. The music itself is just as sinful as it is interesting. We follow the sound of the music, heading deeper into the bowels of the building itself. Until we finally come to the band playing up on stage. The one known as Cyrus, the son of death, is up on stage belting out a song as loud as his voice can do. He's screaming the lyrics, keeping the throngs of patrons inebriated with his melodic tone between the alcohol and his music. Everyone is dancing, grooving and gyrating against each other, keeping in time with the beat of the drum.

Beside him up on stage, the Destroyer, the ender of the circles and the Dark Realms. The one who brought all the dark princes to their knees and destroyed them utterly. The only survivor is Satan, and it's only because he allowed himself to be purified. I glance from him and back over at the Destroyer, and he nods.

"She's far more powerful than she appears to be. Do not incur her wrath. I cannot save you." He says, trying to warn me the best that he can. It's not gonna be a straightforward thing to have her as my mother-in-law. From what I've been told is my mate's father between the two of them. I understand now that my mate is much more than she appears. Glancing over at Satan, we head to the bar and sit watching the performance.

"I have a feeling that we are in for more than what we originally thought of when it comes to our mate." He agrees with me but remains silent. The silence itself is almost killing me.

When the set finishes, the Destroyer motions to Cyrus, then over to the bar where we're sitting. I'm not sure if she's more acutely aware of Satan being here. Or it's possibly me she's looking at. I was never good at reading the nuances of the angels or those of angelic blood. It's not something I ever bothered myself with previously, though I'm feeling at this point I'm going to have to become much better at it because of my mate and her family.

As they approach, I get a little bit of an uneasy feeling in my lower stomach. It's something that I am not very used to. I am usually the one at the peak of the food chain, the one that everyone is afraid of. Whereas right now, I am very concerned about dealing with my in-laws. Facing a horde of demons is easy in comparison. This is definitely a whole new situation for me.

"You're lucky mate number three," the Destroyer says, and I lightly dip my head to her.

"I am." With that being said, she nods to me.

"Satan, why are you here?" Her tone is full of authority and some anger that I just don't understand. Why would she be angry that we're here?

Satan breathes in sharply and then smiles. "Well, I was showing my new friend here around the town since he's never been on the surface before, and we were looking for our wayward mate. I know she's around here somewhere. Though I believe today, she was looking for treats for Michael." Satan wiggles his finger each time he counts off a different thing that he's pretty sure Nikita has been doing.

Something about Michael brings a smile to the Destroyer's lips. "I see," is all she says. Cyrus remains silent, just watching as the banter continues.

"Anything else I need to know?" she asks firmly, but not as coldly as initially.

"Just that I knew we could get my buddy blood, at least, from here. Because they serve it to us. So I figured instead of just staying home since I'm off tonight, I would take him out, show him around so he can find a job for himself to do and contribute to the nest."

Satan's already volunteering me to work. The simple thought of that sends a shiver down my spine. But I guess to be a functional mate in a bond, unfortunately, I need to have a job.

So with that being said, I motion to the club itself. "Are there any open jobs here?"

"I'm sure I can find you something." Motioning with his head, Cyrus gives me the feeling he wants me to follow him through the club. We go back towards where the offices are, down a hidden set of stairs into the bowels of the building itself at the bottom in the basement level. There seems to be a blood bank down here. Humans lined up, getting their blood taken from them, a pint at a time, and it has a reward: they get a free pass to the club. Their admission is that they must donate at least once a month to the supply.

"They do not remember why they make the donation," Cyrus says. "It's part of the magic of the place." I watch as other vampires, more the surface-dwelling, not the demonic type put a glamour over them, and then the thing that gets me the most is that they wipe their memories after donating the blood.

"Do humans stumble out, unaware of what just happened to them?" My curiosity has been aroused.

"For everyone that arrives, we drain them of a pint and then send them on their way. The vampire samples each one, getting ready to take the blood. If they're not up to snuff. Their memories are wiped and sent out the back door." Cyrus and I remain here for several moments, watching the ins and outs of how the club legally obtains their fresh blood. In the corner, several blood mages put their incantations over the blood to preserve it so it does not rot or congeal while it's being saved to be served here at the club.

"Each blood bag is being separated by type, age and status. The rare virgin that comes in, their blood is held for the elite." Cyrus says. He smirks and motions upstairs. "The elite, meaning my mate, and for only her and my children." So that is the secret of the one who shall become Death Eternal. The other one is known as my mate, my Nikita.

"So you've only fed her virgin's blood."

Cyrus smiles and looks back at the production going on behind him, then nods. "Of course. I'd only give my daughter the best. Why not give them the purest ones possible? After all, most of the others have far too many miles and impurities in them to be considered palatable," he says, speaking like a real connoisseur of the different delectable blood types.

Cyrus brings me back out of the bowels and into the club proper where the music's thumping again vibrates my soul. We return to the bar, and there stands Nikita, Michael, Satan, and Thana the Destroyer. She tilts her head slowly, looking at Cyrus and shakes it slowly from side to side.

"I guess you showed him the family business, huh?" By Thana's tone, I can only assume she was not pleased.

"Well, my love, Kitten," Cyrus says as he walks closer to her and wraps his arms around her. "I found the perfect job for our new son-in-law. He will help oversee the production of the club's supply, so neither you nor I have to be bothered with it anymore. And who better than to check the honesty of the other vampires working here than one more ancient and more powerful than any of them?" He says that last part with pride, and I can't help but smile. I have a feeling that this will be a very long, fruitful relationship. My father-in-law smiles at me once more and then waves goodbye before heading back to do whatever he does here in the club.

The Destroyer looks me over once more, then kisses her daughter's brow before walking away. "I don't know if we were just dismissed or if that's normal."

Nikita starts to laugh and looks between me and Satan. "Mom likes you," she says before looking back at Michael. "I have a date with the big guy. I'm gonna take one day, one date, possibly one week, with each of you. To learn about you, to get to know you before we seal the bonds." Her logic's infallible, and it makes perfectly good sense.

I could be perfectly honest. I was concerned about linking my blood with somebody I didn't know. Fate being what it is, you can only trust it so far. After all, one mistake over twelve hundred years ago, trusting Vlad and I got sent to Hell. Well, he still hides in the Carpathian mountains like a chicken. "Well then, you two have a wonderful evening. Satan and I will enjoy our night here. We'll see you back at home on the morrow." Nikita smiles and then comes over, kissing mine and Satan's cheeks before walking off with Michael. I honestly don't know how I feel about this, but the situation has vastly improved.

CHAPTER II
MICHAEL

JULY...

I know Nikita has railed against going to the Mate Trials since it first became a topic of discussion when she was approximately two years old. And honestly, almost fully developed at that point. She fought, cried, yelled, and ripped rooms apart, using the shadows at her disposal to show her disdain for the ancient rite of all those with any semblance of angelic blood. It wasn't until it was her time that I started seeing everything how it really was. It was a construct created by the males, the majority in the population, to assure themselves of the chance of finding the perfect female for them. The Mate Trials, as archaic as it is, have worked for centuries.

But the times and how they are changing, and the more modern forward thinking that most females do now. The idea of settling down and just being stay-at-home parents and moms is far from where it used to be. Most want their own careers and a future and an income of their own. They don't want to be dictated to by the males that are in their lives. I should have realized this with Nikita years ago. And it's now that I sit back, watching my mate and the woman she's becoming that I realize the error of the old ways.

I sat most of the day in consul with some of the older Archangels as we discussed how to go forward with the next several hundred years. Dictating how the female Angels and Nephilim are treated. We've always treated them as delicate flowers, things that must be protected and cherished. Even though the statement is true that they need to be protected and cherished. Protected might not be the correct word. Nurtured, embraced, loved and seen for the powerhouses that they are is probably the more accurate description of how we need to be taking care of the females in our lives.

Nikita shows up at my work today with a box full of snacks, my favorite desserts, and I guess she's been watching me closely over the last seven years. I don't think that she's mad that I'm her mate. I just think that she's mad over the fact that I wasn't allowed to say anything to her all these years. Again, it falls into that patriarchal construct that we were all made to believe was best for the females. Here it is causing problems with my mate. Because I had to lie, basically hide who I was to her since the moment I knew who she was to me. It's not fair to either of us.

Seven long years I've waited, watched, and stood protectively over her as much as I could. Once she went about and lived her life doing what she wanted, within reason. Granted, I know she's not the pure vessel I had hoped for in a mate. But she's perfect and made just for me. The fact that she's more experienced than I am is quite concerning. I had a long discussion with my other brother to figure out how best to navigate this. Nobody really had an answer. Only a few of us had any kind of Dark Nephilim in their bond. So the whole thought of the female knowing more than the male was foreign and quite scary. We ate the snacks in my office at the Police Department and then left and visited her father.

Satan and Mordoc were already there, enjoying drinks and having the time of their lives.

I heard Cyrus offer Mordoc a job with something within the bar, and Nikita's right eye twitched at the thought. I don't know if it was a good or an adverse reaction. But either way, I'm not sure she's too happy about it. Be it the fact that it was probably her one safe place, she could have alone time to gather her thoughts away from the rest of us. Now that whole idea has been shot straight to Hell. But I guess it's Cyrus's brilliant idea to at least monitor the most demonic of her mates. Or as I'd like to call him, the resident demon. I mean, I have much meaner things I could say about him, but that wouldn't be very noble of me. He was chosen for her for a reason, and even though my gut tells me there's something darker in the shadows lurking, waiting for her. I'm trying to be hopeful and believe that as long as he and Satan are with her, nothing bad will happen.

Knowing who her mother is, I don't think many would stand against her. And if they tried, her mother would literally rain Hell down upon them and strike them dead on the spot. A smile graces my lips, thinking about Thana destroying anybody that rose against my mate. Especially if it was in an area I could not get to because of my divine nature. A snapping happens, and the next thing I know, I realize that Nikita's fingers are snapping in front of my face. I blush, caught lost in my own thoughts.

"Where did you go?" she asks. I think she more than likely knows exactly where my thought process went, and I shrug my shoulders.

"Just thinking about your mom razing the earth if anybody were to ever stand against you." She smiles and nods, acknowledging what I said and not denying any of it.

"Very true. But the problem is, I don't need Mom to do it," she says and smiles, her eyes blacken to the deepest shade of black I've ever seen in my entire existence, so black that the idea of the abyss seems lighter. Then the color her eyes have achieved amazes me as an Archangel that my mate would contain so much darkness, and yet she's perfect for me. I can't help but nod at her statement and then laugh softly.

"Yeah, well, that may be true, but anything bad should happen and I'm not able to be with you." I pause in my thoughts and bite my bottom lip. My fear of not being able to be there to defend my mate upsets me tremendously. In a move that shocks me, Nikita reaches out and grabs my wrist. She taps her long claw-like nails on the black band around my wrist, shaking her head.

"No?" she laughs. "I guess you forgot Mom gave you this, didn't you?" Her question catches me off guard, and I ponder it for several moments, then realize the error I just made. I do have a way of following my mate into the abyss. The band created by the Destroyer grants me passage through all the Shadow Realm and deep into the bowels of Hell. I smile and laugh, embarrassed that I'd forgotten.

"I kind of forgot that was there. I've worn it for so long that it's basically like a part of me." My honesty must have struck a chord with her, and she stops and looks over at me, setting her drink on the table before her.

"What was it like? Down there when you were last there." I tilt my head to the side, pondering what she's asked me. Thinking of the best possible way to answer her.

"It's nothing like how it is now. Chaos reigns supreme, and you never knew what would come out of where to try to eat you."

Nikita laughs and then raises the hem of her shirt, exposing her abdomen to me. What looks like a fluffy black tail sits there. She moves the neck of her shirt over, and the head of a large dire wolf rests just over her shoulder and down her collarbone, disappearing into her top. "My great-grandfather will always protect me. I just need to call his name, and he will rise to protect me. I will never walk alone between him and Rex. I will always be safe." She's so confident and so sure that her guardians will always protect her.

I'm almost jealous of a wolf and a dragon. All I can do is nod, agreeing with her because I know neither of her familiars would ever betray her, nor would they ever stop fighting until they knew their owner was safe. I watch her tilt her head to the side slightly as she stares at me, her hand slowly inching towards me and then caressing my cheek.

"This is tough for me. I'm not gonna lie to you." As she says that, her eyes bleed back to the gray-blue they were earlier. "I'm having issues dealing with the fact that you were like a family member." And there's the crux of her problem.

Knowingly, I nod and let out the breath I didn't realize I was holding. "I'm having the same problem. I helped raise you, watched you grow and yet the moment I saw your wings when you were less than a year old, I knew you were mine." My admission makes my heart ache; by human standards, it would be disgusting. But it wasn't a romantic love at that point. I just knew who she was to me. I knew what she was destined to be for me.

It's only recently seeing her wings again this many years later in their full glory. That they've taken on a different quality to me. The long powerful lines the muscles as they flex in her wings and the middle of her back. The sheer power in flight that she has and the thing that is the most enticing of all is how intelligent she is.

Nikita knows things long before anybody else does, and she has no problem telling us about them. I smile again, embarrassed by my thoughts. So I know right now. If I were to move, she would see more of me than I'm quite ready for her to take notice of. She extends her hand to me after a while, and I gently cup it in mine.

"We'll get past this together," she says, full of confidence to me. It makes my heart skip a beat, knowing that she's willing to work on this. She looks down at our joined hands, and I watch her eyes bleed chrome like her mother does. She looks up at me with those polished orbs, and even though they look chrome, they almost take on a slight golden hue.

"As much as I had intended to take one of my darker mates first. I've known you and trusted you the longest. I want it to be you." Her soft admission makes my heart thunder in my chest. The smile that creeps across my lips is broad and powerful. She's made me feel infinitely stronger than I ever had in my existence.

"You honor me, Nikita," I whisper to her, leaning over the table, closing the distance between us and pressing my lips to hers. Her free hand sneaks up, and her fingers tangle into my hair, holding me in place as she kisses me back passionately. Embarrassingly enough, the passion she shared with me had a side effect. And now, sadly, my ego's been deflated, and I get to sit here with my pants a little squishy.

My soft chuckle escapes my lips, realizing it would happen. She quirks an eyebrow up, looking at me after we break away. And I shake my head now, embarrassed to admit that I had very little control over myself. "What's so funny?"

I exhale hard and just start laughing. "Hair trigger," is all I say to her. She looks deep into my eyes, then glances down through the table as if staring right at my crotch. Her gaze jumps up again to look me back in the eyes, and her mouth forms a perfect oh. A little shocked by her revelation, she excuses herself from the table. I'm quite concerned about why. When she returns, she has several napkins in hand and offers them to me.

"I don't know what else to do," she says and smiles, happy that she can assist me in some way. Soon after I discreetly clean up the mess I've created, we leave and head out for the rest of the night to get to know each other on an adult level.

CHAPTER 12
NIKITA

After Michael's minor incident, it raised some minor concerns for me. I know that Angels and Archangels don't fornicate outside of their bonds. But I also know that the Dark Nephilim tend to bite and drink each other's blood when bonding. How is he going to handle that aspect?

I allow him to drive my mustang and he's having the time of his life. Texting Satan, I practically beg him to have THE TALK with Michael. After a lot of convincing, he agrees to help with educating Michael so neither of us gets physically hurt in the process. Looking up, I take in the scenery and have no fucking clue where I am. "Um, Michael? Where in God's green earth are we?" Arching a brow, I wait for an answer.

Pulling into the parking lot of what looks like a mansion, the radiant smile he gives me makes my heart race a bit. "Do you ever wonder where the Angels go to have a nice, quiet dinner?" He parks the car in the circle drive and a valet comes over to the driver's side and opens the door. Michael exits the car, then comes to my side and offers me his hand.

Stepping out onto the pure white stones of the driveway, I get anxious. "I don't belong here." My eyes dart around, taking in my surroundings as my car pulls away to be parked.

"Of course you do. You're my mate." Michael's smile is as bright as the sun, and it's almost blinding.

"I'm as close to being a Fallen Angel as one can get." Furrowing my brows, I rest both hands on his chest, staring up into his brilliant blue eyes.

His large hand comes up and cups my jaw as he rubs his thumb over by bottom lip, gazing at it. "Then you are my Fallen Angel. The most precious being in the universe to me. My heart and soul belong to you alone, Nikita. You are my forever." Closing the distance, he presses his lips to mine and I swear I feel a spark between us.

We break apart slowly, and he blushes slightly. His wings are standing tall and proud behind him, and he chuckles. "Let's get dressed for our date, shall we?" He doesn't give me a chance to answer and wraps his wings around me. The luminescence from his wings is almost blinding as I feel a wave of warmth flow from the crown of my head to the tips of my toes. When the heat fades, I find myself in a smoke-gray gown with a beaded fitted bodice that gives way to a flowing satin gown.

Michael opens his wings and I give the dress a little twirl, watching the material float on the wind. "It's stunning. Thank you." The level of detail in the gown and the feel of the material tells me how deep his feelings go for me.

"The gown isn't as pretty as the woman wearing it. It merely is an adornment to accentuate your natural beauty." Michael steps forward and offers me his arm and we head towards the stairs. "You can show your wings here, Nikita. You're my mate." With his encouragement, I allow my wings to unfurl and flex several times. Darkness emanates from every feather, making them seem as if they are alive.

The Angel at the front door steps back, seeing me standing tall at Michael's side. Leaning into his shoulder, I choose to bite my tongue and not say what I'm thinking. I can already feel his disgust at having me in his presence. "My Lord." The man at the door only acknowledges Michael's presence, ignoring me all together.

Michael's eye twitches as he notices the Angel doesn't acknowledge me. His eyes drop to me and he smiles. "Nikita love, shall we invite your mother the Destroyer, here to join us with your father?" His honey sweet tone has a slight edge to it and he's never been hotter to me than right now.

Allowing my canines to descend, I smile adoringly at him. "If that is your desire, my love. Mother would love to join us and bring Father." Raising my hand, blackened flames rise from my fingertips.

"You cannot do that here!" the Angel yells at me and I smirk.

"Why not?" Michael's voice booms and echoes throughout the halls.

The lesser Angel backs up and looks up at him, frightened. "My lord, the dark ones are not allowed to be here." He shudders and looks between us. The fear in his eyes is quite delicious.

The tick in the corner of Michael's eye grows more intense as he stares at the lesser Angel. The sweetest smile graces his lips before his eyes bleed golden. "Brother Uriel, Archangel of truth, I summon thee..." As Michael speaks, he tilts his head back, facing skyward. His voice booms and vibrates everything around him.

A soft laugh escapes my lips as I pass my hand over the raven on my forearm. "Mother and Grandfather, I need you." My smile slowly turns feral as I lift my chrome gaze to face the Angel in the doorway.

Uriel, my mother and Azrael arrive within moments of each other. Without a second thought, I break away from Michael and run to my mother and hug her tightly. "Mom this Angel…" I motion to the one in the doorway, "says I am a dark one and cannot pass. Dark ones are not welcome in the establishment."

Uriel hears me and stops mid-conversation with Michael. "You are not a dark one! Who is he to judge you?" Uriel's fury is focused on the Angel at the door. "Did you test her before refusing her entry?" Uriel crosses his arms over his armored chest, looking down at the Angel.

"My lord, her wings. She's clearly a dark one." He stutters through the sentence, trying to keep his composure.

"Granddaughter, can you still manifest light in your hand?" Azrael asks and smiles, knowing full well I can.

Bowing my head to my grandfather, I raise my other hand and a small fount of holy light manifests in my bare hand. Michael comes over and passes his hand through the light in my hand and smiles. "A dark one cannot manifest light." His gaze warms as he looks deep into my eyes. A slow, easy smile crosses his lips before he turns his full attention on the Angel at the doorway that is now shaking.

"Look at her wings. It's a trick!" he stutters again, pointing at me as if his beliefs are going to change things.

Mom has heard enough and goes into full Destroyer mode. Both of her Archangel mates arrive almost instantly to flank her side. Mom's almost black wings stand tall, proud and heavily armored behind her. I extinguish the flames in my hands and move to stand next to her, proud of who my mother is. "So am I a dark one?" Her voice reverberates like Metatron's as she stands before the man in full armor.

Dropping to his knees quickly, he lowers his head in deference to my mother. "No Destroyer, you are how HE intended you to be."

Azrael steps forward and rests a hand on my shoulder. "Nikita is ascending to Death Eternal after the Mated Ball. She is no more a Fallen Angel than you are." The ice cold gaze in my grandfather's eyes tells me there is no room for argument with him. I know by the quirk of the corner of his lip, he's enjoying setting this Angel straight.

I step closer to Michael and thread my fingers with his and hold his hand tightly. The stories of the Angels being purists were no exaggeration. I've seen how they have treated my father and Gage when they go anywhere. I also remember the stories Raphael told of the first Mated Ball and how my father was almost attacked just because of his wing color.

The Angel begs for forgiveness from the Archangels, claiming he meant no disrespect to me. Claiming that he's learned his lesson and that from now on he will be more tolerant of those of a different feather color. It's now that my eyes do something they've never done before. I see a darkness pulsing, almost ebbing through his veins. Standing on my tiptoes, I kiss Michael's cheek before moving towards the man.

"Hmmm. Grandfather, do you see what I see?" Tilting my head to the side, I study the man closer. There's a darkness in his heart and it's pulsing out slowly, poisoning his body.

Azrael comes to stand beside me and stares down at the Angel before us and also tilts his head to the side. "Very interesting,

Granddaughter. See if you can draw it out of him without killing him. Your mother can do it, so there's no reason why you can't."

"What are you talking about ole friend?" Uriel states before moving to stand beside us in front of the Angel.

"There's a darkness in his heart poisoning him." It's now that it hits me. "Who did you lose? Who broke your heart?" Laser-focused on the man, I feel as though I am looking through him. His heart rate picks up, and I can smell the sorrow on him as it bleeds out of his pores.

"Irina, she was my beloved." A single tear escapes his eye as he stares at the ground. "At the Mate Trials, a Dark Nephilim claimed her." He grinds out the words and his hands become fists at his side as he raises his eyes to meet mine.

I nod along with what he's saying, watching the darkness pulse in time with his words. Extending a hand out, I push my fingers between the buttons of his shirt to touch his skin. The darkness within his heart calls to me and I pull it to me, drawing it out slowly. Inch by inch, the blackened mass gets closer to me. When its tendrils touch my skin, I feel pure, unadulterated hatred. I hiss, baring my canines in reaction to the malice slithering into my hand. The blackened mass ungulates in my palm as if having a life of its own.

"Michael, I need your help." I turn to my mate and he's prouder than a peacock because I asked for his help.

"What do you need, angel?" His voice is husky with a slight gravely tone to it. The pitch he's hitting makes my core react to him.

"I need your light to burn away the corruption in my hand." Poised, I offer him a good view of the mass in my hands.

His eyes widen as he glances between me and the mass. "I don't want to burn you." He takes a step back and his heart thunders in his chest.

A soft giggle escapes my lips as I smile, looking up at it. "If that was a problem, Mom would have never allowed Davina and I to spar using our gifts at full force." Out of the corner of my eye, I watch my mom nod along with what I said.

Michael nods and steps forward. "Tell me what you want me to do."

Cupping my hands, the mass wiggles in the well that I've created. I manifest what little holy light I can and it's not enough to destroy the mass. Michael takes the hint and cups my hands and adds his light to mine. It's an interesting feeling when his power moves through me. It's almost like a cool chill passing through my hands, like running ice water over my skin.

Looking up, Michael's eyes are polished golden orbs focused on the destruction of the mass in my hands. I study him, finally looking at him like a man and not my uncle anymore. When the mass is gone, his grip tightens on my hands, snapping me out of the deeper examination of his features. He's just as amazed as I am, gazing deeply into each other's eyes.

The snapping of fingers pops into the last of the bubble Michael and I are in. Metatron is standing there smiling, looking at the two of us. It's now that I notice everyone else has left already, and he's the last man standing. "I sent the others away. Go enjoy dinner and we'll catch up on Friday." Metatron leans forward and kisses my forehead like he used to do when I was a little girl. With a wink, he vanishes from sight, leaving Michael and me alone.

CHAPTER 13

MICHAEL

MY GRIP ON NIKITA'S HANDS TIGHTENS AFTER WE DESTROY THE DARKNESS between us. Metatron saying goodbye to Nikita before he left was super touching. I can see the love she has for her family and the pleased smile that graced her lips when he kissed her goodbye.

"Would you like to go to dinner here or somewhere else?" I'm not sure how Nikita feels after the Angel disaster.

She turns slowly and looks over her shoulder at the establishment. "If you wish to show me your favorite place to eat. I would love to have dinner with you." She smiles sincerely at me and I don't feel or sense any dishonesty about what she said. I know she goes to great lengths to please those she loves, so I assume I am no exception to the rule.

Leaning down, I kiss her temple and smile against her skin. "Take me where you love to eat." Nikita backs up and her features light up immediately.

"Do you mean it?"

"I do."

Squealing, Nikita bolts over the valet and gets her keys back from him. Without a backward glance, she vanishes from sight and within seconds I hear the motor of her mustang come to life. A soft laugh escapes my lips, picturing the joy on Nikita's face as she gets behind the wheel of that beast of hers. I swear she is her mother's daughter when it comes to the love she has for her car. I can hear Nikita long before I can see her. Not only do I hear the motor, but also the music as well. Shaking my head, I recognize the song playing. Black Sunshine by White Zombie thumps from her speakers.

Pulling up alongside of me, she stops and pops the door open. "Get in! We're going on an adventure!"

Quickly, I get into the car without a second thought and she guns the motor, throwing me back in the seat. The G forces at play are as exciting as they are terrifying, watching my mate shift through the gears heading towards the Autobahn. We head north west away from where her family is from through some of the most scenic routes possible. I watch Nikita intently as her eyes shift colors from chrome to black, then back to her human gray blue. The color changes tell me she's speaking with different members of the family as she drives.

Leaving the expressway, we wind through a beautiful part of Cadet Street in Bergisch Gladbach, Germany. The large white stately manor appears on our left and Nikita smiles. "Chef Joachim is a good friend of mine and I wish for you to try his food." She stops the car and fidgets with the shifter for several seconds before meeting my gaze.

"If it is something that you love, then I would love to try it." Reaching out, I take hold of her hand, holding it for a moment before the valet comes to the driver's side and opens the door.

Nikita steps out, and I'm shocked that she's speaking perfect German. She hands over her keys without batting an eye, then smiles, waiting for me to catch up. I get out of the car and rush over to her side, and she takes my hand, leading me into the hotel. Several people approach her, greet her, and carry on a brief conversation.

Nikita introduces me as her husband to the humans and her mate to the other Nephilim we run into. Her change in demeanor is shocking to me. Then again, she was always the more tactical of the twins. Where Davina is ruled by her emotions. Nikita is cold and calculating, looking at every angle before making a move one way or the other. She explained it as life is like a chessboard. Every move, like in physics, has an equal yet opposite reaction. We must expect the opponent's reaction before making our moves for the best possible outcome.

The hostess comes over and immediately ushers us to a private table in the back of the restaurant. Several candles are lit in the center, and the lights are dimmed. Nikita sits with her back to the wall to see the restaurant. I slide in on her left side and keep watch down the back corridor.

She smiles, looking at me and reaching out to touch my hand. "I hope you will enjoy the dinner tonight." Her eyes dart around several times before locking back with mine.

Gently, I squeeze her hand and smile. "I'm sure I will. I'm ecstatic that you are so open to having dinner with me. What changed?"

Nikita visibly cringes and pulls her hand back. Her mouth opens and shuts several times as if she's attempting to form the words. Drawing in a deep breath, she squares her shoulders and sits up straight, looking at me. Either I'm in trouble for something I'm not aware of, or she is about to drop the mother of all bombs.

"It's like this." She pauses and sips at her wine. "I always had a crush on you." Sighing, she reaches out and grips my hand. "Raphael and the other Angels in Mom's bond called you uncle and so on, so eventually, I felt wrong for having feelings for you." Nikita looks down and away from me. Pain etches her beautiful features, and it makes my heart hurt.

"I understand what my brothers were trying to do. They wanted to protect you from reacting to your base urges." Feeling the heat rise in my cheeks, I let out a half laugh. "I guess their best intentions shot me in the foot." Shrugging my shoulders, I shake my head at the irony of the situation.

"Shot us both." She forces a smile.

"Where do we go from here?" Honestly, besides dinner tonight, I don't have a single clue where to even start the dating thing.

"Baby steps?" Tilting her head to the side, her suggestion sounds more unsure than I feel.

"Baby steps," I agree with her, glad she suggested it. The appetizers arrive and the wine gets refilled. We split the food between us, sharing everything like we used to before this whole mate thing.

The appetizers are consumed in relative silence. It's not uncomfortable or anything, just not typical. "Anything on your mind?" I pose the question seconds before the server arrives with the next course.

Sighing, Nikita sets her fork down and dabs her lips with the napkin before looking up at me. "I'm afraid that my true nature will scare you. I'm very dominant. I bite, I drink blood, and I growl a lot." Flexing her fingers, her nails become talons, then retract again. She smiles, and I watch as her upper and lower canines descend, then retract. I can see where her concerns lie. "I like to chase my prey. Hunting my bedmate makes it... even more exciting for me." She glances down, then back up with fathomless orbs.

A feral smile plays upon her lips, and I stare at her canines. The darker rites of her bloodline are visible. "I'm what's called a primal. I give into my base instincts and desires. Normal vanilla sex is boring to me." The sultry tones her voice hits make my cock hard in a second. Nikita's nostrils flair, and she looks me over slowly as if I'm lunch. "I can scent your desire, Michael." She leans in closer, the tip of her nose touching my throat.

Swallowing hard, I grab my glass of wine and take a deep draw of the crimson fluid within it. "I... I do desire you... I just... Don't know what to do." Honesty has always been my best policy, and dropping the truth bomb seems like the best idea.

Nikita nods, then leans back, looking at me. "I figured as much. Gramps already gave me the heads up about the Archangel protocols and allowances." She sips at her wine as if it's all as simple as learning to ride a bike. "The important thing is, do you have questions? I'm an open book."

The confidence she exudes isn't cocky. She's speaking from a place of applied knowledge where I only have a theory. "I have many questions. My only concern is hurting you."

Nikita almost spits out her drink as she turns to look at me. "You're joking, right?"

"I would never joke about that."

"Oh, well, unless your dick is as thick as my forearm, we're good." She's actually serious.

I look at her forearm, wrap my hand around it, and then think about my girth. "We're good," I state honestly.

Nikita again almost spits her drink, looking at my hand on her arm, then down at the bulge in my pants. "I guess I'll have to find out later if you're right."

Her eyes blacken, then return to normal. "In all seriousness, I know the basic mechanics. You'll have to teach me what you do and don't like." Shrugging my shoulders, I throw the offer out there for her.

"Knowing the basics is definitely a tremendous help." Nikita smiles at me as she finishes up the last of the fifth-course selection. Her body stiffens, and I watch her eyes dart around the room. "There's something here..." Nikita whispers as she moves out from behind the table.

The server attending us comes up along Nikita's side and motions back towards the kitchen. Racing down the hallway, we can clearly hear the commotion in the storage room. With a wave of Nikita's hand, the door slams open, and a man is thrashing around, holding his head.

"He's being possessed! Michael, create a ward to keep him here," Nikita states as she stares down at the man thrashing around.

Without a second thought, I call upon Metatron and Raphael, who bring Thana with them. They arrive in time to find that Nikita has the man and the demon possessing him fully restrained in shadows.

"Reveal yourself to me!" Her voice booms, shaking cans off the shelves behind us.

Darkness ebbs from the man's pores, and once the viscous mass is released from its human shell, the body hits the floor. If a satyr and a goat had a baby, that's the best description I have for Baphomet. Standing over seven feet tall, not counting the horns on his goat's head, he can appear intimidating.

"Death, several of my disciples have been slain and their heads stolen from their still warm corpses." It's odd hearing a human voice from a goat's head. But then again, demons are abominations, and anything is possible.

Before Nikita can speak, Thana steps forward, crossing her arms under her chest. "How long ago?" Nikita shoots her mother a death glare before looking back at the demon before her.

"An hour ago, by human time. Hellscape time two days ago," Baphomet says before looking at Nikita. "I implore you, Death, hunt the killer. He's nothing like I have ever sensed before."

It shocks the other Archangels and me to see Baphomet ignore Thana to focus on Nikita. With a wave of her hand, Nikita sends Baphomet back to Hell. "I have not yet ascended, and still demons seek me out. It's a very curious turn of events." Nikita turns and stares up into my eyes, making me feel like the only man in the room.

"Whatever you need, my sword and shield are yours." Smiling, I bend down and press my lips to her forehead.

"Anything?"

The tone Nikita takes concerns me. "Yes, anything."

Her eyes turn black as pitch, and a feral grin crosses her lips as her canines descend. "Run."

I back up towards the door as the other Archangels and Thana vanish. Oh bloody hell, this is that primal thing Nikita told me about.

"Run, little lamb. The big bad wolf is hungry." Her tongue trails over her lips slowly, and her warning rings in my ears. She's a primal and I'm her prey. Dark Nephilim and Fallen feast on the blood of their mates.

I take off running, and once outside, I take to the skies, hoping my powerful wings will propel me faster than she can move. Flapping my wings as hard as I can, I fly straight towards the cloud cover as the sun sets. My heart is thundering in my chest as I scan the clouds surrounding me. The silence is killing me; I know Nikita is out there hunting me down, yet I am afraid to leave my fluffy haven.

I hear a whoosh behind me, and the next thing I know, my belt falls apart, and my pants almost fall off my hips. Spinning quickly, I look behind me, and there's nothing there. My gut tells me it was Nikita and that she's found me. I hear the whoosh again, and my shirt splits in two, held together only by the buttons in the front. Her strikes are surgical in precision; not once have her talons cut into me.

The next thing I know, Nikita is barreling at me like a runaway train, hell-bent on destruction. I'm not sure what's more frightening, the fact that I'm turned on that she's hunting me, or that I'm 98% sure she could kick my ass if she had to. The minute her hands touch mine, we vanish from the sky, heading to who knows where.

CHAPTER 14
NIKITA

MY BLOOD HUMS WITH THE POWER CONTAINED WITHIN IT. I'M SO CLOSE to my ascension it's not even funny. Hunting my mate is a brand new high. His fear has a sweetness to it, and it drives the beast within me to the edge of sanity. Being my mother's savage daughter, I am just like her. A beast lives deep within my chest. Its voice rings in my ears, and it brings me comfort.

Mother's basilisk has nothing on the creature within me. It screeches for me to find my mate, and its senses tell me where to hunt in the clouds. Finding Michael is a cakewalk, and I decide to slice at his clothing. His angelic sensibilities are cute—antiquated, but cute.

When I can't wait any longer, I charge at him and rip him through the fabric of the current realm and into the Shadow Realm. Mother's castle has already started responding to me as if I own it. By rights, as I take over as Death Eternal, Grandfather's will be mine. Michael and I manifest in my tower room, and as soon as his back hits my bed, I vanish again.

He stands quickly as the tatters of what's left of his dress shirt hit the floor. His eyes scan the interior of the room, searching for me. "Nikita? Where are we?"

"My room." My voice echoes, and the candles ignite around the room, bathing the space in their warm light.

"It doesn't feel like your room." Michael rolls to his feet and starts exploring the interior.

Laughing, I manifest in the room's corner. Midnight wings stand proudly behind me as I watch him. "We're in the Shadow Realm, Mother's castle."

Michael spins to face me, and as he does, his wings flair open, and in the candlelight, I can appreciate their true beauty. Stepping forward, I close the distance between us and reach out to touch the feathers of his wings. "My wings always fascinated you." Michael's tone becomes rougher, deeper, almost breathy as he speaks close to my ear.

Angling my body, I bring my feathers closer to his, lay them over his, and look at them together. "Day and night, darkness and light. One cannot exist without the other."

His fingertips brush over my flight feathers, and I'm hypnotized watching them. "Your feathers are darker then your fathers and grandfathers. Even Lucifer's feathers weren't this dark." His voice holds wonder in it as well as concern.

"You're distracting me." I tilt my head to the side, pulling my wing free from his grasp.

"Is it working?" A nervous laugh escapes his lips as he backs up to the door.

"Slightly. You have a choice. Climb on the bed and do what you're told. Or…" I motion with my head to the door. He should go out. "Run like a good little lamb."

Michael pales for a moment, looking his options over. His eyes dart between the bed, the door, and the hallway just over his shoulder. A mischievous glimmer appears in his eye, and then he's gone in a flutter of golden glitter.

A dark laugh escapes my lips. My little lamb is on the run, making the prize, in the end, all the better. Closing my eyes, I extend my senses, using all the creatures big and small in the Shadow Realm to search for Michael. He's not here. Not one ounce of angelic energy is here. He could have run to several places and the last one I'd like to avoid at all costs.

Moving through the shadows, I arrive at Michael's condo. Mordoc is sitting on the couch with a goblet of blood in his hand, smiling at me. "The Angel flew through here like someone set his ass on fire." Mordoc is hysterically laughing. "He said you called him a lamb and told him to run."

 Smirking, I lean against the wall and run my tongue over my canines. "He is a lamb, and I told him to run." Smiling, I lean forward and laugh slightly. "Half the fun is in the hunt."

Pouring a second glass of blood, Mordoc closes the distance between us, offers it to me, and then clinks the glasses. "May you have success on your hunt." We toast to my impending hunt, and I gulp down the goodness within.

"Sun's coming up soon. I'll see you tonight. Thanks for the drink." I hand him back the empty goblet, then lean forward and kiss his cheek before leaving the room. Stalking through the house, I make sure Michael isn't hiding anywhere.

Just as I ponder my next move, my phone rings, and it's Raphael.

"Nikita, can I ask what may be a stupid question?" I bite back a laugh, I absolutely love when Raphael starts sentences like this. Because there's a one hundred percent chance he accidentally gives me vital information.

"Of course." Heading down the hallway, I make it to my bedroom and open the sliding glass door that leads out to my small balcony.

"What happened that scared Michael so bad? He's hiding in your mother's office like it's going to protect him." Bingo... Raphael, with the clutch blurting of valuable information. But, then again, this could be a setup by him and Michael to throw me off completely.

"Well, not that it's any of your business. I was trying to bond with my mate." Boredly, I look at my nails as I say it just before I get the brilliant idea to text my father. I hear Raphael choking on the other end of the conversation as I put the call on speaker and text my bio-dad. Good old Cyrus is always down to fuck with the Archangels. He heads towards Mom's office and confirms that Michael is not there. Thankfully, he was on shift as the Reaper for the hospital tonight.

"You know, Dad, it's not good for an Archangel to fib..." The line goes deadly silent, and I know it's killing Raphael that I know he's not being honest.

"Who says I'm fibbing?" he snaps back quickly.

"Daddy is on schedule tonight, or did you forget?" I read Daddy's messages, and I can eliminate the hospital from my places to search.

"I forgot. You've got to understand, little one. He's like a brother to me, and he asked me to hide him." The panic in Raphael's voice is almost comical.

"I forgive you," I say quickly before hanging up the phone, trying to figure out where to look next. Mom's office. She's got more than one.

Moving through the shadows, I manifest in Mom's closet in her office. I can clearly hear her talking to Michael, explaining primals and bonding to him. There's a strange discomfort in the center of my chest, almost like a dull stabbing pain. I rub at my sternum, trying to make the ache dissipate. Mom explains to Michael how I grew up wilder than my other siblings. How I rode the wind wild and free when I was with the Valkyrie. How I'm how she wished she could be. I never knew that about my mom. She expresses how she's jealous of my freedom, being born to parents that love me for who I am.

Her words make my heart hurt. I know my mom had it rough. I didn't know it was that rough. She tells Michael about all her problems growing up and how she didn't feel like she fit in at all. She explains how the blood lust kicked in once she and my biological father bonded. That makes my eyebrow raise hearing that the blood lust kicked in afterwards. When the conversation slows down, I turn the knob, seeing Michael with his head in his hands. I want to shield him from whatever is causing him pain.

Slipping in behind him, I wrap my arms around his shoulders, and he stiffens for a moment, then relaxes under my touch. Pressing my lips to his temple, I rest my body against his back and sigh softly. "As much as we need to seal the bond, I don't want you uncomfortable." Closing my eyes, I rest my head against his.

Michael reaches up, holds onto my arms, and rubs the skin slowly. "I appreciate it. The idea of being prey made me uncomfortable." His honesty, in one sense, makes me feel bad and good at the same time.

Hearing his admission really makes me rethink everything I have done up to this point. My instinct drives me in one direction, yet my light mate makes me want to go in the other direction. Threading my fingers through his hair, I watch as the golden locks flow through. I'm almost mesmerized watching how it moves. "I'm sorry that how I am makes you uncomfortable." I lower my head and turn away from Michael.

Michael's large hand grips my wrist, and he pulls me down into his lap. Thick arms band around me, holding me flush to his broad chest. He presses his lips to my temple, holding it there. "You are my world, Nikita. I want my forever with you." His brilliant blue eyes bore into mine, and I feel my heart skip a beat.

Glancing over at my mother, she smiles, then vanishes in a wisp of shadows. I draw in a deep breath and then kill the lights in the room. Once we are submerged in darkness, I move us through the shadows and end up in his room in the condo. Using the shadows, I flick on the light, and he notices we are in his room.

A brilliant smile graces his lips just before he moves forward to press his lips hard against mine. He loosens up and let's go, kissing me more passionately than I have ever felt before. I wrap my arms tightly around his neck and deepen the kiss. Michael actually moans into my mouth and paws at my ribs.

I am trying to respect his innocence and boundaries, but I can't hold back much more. "Michael, I need you. Either we need to head to your bed..." I leave the rest of it hanging. He stiffens for a moment. I feel the minute his resolve engages and he decides to move forward.

Scooping me up as if I weigh nothing, he carries me across the room and lays me reverently onto the bed. His eyes bleed into golden orbs as I look up into them. I watch so many emotions flitter across his features. It's amazing. His fingers grip the hem of my tee shirt, and I can feel the hesitation. His hand literally shakes at the edge of my shirt.

Taking the hint, I reach down, pull my shirt over my head, and throw it onto the floor. Michael's eyes slide slowly, inch by inch, over my chest and bra. I can sense his amazement. Reaching down, I grip the edge of my pants and slide them down. Michael's cheeks flair a brilliant shade of pink. The stretch of fake leather slowly slides over my hips and down my thighs. His eyes blaze a trail, following the material until I tug the ends off my feet.

Reaching forward, I slide my fingers along the edge of his slacks, getting him used to the idea of me getting closer to his crotch. He breathes in sharply before reaching down and assisting with removing his pants. Digging deep, Michael looks up with golden orbs and smiles. "I think I've got this from here, beautiful." Leaning forward, he kisses my lips. I close my eyes, enjoying the feeling. The next thing I know, he is placing fabric over my eyes, blindfolding me. "Trust me, Niki, all will work out in the end." My childhood nickname, I know I am a dead woman now.

CHAPTER 15
MICHAEL

Thankfully, the bookstore had plenty of books on intimate relationships and what to do and when. Granted, it's a written accounting and not applied education that I'm working with. My beloved Nikki lays before me in just her bra and thong, and I feel like my heart is coming out of my chest.

Nikita's skin feels like the smoothest silk under my fingertips. Goosebumps race across her flesh as my fingertips explore her body. Her snow white locks are fanned out across my white pillows, and her creamy flesh is laid out like a decadent meal before me. Swallowing my fear, I drop my boxers to the floor and crawl onto the bed with her. Starting at her calf, I place tender kisses along her shin bone to her knee.

Looking up, I watch her mouth pop open, and her fangs are visible. From what Raphael told me about Thana, it's how a darkling female shows they are excited. Passing Nikita's knee, I kiss her inner thigh. She gasps, and her body tenses for a moment. I know it's not fear that's making her gasp. I'm close to where she really needs me.

Uriel was kind enough to share his knowledge with me when I asked for help. He was more than willing to educate on what females want and need. It was more done as a mercy knowing how powerful Nikita is, she could easily kill me accidentally. My fingers grip her thong, and her hands fly down to cover mine.

"Michael, you don't have to..." Her eyebrows furrow as she tries to give me an out.

Gently, I kiss her knuckles and sigh softly before brushing her hands away.

"Trust me..."

Soon as the words leave my lips, her hands slide beside her, and I remove her thong. The most mysterious and wondrous creation is at the apex of my mate's thighs. Reverently, I kiss her silken folds, tentatively extending my tongue and lapping at it. The sweetest ambrosia hits my tastebuds, and I understand why Uriel said it would become my addiction for a while. Every lick, more nectar escapes her, and moans reverberate in her chest. The darnedest little thing exists above her folds, and seems to be sensitive and the root of her pleasure.

I attack this little root of nerves licking at it frantically. Nikita's moans are music to my ears and, honestly, the greatest sound I have ever heard.

"Fingers... use... your... fingers..."

Her breathless command slightly puzzles me, then I remember the one book I read. Dual stimulation seems to be the key to some women's pleasure. Slowly, I circle my fingertip around her glistening entrance before sliding it deep within her. Nikita's back bows off the bed at the intrusion. Her hips rock of their own volition, and I take the hint to work my finger within her.

"Faster! I'm so close…"

Her wish is my command, and I do as my beloved asks of me. Remembering what I read, I curve my fingers up and set a steady, hard pace. Her hips rock in time with my thrusts, and I can feel the flutters of her muscles gripping my fingers. She cries out and her muscles seem to engorge and lock my fingers in place. They feel like a vice and I can't move anymore. I remember the stories of Thana's alpha locking her mates when she was ready to conceive, and I'm scared and excited at the prospect.

I place kisses at her apex and smile, knowing I pleased my mate. Panting, she props herself up on her elbows and looks down at me. "Are you absolutely sure you've never done this before?" Her words are labored as I feel her muscles pulse again, then release my fingers.

"Positive. I guess I did a good job. Yes?" I look up at her hopefully.

Her eyes widen as she stares down at me. "Um, yes… you gave me an orgasm on your first attempt. You definitely did a good job. Great, even." Her smile and reaction are genuine.

Bolstered by my mate's reaction, I slowly climb up her body, dragging mine along hers, making sure I keep contact with her. Nikita's eyes fluctuate between pitch black and gray-blue. "I don't want to hurt you, Mikey." Her brows furrow in the middle as she looks up at me, concerned.

Leaning down, I nip lightly at her throat and grip her ear lobe between my teeth. A soft whine escapes her lips as her back arches up, pressing her breasts against my chest. Rocking forward, my phallus probes her slick folds. She stills immediately. Lifting my head up, I look down at her. Her eyes pop open, and she stares at me in amazement.

"Are you sure you're ready?" Her hands come up and frame my face. Her eyes search my features.

"Yes, I feel like I've waited my whole life for this moment." Leaning down, I press my lips to hers and move my hips forward, sliding my length deep within my mate's welcoming depths.

Warmth moves over me in waves, blanketing every inch of my being. Wave after wave pulses as I slide in and out, setting a steady pace, enjoying the feeling of her warm depths fluttering around me. Nikita moves with me, meeting me stroke for stroke. Her eyes bleed chrome as I look down at her, then suddenly, she flips us over, and I am flat on my back, buried to the hilt within her.

Nikita's eyes blacken as she stares down at me. "Hold my hips... and be ready for the ride of your life."

I do as I'm told, and the minute I have a grip on her, she grinds herself down onto me. My cock is reaching new places within her, and the sensations have me moaning right along with her. Why have we been forbidden to partake of the pleasures of the flesh? This is incredible and beautiful, watching my mate please us both at the same time. This one singular act is bringing our bond full circle, and the longer we last, the stronger my connection to her is becoming.

Nikita's wings burst free from her back and spread wide. The shadows whip wildly around her, being drawn into her body, fueling her. The more shadows she absorbs, the stronger and more frantic she impales herself on my length.

"I need..." She pants out between thrusts, and when she looks down at me, I understand what she's trying to tell me.

My beloved looks absolutely feral. Her upper and lower canines are distended, her eyes are blacker than pitch, and the room feels as if death itself walks. She needs my blood to bite and feed from me. Pushing myself up, I flip her onto her back and pin her to the bed, stilling my movements. I grip the back of her neck and bring her up to my left shoulder. "Mark me. Make me yours eternally."

As soon as my consent leaves my lips, the burning, sharp sting of her teeth breaking through my skin almost makes me pull away. The fire I feel where she is biting me spreads slowly through my body, electrifying my nerve endings. I pick up the pace, thrusting into her harder and faster than before. Her wings vanish from behind her, and she eventually releases my shoulder. Her tongue laves over my wounds, and a deep rumbling purr escapes her lips.

There's something erotic about her tongue licking up my blood. Nikita stops licking me and returns to meet me, thrust for thrust. "So close..." She arches her neck back, exposing it to me.

"I'm not sure what you need Nikki..." I run my nose up her throat, and she moans, gripping my shoulders, pulling me down to her. Lithe fingers thread into the hair at the nape of my neck until she pulls my mouth to her throat. I don't have canines like her, but she needs my bite. Opening my mouth wide, I place my teeth over the muscle of her neck, then bite down. Slowly I increase the pressure until her depths crush down upon my length, milking every inch of me for all I'm worth. It doesn't take much to tip me over the edge with her, and I come with her. Power floods our systems, and my blood feels as though it's on fire. Releasing her, I pant as her muscles crush my cock in a rhythmic motion until they lock down, holding me prisoner.

Nikita's hand snakes up to her throat, and she digs the tips of two of her nails into her muscles, making herself bleed. "Drink, my love..." She rolls her neck to the side, exposing the two rivulets of sanguine racing down her flesh.

I dare not disappoint my mate, and I lean forward and latch my mouth over her neck. Slowly, I suck at the wounds, and the taste of her blood explodes on my tongue. She tastes like a full-bodied port wine, rich and smokey in flavor with a slight berry after note. Her heartbeat becomes audible in my ears even though I know I shouldn't be able to hear it.

Squeezing my eyes tight, her rumbling purr becomes louder, and a great feathered beast becomes visible in my mind's eye. One huge amber orb with a fiery middle takes up my vision. It reminds me of the eye at the top of that tower in the movie with the hobbits and the ring in it. I release her neck and lick at the wounds she inflicted on herself. I watch the holes close almost instantly, and I'm speechless.

Nikita has the most serene look as her muscles finally decide to release me. Gently I kiss her lips, then roll to the side, taking her with me. Lithe fingers trace over my muscles, her eyes focused on their path.

"Mikey?" Nikita's voice is soft as she looks up at me with her gray-blue eyes.

"Yes, beloved?" Leaning over, I kiss her temple and watch her watch me.

"I feel calmer. Almost dare I say, not so angry." Her lips press against my chest before she rests her temple against the ball of my shoulder.

Arching an eyebrow, I ponder what she had just admitted to. I balanced the darkness within her. Now I wonder what will happen when Satan and Mordoc join the bond. Will she revert to being a loose cannon or remain calm? Pressing my lips to her forehead, I can only smile against her skin. "As long as you're happy, that's all that matters." I'm attempting to be as supportive as possible. I'm happy yet concerned at the same time.

I reach out through the Archangel bond to Raphael and explain what Nikita said and what I saw once the bond snapped into place. The bond goes silent, then flairs to life with him and Metatron, both speaking a mile a minute. The general consensus is that Thana told her mates she wants my nest at the house tomorrow night for dinner. I agree quickly, needing answers to the questions slowly building up.

My eyes move to watch Nikita sleep, and I watch what looks like ripples moving under her skin, and it's worrisome. As much as I try to shrug it off, all I keep thinking about is what Raphael told me about the basilisk that Thana has in her chest. If Nikita takes her other form, they will forever bar her from the Silver City. These fears swirl within my mind as I attempt to sleep. Sleep I feel will escape me tonight. I remain in conference with other Archangels about what they know about Death and the Destroyers bloodline. Someone has to know something.

CHAPTER 16
NIKITA

August...

The end of September is fast approaching, and so far, the only bond I have consummated was the one with Michael. Tonight, Satan and I are supposed to go out to shoot pool and do a bit of bar hopping. I'm looking forward to the date, but with all the strange emergencies pulling me away from my nest, I believe something more sinister is on the horizon.

Rex seems to take on a life of his own, manifesting when I don't summon him. For instance, if I take a nap, I'll wake up with his physical form in the room I'm sleeping in if I'm alone. It's almost as if he's becoming possessive of me. My hand glides over his tattooed form, and it feels as if his scales are more surface than usual. Then again, I have been dreaming of a massive black phoenix that rivals Tiamat's size and power. It talks to me in my sleep and tells me I am stronger than any Reaper that has come before me. It warns me of a second coming of Lucifer that is being resurrected from his ash in Hell's forge by the Balor.

Those brutes want to take their revenge on Lucifer, but since Mom killed him, they have no way to seek their vengeance. It won't shock me if they hire some hellish fiend to attempt the resurrection. They may even accomplish it, which would explain the influx of unstable energy I've been feeling lately.

"Nikki?" Freya's soft voice broke me out of my inner monologue.

"Yes, little one?" Calming almost instantly, I close the distance between my youngest sister and me and hug her tightly.

"I'm scared. Demons are rising almost nightly, and Mom is constantly battling. What are we going to do?" Her eyes are tear-filled, and it pisses me off almost instantly. Freya is the most gentle-hearted sibling that I have.

Stroking Freya's hair from root to tip, I hum the tune Aunt Sigrun would sing to us at bedtime as little girls when we would sleep over. Freya wraps her arms around my waist and holds on tightly. It's now that Satan shows up and takes in the scene. "All will be well, Freya. When has Mom, Davina, and I ever let you down?"

"Never. I don't want to lose you, Nikki. I can't lose you." Freya hugs me tighter, and my resolve almost breaks. I damn near feel a tear surfacing.

We will be strong enough soon. I will rise again.

The voice in my head makes me stop stroking Freya's hair. My eyes lock with Satan's, and he nods, then touches his ear, telling me he heard it too. Interestingly enough, Freya didn't. "When I rise to Death Eternal, I will be almost as strong as Mom." I kiss Freya's forehead, then turn to her to see Satan in his suit waiting for me. "Go see Aunt Sigrun. Maybe sleep there until this is all sorted out." Freya hugs and kisses me goodbye before taking off towards the Tree of Life.

"What was that?" Satan taps his ear and looks around.

"I'm not sure. I can only guess that non-angelic beings can hear it. Let's go see Mom." Reaching out, I grip Satan's hand.

"You know she scares the fuck out of me," he states plainly. His fear of my mother is not a secret in the least bit. To be honest, it's a well-known fact he's terrified of her.

Winking at would-be mate number two, I take ahold of his other hand and drag him through the shadows to where I sense my mother. We arrive in her office at the back of Club Dread. Opening the closet door, Mom and Dad were looking at a map pinned to the corkboard on the north wall of her office. Sensing our arrival, they turn as one to face us. "It spoke again," Mom states flatly as she turns to look back at the multicolored pins on the map.

"Yeah, and Rex has been acting of his own accord." This tidbit of information makes my mother freeze in her motions.

"He does what?" she spins fully and closes the distance between us. Her hand roughly raises my sleeve, staring at Rex's image on my arm. I swear I think I see his eye look from Mom to me.

"Nothing in my memory tells me anything about what I think was happening." Mom's focuses on Rex's image on my arm. Her thumb passes over his muzzle, and her eyes bleed chrome. "It seems like he almost has a life of his own." Mom's gaze raise to meet mine, and I study her facial movement. I have to give it to her. She's not giving anything away.

"What do we do? Or what do you think is happening?" I watch her thumb stretch and move my skin. Under her thumb, I feel what I think is Rex moving of his own volition.

"This is very interesting," Mom says as she moves her fingers several more times before releasing me.

Darting my eyes towards my father, he shrugs his shoulders and smirks, looking at me, rolling his eyes. He laughs softly as he steps between my mother and me. "I'll go visit your grandfather and see if he knows anything. I'll also check with the dragon clans in the Shadow Realm." Dad presses his lips to my forehead, and I can't help but close my eyes at the sensation. The feeling of love that only a parent has for a child wraps around me like a warm blanket. When I open my eyes again, Dad is gone, yet the feeling of his lips on my forehead remains.

Satan's eyes are wide open, mouth slightly agape as he openly stares. Mom moves her focus from me to Satan. "Settle the bond. Your ascension is close, and so is the Ball." Mom leans forward, kisses my cheek, and vanishes from before me.

I focus my gaze on Satan, and he shrugs. Arching a brow, I watch his facial features as he tries to process what he has seen. "Something is on your mind. Spit it out." Crossing my arms under my chest, I lean my shoulders against the wall.

"I never witnessed Dark Nephilims being affectionate. When I was an Archangel, before the fall, the dark ones were cold and cruel, never staying together beyond creating a life and moving on." Pursing his lips, he parses the information he has before continuing. "We used to be sent to destroy breeding nests because the dark ones didn't care if the females lived or died. If they were willing or not." Biting his bottom lip, he breaks eye contact for a moment before raising his hands between us. "There's so much blood on my hands, Nikita. So much..."

His admission does something to the nerves deep within the pit of my stomach. The anxiousness I was feeling about bonding with a Fallen one subsided. Whatever my mother did to cleanse him brought back the ability to feel remorse. Satan's guilt is palatable on the air. It is sour, almost bitter, on my tongue. The scent reminds me of ozone, strong and weighted in the air. I don't like this scent, the guilt of a bond-mate is not something I want to ever smell again.

Reaching out, I grip both of his hands and hold on tight. "There's another war coming, and I hate to say it, but we will need your experience to keep us safe." I try to implore him with my expression, letting him know I will be there for him. My right hand reaches up and cups his left cheek as I rub my thumb over his bottom lip. "I will be Death Eternal. Far stronger than Azrael ever was, even in his prime. I will be bathed in blood by the time this war ends." My gaze drops, and I can almost imagine the blood coating my claws and hands.

You won't fight alone.

The voice echoes in my ears, and I hear the sliding of scales this time. *Fuck, can it be Rex talking to me or another dragonic demon from the abyss?* I look up quickly. Satan doesn't seem to have heard anything this time. *I wonder if he heard him and is ignoring it?*

He didn't need to hear me.

Now I seriously believe I am going nuts. I'm hearing voices in my head by myself. *Am I truly that lonely to manifest a man in my head?*

"I need to go see an old family friend. When I return, I owe you a date." Leaning forward, I kiss Satan's lips, then vanish in the shadows in the room's corner.

The sun has set by the time I decide to go visit Luna and her mate Marco. Her mate is the descendant of the Maelestor Rex that happens to be on my arm. Maybe he knows more about his ancestor than my family is aware of. Midway there, I text Luna letting her know I am coming in hot so that her mate and his clan don't hit me with their acid breath. She replies quickly, and I almost drop my phone. I know I shouldn't be texting and flying, but I am. At this point, I remember to text the guys and fill them in on what's happening. Instead of typing, I send a voice message and keep on my path.

The mountain village Luna and Marco call home comes into view, as well as all the dragon guards clinging to or circling the mountain. Marco is standing on his balcony with a torch in hand, waving for me to land there. Following his directions, I come in for a landing on the balcony rail. "Thank you for seeing me on such short notice."

Nodding, he ushers me through the house and towards the den, where Luna rests with her children near the fireplace. "You sounded distressed in your message. What do you mean by the tattoo talks to you?"

Pulling my leather jacket off, I lay it across the closest chair and roll the sleeve up, exposing the tattoo of Maelestor Rex. Marco does a long whistle as he stares at the dragon on my flesh. "He was a phenom in battle, undefeated all the way up to the end. He sacrificed his existence to be granted this safe haven for his descendants to flourish. Humans cannot see or find this place. Humans overlook the characteristics of our species in human form." Marco moves to the bookshelf and pulls out a book containing his ancestor's histories.

Marco offers me the book, and I take the heavy leather-bound tome in my hand and sit on the arm of the couch. The pages chronicle his birth all the way up to his sacrifice. Most notably, he never took a mate. The females that produced his heirs were not his mate, just females in his nest. "Why didn't he ever take a mate?" The words fall softly from my lips, more a question to myself than anything else.

"That's unknown. Sometimes we wait centuries for a mate to be born or choose a compatible female so our drakes don't go insane." Marco threads his fingers affectionately through Luna's hair as he smiles down at his mate. He knew the moment she took her first breath she was his. Much like Michael knew I was his when he saw my wings shortly after birth. How Marco and Michael managed to wait for their mates to mature amazes the shit out of me.

"I completely understand that my mate Michael's age is unknown, and so are Satan's and Mordoc's. I know they are thousands of years old. The age gap doesn't bother me, to be honest." Smiling, I glance from Marco over to Luna, who is staring up at her mate with pure adoration in her eyes.

"Age doesn't matter, Nikita. What does is how you feel about your mate." Luna smiles as she stands. Skaldi clings to her side smiling and waving at me. Her sweet cherubic cheeks and pouty lips make me think she's an Angel or at least a Nephilim of some sort.

"Back on topic, ladies," Marco says, snapping Luna and me out of our happy little bonding moment.

"Can you persuade my ancestor to manifest?" He tilts his head to the side and then motions to the double doors leading out into the courtyard.

I am not a sideshow piece.

The voice I now recognize as Rex's echoes in my head. "You're not a sideshow piece to me." I rush out as I follow Marco and Luna into the courtyard.

Luna stops and looks at me, perplexed. "Who were you talking to just now?"

"Rex, he's not happy that his presence is being requested." I run my fingers over his image that is emblazoned on my flesh. His scales rise slightly as my fingertips dance over what would be the scales on his neck.

"You can hear him? I thought you were joking." Marco steps closer, watching my flesh move as the scales rise and fall under his ancestor's blackened, inked image. His eyes shift to serpentine slits as he watches his ancestor move under my flesh. As Marco reaches out to touch the ink, Rex recoils, moving up my arm and away from his descendant.

"That's new." My senses are locked on the slithering slide of Rex's body, moving under my flesh.

"Where did he go?" Marco slides my sleeve up the rest of the way, and there's no evidence of him being there.

"He's moved." Walking to the center of the courtyard, I find the clearest area with the least amount of items that Rex can destroy. "Maelestor Rex! I summon you."

Unlike the times before, I feel like my body is igniting from the inside, as though I am being torn apart from the inside out, flesh, muscle, and sinew snapping and stretching beyond normal extent. The excruciating pain makes it difficult to breathe. The ground feels as though its falling away from under me as the muffled screams from Luna the last sensations I feel.

CHAPTER 17

MICHAEL

AN AFTERNOON WITH RAPH AND METATRON IS A MUCH-NEEDED BREAK from all that has been going on. My home has become an enormous pit of darkness, and I can do nothing about it. Nikita ascending to Death Eternal needs to be fueled by complete and utter darkness to handle the realm of the dead.

"How's our Nikita handling having a nest of her own?" Metatron queries as he sips his tea.

"As well as can be expected at this point. We're bonded, and I'm head mate, so I guess things are in order." Smiling weakly, I feel as though something isn't right. Furrowing my brows, I stare at my tea, trying to figure out the feeling.

"Michael, what's wrong?" Raphael reaches out and rests a hand on my forearm.

"You're burning up." Raphael passes his healing light over me. Beads of sweat roll down his temples as he strains, attempting to heal what's wrong. "I can't sense anything. Your raise in temperature is unexplained." Removing his hands, he stares at his palms.

"Maybe it's not him. It might be Nikita," Metatron says, looking me over, concern etched over his features. With furrowed brow and pursed lips, he gawks at me.

As soon as the mention of my wayward young mate sinks in, I stand suddenly and push away. A chill runs down my spine. For the first time in my life, I know fear. Without a moment's hesitation, I take to the sky, heading back to the house to find the others. The afternoon temperature drops steadily as I fly as fast as possible. The prevailing winds assist me in moving swiftly towards my cliffside house.

Landing on the balcony on the second floor, I shove the doors wide open and rush through the house. "Satan, Mordoc, we've got to find Nikita!" I scream as I race through the halls.

"What happened?" Satan pops out of his room, following close on my heel.

"Not sure something is happening with Nikita. I can feel it." That creeping feeling crawls slowly up my spine like a spider crawling up a wall.

"Shit. Okay, we need to get going then! Mor! We need to fly!" Satan overtakes me in the hallway.

The pounding of our boots in the hallway must have awakened Mordoc because he drops out of the attic and lands behind us. "I have a clue about where she went. Is there a living descendant of Maelestor Rex?" Mordoc follows close behind as we head to the main balcony off the kitchen.

We open the doors and launch into the fading light of the evening, taking flight towards the north. "Yes, his great-grandson lives with his people in the mountains close to here. Nikita's family is close to his mate's family." Mordoc swoops down, then banks hard, heading towards the mountains.

Flapping hard, Satan and I are on his six, following behind closely. "How do you know where to go?" It puzzles me that the one who has spent the least time with Nikita seems to know exactly where she is.

"That's easy. My kind can smell death. Since she is a Reaper and soon-to-be Death Eternal, I can smell where she is. As her mate, you should be able to sense her location," Mordoc states coldly as I hear him huff up ahead of us as if I am a child.

Reaching deep into my soul, I search for the tethers of the bond between Nikita and me. The dark wisp that is my beloved mate that coils around my light. Following my heart, I feel the tug in Nikita's direction.

The further I fly, the hotter my core becomes. The sudden pulling and tearing deep within me feels like something is trying to rip its way out of me. "Ahhhh!" The scream rips free of me in time with the roar of a mighty dragon. It takes several moments before my vision clears, and when it does, the largest, most terrifying Skull Dragon rises and circles the mountaintop.

His roar fills the air, and terror seizes my heart. Several smaller dragons rise to meet him, and they vanish into the night sky. Closing the distance to what looks like a castle in the peaks of the snow-capped mountains. We land in what looks like a courtyard and see Nikita in a white-haired female's arms. "I'm Michael. I'm Nikita's mate."

The female beams up at me, smiling. "Oh, my gosh, you are even more beautiful than she's ever described. I'm Luna, her cousin, one of Aurora's daughters." Her lithe fingers thread through my mate's hair with love and affection.

"Thank you for taking care of my mate. What happened here?" The courtyard looks like a war zone. Acid burns, claw marks, and trees broken in half. Ground zero looks like Hell on Earth.

"Nikita's familiar has been talking to her a lot, and being here with his clan and his descendant, he forcefully ripped his way free of her. He took off to the old hunting grounds with my mate and the current heads of this clan." Smiling, she lifts Nikita, allowing me to slip under, embracing my mate and tending to her.

"What can we do to awaken her?" Satan kneels to the right of Nikita and holds her hand in his.

"Feeding her should do it. Having her familiar rip himself free of her body, then leave of his own accord, took a lot of power." Mordoc kneels on her left side. "Open her mouth. I'll start feeding her first." Biting his wrist, his dark crimson ichor flows freely. He presses his wrist to her mouth, and soon, we hear a sucking noise coming from her.

Luna looks terrified of Mordoc, and I remember Nikita saying Luna is an Omega and easily frightened. "He won't harm you. He's one of Nikita's mates."

Her eyes tentatively glance from Nikita and back to Mordoc, and she simply nods.

Mordoc seems to be in a state of absolute bliss. His head leans back as his wings fall limply behind him. The soft sucking noise almost makes my stomach churn, thinking my beautiful dark angel is drinking a vampire's blood. After several moments, she releases his wrist, and elongated canines are visible in her mouth.

"I guess I'm up," Satan says way too happily, cutting his wrist with a pocketknife before offering it to Nikita. Her nostrils flair, and her mouth opens wide. Satan bravely sticks his wrist into her mouth and gasps. "Fuck, her canines hurt." He, too, smiles, eventually getting a sappy look on his face as a pleased moan escapes his lips.

"She's not a vampire. She doesn't have the venom we have that makes the experience painless and pleasurable." Mordoc waves his hand dismissively in the air as if that were common knowledge.

Nikita's color steadily improves as she drinks Satan's blood. Still, that sucking noise turns my stomach. How can my mate survive off of blood? Then I remember some of the legends that talk about the time before time existed. A time when dragons and demons roamed the dark depths of space in an eternal battle. One particular battle created light and the creator all in one gigantic explosion.

Lost in my own memories, the snapping of fingers draws me back to reality. "It's your turn Golden Boy. You're bonded to her. Your blood will do the most good for her." Mordoc's words sink in, and I nod resolutely.

"Nikki, I can't harm myself. You'll have to bite me." Pulling my sleeve up, I expose my wrist and lower it to her mouth. The burning sting of her bite causes the muscles in my forearm to spasm. Soft mewling noises escape her lips as she pulls hard on my veins, drawing my life's blood into her. Her color returns, and she appears to be regaining her strength getting closer to fully awakening.

A roar sounds overhead followed by the loud beating of wings. I watch as the massive Skull Dragon comes in for a landing, except he shifts into a man the minute his feet hit the soil. He's tall and muscular, like all dragon men usually are. He comes to kneel at Nikita's feet, his golden dragon eyes watching her affectionately.

Another dragon man arrives and hugs the woman named Luna. "Ancestor, Nikita was severely weakened since you freed yourself. Can you help her?" Nikita finally releases my wrist and breathes softly, finally resting comfortably.

The one referred to as ancestor simply nods and reaches out, touching Nikita's bare hand. Her eyes fly open, and she sits up immediately. I watch in horror as their eyes lock, and I can feel intense love burn through the bond. A love that mates feel, oh no... A great dragon spirit is her mate. He smiles briefly at Nikita before returning to the dragon emblazoned on her flesh, meant to be her immortal guardian.

Her eyes drop, and she stares affectionately at the ink upon her flesh. A slow, steady breath is drawn into her, and she sighs as she exhales. I've watched Nikita closely her entire life, and I can tell something is brewing below the surface.

"Are you okay?" Satan scoots closer to Nikita and runs his hand over her hand closest to him.

"Hmm?" Her eyebrows raise before her eyes do. "Yes, I believe I am." Her eyes fall again to the ink upon her flesh.

"Legends are telling of the second rising of Maelestor Rex. The stories are painted in a cavern close to here if you would like to see them," the dragon man named Marco offers.

"I'm not sure she's up to it just yet," I reply, trying to look out for my mate's health.

Nikita turns to face me and smiles. "I'm all right, Michael. Worst case, you can carry me if I'm not." She smiles, and I know it's more for my benefit than anything else.

The others can't feel how drained she is or that the manifestation has left her with more questions than answers. Stretching, I watch as Nikita's wings unfurl behind her. Her obsidian wings are large and powerful, like her mother's. The feathers themselves are longer and wider than the average Angel's feathers. She is capable of incredible speed and agility in flight. The only downside is that her wings are heavy.

Nikita launches into the night sky, her black wings blending perfectly into the darkness. One by one, we take flight to follow her as she follows Marco into what we call the forbidden mountains. The Dark ones have used these mountains for rituals for generations, and as we get closer, a chilling grip wraps its tendrils around my heart. I'm going to the one place that angels fear to tread.

Marco dives down into a pit, and Nikita follows fearlessly. The other nest mates follow in after her blindly. I circle the pit several times, studying the opening, and finally descend into the pit. As I dive deeper, the temperature drops faster. A light blazes to life at the end of the pit's tunnel, and a blood-curdling scream echoes up to me.

Reactively I fold my wings in tight to my body and plummet like a stone closing the distance to the bottom. Reaching the bottom, I spread my wings open wide, stopping almost immediately. My feet hit the floor, and my sword blazes to life only to find Nikita standing over the body of what looks like a lizard that looks like a man.

"What happened?" Moving forward, I look down at the misshapen man.

"Lizardfolk live in these tunnels and guard the legends and treasures of my ancestors," Marco states as he walks the room, lighting the torches that line the wall. Paintings line the walls depicting endless wars and battles.

At the head of the cavern, the biggest depiction stands the test of time behind a well of burning oil. The Skull Dragon we saw earlier stands like a sentinel behind a Reaper. Its darkness is all-encompassing. Off to the left, the Destroyer stands with her tri-color wings open. To the dragon's right, a vampire that looks like Mordoc and, oddly, a winged being with light and dark wings. A being bathed in golden light is the one I keep getting stuck on. What does this all mean?

CHAPTER 18

NIKITA

THE CAVE FEELS LIKE AN ODD HOMECOMING. THE DANK COLDNESS OF THE cavern reminds me of a giant tomb. Blackening my eyes, I scan the room, and the murals seem to come to life like private movies just for me. Wars of days gone by replay, and I learn from the past.

The mural that has the men fixated moves slower than the others. The dragon breathes, and the darkness swirls from the Reaper in front of it. From what I can gather, when Maelestor rises again, whatever is coming cannot stand against him. On the opposing wall, a huge black phoenix stands tall. Its color changes as you look at it from different angles.

By the looks of the bird, it's female. Its feathers and head are not as heavily armored as a male's. Crossing the room without hesitation, I am drawn to the depiction of the phoenix. Reapers can assume a form not of their flesh. It's the ultimate sacrifice of our kind, giving up our shot of entering the Silver City and ascending to take our place among the angels. I'm as close to being a Fallen Angel as any living creature can be that was never of the light.

Extending my hand out, I touch the image of the phoenix; it feels like coming home. Her image feels like home as much as my mother's black wings feel like safety wrapped around me. This right here is what I need, not like the wolf of my great-grandfather before me. Not the raven of father's father. Not the panther my father chose. Definitely not the basilisk my mother picked for herself. The histories of our kind occasionally play through my thoughts.

The image before me is the one part I couldn't see clearly. Glancing over, Michael catches my eye, and I see the moment he realizes what I'm thinking. I have chosen my ascended form. Lowering my gaze, I stare at the dirt beneath my feet. A single black feather rests at the base of the painting. The minute I pick it up, my body absorbs it. All that's left is my ascension after I finish my mate bonds.

Turning away from the image, I rejoin the others. "I have a feeling I know what these images are depicting." Staring up at the depiction of Rex in his full standing form. "The end of days, where the warriors of the past rise to defend mankind. Resurrection happens as well as the dead walking the earth again." I glance down and away again.

"I must ascend. I need to finish the bonds and take the mantle of Death Eternal. My Grandfather's powers are waning, and I'm not sure how much longer he can be an effective keeper of the ninth seal." I turn and make eye contact with everyone.

"Whatever you need to do, Nikita, I will support you." Michael's tone doesn't give away my churning anxiety in our bond.

"Some places even Archangels cannot tread, my love." I close the distance between Michael and press my lips against his for a moment. A soft hum escapes his lips as his fingertips brush over my cheek before I pull away. He bows his head resolutely, then backs away.

"Satan, you and Mordoc can go where Michael cannot. We need to tap into our most primal instincts to ensure the future of this world." My eyes linger on each mate one at a time before looking between them.

"My fangs and claws are yours to do with as you, please. My kingdom and army are at your disposal." Mordoc steps forward and drops to a knee before me.

Bending down, I press my lips to his forehead and offer him my wrist. His teeth break through my skin. The initial sting is replaced with an almost euphoria. The euphoria doesn't last long for whatever reason, and I focus my blackened eyes on him. Fingers thread through his thick wavy black hair from root to tip. "We will feast on the blood of our enemies, Mordoc." He releases my wrist and licks the wound, sealing it immediately.

He rises to his feet and kisses my lips, letting me taste my blood on his lips. Wordlessly, he moves off to the side and leaves Satan standing alone. Cautiously, I move closer to Satan. He has so many hidden traumas; I don't want to trigger any of them. Years of torture at the hands of Lucifer, the trauma of being split from his other half. He's literally lost part of himself, and who knows what damage that did to him. His nightmares call to me when he sleeps. I feel his pain and discomfort when he remembers what they did to him.

Extending my hands out, I allow him to make the choice whether to come to me or not. I'm dominant and primal in nature, so my presence can cause more harm than good at the wrong time. He nervously looks at my hands, then over at the others as he tries to decide.

Unfurling my wings, I try to smile at him to bring him some comfort. Flexing my midnight wings seems to have snapped him out of his daze, and he immediately moves into my embrace. "This is all very concerning." Softly he utters his fear close to my ear for only me to hear.

Drawing in a fortifying breath, I enclose us in my wings. The darkness soothes the savage beast deep within me as I rest my head on his shoulder. "We move at your pace, Satan." I nuzzle his throat, forcing myself to resist the urge to bite him and mark him as mine.

"I'm not as fragile as you think I am." Satan's words are hesitant as he tries to wrap his arms tighter around my waistline, holding on to me like a small teddy bear. I would almost swear I feel a shudder move through his body.

"I understand that. But I also don't want you to feel pressured into doing something you're not ready to do." I try to comfort him the best I can, knowing that I am in no rush for him to form the bond with me. Even though it's imperative we get all the puzzle pieces into place before whatever's rising from the darkness gets here.

Michael paces, and I hear his boots thudding against the cavern's stone interior. Rubbing my hands down Satan's back, I try to pass as much calming energy over him as possible before I open my wings up. Glancing around to the others, I look back towards the phoenix, then back to the legend on the wall closest to us.

"I know this comes as a shock to a lot of you, but I already have a very good idea where all this takes place." I motion to the picture on the wall.

"If you look on the upper right-hand side of the image, there's a castle in the distance. The castle itself is the same one that is my mother's in the Shadow Realm. Over here on the left-hand side, there's the twin Spires, the same ones that my father was strapped to the top of the monolith and was being bled out." My eyes dart between my mates and then over to Marco, my cousin's mate.

"I know your people can traverse the Shadow Realm when need-ed." Reaching back, I pluck one of my flight feathers out and close the distance between him and me. "With this feather, I grant you my protection and the ability to lead your people through to the Shadow Realm when I call for you." I wrap the feather around his wrist, and it becomes an obsidian band. "All that you need to do is touch this to the wrist of each of your warriors, and it will grant them the same passage that I have granted you."

Stepping away from him, I look back over at Satan. "We will go on the date as you had originally planned tonight after we've all rested. It's already very early in the morning, and we need our rest." I glance between my mates and the back over to Marco and lightly dip my head to him. "Thank you for all of your help with everything. Your people have preserved these histories that are the most valuable, and I appreciate you sharing them with us greatly."

He bows his head and brings his fist over his heart. "Anything the daughter of the Destroyer needs is yours."

Smirking, I allow my eyes to shift to chrome and then back to black as pitch. "Soon enough, I will be Death Eternal. None shall stand before me." My words echo in the cavern, shaking it to its very foundation. Finally accepting my destiny and mantle, I feel like my nerves are a live wire. Every fiber of my being vibrates with a newfound energy that I did not know existed.

Reaching out to my mates, I place a hand on Michael and Satan. Mordoc moves forward and puts his hands on my forearms. In a matter of seconds, we're engulfed in shadows and gone from the cavern that possibly has predicted my future. We manifest back in Michael's home, down in the basement in the darkest corner where nothing is left standing. Michael, unfortunately, becomes sick to his stomach from the shifting through the shadows. Satan goes to assist him while Mordoc flicks on the light switch.

"I'm sorry for the abrupt change of scenery." I begin the pace the downstairs, setting the things we accidentally knocked over back where they belong. "There are few people and places I trust at this point. It's not that I don't trust Marco and his flight of dragons. But they are creatures of darkness, like most of us here. Sometimes those creatures are easily swayed by a force stronger than themselves."

I walk over to Michael, place my hand on his neck, and start rubbing gently, trying to soothe him from getting sick. "Each time you travel through the shadows, it won't be as hard to recover afterward, I promise." He simply nods at me and then trudges back upstairs. Looking at both of my dark mates, I smirk and then roll my eyes in the direction that Michael had left. "I've got my hands full with that one, don't I?"

Mordoc chuckles and heads towards the stairs. "We definitely have our hands full with that one." I was hoping the ancient one would disagree with me. Unfortunately, even though he sees things the same way that I do. As much as Michael is my mate when we go into the darkness, there's only so much of it that he will be able to deal with. Part of it I want to shield him from. The rest of it, he's gonna have no choice but to endure.

Satan taps me on the shoulder and then bounces a little bit as he stands there, waiting for me to turn fully to face him. "Dress casually for later. And make sure your clothing and your shoes are comfortable," he says, smiling one of the first genuine smiles I've seen grace his lips in a very long time. I nod in his general direction and then head up the stairs myself. I need a shower and some sleep. Who knows what this evening is going to hold for me.

CHAPTER 19

SATAN

It's our first official date night, and I honestly don't know what to wear at this point. I know I told Nikita to dress casually, be comfortable, and wear shoes she'd be able to get around in. But I feel like I need to make an impression on her at this point.

I don't have the power and wealth that Michael has. I don't have the age and the knowledge that Mordoc has. Hell, I live in her father's old apartment he was kind enough to give to me on the other side of the city. And then there comes the issue of her mother. A shiver runs through me as I think about the idea of the Destroyer herself being displeased with anything I do for her child. Huffing out an exasperated breath, I try to settle my nerves by having a shot of some of the whiskey I have hidden in my room.

After belting back a shot, I draw in a nice slow, cleansing breath and look again into my closet. I decide to go simple and chic at the same time. A pair of Levi's jeans and a nice button-down shirt to go along with it. I feel like I've pulled the outfit together well. The jeans scream casually while the button-down dress shirt says I'm taking this seriously. I move before the mirror and run my comb through my hair for about the millionth time. It doesn't matter how many times I do it; I still feel like something's out of place with me. I go to the sink and splash more water on my face, trying to settle the nerves slowly building. The ticking of the clock as each minute passes seems to ring louder than Big Ben itself. The tick tick tick tick is slowly driving me insane.

I feel the temporal shift when Nikita finally rises from her nap. Nap, who am I kidding? Most of us fell into a deep slumber trying to recover from being up all night, going into the cavern, and learning about what may come for us. I hear her moving down the hallway and into what sounds like the bathroom. I close my eyes and focus on the surrounding sounds. The water in the shower runs, and I can almost imagine what my mate looks like stepping under that heated water. A soft moan escapes my lips as I envision what she looks like in all of her naked glory. Rolling my eyes, I adjust myself in my jeans. Damn it, I did it to myself again. A short, soft chuckle escapes my lips as I mentally chastise myself for giving myself yet another boner.

I almost feel like a pervert standing here listening to the water run, imagining that I was those droplets of water running down her flesh. I know it's not a bad thing we are mates, but we have yet to take that step in our relationship. To be honest, I fear what her mother will do if I don't please her daughter. As much as Thana claims she doesn't have a favorite. Her darkest daughter, my mate, seems to be her number one priority.

Thana has always tried to be fair with her children, but the light children gravitated towards the Archangels and the regular Angels versus their mother. More often than not, I would sit at the bar trying to keep the tears from rolling down Thana's cheeks when Davina shunned her because she was more darkness than light.

I can only imagine what's going to happen when Michael fathers his first child. Will it be dark like the rest of us, or will it be born of light? Most times, they do not give a dark Nephilim female an Archangel or an Angel of any sort. In theory, dark and light cancel each other out. Nikita is as close to being a Fallen Angel as anyone could get without actually having fallen. She has the typical fiery temperament, the predatory gaze, the drive to hunt, and an almost insatiable taste for blood. All three are the markers of the Fallen. I guess that's why she's going to become Death Eternal. Even Azrael, the current head Reaper, and the Angel of Death is not strong enough to gain that title.

A shudder moves through me, thinking about what Nikita might do to me if she loses her temper or I don't please her. Lost in my musings, I don't register that the shower stopped nor that there's a light tapping as if someone gently tapping on my bedroom door. It's not until, I'm guessing, the third or fourth time that whoever is knocking opens the door and steps in. Nikita taps me on the shoulder, and I damn near jump out of my skin. She stands there cackling hysterically, holding her sides as she bends over, her face flush. "You should have seen the look on your face!"

All I can do is shake my head as I look at her. "Nikita, one. Satan, zero." I announce today's score, and she beams the most positively radiant smile I've seen today. In her human guise, she looks as if she could be an Angel. Creamy light caramel skin, beautiful pale grey eyes, and almost white blonde hair. These beautiful distractions hide the demon that lurks within. "Are you ready to leave, beautiful?"

The word slides like silk off my tongue as I extend my left elbow to her. She wraps an arm around mine and pats me on the bicep. "Lead the way."

I'm shocked that she's allowing me to orchestrate this evening. She's far more dominant than I'll ever be, and that she's letting me have control is amazing. We head downstairs and out into the garage. Within it is my Jeep Wrangler. I don't have the need for speed she does, nor do I have a ton of cash like Michael does to keep the expensive car he drives. Mordoc has nothing up here, so I'm guessing at least I have that on him.

I open up the passenger door and assist Nikita into my lifted Jeep. She buckles in, and I close the door behind her, then run to my side. Climbing into the driver's seat, I start the Jeep, pop the clutch, and put her into first gear. We start down the driveway, and I notice Nikita looking all around the interior of my Jeep. "I didn't know you owned this?"

Nikita's question catches me off guard. "Oh? I didn't know you paid much attention to even theorize what I drive." Gripping the wheel a little tighter makes that crinkling noise as I rub my hand back and forth, ringing the top of the steering wheel.

"That's not what I meant..." she practically stutters through the first half of the sentence. "What I meant was, I never would have pictured you as a Jeep guy." She turns slightly in her seat, angling her body towards me while I drive.

Shrugging my shoulders, there's not much I could say. "What type of vehicle did you think I drive? I've only been up here a short period compared to you and your family." Seven years isn't that long compared to the time her family has been here. My existence on this earthly plane has been as long as she's been alive. Except I think she may be alive longer than my existence here by maybe six months, give or take. Nikita stares at me for a few moments and then taps her index finger on the tip of her chin.

"Well, I can almost picture you driving maybe an Audi. Or perhaps a Camaro." She ponders the current types of vehicles, still not settling on something she believes I'd drive most definitively. Shaking her head, she laughs. "Maybe I'll let you drive my car later, see if you like it. I'm due for an upgrade soon, so you might as well have it if you like it." Thankfully, we come up to a red light when she drops that bomb on me. Shocked, I turned to face her.

"You've got to be joking. You would give me your car?" I can't believe those words might have come out of her mouth.

She leans her head against the headrest as she watches me. As I look at her, I monitor the traffic light, making sure it hasn't turned green. "Of course I would. You are my mate. What's in the nest is for everyone to use." She smiles, and it's exactly as Raphael explained it to me. The wealth of the nest becomes everybody's the minute that we add the female to the bond.

Nikita laughs as she points at the now green light ahead of us, and I resume driving. "Besides, Michael's the rich one out of all of us. He's been here for like thousands of years." As she says the word and rolls her eyes. She's not wrong. The man has been alive for thousands of years and has worked amongst humans for as long.

Nikita definitely pulled off a miracle by distracting me by talking to me about cars. For the rest of the ride, she would pull up different pictures of vehicles that she thought would be excellent for her to replace her car with. She looks at everything from a big black diesel truck like Aurora. All the way to the Lexus like Raphael drives. Frankly, I'm not sure why any of them have vehicles except for attending the occasional human party.

We arrive outside of our destination, and I park the Jeep in the last remaining parking spot, shut it off, then jump out and run to the other side to grab Nikita's door for her. Gripping her around her waist without thinking, I lift her up and help her from the Jeep, setting her feet on the ground. I adjust her sweater and make sure there's no dirt from the Jeep. While I'm trying to attend to her properly, I hear her giggle.

Looking up at her, I see a very warm, loving smile gracing her sanguine lips. There's a sparkle in her eyes that wasn't there before. She's looking at me as if I am the only man in existence at this moment. My heart flip-flops in its chest as I stare back at her. I watch as her gaze rises, and she notices the sign on the awning behind me.

"Are we really going to throw axes?" The excited tone of her voice tells me I have chosen well.

"I figured, with all the time that you had stayed with the Valkyrie, that axe throwing would be appropriate." I smile and offer her my arm again, trying to be the dutiful gentleman. Without hesitating, she wraps her arm around mine and rests her hand on my fore-arm. I feel like a king amongst men walking proudly towards the door with her. I slip my arm away from hers for a moment just to open the door for her, allowing her to enter before me.

Once inside, the loud music and thumping bass makes my chest vibrate. The further we go, the happier Nikita seems to get. The music that they're playing is right up her alley.

I exchange high fives between myself and the owner. "Now, who's this beautiful lady you've got with you?" Justice questions as he lightly dips his head to Nikita.

I smile proudly and motion to my mate. "This is Nikita Dawn-strider, the daughter of the Destroyer and my mate."

Wide-eyed, Justice looks between Nikita and me. Several emotions flicker over his visage before he tries to rein them back in. "It is an honor and a privilege to have you here, Death Eternal." He bows his head in supplication and drops to a knee before my mate.

Nikita gives me a look that I'm not sure what it means. She steps forward and places her hand on top of his head. "Rise." This is all that she says, then looks back at me. I can't tell if I'm in deep shit or okay.

Justice stands quickly, gathers two crates of axes, and walks us down the hallway. Several turns later, we end up in what looks to be a party room. "I know you reserved only a single lane in the store's front. But given who your mate is, you can have the run of the party room. You have bullseye targets, mannequins, and several other items you are welcome to throw the axes into. Above all else, enjoy yourself." Justice says with a flourished bow, then backs out of the room, leaving Nikita and me to start our date.

I can only hope this is the right move for me.

CHAPTER 20
NIKITA

Satan's idea of a first date is an absolute stroke of genius on his part. The only downside to what he chose to do is the shop owners' acknowledgment of who I am. I am not, shape or form, looking forward to taking the mantle of Death Eternal. And to be reminded of it when I'm supposed to be having a good time out with my mate is almost a mood killer.

I walk around the interior of what they're calling the party room, looking at all the objects we can throw axes at. "Which do you want to hit first?" I ask Satan. Hopefully, he has a plan of attack for this adventure.

"Well, I was thinking about going after the mannequins because it would simulate us going into war." Shrugging his shoulders, he looks at me curiously, then concern etches his beautiful features.

Closing the distance, I lightly caress his cheek and get him to focus his eyes on me. "We do need to practice, and this is probably the most thoughtful gift I've ever received." Smiling, I move in close and kiss his lips gently. The darkness within me wants to chase, hunt, and make him mine completely. A deep rumble echoes in my chest as I stare at him.

Satan's eyes blacken almost immediately in response to the rumble. It's predator versus prey at this point. He could be a skilled predator if he wished it, but after all the years of damage, I'm not sure how much dominance is left in him. "I hoped that this treat would please you," he says as he rests his forehead against mine. "What do you get the girl that has everything?" He pulls away from me and picks up two axes in his hands. "My answer was to take her out and allow her to throw sharp objects at targets to her little black heart's content."

I watch him as he throws his first two axes at one mannequin. The first embeds itself in the mannequin's forehead. The second lodges itself in the chest of the same mannequin. Both are killing blows, striking with precision, guaranteeing a fatality. "That's impressive. Can I try?"

Satan, being the gentleman he is, reaches down into the crate and offers me two axes, handles first. I test their weight in my hands, turning them repeatedly, getting a feel for them. They're not too heavy, and I'm quite shocked they're decently balanced. This should be interesting. I take aim at the first mannequin, sinking the axe deeply into its chest, burying most of the blade. The second axe I throw, but instead of aiming the blade vertically, I aim horizontally and take the head off the mannequin. To say that Satan is speechless upon seeing the head of the mannequin decapitated is an understatement.

Just as I turn to face Satan, there's a disturbance in the surrounding air. The cold icy chill and the sudden scorching heat warn me that someone is coming through the veil. We move quickly to stand back-to-back, searching the room for the intruder. No one is in the room with us, but that doesn't mean they're not in the building somewhere. We grab handfuls of axes and depart the party room as quickly as possible, running out into the hall. Screams echo from the front of the building.

Satan and I take turns knocking open every door, checking them on our way to the front. By the time we arrive, the other patrons are in a life-or-death battle with a hoard of minor demons. It's not a species I have seen before in all the battles I've engaged in with my mother. This must be part of that influx we've felt deep in the Shadow Realm.

Satan throws axes at the minor demons, cracking them in the middle of their foreheads and knocking them down one by one. Once he's out of axes, he slaps the palms of his hands together, making a mighty crack. The shockwave of energy goes flying out before him, knocking all the demons over and everyone else that's in its path. Once he's knocked down all the demons, he pulls his hands apart, and a blazing sword comes to life. Arching a brow, I study my mild-mannered mate, acknowledging the fact that there's more to him than what first meets the eye. Without question, he dives into battle with these minor demons, slicing through them like a hot knife through butter. The harder he fights, the more impressed I become with him. He, like my mother, forged in battle is a phenom in his own right.

The next wave of demons seems to manifest out of thin air, and it's now my turn. Raising my hands, slowly scaled gauntlets cover me from fingertip to elbow, serrated blades, much like Auroras, shift rising along the length of my arms. I unfurl my wings and allow my blackened armor to move over my body swiftly. I wear what is called dragon armor, which my grandfather Azrael imagined as one of the strongest armors known in the Shadow Realm. The minute the armor completely covers my body, the smaller, lesser demons stop and stare, then drop to their knees before me. As Death Eternal, I almost outrank my mother. Staring down at the little ones, I raise a single hand and wave it, opening a rift back into the darkness. Within seconds, these new demons pile through the void I opened, disappearing into the darkness.

Immediately I summon my sister Davina, and she helps heal all those injured in the attack. Mom, Raphael, and my father arrive to assess the damage. "You did good, Nikita," Mom says as she pulls me in tight to give me a hug. The moment she embraces me, my armor melts back to the jeans and sweater I wore earlier.

"Thanks, Mom," I say solemnly, looking at the few people who died in the attack. "Someone did not think this out." My statement is devoid of emotion as I look over the injured and the fallen.

"It really wasn't," my birth father says.

Cyrus picks up one of the dead demons and holds it out in front of him, turning it this way and that, studying it. "This appears to be a hybrid. A mix of an infrit and one of the smaller sub dwellers. I wonder why this was done."

Dad's assessment of the two species makes me think. I move closer, lifting the demon's clawed hand and then looking at its back, scales, and tail. "It's peculiar indeed. It's almost like they genetically spliced them together perfectly. Look at the scales. The scales protect what would normally be a very soft body of the infrit. The infrit itself can't survive without being bathed in fire. But this lower dweller, I believe this is one of the cave varieties: their armored scales keep its body heat inside and contain their flames."

As soon as I make that assessment, my mom moves closer, turns the clawed hands, and looks at the scales. "I believe you're right, Nikki."

I tilt my head, puzzled, looking at my mother in disbelief. She actually said that I was right. Nodding slowly, I take the demon away from my father and flip it around in my hands several times. Raising my right hand over it, I draw on what little essence is still left within the carcass, trying to figure out exactly where it may have come from. Nothing that I can sense from it gives me a direction to look in, but one thing it tells me is that this was created by magic.

"Who do we know is strong enough to splice lives together?" I aimed the question more at my father than at my mother. He paces back and forth, pulls out his phone, and walks away from me curiously. I watch him for several moments before he turns back and hangs up the phone.

"Okay, so here's what your grandfather tells me." Dad, always one for the dramatics, pauses for an extremely long time after making the initial statement before continuing. "Only three demons can do that, two of which I believe your mother already killed. The third one, well, he's been a little slippery." He looks over at my mother and then back around at me again. "It's one of the spell-casting clans down there. I believe he worked for Beelzebub for almost a thousand years. He was to create the armies for him and make any modifications needed to the demons that already existed."

If what Dad saying is accurate, then I know exactly where I need to go. "Does he still have that fortress on the fourth ring, or did he move to his other hiding place in the ninth ring?"

Dad taps his chin thoughtfully and then looks over at my mother again. "He's currently hiding on the ninth ring. Well, I wouldn't say he's hiding, per se."

The way Mom says it definitely has me puzzled. "If he's not hiding, what is he doing there?"

"That's easy," my father says. "He is exiled from the caverns in the abyss, and it's the only place he has left to go to that's safe for him."

"Hmm." I pace, and Satan stands there staring at me, watching my every move like a hawk. "I don't believe the abyss is safe for Michael to traverse with me so it's going to have to be Satan and Mordoc that comes with me." Tapping my index finger on my bottom lip, I parse out all the information for the trip.

"But neither of them are bonded to you!" My mother says forcefully as if that's going to change things. Whipping around quickly, I come face to face with my mom and stand toe to toe with her, looking her straight in the eye.

"I understand this." I match her forceful tone and grit my teeth afterwards. "I mean, I could easily take them to bed tonight and seal the deal in less than an hour. Would that make you feel better?"

I watch my mother and my father both cringe at my statement. Raphael has his fingers in his ears and is walking away from us. Satan simply tilts his head to the side, looking at me like that is a good option.

"You can't be serious!" my mother says, throwing her hands up in the air.

"Why not? Nothing ever stops you from taking multiple mates to bed at once, does it?" I tilt my head to the side, waiting for her to say something different when all of us present already know that I spoke nothing but the truth. Mom doesn't even try to deny the fact. She simply drops her head and starts shaking it.

"Do whatever you need to do. It's apparent that whatever's going on in the Dark Realm is ramping up, and it's getting more dangerous by the day," Mom says, and the worry I can see etched across her brow makes it that much more real. I nod slightly and then grip Satan's hand, leading him away from the room.

"Where are we going"? His tone cracks at the end, and I can sense his nerves are kicking up.

"Nothing to worry about. We're just gonna grab mate number three and settle this bond. As much as I'd like to keep going the romantic route with everyone, I don't think we'll have time to." I can hear him gulp in the background, his nerves definitely getting the best of him.

We head out the front door and go straight to his Jeep. He helps me slide in, and I buckle my seat belt. Next thing I know, he's in the driver's seat faster than I had expected. Within moments, we're tearing off down the road, heading back to Michael's condo. I'm not sure how comfortable Michael's going to be with what's about to happen, so I shoot him a text message warning him about what's coming next.

He responds quickly and says he's heading into the precinct for most of tonight. Do what we need to do to make sure the bond is settled and safe. He tells me he loves me, and my heart flip-flops slightly. I am also slightly concerned, especially about his puritanical sensibilities. He knew what he was getting into with me, so hopefully, he will adapt quickly.

CHAPTER 21

SATAN

WHAT WAS I ACTUALLY THINKING? SHIFTING THROUGH THE GEARS ON MY Jeep. I speed through the roads heading back to Michael's condo. Every shift feels like one step closer to my doom. This isn't a random hookup; this isn't a succubus trying to better her standings in the nest. This is my mate. Everyone and everything that came before her is absolutely meaningless and pales in comparison. The darkness that used to live within me being gone concerns me. Every inch of her is a predator. She exudes confidence and dominance like a flower does pollen. Every breath that she takes commands a room. Every word that she utters, everyone within earshot hangs upon.

I am nothing but a redeemed Fallen angel. I will never hold the place I did before I fell, nor will they welcome me back into the Silver City, no matter how much I atone. My biggest task right now is to keep my mate safe and prevent the end of the world. Nikki isn't the only one hearing whispers in the dark. I've been listening to the lesser demons speaking about a greater force coming. The greater force they're talking about just so happens to be my destroyed other half. I'm not sure how Baylor managed to pull it off. But somehow, Lucifer is in an egg in the pits, incubating in the hottest magma possible. I guess he's bringing a whole new meaning to 'forged in fire.'

I listen to Nikita tap away on her phone as she sends out messages to whoever is on the other side. I try not to be nosy and look in her direction. But the suspense is killing me. "Is everything okay?"

Listening carefully, I hear the moment that she draws in a deep breath and sets her phone down on her lap. The creaking of the leather and this slide of her denim across it draws my attention briefly. "I was warning Michael about what's coming tonight. I don't believe his delicate sensibilities would allow him to remain in our presence."

Processing her statement, I understand where she's coming from. Doing the things that we will be doing tonight may not be very high on his list. There will be blood, there will be bondage, and there'll be chasing and hunting. But most of all, there will be sex on every single surface possible.

A forced laugh escapes Nikita's lips as her hand ends up gripping my upper thigh. Blood rushes directly to my member the instant her fingers creep up my inner thigh. I draw in a sharp breath and wait to see what else is going to happen. "I'll be honest with you, Satan." Her voice sounds breathy, and she flexes, her fingers gripping me tighter when she says my name. "It's nice not having to be afraid of letting loose with you two completely."

I listen to the leather creak again as she moves in the seat. Glancing in her direction, I see that she's turned herself to face me fully. Her eyes are black as pitch, and her canines have descended fully. The thick scent of her arousal is slowly filling the cabin of the Jeep. Her thick feminine musk makes my own canines descend. A deep burning urge to satisfy my female rises, quelling any subtle fears I may have had to this point. Clearing my throat, I smile so my teeth can be seen. "It's nice to be wanted so desperately." My voice ends in a purr, and I draw out the last few syllables.

Nikita's other hand lands on my thigh and then slides up and over to the top button of my jeans. With the flick of her finger, it's undone, and I can feel her inching the zipper lower. My shaft is at full attention, subtle pulsing from it. I know I'm already leaking with anticipation. Arching my hips up reflexively to her touch, I hear her breath taken sharply. "I'm not exactly slacking," I say, trying to bait Nikita just a little.

"I see this." A rumbling escapes her lips as, out of the corner of my eye, I watch her bend forward over the center console. The wet heat of her tongue flicking over the tip of my length makes me buck my hips up in response. She continues to lick every available inch while I'm driving. I white knuckle the shifter and the steering wheel trying not to sink my fingers deep into her thick white hair and jam her down onto my length. The darkest part of me wants to pull over right here and make her scream my name.

They keep saying that the vampire is the dark horse inthis family. That little misconception makes me laugh hysterically. Even though I play the part of the meek, quiet, well-behaved Fallen one, I am nowhere near either of these. My little dark angel in my lap is going to learn that quickly tonight. She thinks that she's the dominant here. A soft laugh escapes my lips as I think about all the dark things I plan to do to her when we get through that front door.

My little minx teases me, licking me ever-so-gently but not yet taking me within her mouth. "Naughty naughty little Nikki." The words escape my lips. My first audible, deliciously wicked thought escaping.

Nikita sets up almost instantly and stares at me wide-eyed. I half smile again, showing my sharp canines. "Remember, baby, I may only be half of Lucifer. Which half did you get in the end?" My voice is a continuous growl as I let the word slide like silk over my tongue. I can see the shiver run through Nikita, and her scent blossoms again. A fun little game of cat and mouse when we get home. The vampire is going to be direct and go for a head-on attack. If I don't beat him to the prize first. We round the corner coming up to Michael's condo, and Nikita bounces in her seat, eager to make it through the front door to receive the dark promise I've made to her.

The minute I park the Jeep in the garage, Nikita's off like a flash running through the house, giggling maniacally. Shaking my head, I undo my seat belt to put myself away and zip and button my jeans before exiting the Jeep. Slow, careful steps carry me through the house, and I pass Mordoc. He sees the darkness of my eyes, and a feral grin crosses his lips.

"When you're ready to tap out, give me a holler. I'll come in for round two." We high-five, and I go in pursuit of my game.

It's easy to track her right now. Her scent is exploding all over the condo, but I find the trail of clothing most interesting. My little minx is looking forward to our game, and I will not be the one to disappoint her. I know she won't be in her room. Oh no, that would be way too easy. She won't be in my room either. That'd be way too obvious. Mordoc's room is a possibility but doubtful because she knows the two of us need to take her tonight.

That leaves one of three options: the living room, Michael's room, or the main bathroom. I detour through the house and go to the living room. There are no obvious signs that she's here or even was here, except on the way out of the living room, I find her T-shirt crumpled in a ball cast into the corner going down the hallway. There are two things down this hallway: everyone's bedrooms and the main bathroom.

 She could try throwing me off her trail, but I think my little dark Angel wants it too much. I check Michael's room first, going past mine and Mordoc's and, of course, the main bathroom.

Michael's room, unfortunately, is empty, quite disappointing if you ask me. I pop my head into my room to check every closet door under the bed and behind the heavy drapes that I have near the windows; no sign of my wayward mate. Popping into Mordoc's room next yet again, no sign of her. I even lift his bed in the closet to make sure she isn't hiding under it. The last stop is the main bathroom. This thing is mammoth. There's a whirlpool tub, a sauna, a shower that can fit at least three to four people in it, benches, massage tables, and the works. I don't think Michael thought of it when he constructed the room. We could turn it into the perfect dungeon.

I search just about everywhere and still couldn't find Nikita. I hear noises when heading back in the direction that I'd last seen Mordoc. Pausing, I listen carefully to discern exactly what's happening. A crash, a bang, and the sound of something breaking echo through the house. Running in the commotion's direction, I pull up short as a vase goes whipping past my head to shatter on the wall behind me. Mordoc and Nikita are in full battle mode. Claws and teeth are bared as things fly around the room as they lunge, tackle, and claw at each other. I'm not sure exactly what's going on until Nikita sinks her teeth into his throat, and he moans, then I realize. This is the way of the dark ones different from myself. Apparently, some of Nikitas' darker rites line up with how the vampires are. With each strike, a piece of clothing is ripped from Mordoc's body. Her blackened talons and what appear to be dragon armor cover her forearms with blades resembling razors.

She gets him completely stripped and then plunges herself down onto his length, seating herself firmly on his lap. Her talons sink into the ground behind him, holding them firmly in place as she leans down and bites his throat again, fucking him hard and fast. I've never seen anything so aggressive in my entire life.

Nikita shoves her wrist into Mordoc's mouth, and they come hard together to the point that Nikita's wings burst free from her back. Nikita rocks her hips slower than before until she finally comes to a stop. Mordoc releases her wrist and licks the wounds clean, healing them. She leans down and licks her blood off of his lips, and smiles.

Her head suddenly whips to the side, and her blackened eyes lock on me. Part of me wants to run. The other part says fuck, I was a Prince of Hell and bow to no one. Perhaps that sudden development of a spine may not have been my most brilliant idea. But I will be damned again if I am to live in fear of my mate and her blood lust. As she stands, a feral grin crosses her lips, leaving Mordoc a sated lump of flesh on the floor.

A deep purr escapes her lips as her canines descend again. Her steps are slow but sure as she closes the distance between us. "You better run, Satan. I'm still hungry." Her tongue flicks over her lips, slowly coating her top lip. I can remember the feel of its wet length running over my cock. The memory alone hardens me almost instantly.

"No running, beautiful. Though a fun game of hide and seek would be interesting." As soon as the last word leaves my lips, I vanish from sight. Nikita isn't the only one able to move between realms effortlessly. Perhaps I'll take a vacation in the lust ring and show Nikita a side of me she hasn't seen before.

CHAPTER 22
NIKITA

And then there was one. Sealing the bond with Mordoc was fast, hard, and carnal, just the way his species loves it. Even with him being a vampire Lord, he was no match for my strength, speed, and agility. The bonds need to be settled, and every moment I delay, I feel as if the icy fingers of whatever is building behind the curtain are getting closer to wrapping its glacial fingers around my neck.

Turning around to see Satan standing there, having watched Mordoc and I seal our bond, is kind of exciting. But on the other side of it all, I worry about what trauma Satan has endured. I slide free of Mordoc, leaving him a molten heap of sated flesh on the floor. Turning to face Satan, there's a new look in his eye that I haven't seen. He's exuding a level of confidence that, in the last five years, I've not witnessed previously.

When he hints at a game of hide and seek, there's a wicked gleam in his eye. The lines of his face harden as his lips pull tight in a firm line. He looks like a ruler, not a scared little boy. I watch him vanish from sight, and all I can do is smirk. He forgets I am good at tracking angels, demons, and fallen. His life force has a unique signature to it. A little good with a little bit of evil mixed in just the right proportions. The divisible line within him between the two waivers from side to side on any given day. The power struggle between light and dark ebbing and flows back and forth like the waves during the tide change. Sometimes it's subtle and smooth; other times, it's violent, harsh, and massively destructive.

But I know the man behind that false bravado. The man I find occasionally at night curled into a tight ball whimpering from the nightmares he's enduring from the torment of the last thousand years. Much like most of us, he's broken in some way, shape, or form. If I'm being honest with myself, I'm broken as well. Maybe not to the extent he is, but broken just the same. Glancing back at Mordoc, who is sleeping on the floor right where I left him, I huff out a small laugh before I, too, vanish and decide to go on the hunt for Satan.

This new game of cat and mouse that Satan and I are in is delectable. My blood thrums in anticipation of trying to locate him wherever he's hidden. Being the excellent hunter I am, I head directly to his room. It may be the most obvious place for him to go, but it is not him that I am looking for here. Some of our favorite possessions almost take on their own life, picking up pieces of our aura and essence.

Heading directly to his closet, I open the door swinging it wide, and look towards the back. There, in an embossed leather sheath, is his prized possession. His sword is from when he was a ruler in Hell. Reaching in, I grab hold of the onyx hilt that is gold inlaid with his name etched in a filigree scroll. It's ornate and quite beautiful. Almost a piece of art all by itself. Drawing the sword, I look along the edge of the blade. They're minor scratches in the metal, slight gouges, and other spots from battles from years gone by. I grip the blade and the hilt and close my eyes, focusing on the energy contained within. We exude most of our life force in battle, fighting for our lives. Using this sword, I should be able to do a simple locator spell, and I will know exactly where the wayward mate number has gotten himself to.

Oddly enough, the initial place that I sense him is my father's club. He remains there only for a moment and then is gone again. A semi-feral smile plays upon my sanguine lips as I pay attention to every jump he makes, trying to escape my detection. Father must have warned him of my ability. It's kind of funny, and it makes me laugh. The simple fact is that he is jumping around like a jumping bean, thinking that will save him. Maybe in his mind's eye, it will, but I know where he's heading.

I move through Michael's home as I open my eyes and head down the stairs. Just as I reach the bottom of the stairs, still holding on to Satan's sword, Michael walks through the door. "Nikita, where are you going?" He motions to the sword and how I'm holding it. The blade itself is pointed straight down, one hand on the blade, the other on the hilt, and I can't help but laugh a little.

"Funny that you ask me that." Closing the distance between us, I set the sword against the wall and wrap my arms around his waist, hugging him. Gently resting my head on his chest, I angle my face to look up at him. "I'm hunting Satan." Smiling broadly, I can see the bewilderment crossing my innocent mate's face.

"Why in God's green earth are you hunting Satan?" He kisses the crown of my head and rests his cheek against my hair.

"Well, Mom told me I needed to settle the bonds quickly. He decided that playing hide and go Satan was a good idea," I say sarcastically. "My primal nature is excited that I have to hunt him. But what little angelic blood that's in my veins exists is concerned that we may cause additional damage by hunting him."

"So? I'm guessing hunting him is bad?" Michael pulls back to look down at me, puzzled.

Pulling away suddenly, I pace in front of him. "It's fantastic and horrible all in the same breath." Michael prepares to open his mouth and question me. I raise a single finger and silence him. "It's fantastic in the sense that my predatory nature is thrilled that we have to hunt him." My index finger taps my bottom lip as I figure out how to phrase the next sentence. "But I'm concerned about triggering the damage he already has by hunting him." I take hold of Satan's sword and extend it in front of me. "It's literally a double-edged sword. Do as my instincts demand, and it's awesome or horrible."

Understanding dawns on Michael's features, and he slowly nods his head. "That is a conundrum. In one sense, you want to do what your instinct is driving you to do. But your instinct is also telling you to protect your possibly fragile mate." Damn, Golden Boy's understanding is far greater than I expected him to. He smiles at me again and kisses my forehead. "Hunt him, but be aware of his body language. Don't lose yourself completely to the beast if you can help it." Michael kisses me on my lips softly and then gives me a smack on my ass, sending me out the front door and closing it behind me.

I can't decide if I was just dismissed by my Archangel mate or encouraged by him. One thing I know for sure is Satan is no longer in the Earth Realm. I can also determine he's not in the Angelic Realm because there is no place to hide. So the focus of my hunt is going to be the Shadow Realm. Walking around the back of the house, I leave what light was being cast by the front porch, and into the darkness, I step. Within seconds, I'm slipping through the shadows and into the Shadow Realm.

Wings of midnight burst free from my back, and I take flight heading towards what will soon be my castle. It's not as large as Mother's, but it's still a grand and imposing fortress. I land on the tallest battlement and look out across the realm. I know it will only take a matter of moments before my grandfather joins me up here.

"I've had a lot of visitors tonight." My grandfather's deep rough voice calls from behind me. I turn to see him and rush into his arms. We encapsulate each other in our wings, snuggling, and sharing in the darkness that is our bloodline.

"Let me guess, wayward mate number three arrived here a little while ago, trying to find a place to hide." My grandfather's chuckle tells me all that I need to know. We release each other from our embrace and allow our wings to rest behind us.

"You know and I know, little one, that I cannot and will not take part in anyone's mating rituals." He visibly shivers while making the statement, then looks awkwardly away from me.

"Trust me, I never want any maternal or paternal grandparent involved in any way, shape, or form of anything I need to do behind closed doors." At the very thought of that, I cringe, and bile wants to creep up my throat.

"I'm glad we can agree on that, then." Azrael chuckles and then leads me down into his fortress. As we reach the lower levels, I hear the sultry tones of Azrael's fated mate Lyra. As interesting as it is to say, he's actually mated to a siren. I didn't even know those things existed. Apparently, they do, and we can find the last ones in the river Styx.

"Nikki!" Lyra practically sings my name as she comes running across the marble floors. Wrapping me up in a tight hug, she kisses both of my cheeks excitedly. "I'm so happy to see you! And you have such a catch!" She sounds like one of those California surfer girls with how she says things. It's almost comical.

"Thank you." I smile, blushing slightly. "I also have a vampire Lord as a mate and Michael."

She's stage whispers to my grandfather, asking if he was the creepy uncle with a staring problem when I was little. I laugh and nod along. "Yeah, one and the same. He saw my wings when I was really little, and unfortunately for him, he knew at that point who I was to him and had to wait until now."

Lyra visually cringes and shakes it off. "That had to be the most epic set of blue balls to ever occur in history." I don't know if I'm more stunned or just at a loss for words staring at her, not having thought of it that way.

"I, um, never even gave that much thought, to be honest." Definitely in shock; not in a very good place right now. "I should really get going." I make my way towards the front door. "I have a mate to hunt and not that much time left. The Mated Ball is in two weeks."

"You don't have two weeks, Nikki," Azrael says as he looks at the watch on his wrist. "Remember, time moves differently down here. A single day is five up there." He taps his watch, reaches into his pocket, pulls out a pocket watch, and hands it to me. The clock face differs completely from one you would find on the surface. Instead of having a 12-hour clock face, it has a sixty. So every sixty hours is two and a half days, and it takes one hundred and twenty hours for the sun to rise and set and then rise again. So what would be a twenty-four-hour day for us is five days' worth of time.

Shaking my head, I look around quickly and then bounce up and kiss my grandfather's cheek. "I best be going then." I rush over and hug and kiss Lyra before running out the front door and taking flight again. Satan's not in the Shadow Realm, so he must be down in one of the rings. I know which one he went to. It's not all that difficult to figure out he went to the Lust Realm. He's probably hoping all the scents and sounds will disrupt me and throw me off his trail, it might, it might not there's only one way to find out.

I arrive at the opening of the pit and dive down slowly, passing ring after ring, watching each of them, making sure that nothing is out of place and that nothing new has arisen that I am unaware of. Once I reach the Lust Ring, I already feel the disturbance in the force. He's definitely here and close to where I was held as a child.

Walking back through the casino district that brings back happy yet confusing memories, the succubus den is a favorite of most male demons, and by the feel of it, Satan's here. Shifting forms, I enter the casino. I'm wearing a simple black dress. I hide my wings with my dragon tattoo on full display on my right arm.

Under my skin, I feel Rex moving around uncomfortably. Part of this feels like I may walk into a trap, but I know my mate's here. He better not be in any sort of trouble. Otherwise, I'm going to be quite pissed off.

Traveling through the different casino floors, I can sense that I'm getting closer. The top floor is where the succubi held me, and it's exactly where I sense my mate is. I raise my hand, and the doors open. Dozens of succubi walk around in next to nothing, kissing and hugging each other like any other day. I move further into their nest, and there's my mate sitting on what used to be the succubus' queen's throne, a glass of blood in his hand and four demonesses at his feet.

A deep growl escapes my lips, and I feel my canines elongate. Anger doesn't even describe what I'm feeling; jealousy, maybe.

But the sheer audacity of him being here has set something off deep within me that I've never experienced in my life. Possessiveness. It's the only word to describe this feeling. He is mine. They don't belong anywhere near him. A strange rolling in my blood is almost an undulating mass beside the dragon. It's not until it's too late that I realize what it is. I'm a lot closer to my ascension than anybody anticipated. And I feel Hell as if it's a freckle on my skin. As the growl deepens in my chest, the building beneath my feet starts to rumble and quake in time with it. The look of concern crosses satan's features as the succubi take off, scattering in all different directions, leaving immediately at the top floor of the casino immediately.

CHAPTER 23
SATAN

 HAVE OFFICIALLY MESSED UP ROYALLY. SEEING THE LOOK OF PURE darkness in my mate's eyes makes my heart clench and robs me of breath. I knew the minute that she had entered the rings, having lived here for thousands of years. I feel the interpretation of her journey for a mere moment. I'm not sure exactly how much of her youth she remembers clearly. This is the same place where the succubi held her hostage. On Lucifer's orders, they stole her, and they were planning to make her into one of them. The prolonged exposure to their level of darkness snapped something within her. It may not have been clear, but I'm seeing it now.

The woman I see before me has an unspeakable power ebbing from her every pore. The rings themselves respond to her emotions. This recent development can be catastrophic on a level never seen before. She has claimed two out of three of us in the last thirty-six surface hours. But she doesn't realize that her journey from the Shadow Realm to here took almost three surface days. Even though it was merely a couple of hours here, the deeper she goes into the rings, the faster the time on the surface moves. If she had stayed in the Shadow Realm, what would have been a sudden rise in the sunset would be approximately five days on the surface. But for each ring she descends, it increases by a day. Those negligible factors run through my mind as I do the calculations. Fuck, we need to seal our bond, then move through the shadows back to the surface. We have less than four surface days left before the ball.

"How dare you!" Nikita's words lash out at me like the crack of a whip. Physical searing pain burns across my chest just from her words. Every step on the earth rumbles deeper and stronger than it had before. If she doesn't get her temper under control soon, this building will fall, killing everyone within it.

"Nikita." I raise my hands in a placating manner as I rise slowly from the throne, approaching her. "You need to calm down. You're going to destroy this building."

"What do I care if I destroy this building?" Her eyes blacken, and her upper and lower canines descend. They've changed. Long sharp dagger looking teeth replaced her canines.

"If this building falls here and now, it will also fall on earth." I enunciate my words and look down at her, trying to drive the point home that her tantrum will eradicate countless human lives in a blink.

Her eyes dart around briefly and then returned to me. The earth-quake slowly subsides as she crosses her arms under her breast. "It still doesn't excuse why you're here. This, of all places!" She throws her arms out to the sides. This was exactly my judgment error.

"I didn't know this would affect you. For that, I am deeply sorry." I kneel before her and bow my head. Her mother might have puri-fied me, but that doesn't remove the fact that I'm still the last living Prince of Hell. It takes several moments before Nikita threads her fingers through my hair.

"We're running out of time, Satan."

"I know." Rising to my full height, I extend a hand to her, and when she takes it, that leads her back through the casino to the hotel portion. Riding the elevator like a normal visitor amuses her. She studies her reflection in the mirror, and because of how they're angled, dozens of her are in here with me. But unlike her, my presence doesn't replicate.

Arching a curious brow, she looks at me and then at the mirrors, trying to make sure that her eyes do not deceive her. "There's only one of me, beautiful. Part of the magic and the curse of this place."

"What do you mean, the curse of this place?" She stops staring at me in the mirror and turns fully to face me just as the doors open.

"Being a Prince of Hell, to replicate me would also replicate my power. The big guy put limitations on us."

She ponders the thought for several moments, then accepts it. Taking her hand, I lead her through the upper floor to the penthouse suite. Biting the tip of my finger, I touch it to the seal on the door. "The penthouse suites are reserved only for the Princess of Hell." I say it as if it's common knowledge entering the suite before her. "Even though, once upon a time, I was one of the more fearsome princes, I'm not sure what my absolution has done to me. By reputation alone, I maintain control here. I would hate to know what would happen if they found out that I'm half the man I used to be."

Nikita moves around the suite, studying every nuance that it offers. Her clothes change from a battle outfit to a beautiful flowing black dress with their hair hanging down her back, the stark white against the black a beautiful contrast. She doesn't linger long in the main sitting area. No, my mate heads directly to the bedroom. Gulping hard, I follow behind her, and as soon as I step foot into the room with the flick of her wrist, the door slams shut and locks behind me. I've never been the prey and always the predator, but seeing that look in her eyes, I know I'm in trouble. She moves forward efficiently and extends her hand out towards me. The minute her fingertip contacts the material of my shirt, it disintegrates. Every stitch of clothing on me falls to ash at my feet. Her eyes turn from pitch black to polished chrome as she stares at me. That is the Destroyer's gaze, yet Nikita can do it.

"Hmm, so this is what a Prince of Hell looks like." The words roll off her tongue like silk off the edge of a bed. The syllables slide smoothly, almost hypnotically, as she speaks. "I wonder exactly what a Prince of Hell is capable of doing." She smirks, looking at me, and I know her predatory nature is used to being dominant.

Not today.

"Wow, I guess you're about to find out now, aren't you?" Spreading my wings wide behind me, I take control of the room. Nikita looks around in shock when the room stops responding to her. A deep throaty laugh escapes my lips as I watch panic move over her beautiful smooth features. Eyes wide, her head lit whips from left to right, then back at me. She's not going on the defensive. She knows I will not harm what's mine. My guess is that she does not like that the tables are turned.

"I need your consent, Nikki. Your consent to do anything and everything to bring you the utmost pleasure. No matter what it is." I hit that deep tone that I've watched her shiver over, and it has the same effect now. Her head nods, and I laugh. "I need to hear the words, Nikki. You need to say the words." I enunciate the second sentence, pausing dramatically between words to drive home the importance of her verbally giving consent to what we're going to do tonight.

"Yes, Satan, I give you consent to do whatever is necessary to give me the utmost pleasure that I've ever felt in my entire life."

No sooner does she finish speaking than my heart soars. "As you wish." I pause dramatically, watching her mouth drop open into the perfect o. Raising my hands, the room shifts, and it catches her off guard. Leather lashings whip out of nowhere, entangling her wrists and ankles, pulling her swiftly across the room and over a padded dolly. She's laying over it on her stomach, ass in the air, her dripping wet sex bare to me. The lashings did the job for me. By removing her clothing, they set her up perfectly. Getting closer, I run my fingertips from her tailbone up her spine and into her thick white hair. "The fun's about to start, beautiful. Hold on for the ride of your life." She shivers with anticipation, and I know I cannot wait.

I grab first the suction stimulator clamps and place them on her. The pulling, sucking sensation, and the dual stimulation of both breasts at the same time make her moan and wiggle on the dolly. My hands run down her sides, over her hips, then down her thighs. I stand behind her, then drop to my knees, eye level with her moistened folds. Shifting my tongue, I turn it into a serpent's tongue, long on the tip. I use it to lap at her hungry sex, torturing her clit, teasing it frantically, and then stopping the moment I see her muscles pulse slightly, keeping her on edge for the better half of ten minutes. When she least expects it, I press two fingers into her, curving them down, finding her g spot, and rubbing it slowly in concentric circles as my tongue flickers over that sensitive bulb of nerves. The minute her core flutters around my fingers, I pull them out immediately and stop flicking her clit.

"Please, Satan, please, I can't take anymore." Nikita strains against her restraints as she tries to rub herself against the padded dolly.

Not yet. I give her a quick smack on her ass cheek, watching it jiggle from the impact. A faint pink imprint of where my hand had landed remains at the point of impact. I move forward and release the nipple stimulators and reapply them with more suction than before. An almost keening cry escapes her lips as she arcs her back. The stimulation, I can tell, is getting to be too much. Or is it just enough? Slipping behind her, I grip my length and rub my juices from tip to root and back again, watching her pink, engorged pussy slightly pulsing on its own. Without warning, I thrust forward, burying myself as deeply into her as possible. We both cry out at just about the same time. She fits me like a glove, and as tight as her muscles are gripping me, I know I won't last long. Damn me for teasing both of us. I grasp a hold of her long hair and wrap it around my wrist, tugging on it as I set a punishing pace, pounding into her as deeply as I can get.

She's a moaning mess, fluid everywhere, dripping down my inner thighs with how wet she is. I feel the telltale flutters just as my sack starts the tighten. Doubling my efforts, I reach forward, gripping her breast, removing the one stimulator, and rolling her nipple between my fingers. She detonates around me, and I swear all I can see is stars. The most blinding, euphoric feeling I've ever experienced in my life rushes through me just as my orgasm overtakes me. Pulse after pulse myself deep within her, knowing full well we're safe; it's not her time yet. My erratic movements set her off again, and this time she crushes down around me, almost holding me hostage. I become concerned that maybe I was wrong. Maybe it is her time, and then she suddenly releases me.

The minute her body relaxes with the leather bindings releases her wrists and ankles. I scoop her up, fall free from her body, and carry her to the ensuite bathroom. Setting her on the bench, I move to the Whirlpool tub and fill it with bubble bath and hot water. It may be a huge mistake because of the bubbles I'm about to create, but if I ease her muscles and make her feel pampered, the mess will be worth it. I turn on the jets once there's sufficient water, and the bubbles multiply. Nikita eventually joins me at the side of the tub and starts laughing as the bubbles take over. I help her in and get her in the one cradled seat, then wash her hair as she relaxes.

"Who would have thought that you would have been exactly what I needed?" The words fall from Nikita's lips as she closes her eyes, leaning back, trusting.

"Sadly, love, we can't stay terribly long. If we move through the shadows, it'll give us two days before the ball. If we go back to the traditional way, we're going to miss it by six."

Stating the way the time moves makes her eyes pop open. She stares at me in disbelief. "I didn't think about that."

I bend down and kiss her forehead and smile. "That's okay, I did, and once we're both cleaned up, we'll move through the shadows and get home in plenty of time." I kiss her forehead again. "For now, lay back and let me spoil you. It's my honor to be able to take care of you." Nikita relaxes in the tub, allowing me to take care of her needs. Before long, she's fast asleep, floating in the soothing water. Moving closer, I wrap my arms around her and move us through the shadows back to Michael's home to get ready for our debut.

CHAPTER 24
NIKITA

The first rays of light break through and land on my face, rudely waking me up before I'm ready. Reaching out blindly, I pat around me, find a wing, and pull it over me. Slowly opening my eyes, the feathers over me are an opal white. A soft chuckle escapes my lips as I turn to press my face into Michael's chest.

"Good morning Nikki. Ready for your big night?" he whispers as he lifts his wing to look at me.

"My big night? I don't get it." Scooting up his body, I move until I rest my head on the pillow beside him, able to look into his blue eyes.

His fingers thread through my hair slowly. "The Mated Ball is tonight, and we get to present the nest to the world." Pride blossoms in his voice, and a radiant smile graces his lips, soothing some of my anxiety about it.

Reaching up and running my hand up Michael's neck until my thumb caresses his jaw's sharp lines. I drop my gaze to follow the path that my thumb takes as I try to plan how to present to him what I feel in my gut to be true. "I don't know how to say this, Michael. But the nest isn't complete. We're still missing someone." His brows knit in the middle as he looks down at me. His eyes dart over my features as he tries to figure out what I'm saying.

"You have all of your mates, Nikki. We're not missing anyone." His soft, calm tone would put me at ease on any other day. But the anxiety building in my chest tells me the statement is more for his benefit than my own.

Running my hand over the tattoo of Rex on my forearm, I can't help but think that he is the one that's missing. Michael's gaze follows the direction that I'm looking, and he slowly nods his head. It didn't take as long as I thought it was going to for him to make the connection.

"I'm not sure how that's supposed to work." He takes my hand from his neck and turns it this way and that, studying the tattoo on my forearm. "How does one free a being from its existence of servitude?"

Michael's question hits the nail on the head and poses the biggest obstacle I've faced yet to date. "Indeed, how do we free Rex permanently from his life of servitude? I'm not sure. What I know is that he should be with us." I say it with as much conviction as I can muster. I'm not sure which of the family members could help us. But I know in my heart I need to try.

Michael nods, slowly rolls away from me, and gets out of bed. His sleep pants hang low on his hips, and that perfect V I love tracing with my fingertips is on display. He flexes those opalescent wings of his before putting them away. "I'll see what I can find out for you," he says before stepping into the bathroom. The sound of the shower starting catches my attention, and I can't help it that my attention is divided between wanting to join him and finding out how to free Rex. I fire off a quick text to my mother and grandfather, figuring that between the two of them, one of them should have a clue.

Several moments pass before rapid-fire text messages hit my phone. Mostly it's my mother answering my most direct question: if it's possible. According to what she knows, the answer is yes, and oddly enough, it's like some of those stupid fairy tales we get told as children. True love's first kiss. Since Rex never took a mate, he never experienced what it was to be loved. With me being as dark of nature as I am, I'm honestly not sure if I can provide him with what he needs. It may just be my insecurities, but that's what I believe. I rise from the bed finally and make my way through the house.

Downstairs in what should have been the living room now looks like a high-end retailer vomited all over the interior. The blackout curtains are drawn tight. I catch Mordoc and Satan running around in circles, putting the dresses in the order they find most attractive. There's everything from white, about the same color as Michael's wings, to black, which is blacker than pitch.

None of the ridiculously girly colors are included in the color palette. Various shades of red start at what I call blood red, going to the deepest, darkest burgundy. Shades of white to black with all the grays and metallics in between. They represented deep blue and dark green, all on the various racks lining the living room. Various lengths and cuts of gowns are represented in each of the colors. There are three main racks, one with each of the mates' names over the top and two other racks of additional dresses that have not been claimed by anyone. To keep the peace in the nest, I really don't want to pick off any of their racks. I'd rather go to one of the two freestanding racks and pick something of my own. So at least that way, it doesn't appear I am showing any favoritism.

As I move towards the unclaimed dresses, my mother, grandfather, Raphael, and Metatron arrive in my living room. Shaking my head and rolling my eyes, I close the distance between my mother and me and wrap her up tightly in my arms. Now, of all times, I need her more than anything. I am, however, shocked that Raphael is here and not with his perfect daughter.

"I came as quick as I could." Mother states as she looks at the dresses on the racks.

"I know you're not here for a fashion show." I lean against Mordoc as I face my mother and I can tell she's forcing a smile on her lips.

"I don't believe what you desire most is possible." Wringing her hands in front of her, she stares at me. I'm guessing, hoping for understanding.

"What do you mean it's not possible? You're the Destroyer. You have the powers of Heaven and Hell at your fingertips." I drive the point home, pausing between words. I can feel Rex moving under my skin, as well as a second entity. The one I shall not name or tell the others exists.

"It's exactly as I said, Nikita. It's not possible. He willingly submitted himself to be a guardian. He would have to free himself." Mom's statement hits me like a Mack truck slamming into me. This entire time of searching for an answer, and it's been within his grasp this entire time.

Nodding my head, I turn in Mordoc's arms, and he wraps me up in his leather wings. It's a different comfort that I'm seeking from him versus the feathers of my Fallen and Archangel mate. His is nothing but darkness and malice unless it comes to me. I feel his lips graze the shell of my ear. "Once the ball is over, we need to return to the darkness, and perhaps there he can rise." Mordoc's statement makes sense. Perhaps all it will take is returning to the Shadow Realm to empower him enough to rise. I nod gently and press a kiss to his cheek before turning and pushing his wings open to face everyone present.

"Let's get this bullshit over with. We all know how much I love dresses." I say with this much sarcasm in my voice as possible. Mom is smirking, and the Archangels are smiling their approval. I glance over at Satan and Mordoc. They, too, had caught on to the sarcasm in what I said. Yes, tolerate the archaic patriarchal bullshit free mate number four, and ascend to the mantle of Death Eternal. Easier said than done.

My birth father arrives when Michael returns, and they head to the corner of the room, looking over parchments. Grandfather and mother join them almost immediately. Rolling my eyes, I pick several dresses from the free-standing rack and one from each of my mate's racks. I did that more for show than anything else. What the others don't know is that Aunt Sigrun had a dress fashioned from dragon scale and mythril. As she put it, it's a dress befitting a warrior queen.

Carefully, I slip into the dress Aunt Sigrun made for me. I smile, looking at how it hugs my curves. I feel beautiful and powerful in it. The dragon scales are as black as my feathers, and the mythril is polished bright like the edge of a blade. The dress's bodice is covered in fine mythril chainmail with dragon scales dangling off it. It looks like armored snake skin covering my chest and ribs. Aunt Sigrun showed me how effective the armor is by trying to drive her sword through it. Not a single scratch on the entire bodice.

Using some of the mimic magic my father taught me, I pick the dress that Michael favors and glamour my dress to look like it. I will bring the shock factor tonight. If Mom is right, there may be an attack like what happened at hers, either at the ball or shortly after. I move across the room and look at myself in the mirror. Dressed like this, I look like I could pass for being an angel. White blonde hair and light eyes in a white dress scream angelic. They don't see the demon inside until I unfurl my wings.

Grabbing my phone, I open my music app and cue up *Jekyll and Hyde from FFDP*. The first few lines ring so true to me eighty percent of the time. It's not even funny anymore. Using the shadows, I style my hair in loose curls down my back. Pinning the left side up the braid that the Valkyrie had put in, my hair is on display. It doesn't take long for me to put the finishing touches on my look for this evening. It's now that I notice Rex is missing. Turning frantically in front of the mirror, I can't seem to find him anywhere.

"Nikita, it's time to leave." Michael stands smiling in the door frame. His tux is fitted to his frame perfectly. His hair is tied back, and his beard is trimmed close to his face.

"You look very handsome this evening, I must say." Bouncing up, I kiss his cheek as I take his offered hand.

"You're too kind, Nikki." Michael kisses me reverently. His lips against mine make me feel as though I can do and be anything.

Melting into his arms, I almost forget that we are expected elsewhere. I want my Archangel mate to ruin this dress. I want him to lose control and take me hard and fast with reckless abandon. He's too much of a gentleman for that. Just once, I would love for him to let loose and allow his desires to take the wheel. He breaks the kiss suddenly, as if remembering himself. "We're gonna be late," he whispers against my lips before leading me out the door and down to the waiting car.

Something isn't sitting right with me as we climb into the car. Satan and Mordoc are already in their seats. Surprisingly, Satan is in a light gray tux, and Mordoc has chosen to wear a burgundy and black tux. "Everyone looks so handsome. Thank you for dressing up."

The dark half of the bond looks at me puzzled, knowing full well that the word thanks never fall from my lips. Michael beams at me, his eyes churn golden, and I swear his face almost glows.

The glow fades suddenly from his face, and he looks around quickly. "We're going the wrong way." He crosses to the other side of the limo and looks out the window. "This isn't right..." Michael moves to the glass separating the back from the driver. His hand shatters the glass, and there is nothing but a solid black mass on the other side. "Get out!" Michael roars.

CHAPTER 25

MICHAEL

A malevolent being has hijacked our limo, and there's nothing here for me to physically fight. I yell for the others to get out, and they can't. When I try to, I feel I can. "Nikki, I have to get you out of here." I caress her face, trying to get her to see reason.

"Get the others out first." For the first time in her existence, I see genuine fear in her features as she looks at the others. "Please Mikey, please save them first." Her eyes dart to Satan and Mordoc, then back to me. Her eyes churn midnight, then tiny microscopic flecks of gold emerge.

The sacrifice... I don't say the words other than to myself. Resolutely, I nod, giving in to her desires. Reaching out, I take hold of Satan, pulling him with me out of the limo. As I emerge and set him free, I reach out to my brothers and alert them to the issue. Metatron and Gabriel arrive just as I pull Mordoc out.

"Why is this happening?" Gabriel shouts as we fly after the limo.

"The sacrifice!" My voice breaks, knowing full well what must happen next.

"It's too soon! She can't!" Metatron screams as he flies ahead of us.

We race after the limo, and it seems to move faster than it should. Blackness encompasses the interior of the front of the limo. We tear at the steel and rip panels off one by one. Working together, we take the limo apart, and Nikita isn't in there anymore.

"Where is she?" Tearing the limo to shreds, we cannot find any clues about where Nikita is. There's not even a piece of her dress or a lock of her hair.

Gabriel also searches what was left of the interior of the limo. "I'm not even sure how this is possible. It's as if they constructed it to trap the dark half of the bond." He runs his fingers over the metal and then the leather of the seats. The way he stares at his fingers, I know he's seen something.

"What did you find?" Anxiously, I move forward and try to see what he's seeing.

Gabriel holds up his fingers, and a black opalescence coats his fingers. "Only a Fallen one would have this sheen on their feathers." Metatron joins me, looking at the residual presented to us.

Reaching into the car, I wipe the same silt off the seat and examine it. "Good grief, is there any chance they resurrected Lucifer?"

We freeze and stare at each other. My heart sinks. The general feeling is that, yes, it's possible. Before I can ask my next question, Thana and Cyrus arrive. The rage written on Thana's face speaks volumes.

"Where the actual fucking hell is my daughter!" Thana's voice booms and causes the remnants of the car to shake.

"We're not sure. She told me to get Satan and Mordoc out because they were trapped, too. When I tried to return for her, I couldn't get into the car until it stopped." Running my hand down my face, I feel nothing but despair seeping into my heart. My gaze drops to my bloodied hands before looking at what's left of the car. "How do we find her?" Immediately, my eyes whip up to meet Thana's chrome gaze.

Thana paces as she stares at the car. I swear if she stares any harder, the thing will ignite. Thana suddenly stops moving, and her eyes blacken. I watch as she looks around without moving.

"What's she doing?" I stage whisper to Cyrus.

Arching a brow, he sighs. "She's using some of the abyssal creatures to search for Nikki."

"Mordoc and I can go start searching." Satan moves forward, offering himself and our other bond mate to lead the hunt for Nikita.

Thana double blinks, and a soft smile crosses her lips. "I appreciate the offer. She's in the deepest pit of Hell. The void beyond the ninth ring."

Satan gasps and steps back. "How?" Satan pales, and Mordoc shakes his head.

"What isn't everyone telling me? I have a right to know!" It's the first time I've felt this level of anger boil up, and I'm not sure where it's coming from.

"Michael..." Metatron moves to stand before me, both his hands gripping my shoulders. "It's the one place Lucifer knows that most of us cannot tread." He lowers his head, and I feel like there's a rock in the pit of my stomach.

Thana moves closer to me and rests a hand on my shoulder. "We need the skull dragons. They are born of the abyss. The vast space beyond the ninth ring is the abyss." Her smile broadens, then the most psychotic laugh escapes her lips. "Maelestor Rex will rise again!" she screams and fist pumps, doing what I can call a victory dance.

"Mind filling the rest of us in?" Gabriel tilts his head, clearly as puzzled as I am.

Laughing, Thana hops up and sits on the wreckage of the car. "Think big picture. Rex is a skull dragon that gave his life to the Reapers in servitude. The abyss may give him enough juice to rise again. Permanently." The finality Thana says those words with rocks me to my core.

"Fuck!" Satan exclaims as his wings open wide behind him. "Whoever took Nikki has no clue what the hell they just unleashed upon themselves. Even if they just exchange bites, she will be stronger." He turns his gaze upon me, and I know deep down what he's saying is true.

"Any clue what Reaper form she chose? We all have to choose one." Cyrus looks back at the three of us expectantly.

"No." Mordoc's tone hints at his concern.

"She didn't say anything to me." Satan looks at me, then back at Thana.

"I'm not shocked she didn't say anything. To choose a form is to lock the gates of the Silver City to you forever." Thana's sad gaze turns to Metatron, and he lowers his head slightly.

"She's practically a Fallen Angel without having to fall." My eyes drop again to the blackened sheen on my fingers. Then it hits me. "The cavern that Luna's mate took us to. It had Rex painted on one wall, a huge chromatic dragon on the other, and a black phoenix." My heart drops suddenly, realizing what my crazy mate may do to save herself.

"Are you saying that Nikita will become a dragon? Or that Rex will rise again and save Nikita?" Satan looks back and forth between Thana and me before looking towards Mordoc.

Arching a brow, he shrugs his shoulders. "It's possible."

"What's possible?" I can't help but ask, though I honestly don't want the answer to.

"Everything..." Mordoc's tone doesn't leave any room for further questioning.

If what he says is true, the world as I know it will tilt on its axis and possibly spin in reverse. Best-case scenario, Rex rises and helps Nikita bust free of the abyss. Worst case, Nikki takes on the dragon form. I can only guess it is her last-ditch effort to save herself and everyone else.

As the thought crosses my mind, my heart sinks and feels as if someone has wrapped their hands around it, crushing it in their grasp. Spots dance before my eyes as I hyperventilate. Gasping breaths escape my lips as my eyes dart around as I try to get a grip on what's happening.

"Breathe." Thana grips my face, staring deep into my eyes. "She's a fighter. There's nothing that will stop my daughter." A slow smile creeps over her crimson lips just before her eyes blacken. "I'm sending reinforcements to assist Nikita. It's up to her now. She needs to ascend and do it quickly." Thana's words hit like a punch to the gut.

Satan, Mordoc, and I stare at each other and then back to Thana after she falls silent. "You expect us to stand by and wait for her to return to us?"

Cyrus shakes his head and steps forward. He raises his hand, stopping Thana from talking. "I don't expect you to do anything. There's only so far you can go, Michael, without risking your immortal soul. You will fall if you descend into the abyss. Understand that fact." Cyrus's eyes blacken, then he turns his head and looks away.

Thudding hard, my heartbeat drowns out everyone's voices. I see their lips moving but nothing is reaching my ears. To fall is to not be counted within the ranks of Archangels for all eternity. I'll be permanently ostracized from the Silver City. Paradise will be lost to me forever.

Resolutely, I exhale louder than I mean to. "We will do whatever is needed to be done to get Nikita back in one piece." I lock my gaze on Gabriel and Metatron. "If I need to fall, then so be it. As long as Nikita is alive and safe."

My armor blazes to life upon my body. Staring at the armor, I take in the details of the scrollwork forged so many thousands of years ago. Reverently I graze my fingertips over the intricate details taking in the finery one last time.

The weight of a hand on my shoulder drags me out of my self-mourning. Looking over, only Metatron is left standing beside me. "Sometimes, to rise, we have to fall. If falling is how you save your mate, then so be it. I will stand beside you until the bitter end." Metatron embraces me tightly, and I feel at peace with what I may have to do.

I stand watching as my brother-in-arms takes flight back to his mate. My bond mates, on the other hand, stand there staring at me. They look to me for the answers, and I have none. For the first time in my long life, I don't have the answers or idea of where to start. In all the wars I've fought in, fighting an unknown enemy makes it impossible.

Shaking my head to clear the dark thoughts that have tried to take root there. "We need to get to the Shadow Realm and the Destroyer's Castle. Once there, the war room has maps of the rings and the entrance to the abyss."

"Let's go then." Satan sounds serious for once and opens a portal to one of the Dark Realms.

"Where are we going?" I walk to the edge of the rift and watch Mordoc walk through without question.

"The lust ring where the seat of my power is. Mordoc's is at the edge of the abyssal rift. We'll gather our forces and then descend into the rift. You can wait at the edge for us to rise."

CHAPTER 26

NIKITA

I FEEL LIKE EVERY BONE AND JOINT IN MY BODY HURTS. THE THICK SCENT of sulfur and blood fills my nostrils. The metallic tang almost makes my stomach growl. There's a scent here; I swear I recognize it. But it can't be. Mom destroyed Lucifer utterly. Or did she? Forcing my eyes open, I look around and see that I am chained to a cavern wall. Sharp stones dig into my spine, and water drips down onto me from the stalactites. The water smells like rotten eggs and is absolutely ruining my dress.

Lining the cavern's ceiling are what look like bats, larger than the bats on the surface. I make a squeaking noise to get the bat to turn its head; the minute it does, I have it. Blackening my eyes, I use the bat to reach out to my mother. Son of a bitch, she already knows I'm in the abyss.

"Nikita, what can you see?"

Glancing around, I let her see through my eyes. It's a regular cavern, with nothing out of the ordinary in my line of sight. *"Not much. Can't hear anything other than the dripping of this sulfur water."*

Mom is silent for several moments. *"Your Grandfather and I are looking over the abyssal maps trying to get a better idea of where you are. Is Rex with you?"*

My heart sinks as I think about my missing familiar. *"No…"* Looking around the cavern, I make sure no one is there. *"Did the others make it out? Did Michael save them? Are they okay?"* I can't believe I didn't think about them until now.

"Yes, Michael saved them. He's also thinking about descending into the abyss after you." Just when the sinking feeling of despair was almost abating, Mom had to say that.

"No, don't let him! He can't fall!" I want to cry. Tugging at the chains that bind me to the wall doesn't do a damn thing. The more I struggle, the tighter the shackles get around my wrists.

"Now that's a naughty-naughty thing to do trying to get loose." A sultry voice echoes through the cavern, and I lose the connection to my mother.

"Who's there? Show yourself, coward!" Gripping the chain, I tug even harder than before and hear the metal pin move slightly in the stone.

Next thing I know, I'm blasted in the chest by an unseen force, knocking the wind out of me. A man with a metal mask over his face walks into view. "You know exactly who I am. Your gut should have given you a clue by now." He leans against a stalagmite staring at me. Glowing crimson eyes are all I can see behind the mask.

Laughing, I throw my head back and let loose with a full-on belly laugh. "Oh Luci, what have they done to you? This isn't Phantom of the Opera. Masks are so 15th century." Arching a brow, I lean forward. "Are you gross under there? Are you Night of the Living Dead under there? Flesh falling off your face under there?" I can tell I hit a nerve with him as I watch his hair ignite. I want to laugh again and call him Hades, but I choose to not poke the bear again.

"Yes, very Night of the Living Dead. Thanks to your mother…" he growls out as he manifests a sword from nowhere.

"Oh, shit…"

"No one can find this cavern. It's warded, and some of the most venomous deep dwellers guard the entrance." I swear I can feel the smirk that's probably under his mask from here.

Holding my head up high, I try not to show exactly how deep his words have just cut me. Turning my head away, I look down the cavern into the darkness and see a set of green eyes glowing close to the ground. Rex has green eyes, and I can only hope it's him. "Well, I guess I'm stuck with you then, I suppose." Yawning after I make my statement, I look back at him, bored.

Narrowing his eyes, Lucifer stares at me. "You're up to something. I don't know what it is, but you're up to something." He taps his fingers on the black mask as he looks around the cavern. "You'll tell me when you're hungry enough. Until then, you can starve." He roars and shakes the very foundation of the cavern, making rocks fall from the ceiling.

Lucifer suddenly turns and stomps out of the cavern to who knows where. Once I'm sure he's gone, I look back toward where I saw the green eyes staring at me. The dog-sized Skull Dragon emerges from the shadows and stalks forward. It's not Rex; it's some other dragon I'm not familiar with. The dragon shifts, and a naked woman stands before me. Scales line the bridge of her nose and under her eyes.

"You shouldn't be here." Her voice is more of a hiss than clear spoken words.

Lowering my head, I whisper to her, "Can you help me? I need to get out of here." Moving my arms, I draw her attention to the chains and shackles that bind me.

She looks at the chains, and I hear a low growl, almost rumble, before she spits on the chain closest to the wall. The hiss of her acid spit hitting the metal eats away at the link in the chain. Her head suddenly whips towards the mouth of the cavern, and as fast as she shifted, she's back to being a little dragon on the ground.

"What's going on in here?" Lucifer screams, drawing my attention back to him. He forgot the mask, and the flesh of his face looks like a burned marshmallow. Cracked and flaking skin barely hanging onto the muscles of his face move with every expression.

I try to angle my body to hide the melting chain, but it doesn't work. His nostrils flare before his eyes burn a brilliant crimson. "How dare you!" His hand goes to my throat, and he squeezes until spots dance before my eyes.

"What are you doing, Lucifer? I told you to keep our pet safe for now?" A tall man steps into view, and I instantly know who he is.

"Mephistopheles, I guess Mom missed killing you. No worries, she won't make that mistake twice." Smirking, I stare at him openly, knowing full well my mom is working on tracking my exact location.

Scoffing, he draws a sword I've only ever heard about in nightmare stories. The Muramasa sword is one of the most cursed swords in all of history. I try my best to school my features, but it's too late. The sickeningly broad smile that crosses Mephistopheles's face tells me I failed on an epic level.

"Poor little Nikita. You won't live long enough to see your ascension." Glancing over at Lucifer, he almost looks concerned.

I can't help but openly stare at Mephistopheles as a frigid chill runs up my spine. The faint whispers of my mates filter through the pounding of my heart in my ears.

We'll be fine… He can't hurt us…

The voice filters through, and I feel something move within me. It's not like when Rex would move. No, this is almost fluid, like water. I know I'm going to possibly die. The sacrifice was something I read about in the journals that my grandfather had about the mantle of Death Eternal. Usually, the Reaper is tested, dies, then is reborn as Death Eternal. Ordinarily, it's a ceremony. I'm not sure either of these fools killing me will work the same. The way Mephistopheles keeps looking at that blade, I know my time is coming to an end. Drawing a deep breath, I recite the last rite in my head. I need all the help possible to survive this.

Darkness rise, shadows fall.

Listen ancestors to my call.

Death Eternal, on khlōros, I ride.

The fourth seal has been broken. It's now my time.

I have made my sacrifice, this form is forfeited.

Through my death, I shall rise

Rebirth through blackened flames

"I will rise again," I say the last line aloud as I lock my gaze with Mephistopheles. His eyes widen as he charges with the sword out in front of him. I hear the scrape of metal on metal, then the sharp pain and burn. My blood feels like it's on fire. Looking down, the hit of the Muramasa sword is planted firmly between my breasts.

Crimson ichor blooms from around the hilt and down what's left of the white gown covering my warrior's dress. Samael's wolf rips free of my body and goes on the attack. The raven on my forearm takes flight, I guess, to find my mother. Rex finally manifests not as a dragon but as a man. I'm gasping for air, feeling my strength fading. Mephistopheles missed my heart but did enough damage that I will not survive this.

Rex looks at the hilt of the sword and snaps it clean off of the blade, then slides me free from it. I'm fading in and out, and the next thing I know, I'm in his arms. He's managed to staunch the bleeding for now, but I don't have long.

"Bite me," he says softly, raising my mouth to his shoulder.

The bond... Weakly I sink my canines into his flesh and taste his blood. I can feel the pressure from him biting me, but there's no pain. I black out again for how long, I don't know.

So, cold. Is this what death is like?

"Nikita, open your damn eyes this instant!"

Mom?

"Damn it, Nikita, open your eyes!"

Forcing myself to obey, I fight through the exhaustion and open my eyes. Everyone and everything is blurry. So tired. Hands contact my skin, and they feel so warm compared to me.

"It's almost time." I hear my grandfather's voice break through the haze.

"I failed her." Michael, he blames himself.

"You didn't fail her. I didn't rise in time." Rex, he's still holding me.

Another set of arms takes me away from Rex. I know that cologne anywhere. My dad has me. "You can rest now, my little nightmare. Daddy will see you soon when you rise again." Quivering lips press to my temple as my last breath leaves my lungs.

CHAPTER 27

MAELESTOR REX

The shift comes faster than it has in the past because I have taken a mate. My beloved lies dead in her father's arms, surrounded by her other mates and family just outside the Destroyer's castle. I watch as the others say their goodbyes to her old body before Cyrus lays her in my taloned hand.

I wait for the others to move far enough away before I allow my ignitor to click, and I breathe fire instead of acid this one time. Nikita's scent has changed, and I know what beast lays dormant in her chest. My flames, the fire of a loved one, will free her from this husk to be born again. She recited the words, and I heard every single one. Skull Dragons have been one with the Pale Rider since time was numbered. She is the first of the horsemen to rise and be reborn upon this plane.

Pouring my heart and soul into my flames, I burn away her past sins as other family members arrive. Pausing for a moment, I bellow, summoning my family for the rising of the Pale Rider. Listening carefully, I hear the return calls of my family. Using the bond shared within my bloodline, I summon all of my descen-

201

dants to my side. Skull Dragons black out the sky as they come from all corners of the Shadow Realm and the Earth Realm.

The swarm grows, and I watch the smile on the Destroyer's face as several kin land. A small wolven female with a white Skull Dragon hatchling arrives upon the back of my descendent. The little one enthusiastically breaks free of her mother and blows her hatchling flames to help me. The husk of my mate falls away to ash, and my task is done. Shifting back to my human form, I raise my hands to get the dragon's attention, as well as the Nephilim present.

"It has been over a millennium since I last stood before my kin as a man." Pausing, I look at the others. "I beseech you. Lend your voices and help the Pale Rider and my mate rise."

Locking eyes with the Destroyer, I can see the pain of a mother suffering the loss of her daughter. Giving her a nod, I make eye contact with Azrael, whose place my mate will take.

"Dragons! My kin. Let us begin!" My voice carries, and my kin lower their heads, letting a deep rumble escape their maws. The reverberation causes the dirt beneath our feet to shake with their power.

— "I CALL UPON THE POWER OF THE FOURTH SEAL!" "THE POWER OF CREATION AND DESTRUCTION," "TO THOSE THAT HAVE PASSED BEFORE US, AND THOSE YET TO COME." "IT IS TIME FOR THE PALE RIDER TO RISE. TIME FOR DEATH ETERNAL TO WALK THE EARTH ONCE MORE." "KHLŌROS COME FORTH! BID YOUR MASTER TO RISE!"

I can hear the thundering of hooves over the rumble of the dragons. Fire bathes the countryside as a herd of Nightmares gallop towards us. A single stallion walks away from the herd and bows before the ashes. He stomps his front hooves, and soon the other horses join him.

All eyes turn to the ashes swirling counterclockwise before me. In the center of the maelstrom, embers begin to ignite and spark to life. Those surrounding the Destroyer, I can only assume, are her mates. They cling to each other, watching the embers. Every second that passes, new embers ignite, joining the others. I already know what my mate will become, and it hasn't been seen by human or Nephilim eyes since the dark times.

With each stomp of the stallion's hooves, his black coat loses its color, and the fire around his hooves blackens. The more the stallion changes, the faster the embers swirl, increasing in size and number.

The stomping seems to have gone on forever when, in reality, it's been almost an hour. At the final stop of his hooves, the last of the black fur falls away, and he rears up for the last time as the ashes burst into flames. Silence falls over the group as we stare anxiously at the blaze.

The heat intensifies, and the flames pulse rhythmically. Pulsing embers and flames remind me of a heartbeat. The lub-dub of the embers is almost soothing as I watch. Deep within its core, a dark mass is forming. The others have noticed it and move closer to the blaze.

The fiery white mass pulses faster the longer we stare at it. Nightmare Stallion lowers his head and whinnies, then tosses his head around. The rest of the herd returns his call, amping up the excitement.

In a sudden burst of power, the flames rocket up into the sky like a volcanic eruption. A large black phoenix rises from the column and screams across the painted sky. The bird is huge, its wingspan greater than twenty feet wide. The bird circles overhead, and I take in its features. Its tail reminds me of a peacock's tail feathers, except they are made of blackened flames. The bird's broad wings flap gracefully as she moves, the fire trailing behind her.

Losing altitude, the bird plummets to the ground in a burst of obsidian flames. When the fire recedes, Nikita stands in a wispy black gown, her skin almost porcelain and her lips as red as a rose. Her long white hair seems to moves of its own volition like a banshee's mane. Her eyes slowly turn towards me, and I feel rooted. Nikita's steps glide over the scorched earth soundlessly as she closes the distance between us. I watch as her lips part, and sharp upper and lower canines are visible.

"Maelestor Rex, I presume?" Nikita slowly tilts her head from left to right as she studies me up close. Her pale lithe hand reaches up and cups my beard, pressing it flat to my jaw.

"Yes, my love. I've waited a long time for you." Tilting my head, I lean into her touch as I reach out to rest a hand on her hip, allowing her to choose how close she intends to get.

Nikita moves in and buries her nose against my neck just under my beard, and inhales deeply. Her fingertips tense, pressing hard into my hip as she stands on her tiptoes to get closer to my height. Her hot breath washes over me, making my body thrum with anticipation. My mate examines me up close, testing how much I trust her by allowing her this close to my throat.

Her lips press just over my pulse before she returns to standing at her normal height. As she turns to face the others, her dress morphs into black leather armor I've never seen before. It's more aggressive than the armor that her mother, the Destroyer, wears.

Smoke and shadows bleed from the armor as easily as I draw breath. Her amber eyes glow like a fire has been ignited behind her pupils. "I have been hunted and killed. Separated from my mates for what seems like an eternity." Her voice projects as she turns slowly to face each family member.

"Who killed you?" Cyrus fires off. I can feel the rage of her father from where I am standing. Honestly, I don't blame him. I want the party responsible's head on a platter.

Laughing, Nikita closes the distance between herself and her father. "Lucifer and Mephistopheles, actually. They possessed the Muramasa sword." Shaking her head, she turns and walks towards Khlōros. Nikita pats the horse's flank, looking his corpse-like appearance over.

Thana's audible gasp draws Nikita's attention away from the horse for a moment. "The sword was driven through my chest. I can only assume it nicked my heart and probably a blood vessel. As I stood there dying, I heard Samael's voice in my head. He told me what form to take to become Death Eternal." A sick, twisted smile plays upon my mate's lips, and my heart swells with pride. "No matter how many times I am killed. I will always rise. I am now Death Eternal."

Nikita finally moves away from her horse and then over to Azrael, the head Reaper for as long as I can remember. He was in charge since I was a hatchling. Her hand caresses his cheek, and he bows his head to her, smiling. "Rest, Grandfather, I will command the armies of the afterlife and carry the souls of the departed from now on." Waves of shadows and power ebb and flow between them in almost a cyclic motion.

When Nikita is finished, Azrael looks thirty years younger and stands a little taller. "What did you do, Granddaughter?" He touches his face hesitantly, feeling the change in its texture.

"That's easy. I gave you back the years that were stolen from you. All the time you lost waiting for your replacement to be born. Consider it a gift." Nikita kisses Azrael on the forehead, then moves to be reunited with her other mates.

I'm not sure who is more excited, Mordoc or Satan. It's Michael I am concerned about. He's standing there frozen in place, staring blankly into the group of people. It's as if he can't believe our mate is alive. Crossing the distance between us, I rest a hand on his shoulder. "Are you okay?" It's the only thing I can think of asking that's appropriate at the moment.

"I think so? How? I mean, she was born to die?" He looks sadly between Thana and Nikita.

Exhaling loudly, I look down at the scorched dirt below me. "Those of us that started out as mortal, I guess you can say we were born to die. Nikita had a destiny written in the stars ages ago. The Riders will rise again and set things back in order." Forcing a smile, I grip his shoulder as I watch Nikita's siblings swarm her, hugging their sister tightly. What Thana doesn't realize is that she is the origin of the rebirth of the riders of the Apocalypse.

I laugh to myself as I turn my attention to the little white skull dragon at my feet. She is born of my descendant and his wolf mate. Crouching down, I let the little one approach me, and she uses her horns to knock me over. It's amazing how feisty the little ones can be when they have no clue how dangerous what they are doing is.

A hand rests on the top of my head, and I turn to see who it is. Nikita stands there with a broad smile. "We are heading to my castle now. I'm famished and a little tired." Laughing, she smiles the most brilliant smile I've ever seen. "After all, I've been mostly dead all day, and resurrecting takes a lot out of a girl, ya know?"

Chuckling, I stand up and dust myself off. "I will have to take your word for it. Lead the way, my love, and I will follow." She nods and walks towards her horse.

The minute she gets close, Khlōros bows down, then moves its foreleg for Nikki to get onto his back. Gracefully, she mounts him, and her outfit changes again. Instead of the black Reaper gown of yore, she wears a pale gray cloak that covers her head. The fabric appears to be tattered and older than her young years. It floats around her as if a strong breeze is moving it. The long flowing sleeve raises, and her hand slides free. I'll be damned; it's nothing but bones.

What does this mean for the future of this family?

CHAPTER 28
NIKITA

It's like the song from Skillet. I'm back from the dead tonight. Looking at my exposed hand knocks me for a loop. I have a skeleton hand instead of my flesh one. *What the actual fuck happened to me? Can I still have children? Am I dead and I move?* The Crow reference makes me giggle as I watch the Firemares choose which mate it wishes to take with us. Picky little bastards. When my last mate mounts his horse, I turn Khlōros towards what used to be Azraels' castle to the north.

My horses' hooves are soundless as we move over the various terrain on the way to the other side of the Shadow Realm. Interestingly, none of my mates protested and mounted their horses instead of flying. It may just be a unified front thing, or they just really wanted to ride a horse.

The castle comes into view on the horizon, and the spires reach high into the blackening sky. It's more of a gothic-looking castle. I would be sure if it was on the surface, it would most definitely be haunted. Dead trees reach towards the sky, casting their shadows over the structure of the castle. As we get closer, the deep cut marks in the granite tell the tale of all the battles that laid siege at its foundation.

Sliding from Khlōros' back, as soon as my boots hit the ground, my clothing and body return to normal. My eyes scan my hands, and I am amazed at how simply getting on my horse's back changed me. Khlōros touches my arm, and he, too, becomes a tattoo upon my flesh.

Thirteen stairs rise from the scorched earth and lead to the castle's front doors. The large stone double doors scrape open, and a blast of cold air hits us from the interior. I lead the way into the interior of the castle and every candle and lantern ignites. Before I can turn to my mates, my grandfather and father appear before me.

Without hesitating, I dive into my daddy's arms and hug him like there's no tomorrow. "Shhh, Daddy is here." Cyrus places his lips on my temple, and I can feel him exhale roughly. A tear hits my cheek, prompting me to pull back and look at him.

Blood tears streak down my father's and grandfather's faces. Reaching up, I wipe the tears away and smile. "I'm okay, Daddy, I swear. If it wasn't for Rex's quick thinking, I might not have resurrected." Closing my eyes, I hug my father tighter.

"You got lucky, my little nightmare. I'm glad that you learned the rites when you did." Dad's voice breaks, and I can see him struggling with the emotions. Pain is etched in the creases around his eyes and the quiver of his lips.

"We knew my ascension was coming. We just didn't anticipate the how of it." Forcing a smile, I kiss my dad's cheek before going to hug my grandfather.

"The legends of the Pale Rider were understated, to say the least. Nowhere in any of the texts did it say you had to die to be reborn." Azrael presses his lips to my temple as he hugs me tightly to him.

A laugh escapes my lips as I hug him back just as tightly. "Legends are just that, legends. Stories passed down for generations, first verbally, then finally written. Details get missed sometimes." Shrugging my shoulders, I step away from my grandfather and look at my mates.

"I'm sorry I scared you guys. I didn't know this was going to happen this way." Glancing down, I gather my thoughts before finishing.

There are at least a half dozen things I know are true now. "First and foremost, I need to finish my bond with Rex." I stress the word need as I turn and stare at him. Fire and hunger burn in his eyes as his gaze rakes over my form." I can damn near feel his hands running over me as his eyes move from my toes to meet my eyes. My heart beats a staccato as I can only imagine the thoughts going through that damn man's head.

"The next bunch of truths I know is that, once the bonds complete, I still need to present my guys before Uriel to be judged once and for all." I look over at my mother, who nods slowly, agreeing. My father rolls his eyes, sick of the Angelic rule how has been for as long as time has been numbered.

My grandfather is the one that surprises me as he tilts his head, smiling. "I have a shocking truth for you." The dramatic pause that he takes next makes me want to giggle. Grandfather gets like this when he knows he's going to stick it to the Archangels.

"Well, come on, Gramps, you need to tell me. That look in your eye tells me it's going to be something devilishly delicious." I let the words roll off my tongue, and I watch Michael cringe out of the corner of my eye.

Laughing, my grandfather walks back and forth, pacing in front of us before he stops short and stares at me again, folding his hands in front of him. "Depending on how you present yourself to Uriel, you can't be judged."

Furrowing my brows, I look between my four mates, each one just as puzzled as the next, before I look back at my grandfather. "What do you mean, depending on the form, I can't be judged?"

"Well, that's easy. The Pale Rider predates the choir of Angels." Azrael's statement creates more questions than answers.

"I thought you were the Pale Rider, Gramps, since the Pale Rider is death, and you have been death." I'm still lost because I can assume a form that should have been his by all rights.

Michael steps forward and raises his hand, stopping everyone. "The Pale Rider existed during the Dark Ages. The time before good and evil was clearly defined, and the Azriel we have been waiting for was a female. Since women can bring life into this world and, with a stroke of their hand, death at the same time. They are creation and destruction all in one body." Michael stares at the ground as his eyes burn golden, even though I cannot see where his pupils are looking. The pain etched in the corners of his eyes and in the furrow of his brow tells me that something much darker is yet to be uttered from his lips.

Closing the distance between us, I reach out and take his hands, looking up at him. "If I am to be the next rising of the Pale Rider, then so be it. I have one of the most powerful Archangels at my side as my mate and, of course, my eternal love." Bouncing up, I kiss his lips softly. "I have a demon vampire, probably one of the oldest amongst us. His wisdom will help guide this family beyond the knowledge that you already have. We have Satan, who has been on both sides of the line of darkness and light, to be a voice of reason and neutrality. Finally, we have Rex, who joins us from a time long forgotten. It was a time when chivalry and doing what was right was at the forefront, even if it meant wiping out a population to save those you love. He is the epitome of sacrifice."

I say those words as I look deep into his now serpentine eyes. Hopefully, he can see the love and pride in mine shining back at him. I look back and everyone else and then motion towards the castle. "Let's go in and have something to eat and drink. Let's relax and enjoy this time together."

Tomorrow is never promised or guaranteed. It's never a thought that easy to come to accept. As I lead my family into my new home, I hear stone sliding across stone. I remember hearing stories about this when my mother took over the Destroyer's castle. My grandfather's castle is now reshaping itself to fit my needs better. He stands alongside me and threads his fingers through mine, smiling, proud of what's happening.

"Every time a new Reaper takes over, the castle itself reorders itself to fit the desires of the one now in power." His tone echoes through the building, bouncing off every wall reverberating, making it sound like he's repeating himself multiple times.

"It's still a little freaky to get used to, Grandpa." I bump shoulders with him, then move into the Great Hall to the right. Stones are flying through the air as others slide across the ground as the castle changes itself right before my eyes. "How does it know what I need it to be?" I turn and face my grandfather, waiting to see what answer he will give me.

"That's easy, little one. It reads you. It's able to figure out your purpose in this lifetime, and it's adjusting to meet and anticipate those needs." We narrowly move out of the way of several blocks flying past us. Five stone thrones rise up from the granite floor. I stand there staring, amazed at the Thrones' construction. The one in the center, I can only assume, is mine. A large black phoenix is carved right into the stone over where my head would be. A dragon sits directly to my right. To my left, what appears to be a halo is carved into the back of the throne. The next one has a bat carved into its back, and the last a tilted crown. The throne that represents Satan puzzles me the most; the symbolism behind the tilted, cracked crown isn't lost on me. He would have been the strongest of the Fallen angels when he was whole. But having been divided from his other self, he is not what he used to be.

Turning to face everyone, I bring my hands together in front of me. "Grandfather, I don't know how you would normally order food and beverages here, but let's get that started so my family and I can settle into our new home."

"Are you serious?" I hear Michael's voice rise up, and it stops me in my tracks. We're on the other side of the Shadow Realm, the neutral ground where Archangels that have been granted permission can tread. So his reaction doesn't make sense.

"What seems to be the trouble?" As I close the distance between Michael and me, I can see he's seriously having issues with all the changes.

"I don't know if I can handle this." His brutal honesty rocks the very foundation of where I thought our relationship was.

"Handle what? My death and rebirth, or living here?" The other guys back away. I guess maybe something with myself is changing and giving them a visual cue that it's not safe to remain that close to me.

Michael throws his hands up in the air and starts to pace. The waves of agitation are upset, and the most concerning undercurrent is the feeling of betrayal. I stare at him, hoping and willing him to come to his senses. "I can't do this right now." Michael's tone almost sounds final. Before I can get too close, he vanishes from before me.

I stare at the empty space where he stood several moments before. Shock, hurt, and disbelief war within me. Part of me wants to storm the gates of Heaven and burn it to the ground. Sadly, the other half of me accepts that perhaps with all these changes, I'm more than what he can handle. Plastering a smile upon my face, I motion for my grandfather to proceed. My heart feels like it's shattering in my chest. For now, I need to shelve Michael's blow-up and get my family settled for the night. Dying takes a lot out of you, and if I'm honest with myself, I'm not strong enough to go much further than dinner and bed.

CHAPTER 29

MAELESTOR REX

As long as I have existed, I have never wanted to storm the gates of Heaven as much as I do right now. The growl of my dragon breaks loose of my human lips, and it makes everyone's head turn in my direction. I can feel my scales running just underneath the soft, pale human flesh covering me. Death would be too good for Michael at this point. It would be a mercy that I refuse to grant him. Huffing out a breath, smoke bellows from my nostrils as I hear the faint click of my ignitor in my chest. Unlike other shifters, dragons can not separate their beast from man as easily. It's especially difficult when one's mate has been physically or emotionally hurt. Nikita has been harmed in the mental and emotional sense, and I'm not sure if there's a fix for that.

Michael had better hope Nikita gets to him before I do. As the goddess is my witness, he will not walk away from me unscathed. One does not harm one's mate in any shape or form. It's beyond unacceptable. I'm amazed that her other mates allowed him to get away with this atrocity. I guess, in a sense, they don't build males like they used to. Sadly, most of the males these days barely pass for being men. They may have the correct equipment between their legs, but they lack the fortitude and the moral compass to do what's right for their mate and their family before all else. Most are narcissistic little boys trapped in an adult male's body. It sickens me what these poor females are stuck accepting for mates. Back in my day, we would have slaughtered the males who were not worthy of the females we were fighting for. Male-to-male combat was how mates were chosen for the few available females. It appears in this time period, yet again, the males outnumber the females. Except for this time, the genetic pool has become a lot more shallow.

I follow my mate and her grandfather through this grand castle, watching it morph and become exactly what she needs. I believe this lifeless monument has more sense in a brick than Michael has in his entire body. It at least knows to provide a stable foundation and a sound structure to shelter my mate from whatever is coming.

Satan comes to stand beside me. I can see in his eyes that he wants to say something. "Out with it." In my mind, it's better to get right to the point than the play idle little children's games with extra words that are not needed. I have always been a man of action; instead of saying they were gonna do something, I just did it. I guess you could say I come from the school of thought. It's better to beg for forgiveness than ask for permission. Sometimes, when it's a life-and-death situation, it's better to react and apolo-gize later than to not respond and die where you stand.

Satan hesitates. I guess not expecting my response to be as blunt as it was. "Michael royally messed up." He looks down and away, and I see that he's rather distraught. He's too emotional for my liking. Delicate emotions are more of a woman's place than a warrior like me. But then again, his ability to get in touch with his feelings probably will give him an advantage over me in some instances.

"He did royally mess up." I motion ahead and have Satan follow me into the next available room. Interestingly enough, Mordoc follows as well.

"What do you propose we do about this fiasco?" Mordoc states plainly and with an aggressive undertone. I like the bloodsucker better every moment.

"Nothing yet." Glancing around the room, it appears to be an old sitting parlor with hundreds of books lining the shelves. I lean against the fireplace, resting my elbow on the mantle as I look at the other two. "For now, our priority is to keep Nikita happy and comfortable, no matter what has to be done." Both males nod, agreeing with me, which goes a lot easier than I thought.

"You need to complete your bond with her," Satan states the obvious, and I almost want to laugh. If I wasn't sitting here having to deal with these two knuckleheads, that would be my utmost priority at this point.

"Duly noted. I plan to attend to that as soon as possible. For now, I needed to make sure that this family unit." I stop and motion to the two of them before continuing. "Is as solid as it can be, to build a house on a crumbling foundation doesn't help anyone."

Satan looks a little puzzled while Mordoc understands exactly where I'm coming from. He looks over at Satan and rests a hand on his shoulder. "I think Rex means that if the three of us cannot support Nikita at her worst, we do not deserve her at her best."

Interestingly, the leech understands exactly what needs to be done. I nod my head along with what he's saying as a pleased smile graces my lips. "If you will excuse me, gentlemen, I need to find our mate." I depart quickly, not giving them any time to say anything further.

I follow her scent through the hallway like a moth to the flame. I weave in and out of corridors rooms only to finally arrive in what appears to be the throne room. Standing in the center is Nikita, with her obsidian wings spread wide. She's orchestrating the reconstruction of the room to fit her needs.

Brick and mortar fly around like feathers on the wind. I guess she senses me in the room because she slowly turns to face me. She's a vision of divine darkness, beauty, and lethality all in one package.

I stand here in awe of the beautiful woman that has bewitched me from the moment they emblazoned me upon her flesh. "Can I help you, Rex?" She closes the distance between us without hesitation. I watch her as she moves with the fluid grace of a predator.

Wrapping my arm around her waistline, I draw her flush against me and plant a kiss at the corner of her lips. Close enough yet just far enough away to entice her.

"You're playing dirty." Her statement makes the corner of my mouth raise slightly before I pull away and wink at her.

"But of course, I'm not dead after all. It's not fun to be boring and predictable." I look around to see how the changes are going with the throne room. I move to sit on the bench close by and watch her.

"Am I entertaining you?" Nikita tilts her head to the side as she watches me.

"I can think of much more entertaining things we could be doing." Shifting my index finger to a talon, I cut the top button off my shirt as I stare at her.

"Is that so?" She closes the distance between us and bends to look me in the eye.

Reaching up swiftly, I grab her throat and give it a gentle squeeze. "That is so. Because I say it is." She tries to break loose from my grip, and I merely tighten it using my thumb, index, and middle finger to apply pressure to the muscles on the side of her neck, yet not to her trachea. When she realizes what's happening, she stops fighting and stands there, waiting to see what I'll do next.

"Be a good mate and lead us to the bedroom. You and I need to attend to some finalities post haste." Her eyes light up almost immediately when she understands what I'm hinting at. It's kind of interesting to watch the shift in her personality.

I release her from my grip, and she turns on her heel and runs from the room. Watching a primal want to be chased is an interesting turn of events. Shaking my head, I start pursuing her, making my blood boil with anticipation. I pick up the pace when I no longer hear her footsteps in the hallway. My fatal mistake was not looking up. Nikita drops from the ceiling, tackling me to the ground. Her canines go to my throat immediately. A twisted smile plays upon my lips as I feel them sinking deeper into my flesh. "Oh, this is going to be fun."

Nikita leaps off of me and tilts her head to the side. Blackened orbs stare back at me, and I am lost in the fathomless depths. "You may be my mate, but I will not be dominated." The growl in her voice is hot as fuck, and I feel myself harden thinking about it.

Her eyes drop to my crotch, and she smirks. "Hmmm. Someone looks interested. Better keep up, old man." She takes off down the hallway again, vanishing in a wisp of shadows.

Getting up, I dust myself off and start laughing. "What's so funny?" Mordoc apparently witnessed the entire event.

"She thinks she's going to dominate me." I laugh all over again, thinking about how absurd that idea is.

"I don't see how that's going to work out in her favor," Mordoc states and leans against the wall, crossing his arms over his chest.

"That makes two of us." He laughs as well. "If you need me, just holler." The vampire's swagger amazes me. He saunters down the hall and off on his merry way.

Turning on my heels, I pursue my mate. Her scent is as potent from a distance as it was when she stood right before me. After three more turns, I arrive at what looks to be the main bedroom. Nikita is standing with her back to the door with her wings unfurled as she looks out a bay window. Taking several steps into the room, the door slams shut behind me. Turning to look behind me, I see the door is gone, and only a wall remains where the door once was.

I spin to face Nikita again, and she's gone. I swear this female is going to be the death of me today. First, the door disappears, and now she's gone as well. Looking around the room I'm standing in, much of the furniture has shifted since I first arrived here. The bed has almost doubled in size, the sitting area is now gone, and I hear running water in the distance.

Crossing the room, I follow the sound of the water and come to what appears to be a large main bathroom. It looks more like an oasis than a bathroom. There's a swimming pool in the center and what looks like a giant shower stall that could probably fit at least four to five people. Nikita is standing under the shower head, bathed in rivulets of water, lathering herself, allowing the suds to roll down her curvy body. It's been more years than I can remember since the last time I was able to touch a female. And what makes this even more special is that she not only carried me upon her body and gave me life again, she is my fated mate.

All those years when taking random females to warm my bed, never once did I dream of this day ever coming to fruition. The smirk playing upon her crimson lips tells me she knows I'm here. She's just taking her sweet time to get to me. Closing the distance between us, I lean against the nearest wall to the shower stall and watch as her lithe hands run over her frame. She inches her hand slowly down her body, caressing every curve, making me mad with lust.

"Don't think I don't know you're there, Rex." The moment she speaks, it's as if the Angels are singing.

"I figured as much, my love. Please, don't let me interrupt you." A smile graces her lips again.

"I wouldn't dream of it. It's been a rather eventful day in Hell. Dying, resurrecting, and now preparing to take my last mate," she states the obvious and the burden of her day so calmly you would think it was like any other Friday afternoon. One where you would go and pick up the children from your parents' house before returning home for a normal supper. My poor mate is handling all these trials and tribulations with the grace of somebody well beyond her years.

I glance away for a moment, taking in the bathroom's layout, and when I look back again, she's gone. This seems to be Nikita's favorite game to play. Now you see her, now you don't. If I was her, I would return to my bedroom and dress, so that's where I go. There she is, as predicted, standing in front of her armoire, slipping on a blood-red silk nightgown. The gown leaves nothing to my imagination; after all these centuries, I don't know how much more patient I can be. A deep growl escapes my lips as I stalk towards her. With a flick of her wrist, I end up flat on my back, staring at the ceiling. Soon, she's standing over me, looking down and smiling.

"Oh, how the mighty have fallen." She drags a clawed hand over my clothing, slicing the fabric over my chest.

I can only imagine what my little vixen has in store for me tonight.

CHAPTER 30
NIKITA

Rex has no clue what he's gotten himself into when it comes to me. With each mate I have taken, my power has grown exponentially. With a flick of my wrist, I have put Rex flat on his back, and he's not happy.

"What's the matter, my love? Don't like a dominant female?" Grinning, I move to sit on his chest and look down at him.

Shaking his head, the initial anger fades, and he almost looks sad. "I'm sorry I wasn't in your life sooner. I am aware of how poorly the Dark Nephilim have been treated, and it's why you need to be in control." His brows knot in the middle as he plans his next sentence.

During the silence, I let his words sink in. Yes, I have witnessed the division between light and dark Nephilim grow in my relativity brief life span. The hostility between the two is insane. And for what? A war that happened over a thousand years ago that most of us were not involved in. "My need for control is directly related to my personal safety. I need to feel safe."

Rex pushes himself to sit up, and I slide down onto his lap. Powerful arms wrap around me as he holds me flush to his chest. "I'm sorry no one has ever made you feel safe enough to relax and trust your mates to keep you safe." His statement knocks me for a loop.

Sitting back, stunned, I stare at him, trying to parse what he just said to me. Has my desire to be safe driven me to need to be in constant control? "I never looked at it that way before." Leaning forward, I rest my head on his shoulder, and he hugs me tightly.

"It's always hard to look at yourself sometimes. It took me many years to realize I was no better than the tyrants before me." His fingers thread through my hair slowly. The slow strokes he takes to remove the knots from my hair are soothing, and I rest for a little while. "You've had a rough day. You've died and been resurrected. That's no easy feat to deal with. I'm here to listen if you need me to." He presses his lips against mine, pushing his affection and strength toward me.

"Make me forget today. Make me forget I died." Pulling back, I search his eyes, and he nods resolutely.

Impressively, he holds onto me and stands up, carrying me across the room. Gently, Rex deposits me on the bed, stands back, and strips. Rex knows he's teasing me as he unbuttons his shirt slowly, exposing his chest to me. He has dozens of scars; barely any of his chest is unscarred. Rex moves forward and lays his shirt on the end of the bed. He sits next to his shirt, removes his shoes and socks, and drops them to the floor. Crawling up the bed, he lays himself over me, keeping his weight off me. "You can tell me no, love. I can hold you until you sleep if that's what you want."

Reaching up, I thread my fingers through his beard and pull him down to kiss him. Our tongues battle for dominance, and eventually, I relent and let him control the kiss. Something within me shifts when I let go. Other feelings surface love, happiness, and relief floods my system. Rex controls the tempo of my emotions like a seasoned pro. Breaking the kiss, his lips move across my jaw and down my neck to where he bit me when I was dying.

"I want to leave my mark this time without rushing." His teeth lightly grip my flesh over the old mark, making my core pulse in response. Unconsciously, my body arcs, pressing myself against him.

My canines descend at his declaration. The low ache in my belly is getting hard to ignore. Turning my head, I attempt to bite at him, and his hand comes over my mouth, stopping me. "Be a good girl and wait." He kisses my nose, pulls back, and flips me onto my stomach. The way he spreads his fingers out, his hand almost spans across my back.

Sharp points touch the tops of my shoulders, then drag down. The sound of ripping fabric echoes in the room. He just used his talons to slice my nightgown off of me. The silken material falls off me, and I shiver from the chill in the air. *Damn drafty castle.*

Fingertips trail down my spine to my tailbone. My skin feels electric, nerve endings sparking to life with every touch. For once, I remain silent and let this play out. I'm very curious about what Rex is going to do. He's the first male I've allowed in the driver's seat when it comes to sex or anything for that matter. Lips press between my shoulder blades, drawing me out of my inner monologue.

Closing my eyes, I revel in his hot breath and lips upon my skin. His hands grip my waistline before he props my hips up and uses his talon to cut my underwear away. He drags the material up over my pussy, teasing my clit as the material leaves my body. Cool air hits my silken folds just before he drags his tongue from my clit up through my folds.

Moaning deeply, I force myself to remain still, fearing he will stop what he's doing. "Good girl… It's so much better when you allow someone to take care of you, isn't it?" He nips my ass cheek, and I hiss slightly.

"Yes, Rex, please… I need you." Turning my head to the side, I watch the pleased smile that crosses his lips.

I watch him move from the bed and remove his pants, letting them fall to the floor. His large member juts out proudly before him, already weeping pre-cum. I clench my thighs in anticipation. He grips his length and gives it a long slow stroke, making me watch.

Rex moves faster than I expected, flipping me onto my back and throwing my calves over his shoulders. Squealing, I paw at him, trying to gain some sense of balance. He full-on belly laughs at my reaction, then thrusts forward, burying himself deep within me. Gasping, I grip his forearms tightly, feeling how full I am and the warmth spreading of the bond settling into place. I can feel the fibers of each of my mates within the bond blaze to life now that the last piece is in place. Drawing in a deep breath, I feel balanced and relieved all at the same time.

Rex sets a punishing pace, thrusting hard, fast, and deep within me. Every thrust knocks the headboard against the wall to the point the other mates burst into the room. They stop short, and I watch the glow of Rex's dragon in his eyes and then the flare of scales across his face. His dragon is getting possessive, which may not end well for my other mates. Curling up, I make enough room to unfurl my wings, then use them to push me up and flip Rex onto his back. Staring down at him, I let the blackened flames of my phoenix dance across my feathers.

"Be a good boy and finish what you started." As I speak, I let my upper and lower canines descend and bare them at him. His dragon immediately settles, and he moves again. His slowly rolling thrusts reach every sensitive spot within me. Rolling my head to the side, I crook a finger at Mordoc and Satan. "Either join in or get out," I growl, baring my teeth at them.

Mordoc's clothes hit the floor faster than a dress on prom night. He's at my side in seconds, kissing my chest and neck. Satan strolls over like he's walking through the park. The casual way he slowly removes his clothing is almost a strip tease. He slides himself up behind Mordoc and rubs his ass. The sight of him touching my other mate sets my nerve endings on fire.

The second Mordoc moans from Satan penetrating his ass, I cry out my release. My core crushes around Rex's length, milking him for all he's worth. His thrusts become erratic, and soon he comes, and I can feel the pulsing of his cock deep within me.

I watch, mesmerized, as Satan holds Mordoc, his hand tight around his throat. I had an inkling that Satan had a breath play kink, but I have never witnessed it for myself. Pulling free from Rex, I reach out, gripping Mordoc's length and stroking it slowly in time with Satan's thrusts.

There's a shift on the bed behind me, and the next thing I know, Rex is standing over me, waving his cock in Mordoc's face. "I feel one fang hit my cock, and you will know a pain you will never forget." Roughly, Rex grips his hair and shoves his dick into Mordoc's mouth.

The guys have their rhythm, and the slapping of flesh sends my senses off the deep end. Gripping my breasts, I roll my nipples between my fingers almost in time with the phantom pulses in my core. Satan's eyes are locked on me as he ruthlessly fucks Mordoc. "Babe, join in. Mordoc's cock is lonely." No sooner does Satan mention it than Rex moves off to the side, and Mordoc's cock is bounding free, waiting for me.

Moving closer, and turn my back to him and drop onto all fours. Rex stops fucking Mordoc's mouth long enough for my vampire to slide his length through my wet folds. "This is as close to Heaven as I'll ever get." He thrusts forward, burying himself deep within me, and I rock forward, using Rex's leg to steady me.

With every thrust, I get knocked forward. Every chance I get, I bite Rex's thigh, and the scent of his blood drives Mordoc insane. He bucks harder into me, thrusting deeply until Satan tightens his grip. It's an interesting power dynamic between them. I'm honestly not sure who is the dominant or submissive sometimes.

"I'm getting close," Satan yells from behind Mordoc.

"Me too," Mordoc chimes in as his hands work frantically over Rex's length.

"Almost there," I pant out, teetering on the edge of sweet oblivion.

Laughing, Rex takes his length and strokes it faster, inches from my face. Mordoc wraps his arms around my ribs and lifts me up so that I'm kneeling. That sudden change in angle sends my orgasm crashing through me. I cry out, my release lasting only moments before Satan reaches forward and shoves his wrist in my mouth. Taking the hint, my canines descend and break through his skin.

The familiar hiss of the guys all exchanging bites is music to my ears. The slurping of blood and the heat of each other's bodies is comforting. As we start coming down and slowly breaking apart, my mind drifts to Michael.

Turning away from the others, I slide to the edge of the bed and head to the bathroom to shower. Scorching hot water caresses my body loosening my tense muscles. Even from here, I can still hear the guys having sex with each other. Shaking my head, I close my eyes, trying to focus on wayward mate number four. He is a maelstrom of emotions; I know he's having issues processing. It's tough for one as pure as him to deal with those of us of the dark blood.

Lathering up my hair, I reach out through the bond to figure out where Michael is currently. My senses are muddled down here. Part of what I'm sensing is that he's having dark thoughts. The other half of what I am sensing is that I believe he's in my father's club. I finish washing and conditioning my hair, then scrub the rest of my body. The long, relaxing shower I had planned for myself has been shot to hell.

Wrapping a towel around my body and one around my hair, I step into the now-silent bedroom. The guys are in a huge pile of limbs and sweat, with satisfied smiles on their lips. The only one left awake is Satan, who is braiding Rex's hair. I make a quick motion with my head to get him to follow me out of the room.

Darting through the castle, I head towards the other master suite on this floor. "What's so urgent?" Satan says as he walks into the room, toweling himself off.

"Michael is on the precipice. I believe he is planning on falling to join us." Throwing my fear out there makes it even more tangible than before.

"We should go to him. What would his falling do to the bond the way it sits?" Satan manifests a suit on himself and straightens his tie.

I ponder my outfit for a moment, then decide my black jeans and blood-red sweater combo would be best suited for this misadventure. "Honestly, I'm not sure. My dad or mom would definitely know. I'll summon them to where ever we find Michael." With the plan settled, Satan and I take off to the void between Heaven and Hell.

CHAPTER 31
NIKITA

Gripping Satan's hands, I try to focus on wayward mate number four. When I finally get a lock on him, I'm shocked to sense him at the edge of the void. The void is a place that Angels fear treading. It's between Heaven and Hell and between life and death. There's no telling what it will do to an Archangel if he chooses to fall. The Angels fell through the same massive power source to follow Lucifer after the first war. Unfurling my wings, I spread them wide and then wrap them around Satan and me, moving us the fastest way I know. Ripping through the shadows, we arrive not even fifteen feet from Michael. Unfurling my wings and allowing them to hang open behind me, I extend my hands out in front of me in a placating manner. "Michael? Sweetheart, please back away from the edge," I beg him.

The sadness in his gaze makes my heart break looking at him. He glances back over the edge again and then back at me. "I'm the odd man out," he states resolutely. His eyes turn again to look down and over the edge. "You would be better off if I fell and I was like you. I wouldn't be holding the family up. I wouldn't be the stick in the mud that I get accused of being." His gaze pins Satan in his spot. He turns quickly again to face me. "You have a dragon king and a horde at your disposal. What use am I?"

We've stumbled now on the crux of the problem. Michael feels as though he has no purpose. Carefully, I step forward slowly, trying not to literally send him off the deep end. "Is that what is plaguing you? That you feel you have no purpose in this family." I step closer to him yet again, and he's not flinching, which is a good sign.

"You are the daughter of the Destroyer and now Death Eternal. My entire purpose of being your mate to defend you is a moot point." His voice is strained with raw emotion as he fights to hold back his tears.

I attempt to see things from his point of view, and still, to me, it makes no sense. "How can you say it's a moot point? I will always need you." I try to stress the needing part, hoping his sense of purpose and responsibility overrides his self-depreciation. But honestly, I'm not sure if anything will work now.

"You've always been a good girl, Nikita." His tone is sad and wistful at the same time. His eyes take on a faraway look as a smile slowly creeps across his lips. "I had a harder time keeping Davina out of trouble than you." He smiles and lets a half laugh escape his lips. "She was an absolute handful when she was little." He states plainly and then returns his gaze to the precipice. "I just want you to know that I would change nothing. Well, minus the part where you died, that I would change. Without a doubt, I would die for you a thousand times over. Even if it meant repeatedly dying for all eternity just to keep you safe." No sooner do those words leave his lips than he dives over the edge, not even attempting to unfurl his wings.

Without hesitation, I run to the edge, spread my wings, and leap, ready to dive to catch up to Michael. Powerful arms wrap around me, catching me, and it's Metatron. Being bigger and stronger than I am, he carries me back up and sets me on the edge. I pound my fists into his chest, screaming to be let go. The only thing I can see is the sadness in his eyes. Tears threaten to fall, bubbling right at the edge of his eyelids.

"This is his choice. Free will and all." Metatron's defeated tone makes my heart feel like a lead sinker.

I stare over the edge, watching Michael pass through the storm clouds separating Heaven and Hell. An almost atomic-level blast radiates from his point of impact, sending a tsunami of power out in all directions.

Boldly, Satan takes me from Metatron and pulls me flush to his chest. He holds me as silent tears roll down my face. The mate that I have known the longest just chose to fall. My bottom lip quivers as I attempt several times the form the words that need to be said. He kisses my lips, stopping them from moving, and stares deeply into my eyes, trying to push all his love for me through the bond.

It doesn't take long for the others to arrive. My other two mates, both of my parents, and the rest of my mother's mates. Metatron and Raphael seem to be the most damaged by this transgression. They stare at each other hopelessly and then embrace, trying to comfort one another, having lost one of their brothers in arms. I know through the bond he's not dead, but I also know he's not the same. It feels as though he's being ripped apart to me. I cry out, screaming, falling to my knees as I feel like I'm being torn into. Satan falls with me, clutching his chest, and as I look at the others, we're all in the same position.

"I've never seen this before," Uriel, who I hadn't even noticed arrived, states as he looks between us. "It is unheard of for Dark Nephilim to be able to feel when an Archangel falls." The nonchalant way he dismisses my species and what my mates and I are going through hits a whole new level of rage for me.

Forcing myself to my feet, I move to stand before him. "Do you think we are all that heartless?" My statement leaves little room for him to deny how it sounded to me.

"No, but you weren't raised as a Dark Nephilim either." His powerful tone reverberates against my chest, making me grit my teeth even harder, strengthening my resolve.

"You're right; I wasn't. I was raised to be a strong, independent female. I was raised to stand up for what I believe in." Getting within inches of him, I press my index finger against his chest. The armor under my finger heats up as I stare into his eyes, daring him to say something else.

"A lot of this hatred," I say, looking at everyone present, "is taught." My words cause the Angels and Archangels gathered to stop their conversations and stare at me. "Think about it," I say as I move away from Uriel, flexing my wings, then putting them away. "I was raised with Light and Dark Nephilim in my family group." Laughing, I turn to look at those gathered. "I am as close to being a true-born Fallen as anyone has ever come. The product of the Destroyer and the son of Death himself." Laughing again, I pace along the edge, "By all rights, I should be a monster."

I fan my fingers wide and then lay them over my heart. "I should be the one that is feared. And yet everyone worries about Davina and her temper, not mine. The one ascended to Speaker is the one whose temper and wrath everyone worries about." Arching a brow, I fix Raphael in his place. He winces, knowing I speak the truth.

I step away further from Uriel and come to stand before Raphael. "Your perfect daughter, my twin, has always been viewed as more of a threat than I am." Raphael visually cringes as he stares at me. "Do you know that most young Dark Nephilim go to sleep afraid that an Archangel is going to kill them in the middle of the night? Just because of what color their feathers are?" I say before stepping away from him. I look down over the precipice, finally feeling that Michael's getting control of himself.

Shaking my head, I huff out a half laugh. "Death walks, and War has been resurrected." I raise my eyes as I make the statement about War. I make eye contact with everyone. The only person who gets what I just said is my mother. Both hands fly up to cover her mouth as she stares at me in shock.

"Nikita, are you certain?" Mother says as she rushes forward and takes both my hands in hers.

"Yes, I am."

Mom spins away from me, running her hands roughly through her hair before she stops and stares at everyone else. "According to Grandfather's memories, when the riders rise, the apocalypse comes. There will no longer be segregation between Heaven and Hell. They will both just simply exist." The remaining Archangels gather the bunch up in a heated discussion.

"Nothing ever changes," I practically growl out as I stare at those white-winged mother fuckers. Sadly, my mother lowers her head. She has nothing to say at this point that would change my mind.

"Nikita, they're not all bad." The strain in her voice tells me that even she's having an issue dealing with what's happening.

"How can you say that!" I scream at the top of my lungs, then motion towards all the Angels gathered. "Look at them. I mean, really look at them!" Mother turns her head slowly and tries to look at them differently. "Their brother just fell." I enunciate my words, trying to stress exactly what this means. "They don't seem to care."

Feeling defeated I sigh and look down at my feet briefly before looking back up at my mom. "Tell me I'm wrong." Mom looks back and forth between her mates and Uriel, now seeing this for what it truly is.

"I'm sure they'll figure something out." Mom's furrowed brow tells a completely different tale than what the words coming out of her mouth.

"I'm sure they will. They'll try to figure out how to either extinguish my bond," I motion to my mates and down towards the abyss, "or just Michael."

I can tell the moment the gears turn in Mom's head as she looks from me to her mates and then down into the blackness Michael disappeared into. She stares with her chrome eyes down into the eternal darkness of the storm that wages in the void. "If your mate is truly War resurrected, there's nothing they can do to stop him." Mom turns her head and looks at me as her eyes fade from Chrome back to their natural color.

"I can only hope you're right." My tone is icy cold. I don't care if there is a Heaven or Hell left after this is all over. *There are only two things I know to be true. The first is that because of the segregation between the races, my mate has thrown himself into the void to cross-over and join us. And two, if they even try to raise a finger against him —a feral grin crosses my lips—none of them, family or otherwise, will be left standing.* I turn and look at my mother with my abyssal orbs. *I will burn them all asunder, leaving nothing left.*

The earth shakes under my feet. Instinct drives me to run to the cliff and look over the edge. Hundreds of specters walk up the stone face heading right for us. "Back up!" I scream to the others, then take on the form of Death. My horse manifests beside me, and I climb up upon him. Extending my right hand out, my scythe blazes to life, ready to kill whatever comes my way.

CHAPTER 32
MICHAEL

I REMEMBER THE FALL AS CLEAR AS SEEING THE FIRST SUNRISE. THE temperature shift alone was enough to set my senses on fire. Then it was literally blazing heat tearing up my flesh as I moved through what seemed to be a hurricane. Eventually, there was peace, calm silence, and nothingness, voices from the past echoing in my mind, showing me all the wrongs I had committed.

It showed me all of those that I have tortured, and murdered, all because of divinity. We say that the humans are blasphemous when they kill in the name of religion, yet we, the Archangels, are no different. We kill because of a wing color because of an order we follow blindly. I am no better than the humans that they send us to protect.

The talk of a being called War reverberates numerous times. Neither divine nor evil. War brings about justice to those that cannot claim it for themselves. It's not the war that the humans wage or the war that the Angels have already waged. This War is different. This War means the ultimate sacrifice, my time within the Silver City. My mate and my brethren, who are her mates, will never see the interior of the Silver City just because of their wing color. Only I would be the one to walk in there whenever I feel like it and taste paradise for eternity. I can't do that to Nikita. I can't leave her alone. My voice breaks as I scream into the storm. A deeper voice speaks, one that I have never heard, and it says to rise.

I feel as though every fiber of my being is on fire. My muscles are stretching, flexing, and spasming out of control. This has to be the most excruciating pain I have felt in my long years. The voice repeats over and over, "Rise." The louder and stronger it says the word, the more the pain intensifies.

I can only imagine what my Nikita went through when she died and was reborn again. If my pain is half of what she felt, I do not know how she survived. Glancing down at my form, I see that it's changing. My hands are larger, forearms and arms are thicker. I would almost dare say that I appear to be monstrous. I was unaware that Angels could change, unaware that Archangels can become more than what they were originally intended to be.

As the pain continues, flashes of my old life dance before my eyes. Memories of battles past and my current love. I question every-thing that I know. Everything that we were raised to know as it being the divine truth. There are things beyond being an Archangel, apparently. There's a power beyond the creator we were told does not exist. Why were these truths hidden from us?

The voice says, "Rise" again, and this time I claw at the very fabric of my sanity. I'm not sure what it means when it says rise. I'm also not sure of what I'm going to become. I am not the same man I once was. My only concern is if my mate will accept me how I am now. I know I've changed. As the voice repeats the word rise again, I pay closer attention to its subtle undertones. I recognize that voice. It's a voice I haven't heard in almost eight years.

"Samael!" I call out to him the original Destroyer that heralded the apocalypse. The man who is also the great grandfather of my mate.

"Ah, so you finally figured out who I am." A deep laugh escapes and surrounds me. The old man was always a trickster.

"Why me? Why do I have to change?" I know we're not meant to question those of a greater station than ourselves, but this is one thing that I definitely need an answer to.

"With how the world is going and how man is changing its land-scape, we must be prepared to start over." His statement is brief and, unfortunately, makes sense.

"We have Lucifer yet to deal with. He has risen again. I have to help Nikita." Hopefully, pleading with him about saving his bloodline will expedite my return to the land of the living.

"Lucifer can wait. I have half of the riders now resurrected. I need to resurrect the other two." His statement puzzles me, and then I realize it.

"Davina?"

"See, you are smart," Samael says almost sarcastically. Part of me wants to be angered by the assumption that I was stupid. But the other part is more concerned that Davina or her nest mates are next on the list.

"Who is the next to fall?"

Laughter bounces around me. "No one needs to fall. They just need to become more than what they are."

"Who is left to rise?" I figure posing my question differently would make more sense.

"One from your mate's twin nest, the other her brother." With the finality in Samael's tone, I know there is no room for conversation.

Nikita has several brothers, so it could be any of them. As for Davina's nest, the selection is not as difficult. The oppressive feeling that had surrounded me earlier is gone, and I have a feeling that Samael's presence has left. I try to unfurl my wings but they do not respond. I try again, and still nothing.

When I finally stop falling, I land on a ledge somewhere in the clouds between the Shadow Realm and Heaven. My wings have been taken from me, and this new massive body given to me obviously cannot fly. Not only did I give up paradise, but I also gave up the sky. A great piercing cry fills the air as a familiar feeling washes over me. Intense heat surrounds me, and within moments the great black phoenix that is my mate is beating its wings, hovering almost perfectly in front of me. The bird cants its head from left to right, staring at me, observing the changes. Without hesitation, it reaches out and grabs hold, picking me up off the ledge and flying back up the cliff face.

We return to the others, and she sets me down before landing a good twenty feet away. Shaking out her feathers, she stares at the new form I've been given. She takes several moments before she shifts back and then closes the distance between us. I am easily over eight feet tall now, who knows how heavy, and my mate looks like a little pixie beside me. The minute she wraps her arms around me, I calm down, and the rage dissipates, then I shrink back down to my normal size.

"So War exists," Azrael states as he moves closer. "War and Death go hand in hand, so it makes sense that you two are in the same nest. That leaves only Famine and Pestilence yet to rise." Azrael looks over at Cyrus in silent conversation. I know those two have an idea of who the others are. This will be something to ponder later.

Nikita pulls away suddenly, a knowing smile playing upon her blood-red lips that almost concerns me. She whistles loudly, and within several moments her horse and the herd of the firemares gallop towards us. The tall ghostly stallion, the pale horse that my mate rides on, moves to stand before her and bows its head. A second stallion moves forward. As it stomps its feet, the black fur falls, replaced with a color as red as blood. With each stomp, the color changes faster. Nikita pets her horse as she stares at me, watching my horse undergo its transformation. Its size and bulk increase, I can only assume to match what my new form requires. It takes much longer than I would have thought, but when it is done, a massive blood-red stallion with its hooves on fire stands before me.

"Climb up. Mount your horse and forge the bond," Nikita says as she grabs hold of her horse's mane and climbs up. The minute she is seated properly, gone is the mate that I know, and the Pale Rider known as Death is before me.

Nikita extends a hand as a flaming black scythe forms. She uses the end to point at me and then my horse. Taking the hint, I take a running start, leap, and land on my horse's back. The shift isn't that painful this time, and I stare at myself in my black armor mounted upon my blood-red horse. As I extend my right hand, a claymore-like sword forms in my hand and blazes to life covered in hellfire. As I look over at the Pale Rider, she nods and takes off. There must be something she needs to show or teach me, so we take off at a gallop after her.

Our horses seem to fly over the great plains of the Shadow Realm, passing through the Great Desert and around the Swamp of Despair. We ride for almost an hour before we come to a vast lake.

The water looks like liquid tar and moves with a life of its own. Nikita slides off of her house and shifts back to her Nephilim form.

I slip off of my horse and shift back to my Nephilim form minus my wings. Sighing, I make one last attempt at freeing my wings. Nikita turns and looks sadly at me. "Unfortunately, War is a foot soldier. I'm sorry it robbed you of flight." Nikita rubs her hands together, then closes the distance between us and hugs me tightly. "I thought I lost you."

She pushes up on her tippy toes and kisses me softly. The pillow-soft feel of her lips against mine reminds me I'm alive. The warmth of her body gives me solace and strength I didn't know I had before. Somehow, someway, the fall gave me a peace I never knew was possible.

"I'm right here with you, now and forever." Pressing my lips against hers again, I feel all the anxiety melting away slowly.

A deep moan escapes her lips before she pulls back. "Do you know what War can do?" She tilts her head to the side and backs away, putting space between us.

"No, what can this new form do?" Turning to face her, I wonder exactly how much she knows.

The radiant smile that crosses her lips is almost blinding. Nikita raises her hand out in front of her, and I mimic every movement she makes. Waves start on top of the black water ebbing and flowing with every flick of my wrist. With every movement we make, it almost seems as if we're doing a dance in Tai Chi. She takes a deep breath and then throws her hands skyward, quickly with force. Mirroring her movements, I thrust my hands up, and I feel like a sudden shockwave of power moves through my body, electrifying every nerve ending until there's almost a second beating pulse in my core. She brings her hands down and holds them in front of her with her fingers caged as if holding a ball of pure energy. I follow her movements exactly, except there is a mass of energy in my hands.

"Picture an army rising from the black abyss before you." Her words flow smoothly and calmly over her lips.

I envision a large, heavily armored skeleton army with long swords and shields strapped to their bony forearms. "Now picture that army rising to do your bidding, freeing themselves from the River Stix, and coming straight towards you."

 I do as she asks, and I envision my army rising, hearing clicking and the clank of the armor as it moves in my head. Closing my eyes, I focus on the vision that I'm trying to conjure. A vast, unnumbered army of soldiers. All coming to do my bidding and serve me as the God of War.

Her lithe hand rests on my bicep and gives it a gentle squeeze. "Launch the orb into the water," she says, and I open my eyes to look down at her. With a confident nod, I thrust my hands forward, opening the cage and releasing the orb into the waters.

Unbeknownst to me that this must be the tail end of the water from the river Styx. The unfathomable amount of souls trapped in this inky mass before me is mind-boggling. She keeps a hand on me, and I can only assume that War needs Death to raise the army. Without voicing my question, I turn to face her.

A soft laugh escapes her lips, and she smiles and shakes her head. "This only works with us being in tandem. You need Death to summon the dead. I need you to control them. I can kill beings with just a glance and reap their souls by just thinking about it— dropping their corpses on the battlefield, raising them from the dead." She smiles and stares at the water as it starts to move violently.

"I can only give them a purpose for a little while. You, on the other hand, they will rise up and wage war for you and not stop until they are unable to move. That is the difference between you and me." She rests her head on the ball of my shoulder, wrapping her arms around my bicep. We watch the movement of the water intensify, and what sounds like a stomping of a herd of elephants is the next thing we hear as the domes of the dead start to rise from the blackish water. Skull after skull starts to make itself known. Soon enough, we'll have the army of the dead at our fingertips.

This may be the single best and worst day of my life.

CHAPTER 33
SATAN

I CAN FEEL THE SHIFT THE MOMENT IT HAPPENS. MICHAEL HAS ACCEPTED his mantel and has summoned the army of the dead. Turning slowly, I watch Mordoc and Rex look in the direction that Nikita and Michael had gone.

"It is done..." The finality of Mordoc's words sends a chill down my spine.

"What's done?"

Laughing, Rex slaps a hand on my shoulder. "Nikita and Michael are heralding the end of days." A sinister smile creeps across his lips as his eyes shift to his dragons. "No longer will the Angels be the authorities."

Mordoc moves to stand before me and tilts his head to the side, those blood-red eyes of his boring into me. "If all the Riders rise, the End of Days begins."

"What do you mean, if? You say that like they have a choice."

"They do," Rex chimes in and points towards the beam of crimson light that marks where our mate is. "Michael chose to fall. He accepted the additional power offered to him when he fell. He didn't have to become War. I can only assume that it was a natural transition for him because he's been a warrior since his creation." Laughing, he looks over his shoulder as he walks away from the group. "I would have accepted the gift as well." He shifts into his monstrous black Skull Dragon and takes flight toward the beam of light.

Mordoc, that fucker, just winks at me, then launches up into the sky, following behind Rex. I have other plans, using the shadows I manifest in the Destroyer's castle. "Thana? Cyrus? Anyone?" I keep yelling the names as I walk through the spooky halls of her castle.

"In here, Satan!" Thana's voice does that weird reverberation thing that Metatron's does, and I can tell she's in the war room.

"We have to stop them," Raphael's tone drifts down the hallway.

"How do you propose that?" Sounds like Metatron is trying to be the voice of reason.

"My daughter is not a threat. You light fuckers are so used to oppressing others that any threat to your power, your answer is to kill it," Cyrus' voice booms louder than I have ever heard from him before.

"Guys, settle down. We need to look at this from all angles," Thana sounds exasperated.

As I turn the corner and enter the war room, I see the entire family is gathered. Even Davina and her mates have made the trip to the castle.

"Sorry you had to hear any of that, Satan," Thana apologizes, and I can see the exhaustion threatening to take her.

"It's fine. I came to talk to you about the exact subject you're currently on." Approaching the table, they make room for me, and I look down at the maps. "It's not what you think it is." I move the dragon and the bat icons over to where the ones representing Michael and Nikita are.

"What do you mean, it's not what it seems?" Raphael rests his palms flat on the table, leaning forward, trying to intimidate me.

"Well, like Cyrus accurately stated, you're lost in your delusion of power and control. Both are constructs that, through fear-mongering, you've used for centuries to control the Fallen and Dark Nephilim." I make it a point to make eye contact with every family member at the table. "Through Thana and now Nikita and Michael, the Dark Nephilim have voices that will not be silenced, and it scares you." The amount of joy bubbling up in me is empowering because I am finally speaking my truth.

"I'm not scared of them," he states flatly and breaks eye contact first.

"Liar. You and the other Archangels are terrified." Flexing my mottled wings, I stare at him. "Change is scary, Raphael. It always is. Either you progress with the times and help mold the change they are going to bring about, or you will inadvertently bring about the End of Days because you're trapped in outdated ideals."

I hazard a glance in Thana's direction, and she's smiling at me. Dare I say, she looks proud of me. "You have provided valuable counsel, Satan. Thank you for your perspective."

"He's a Fallen. What say does he have?" A voice I haven't heard in forever speaks up. Uriel moves forward, and I get to stare at my long-lost brother.

Thana moves quickly and stands between Uriel and me, her armor manifesting on her body as she holds a sword pointed at Uriel. "He didn't choose to fall. Lucifer did, and his conscience split off, forming Satan." Her free hand motions back at me. "Out of all of us, he can see both sides for what it is, just like I can."

Uriel backs down and steps back into the gathered people. Davina steps forward, her wings luminescent, and she looks me over. "My sister has ascended to the mantle of Death Eternal?" Her soft question rocks me to the core, and I nod at her. "As Speaker, I will stand with my sister." She takes a firm stand and turns to face her father. "You think about going against Nikita? You will be going against me." For Davina to stand against her father is huge. She turns and faces me, "Tell my sister I will stand with her."

Davina vanishes in a flash of light and leaves me standing there, staring at the rest of the family. Bowing deeply, I back out of the room and use the shadows to catch up with my family.

All I see as I crest the horizon is the army of the dead standing in formation before Nikita and Michael. Landing beside them, I look over the masses gathered before them. "Well, this is new..."

Nikita chuckles, then leans over and kisses my cheek. "Yeah, I'm teaching Michael about combining our powers." Beaming, she looks up at Michael with that love-sick look in her eyes.

"They have come a long way in the last few hours," Rex chimes in.

"Where did you go?" Michael looks over the top of Nikita's head at me.

Breathing in deeply, I fold my hands in front of me and smile. "I went to see your mother, Nikita."

There's the slightest flinch when I say I saw her mom. I have to give it to Nikita. She has her features perfectly schooled. Even through the bond, I can't feel the turmoil I know is there. Her only tell is the change in her heart rate. It elevated for several beats, then calmed back down again. "And?"

"Davina stands with you. Change needs to happen, and it starts with us. The Archangels are afraid of the shift in power." My statement makes Nikita turn fully to face me.

"Let me guess, Raphael has an issue with what we've become?" Michael wraps his arms around Nikita as they look at me.

"Him and Uriel. I would also safely assume the entire choir is up in arms over it."

Nikita pulls away from Michael, unfurls her midnight wings, and flexes them several times. "Uriel could potentially be a problem." Her obsidian orbs turn on us, and she looks back at the army behind her. With a wave of her hand, the bones fall and liquify, returning to the lake of souls.

"I don't think so. Davina made a firm stance, and as Speaker, he would really have to push to go against her." Watching my other nest mates react to the news is interesting. Nikita is calm, and I'm almost guessing they expected their reactions. Mordoc shrugs, having seen the oppression of the Dark Nephilim for centuries at the hands of the Archangels. Michael looks distraught over the news his brothers may rise against us. Rex loves the idea of going to war, so he's prepared for anything the Angels have to throw at us.

I'm honestly not sure how I feel about the entire situation. "Don't forget, we still have Lucifer to deal with besides all of this." I motion to where the army stood and how Nikita and Michael have changed.

"It's at the forefront of my mind, Satan. Trust me, we will deal with your other half and make him pay for killing me." Nikita's hand rises and rubs at the spot where the blade went straight through her chest.

Boldly, I move forward and pull her away from Michael and hold her tightly to me. Her arms slowly band around me, and she rests her head on my collarbone. Initially, she didn't put her full weight on me. Gradually, I feel her melt into my embrace. An inaudible sigh escapes her lips as I tighten my arms around her body. Even the strongest of us need the love and support of our family. Looking away from Nikita, I motion with my head to get the others to join us. One by one, the other mates wrap their arms around us and hold on tightly. We can finally be the family we were meant to be.

"Well, this is heartwarming." The level of sarcasm can only mean one person's arrival. Davina stands there in all of her celestial glory. You would almost swear that her wings are bioluminescent with the light radiating from them. She moves forward, and the rest of us part ways to allow her to get closer to Nikita. The smile that crosses my mate's lips makes me happy. She's actually over-joyed to see her sister within her own realm. "What brings you here, Davina?"

Laughing, Davina closes the distance between her sister and herself. "Well, I see the rumors of your death were greatly exag-gerated."

They both share a short, forced laugh, and Nikita shakes her head no. "Unfortunately, sister, it wasn't exaggerated. I did die."

"How can that be?" Davina moves closer and runs her hands all over her sister's body, trying to understand exactly what has happened.

"Well, that's easy. Lucifer had found the one sword that can kill immortals. And he drove it through my chest." Nikita changes her clothing on a whim. The light gauzy dress surrounding her has a front she can untie. When she does, she exposes the two-inch-long scar over her heart.

"How can this be?" Davina extends her hand out, and it trembles before touching the scar in question.

"Grandfather and Great-Grandfather have told me many times that I would rise to be Death Eternal. None of the scriptures are tomes mentioned how it was going to happen." Nikita takes Davina's hands and walks to the edge of the lake that contains the waters of the River Stix.

"Much like how taking our mates changed you." Nikita smiles fondly and touches Davina's glowing wings. Her lithe fingers dance over the edge of the feathers at the bend of her wing. Still staring at the feathers with sheer joy and wonder on her face, she turns back and looks down at her sister. "There are simply things we just don't understand, and that's okay."

"When I was in the cavern dying, great grandfather's wolf spoke to me and told me I had to choose a form in order to live. Initially, I thought of choosing a dragon, like Rex." The smile that graces Nikita's lips as she looks over at Rex is nothing short of pure love and adoration. Looking back down at Davina, the same smile remains in place. Nikita breaks away from her sister and wades into the River Stix up to her knees. "My initial choice was a dragon, one of the great chromatic wyrms. But Dragons cannot resurrect, not even the mighty Skull Dragon." Rex bows his head to her, smiling.

Stepping back out of the River Styx, Nikita spreads her arms open wide. As black flames dance over the obsidian feathers of her wings. "I chose a phoenix. Not just any phoenix, a nightmare phoenix." Davina gasps, hearing Nikita's choice. "Unlike your standard fire phoenix that holy water can extinguish and kill. As long as humans and animals dream, I can resurrect. So as long as anything draws breath in this existence, I can never die." When Nikita says the word die, the River Stix's water bubbles and churns violently. Thousands of skulls rise from the water behind her. As far as the eye can see, the tops of skulls and eye sockets stare at us from the blackened waters. Nikita smiles, puts her wings away, and then lowers her arms. The vast army behind her lowers back into the water's depths, not to be seen.

"You see, dear sister, as Death Eternal, all things that have died are under my command, be it down here or upon the earth." Nikita walks past Davina and passes us, heading back towards her castle. She stops and looks over her shoulders at the rest of us. "I will not bring about the end of days. Just the end of Lucifer." As soon as the sentence is spoken, she vanishes from before us, not leaving a hint as to where she's gone.

CHAPTER 34
THANA

 what both sides of the veil are going to do. On one side, I have my daughter, who has grown exponentially in power and, as far as I'm concerned, is probably stronger than I am. On the other side, I have two of my mates and my daughter's twin. Raphael seems to have the most difficulty with the changes in Nikita. We all knew, given my lineage, that eventually things out of our control might come about.

"What do you plan on doing?" Metatron's soft tone soothes the frayed edges of my nerves as I stare at the map of the Shadow Realm and the nine layers of Hell.

"Nothing yet." I glance at him over my shoulder as he wraps his arms around me, holding me tight and flush to his chest. His rhythmic breathing calms me down and helps me refocus on everything at hand.

I shift all the chess pieces onto the board, watching them move about the map. No matter how many times I place the one for Nikita on the board, it shoots off the map and onto the edge.

Moving over to my second table, the map of the Earth Realm, I try to set her chess piece on there. Again, it shoots off the edge of the map to sit on the table. My last guess, and it's a long shot. I move back over to the third table, where the Angelic Realm is, and set her chest piece there. It vibrates and does not move. The reaction of the chess piece puzzles me, and I try to place it in different places on the map. When I arrive at the Tree of Life, it practically jumps out of my hand and lands dead center.

"Nikita has gone to seek her aunt's counsel." Just as I get ready to move away from the map, piece after piece that represents my children gather at the tree. Nikita has essentially gathered all of her siblings in one place. "This can only mean one thing," I say out loud, mostly to myself.

"What do you mean, it means only one thing?" Metatron watches as the chess pieces move to the Tree of Life.

"She is preparing to go to war or something far worse." Backing away from the table, I look at my mate and give him a firm nod. Wrapping me up in his snow-white wings, I feel the pull as he rips us through whatever that white light tunnel the Angels use in the Angelic Realm. Once arriving there, we take flight, heading straight to the Tree of Life. There stands Nikita with Sigrun at her side, and she's updating her siblings about what's been happening. My daughter looks like a general getting ready to go to war, how she's commanding everyone's focus on her. I'm frightened and impressed at the same time.

"Glad you could make it, Mom," Nikita says with a smile, and she laughs. "Sorry about the impromptu meeting." She motions to her siblings.

"Do you not want the adults here?" I need to know the answer, so I might as well pose the question.

"Technically, we're all adults here, Mom," Freya says from off on the side. She's the most outspoken of Gage's children and keeps her sister Arielle safely behind her.

Damien, Nikita's full brother, steps forward and smirks just like his father. "We have to be prepared for everything. The balance and fate of the world rest in our hands." His father's cocky nature is not lost on him at all. He motions back to his siblings, and the other nine nod along with him.

To my surprise, Christian's first-born son Ben is also among the numbers. "I'm kind of shocked to see you here," I say directly to him, and he laughs.

"Do you honestly believe I'm going to let Selene and Samuel have all the fun without me? Besides, what are big brothers for?" He places a hand on each of his half-sibling's shoulders.

It's quite apparent now that the children have already formed their alliances. Even Davina is standing there with her arms linked with Nikita's. One child of pure darkness, the other of pure light. This is how it was meant to be.

"I remember an old prophecy about Davina's and Nikita's birth." Stepping forward, I fold my wings and let them hang relaxed behind me. "It was said that at some point, life and death would be born from destruction." I place my hands on my chest, acknowledging the fact that, as the Destroyer, I am the source of destruction. Davina and Nikita look at each other and then back to me. "One above, one below, that's how it must be. One to help guide the Kingdom of Heaven, the other to help rule in the Bowels of Hell." I motion up and down as I say the words.

One by one, my mates arrive and listen as I describe the prophecy. "Why weren't we made aware of this?" Raphael clearly has his feathers ruffled; he doesn't like not knowing everything. I'm guessing it also has something to do with the fact that he is in charge of the nest.

"That's easy, I didn't think it was an issue until they killed my eldest daughter." When the word kill escapes my lips, even the heavens rumble. This draws the attention of the Archangels up there, and they gather around us. Davina's mates move and stand behind her protectively, offering silent support. Nikita has all of her mates with her as well. The Valkyrie form a circle around us, listening to our words carefully.

"What do you plan to do next, little one?" Metatron has moved forward and taken Nikita's hands in his like he used to when she was little. Melting almost instantly, she snuggles against his chest and wraps her arms around his waist.

"Davina and I have discussed it. We will not bring about the end of days, nor will we allow it to happen. The last two riders will not rise." Nikita pointedly looks at Damian and Seraphina. "I have already consulted with Aunt Sigrun about what we can do to prevent it."

Stepping forward, Sigrun, the queen of the Valkyrie, bows slightly to me and then looks around at everyone else. "There are sigils older than the Choir of Angels."

Hushed whispers move through the Archangels present before she raises her hand and silences everyone again. "The old gods knew of the riders and what they were capable of long before the Angels did." She looks back over at Nikita and Michael, then back at me. "Initially, there were only two riders, War and Death. Out of the riders, they are the most powerful. The apex of their power is their connection, which is why it makes sense that it's Michael and Nikita. War produces Death, and Death needs War. It's a perfect symbiotic relationship. Both can work independently but are stronger together."

Sigrun pulls out an old scroll from the bag on her hip, unfurls it, and spins it to face all of us. It's written in runes that most of us cannot read except for me. "This scroll is why Pestilence and Famine were created. They created those two at the behest of your Almighty. He is a just and wrathful God. The Kingdom of Egypt, Sodom and Gomorrah, and countless others were the reason they created the riders of Famine and Pestilence." Glancing between each of us, we all know the old stories and understand now about their creation. "With the runes that I have marked on the two children that bear the spark of the riders, they will not rise no matter how hard outside forces attempt it."

I step forward, take the scroll from my oldest friend, and skim it. "It also says that we need to protect the first and third seals, that once those two are broken, Pestilence and Famine will rise." Sigrun makes a motion with her hand. One of the other Valkyrie steps forward with an ornate box. Digging through her pocket, she pulls out three keys. Using the keys, she unlocks the box, and the two seals in question are within it.

"I will offer a key to the Kingdom of Heaven. I will also offer a key to you, Destroyer, to hold and keep safe. My people will protect the third key. As you've already seen, it takes three keys to open this chest. Without them and with the seals intact, the last two riders can't rise." She carefully re-wraps both seals and digs down into the sand, settling the seals into them before relocking the chest. Once locked, she offers me a key, then gives the other to Uriel.

It seems now that we appeased the Archangels, knowing that gaining all three keys will be no easy feat. "What's the next order of business?" At this point, I'm not sure who to look at concerning who's running this circus that we call a family gathering.

"Next up, Mom," Nikita says as she steps forward and then spins slowly to look at all the family members gathered. "We prepare to go after Lucifer. Those that are able to make it to the ninth ring will fly with me. Those who cannot will wait and watch on the other rings, ensuring he has nowhere else to go."

I watch my daughter move over to Satan, resting her hand on his shoulder. "It's been many millennia since they have split you in two. The reason that Lucifer can't die is that you live."

Tears well up in Satan's eyes as he stares at his mate, afraid of what she's about to say. "I will not allow you to die. Instead, Lucifer will have a choice." Nikita looks back at me, and I nod because I have a very good idea of what she's about to do.

"I wish to put the two of you back together. Your light with his darkness." I can't even imagine what it's been like to have half my memories and half of everything I once knew no longer within reach. Satan does not belong, not knowing what else he could do.

"If you think that's best, we will try it. Hopefully, it doesn't destroy me." Satan forces a smile, looking at Nikita.

Mordoc moves forward and stares at Nikita. "I will bring the rest of my clan, and we will weaken Lucifer by draining him." Double blinking, I didn't even think about that as a viable option.

"As scary as that sounds, it makes sense. If he's weakened, he cannot fight to keep himself separated from Satan," I say, pondering the ramifications of everything.

"Do you know how long it's been since those two have been whole?" Uriel has that cocky tone to him that makes me want to slap him silly. Gone are the days that I feared him. Now, with the stance that he takes against my daughter, I am not his greatest fan.

"Probably more centuries than I'd like to count," I snark back at him and watch his eyes widen at the tone that I take with him.

"That would be accurate. They have been separated since the fall, literally ripped into two as they breached the veil going into the Shadow Realm. We might not even be able to put them back together again." I'm not about to entertain his level of negativity.

"Nikita, take your family home. Rest, spend time together. I need to do some research before the attack." My daughter breaks away from Metatron and extends her hands out to her mates. The moment they make contact with her, they vanish.

"Go home, everyone, and be prepared to rally at my castle when I summon you." One by one, my children and mates leave. Looking over at Sigrun, she smiles and nods. I know, above all else, the Valkyrie will listen to the rumors up here and report to me.

CHAPTER 35

NIKITA

It has been over a week, and Mother has called several long meetings between myself and Davina trying to put a plan into motion. The only thing the three of us can agree on is Lucifer's utter destruction. Staring at the mirror we are using to communicate with, I can't help but shake my head at Mom and Davina. Neither wishes to budge on their perception of the problem at hand.

Michael has become my rock, my foundation, the steady constant since his ascension to War. I wholeheartedly believe that he was always meant to have this role. He interjects when my mom and sister explain a tactic incorrectly and gives us ideas for a better solution.

"We aren't getting anywhere!"

"How do you figure?" Davina says, crossing her arms over her chest. Huffing out a breath, I can tell she's at the end of her rope.

Softly growling as I run my hands down my face. I turn my back on the mirrors and draw a deep, cleansing breath, trying to get my temper under control. I can feel the blackened flames flickering over my wings as I stretch them slightly. "No one wants to deal with the actual issue. You're more concerned about the riders rising than dealing with Lucifer, who is the entire problem at the moment." Spinning back to face the mirrors, I glare at my sister and mother. The riders are the least of my concern. The destruction of the mortal realm at Lucifer's hands is a more immediate concern.

Poor Michael looks exasperated as he stares at the three of us. He pinches the bridge of his nose and squeezes his eyes shut. Through the bond, I can feel a new rage burning deep within him. Some of it is the anger over being not only flightless but also never able to enter the Silver City that he has lived in his entire existence. Being someone who used to be in control all the time, I'm guessing not having any semblance of control must be driving him crazy.

"Ladies, there's an easy way to solve this." He looks between us and waits to see if anybody says anything. When no one opens their mouth, he releases a relieved sigh, then starts again. "The seals are protected by the three keys needing to be together to open the box. Since they are of divine origin, no simple way can destroy the keys," he states plainly as if it's common knowledge to everyone.

"But there is a way," I state and then look at my mother, who's nodding.

"If we go to lands where the Greek gods are, the one named Hephaestus can destroy the keys," Michael says and then leans back against the desk in the office.

"What good will that do us?" Davina says and leans forward, looking at me. With the tilt of her head, I have her attention, and she's curious.

"Think of it this way," Michael chimes in and steps forward. "You can't unlock a lock if the key is destroyed." He mimics the way Davina is standing.

"Who would go to this realm that we can trust not to screw it up?" The level of sarcasm dripping from her words wasn't lost on me. Michael, who still doesn't understand sarcasm, smiles, thinking he's making progress.

"Funny you mention it. I was going to ask if you and your mates would take this task on." Flexing my wings, I smile broadly at my sister, knowing full well Mom will endorse my suggestion.

"What? Why?" She looks back and forth between our mother and me.

"Davina, this is an important task, and unlike your sister, you can take the shortcut across the Silver City to get there," Mom says as she motions to me and then herself since neither of us can make that crossing. "Take Ben with you and possibly some of your other siblings as backup. Those of us of dark origin will remain here and plan to go after Lucifer." The force Mom puts behind her words is a bit excessive but works nonetheless with Davina.

Mom turns to look at Michael and me and smiles. "You're strategic like your great-grandfather was. Lucifer is the big threat. If he gathers his minions and regains power by siphoning their life force, there could be a huge war on our hands." Mom crosses her arms and sighs. "We need to avoid war at all costs. If it can't be avoided, then so be it. We will initiate the clean slate protocol."

Laughing, I shake my head. "Quoting Tony Stark? Really, Mom?" She laughs and runs her hand down her face.

"I was hoping you wouldn't catch that. It sounded brilliant, didn't it?" Beaming, Mom lights up.

"It did, Mom. Catch my other siblings up on what's happening. I need to fully seal the bond between everyone. With Michael reborn, his tether isn't as strong as it was." Michael gasps behind me, turning slowly. I give him a reassuring smile. "Everything is going to be all right." Reaching out, I take hold of his hand and give it a squeeze.

"I'm so glad you two are doing so well now. It's a shame you both had to die and be reborn for it to happen." Mom's melancholy tone catches me off guard, and I spin again to face her.

Michael pulls me flush against his chest and wraps his arms around me. "I would die a thousand times to be right where I am." Michael's words hit me hard in the feels, and I finally understand what he meant by 'some things are worth fighting for.' Leaning back, I look up at Michael, and all I see is him smiling at me. I understand the nature of the bonds better now.

Without breaking eye contact with Michael, I address my mother. "Mom, I've got to go. I have a few things I need to take care of."

All I hear is laughter. "Go get'em, tiger!" It's times like this I can't take my mom seriously. I can clearly hear the static of our connection severing.

Michael makes me spin in his arms and rests his forehead against mine. "What things do you need to take care of?" His gravelly tone tells me all I need to know.

Sliding my hands down his chest, across his abdomen, and then over the bulge in his slacks. I cup his hardened length and give it a long, slow stroke from root to tip over the material. "I think I found one thing that needs attention."

Tightening my grip on Michael just before I back him out of the room that we're in. Being in what is now my castle gives me much more leverage, which means I can do more things versus in the human realm. Wrapping my arms tightly around him, I pull him through the shadows and into the main bedroom. Without hesitation, I throw him onto the bed and he just smiles up at me.

"What do you think you are going to do, sweetheart?" This newfound spark in him starkly contrasts the soft-spoken, gentle, innocent giant I had started out with.

"Anything I want," I state boldly as I reach out and touch his shirt, making it disintegrate.

He arches a brow at me, grabs me by my wrists, and pulls me onto the bed with him. This new boldness from him is quite interesting and exciting. At the same time, my core clenches at the thought that he might actually unleash and follow his desires now that he's free of those angelic roots.

He runs his hands down my back and over my ass, and I'll be damned. He pulled my stunt of making the cloth and fabric under his fingertips disintegrate. Smirking, I look down at him and let loose a soft laugh. "You learn quick."

"I had an excellent teacher," he states as he curls up, pulls me flush to his chest, and then bites hard on my shoulder right over where his original mate mark was.

I feel the moment his teeth break my flesh and the savage burn that courses through my blood, igniting every nerve in my body, setting my core aflame. The drive and need to have him in me are all-consuming. He must notice when the fire ignites within me and recognize it, because he flips us over in one swift move. His free hand reaches down between us, and he slips his fingers in between my silken folds, finding me soaked to the core.

Without skipping a beat, his fingers plunge deep within me as he thrusts them in and out quickly. I cry out, feeling the sudden rush of my orgasm sweep over me. It's probably the fastest I have ever come in my entire life. Be it from the excitement of his newfound dominance or the need to re-bond with my mate. At this point, it doesn't matter which one it is. All I know is I need him and I need him now. He works me slowly, bringing me back down from that high that we had just achieved. His teeth slowly remove from my flesh, and he laves his tongue over the broken skin, healing it. I reach down between us and make his pants and his underwear fall away to ash.

A hearty laugh escapes his lips as he bucks his hips up, slapping my lower stomach with his length. Lunging forward, I sink my teeth into where my original mate mark was as I wiggle my hips until I line up with his length. Just when I think I'm going to slide down nice and slow, Michael thrusts up suddenly, burying himself to the hilt. Crying out, I release him before lunging forward again, latching back onto his chest.

My cries draw the attention of the other mates, and the next thing I know, three other sets of hands are running all over my flesh. Michael laughs again. "Don't just stand there. Nikita says we need to reseal the bonds." Michael doesn't miss a beat, still thrusting up into me as he talks to the others. Without warning, he flips us onto his back again without withdrawing from me.

"Damn, this change suits you, Mikey!" Satan states as he climbs up the bed to kneel to my right. Reaching out, I grip his erection tightly and feel it throb in my hand. Moaning loudly, Satan falls forward, and I can see him out of the corner of my eye.

The crack, then the sting of someone's hand hitting my ass, makes me release Michael's chest. Looking over my shoulder, I see Rex kneeling behind us, stroking his lube-covered length. "You know what I'm about to do." His eyes change to his dragons and ebb darkness and raw, primal power. Michael slows his thrusts and pulls me flat to his chest. Rex has assumed the spot of the dominant mate since Michael fell, and the change in the power dynamic seems to have settled the nest.

Rex nudges his length against my rosette, easing his way in slowly. Anal seems to be one of his favorite things to do lately. To my surprise, Michael isn't freaking out about Rex's legs touching him. Rex grips me around my ribcage and lifts me off of Michael as he sinks his length deep within me.

"So full…" Moaning, I throw my head back against Rex's chest, and his free hand wraps around my throat, holding me to him.

"Yesss…" he hisses the word out as he finds his timing with Michael.

Mordoc comes up along my left side across from Satan and offers me his bleeding wrist. The scent of cinnamon and desire wafts up from the dripping crimson ichor. "Drink. It is my honor to feed you, nourish you through our joining." I take hold of his wrist and sink my teeth into his flesh.

The burst of flavor sends a wave of power through me and straight to my core. The in-and-out thrusting of Michael and Rex has me almost losing my mind all over again. Mordoc and Satan each reach out to fondle or suck on a nipple as my more dominant mates try to fuck me into submission.

When I have drunk my fill, I release Mordoc's wrist only to reach down and grab ahold of his thick throbbing cock. I set a rhythm between him and Satan as I jerk the two of them off at the same time. Poor Michael may end up bathed in come from head to toe at the rate everyone is going.

"I'm not going to last much longer…" Michael pants as his thrusts become more erratic.

"I've got this..." Rex starts kissing along my shoulder where his mark was, and he sinks his teeth in deep and thrusts up with his cock, burying himself deep within my ass.

The minute his mouth clamps down on my shoulder, my body detonates around both of their cocks. My muscles clench down hard, almost making it impossible to move as my core pulsates around their lengths, milking them for all their worth. I feel an odd warmth wash through me, as suddenly as it started it is over. Rex and Michael come almost immediately, their pulsing lengths driving my pleasure higher and higher.

Frantically I pump Mordoc's and Satan's cocks, trying to push them over the edge with us. Several rough strokes later, Satan shoots his come all over Michael's lower abdomen. Mordoc apparently liked watching Satan cover Michael; his orgasm comes suddenly almost out of nowhere. He comes so hard he shoots Satan's balls, covering them and his lower stomach.

CHAPTER 36
MORDOC

Nikita releases our lengths, allowing the throbbing to slowly subside. Satan looks down at his come-covered balls and stomach and starts laughing. Shaking his head, he hops off the bed and heads into the bathroom. Several minutes later, he returns washcloths and towels to clean up with.

Once free from Michael and Rex, Nikita turns suddenly and launches herself at Rex. Her teeth sink deep into his flesh, and he gasps from the pleasure of her bite. He grips her tightly around the waist as he grinds his length against her stomach. When Rex comes again, it's all over our girl's stomach; she laughs and rubs it all over him.

Slowly Nikita's head turns in my direction, and the look she's giving me is nothing more than pure predator. The humanity switch must be flipped off because she has me pinned halfway up the wall the next thing I know, using her claws to hold me in place.

"I'm hungry, Mordoc." Her canines descend, and she flashes them at me, and for once, I'm concerned.

"My blood is yours, as is my life and eternal love." Her eyes go from blackened orbs to the brilliant amber of the phoenix. Then, her teeth are sunk deep into my shoulder over the original mate mark. I scream from the pain and burn of her bite. If I didn't know any better, I would swear she injected pure silver into my bloodstream to kill me.

Looking over Nikita's shoulder, I see the concerned looks of Michael and Rex. Only Rex dares approach, and when he does, Nikita releases my shoulder and hisses at him before pulling us through the shadows to LaMagra knows where. When the sickening pull of being dragged through the in-between ends, I notice we are in the room I claimed for myself.

Laughing, Nikita licks my blood off her lips before stalking forward. "We need to renew the bond." Her low, sultry tone hardens me instantly. If I didn't know better, I would swear she was a vampire like I am.

"You're using my ability against me..." Smirking, I decide to use my thrall ability on her to its full extent. I watch her resolve waver before all the fight drains out of her. "Silly mate, you can't control an elder." Stepping forward, I kiss the tip of her nose and then gently guide her to the bed.

"What has you so concerned, my Pet?" I've never seen her try to get us all in one bedroom. Perhaps it was her death that spurred this one.

"Lucifer..." she states so honestly, I wasn't even sure it was possible to be that honest. The pitch of the tone of her voice, so even and sure, tells me it is her belief that he is a threat to the nest.

"You know I can summon my nest to fly on our flanks into the pit? Several thousand vampires, dhampirs, and ghouls will go to war at my command." Her face relaxes, and she breathes a slow, relieved sigh. I hate using my powers like this, but her mind is locked down harder than a maximum security prison. There's no chance for logic to get past her barriers unless you find a way to bypass them. Fortunately, because we have fed on each other, I can bypass them with ease. I always feel horrible when I do this, but I also need to keep my love safe.

Nikita nods slowly and relaxes even more before I release her from my thrall. Double blinking, she looks around the room and arches a brow. "When did we get here?"

"You brought us here, love. I believe your humanity switch was flipped off." Her mouth pops open in surprise.

"Did I hurt anyone?" Nikita's first concern is keeping her nest safe, so her asking about the others being unharmed is on par with her core value.

"Everyone is safe, Pet. The others are in the room where you left us, and we are in my room." Alone in my room, it's easy to drop the cold, calculating vampire act and actually show my mate the heart I've hidden for the last millennium. Reaching out, I gently brush away a rogue bunch of white hair that hangs over her eye. A soft smile creeps across my lips as I watch myself tuck the hair behind her ear.

"I've never seen you smile like that before." The tender tone in her voice isn't lost on me. She's as amazed by the action as I am.

Leaning forward, I press my lips against hers before nipping the pillowy soft bottom lip. "I reserve that just for my mate. No one else deserves my smile." Her eyes dilate upon hearing my confession. "You are my heart, my life, my everything." Kissing along her jaw, I get to her ear, then trail my kisses down her throat to the crook of her neck where my mate bite was. Reaching down, I lift her up and encourage her to wrap her legs around my waist as I walk us over to the bed.

We need to re-seal our bond since her death and rebirth. Looking down at my beautiful mate, I see all the scars that the others have missed. All the damage that isn't on her skin. The sadness she buries deep so the others don't see it. Fear that she won't be enough to keep everyone safe even with all the changes she has endured. The most prominent emotion I see is her fear of not being enough for her mates. "Nikita, my precious mate. You are more than I ever could have hoped for." I whisper close to her ear as I kneel on the edge of the bed before laying her down.

Blushing, she pushes herself up onto her elbows and stares deep into my eyes as hers shifts back to her human gray. "I thought vampires schooled their emotions to the point of not existing." Her statement shows how little the Angels know about my kind.

A hearty laugh escapes my lips. "That's where humans make the mistake of wanting to be turned. They think it will shut off the pain they are in. It does the exact opposite." Licking my thumb, I reach down and use the pad of my thumb to swirl it over her sensitive nub.

"When we allow ourselves to feel, we feel so much more than humans can. Our emotions are magnified. We love deeper, mourn harder, and become extremely volatile, especially in the first few hundred years." I'm letting her in deeper than I have ever let anyone, which is apparently a huge turn-on for her. Her juices drip freely from her silken folds.

"I need you, Mordoc." Hearing my mate whine and scenting her need so thick in the air makes it difficult to resist her request.

"I know, Pet, a few more minutes. Trust me, it will be worth it." Leaning forward, I take a nipple into my mouth and suck hard before nipping at it. Her hips buck up the instant I bite her nipple. She's straining, trying to line herself up with my length. Every so often I bump the head of my cock against her clit, letting my pre-cum coat her so I can go back to teasing.

Reaching down, I rub my shaft through her folds, and I damn near come, feeling how wet she is for me. A guttural growl escapes my lips as I try to resist sinking myself balls deep in her. The door-knob's click alerts me that the other player in the game has finally arrived.

Thrusting forward, I bury myself within her, and she cries out, detonating around me instantly. I slide languidly in and out of her pulsing core, enjoying the milking grip of her muscles on my shaft. I roll us effortlessly and press her flat to me. The pop of the top of the lube catches her attention. Looking over her shoulder, she sees Satan there, massaging his length as he steps forward. Scooting down the bed, I plant my feet flat on the floor to give me more leverage for later.

"What do you two have planned?" breathlessly, she asks as she rests her head on my shoulder.

"You'll see. I've discovered something the humans call porn," Satan says, sounding proud of himself.

Nikita's eyes widen as she lifts her head and stares at me. "This will not end well." She looks over her shoulder. "Remember what happened the last time you tried something from the internet? We had to sneak you into the hospital and cut the vacuum hose off your dick."

I stop moving altogether and curl up to look over Nikita's shoulder at Satan in disbelief. The words that came out of my mate's mouth are hard to believe, but Satan's reaction tells me it happened. "You've got to be fucking kidding me. You said you knew what you were doing!" I yell at him as I lay flat on the bed.

Tilting his head to the side, Satan smiles. "The vacuum thing was an honest mistake. One of Thana's co-workers told me it would make my dick bigger." Shrugging his shoulders, he steps between my feet, and I can feel him rest his length on top of mine. I pull out further so he can get further up my length.

Satan gives me a confident nod as he slathers more lube over both of our cocks before we push into Nikita together. Nikita is a real trooper as she breathes through the intrusion. Once we are seated deep within her, we wait until she starts wiggling again.

Nikita is almost one continuous moan as she finally starts trying to move between us. With a nod, I pull out slowly, then move forward. As I move forward, Satan pulls out some. We set the rhythm and feel Nikita trying to move between us as her muscles spasm around us. It's a unique turn of events. This whole sharing with my mate and having another man's cock on top of mine is interesting.

The ripping of fabric echoes on either side of my head as Satan and I focus on keeping the rhythm just slow enough to have a slow-build orgasm. We've spoken at length before tonight about how to make Nikita explode all over our cocks. Michael, in his innocence, discovered the trigger for her.

Fast and hard works wonderfully to get her to come hard, but she's never truly sated from it. The long, languid strokes we are taking are driving her absolutely mad. Looking over Nikita's shoulder, Satan nods at me, and I grab both her wrists. I drag her hands over my head as Satan wraps her hair around his wrist and pulls back. A deep, guttural growl escapes her lips, and I can see her canines descend. She struggles, and that's when I strike and bite over where my mate mark originally was.

Nikita's core detonates around us, crushing down hard, milking our lengths for all they are worth. Satan cries his release and lets go of her hair to fall forward and bite her shoulder, marking her again as his. Feeling both Nikita and Satan tip over the edge, I follow them into sweet oblivion.

Somewhere along the way, we fall asleep and awaken sometime later to Satan snoring with Nikita latched onto her original mate mark on him. She mewls softly as she laps at the wound. I must make a noise because she turns suddenly and stares at me. "We still need to present the nest before the Archangels and Uriel." Her eyes narrow, and I can sense the disdain for the antiquated ways of the Angels.

"I can tell this infuriates you." Gently, I run my fingers through her hair, trying to soothe the beast lurking under the surface.

"All things considered, they canceled the Mated Ball and rescheduled it for a month from today. We will show up only because of who my parents are." The curve of Nikita's lips concerns me. Her smile turns feral as her eyes go from midnight to chrome, then the pure amber orbs of the phoenix. "Michael and I cannot be judged. Neither can you nor Satan. Think about it. You were never an Angel. Satan was a Fallen Angel and then was purified. Michael and I both died and were reborn as riders." She laughs as she turns to head out of my room. "Wake up, sleeping beauty. We need to head back to Michael's and prepare for the debacle of the century."

Nikita leaves, and I'm left with more questions than answers. What puzzles me the most is why do we have to go after everything that has happened?

CHAPTER 37
NIKITA

ONE MONTH LATER...

Things have been quiet, too quiet for my comfort. Nothing seems to be happening in the Bowels of Hell or on the surface. My biggest threat is the ball that is happening later today. My mates are running around like chickens with their heads cut off. Mom is sitting at the table with me, looking at the gown choices and styles we would like to wear. Davina arrives shortly after lunch to look through the style books with us.

It almost feels like how it used to be before the Mate Trials. It's interesting to sit here, passing the books back and forth like nothing has changed. Davina and I compare notes on Michael and his brother, my sister's mate. Thankfully for them, he never saw her wings, so they didn't have as many hurdles as Michael and I.

Michael prepares a late lunch, and the smell of the hard-boiled eggs turns my stomach. I cover my nose with my sleeve and notice my sister is doing the same thing. Mom stands up suddenly and starts screaming excitedly. "It's happened!"

"What's happened?" My mates are by my side in an instant and watch my mom running around before vanishing.

I look up at Michael and arch an eyebrow, looking at him before shrugging my shoulders and going back to looking in the magazines. "What is your mother talking about?" Michael leans down and kisses my cheek before heading back to the stove and tossing the eggs in the garbage.

"No clue. With Mom, it could be anything," Davina answers without looking up from the book.

"True. Remember the time she thought we had the flu, and it was our first molt that spiked the fever?" I supply as I hold my stomach, still feeling ill from the remaining smell of the eggs.

Mordoc enters the room and freezes. Raising a hand, he points at each person in the room and then stares at Davina and me. "Guys? There's no one else here, right?"

"No, there's only the five of us." I do a quick head count. My sister and I are two, Michael is three, Mordoc is four, and Rex makes five. Satan is out picking up the dry cleaning for the guys.

Confirming the head count draws Rex's attention away from the book he is reading. His eyes shift to his dragon's. and I see the bone plates shift under his skin. "I count seven heartbeats." He looks over at Mordoc for confirmation, and he nods.

"Seven? Are you sure?" Davina and I stare at each other, and the color drains from our faces.

A resounding yes comes from Rex and Mordoc, and my chest tightens. If one or both of us are pregnant, this can get very dangerous quickly.

"What do we do?" Davina stands up and starts pacing the room.

Before we can go into a full tailspin, Mom arrives with my birth father and Raphael in tow. "Mom!" Davina and I scream as we dive into her arms, almost knocking her over.

"Shhhh, little ones. Mommy is here, and so are your daddies." I look over at my father, release my mother like she is on fire, and dive into Cyrus's arms.

"Hey, it's going to be okay, my little nightmare. No matter what the outcome is, everything will be fine." Dad rests his head on top of mine, holding me as tightly as he can.

Within moments Davina's mates arrive. I can only guess summoned by Raphael. "Now, I am not sure how this will work or if it will be effective with Nikita." The way Raphael says it makes me want to go into a rage.

"What do you mean by that?" Rex steps between Raphael and me, and I swear his muscle mass doubles. It must be something that the dragons can do.

Raphael takes several steps back and bumps into Michael's broad chest. "Please clarify, old friend. Rex is worse than a malinois protecting its human." Michael's analogy must have hit home with Raphael because his eyes widened.

"What I mean is that I may not be able to sense her since she's a rider now. For all we know, my daughter can carry twins because Nikita might not…" Thana slaps a hand over Raphael's mouth, stopping him from finishing that sentence.

"Might not what?" I growl out as I stalk forward.

Raphael visibly gulps and sidesteps away from Michael. "Have children. You might not be able to have children." His eyes nervously dart back and forth between my mates.

"Oh? Is that all?" Shrugging my shoulders, I walk away from Raphael and grab my cranberry and blood that Michael had made for me.

"You don't care?" Raphael asks incredulously.

"Not even in the slightest. If we can have children, wonderful. If we can't, then that's fine as well. We can always adopt if we feel the need to have children." Yet another holdover of the patriarchy is that the family unit is defined by having children.

Mom smirks at Raphael, holds up three pregnancy tests, and hands one to Davina and me. "The three of us will test ourselves and place the tests into this box. Three minutes after we do the last test, we will pull the sticks and see." Mom runs and ducks into the bathroom first, and Raphael looks panicked at my father.

"Get over it, Golden Boy. You know Thana loves babies, and if she is, so what?" Cyrus has the best attitude about the situation as far as I'm concerned.

Mom comes out of the bathroom and drops her stick into the box on the counter. Davina heads in next, and Raphael paces. Rolling my eyes, I step away from my dad and wait for my turn. Michael stops me before I head into the bathroom. "No matter what, this..." he touches the stick, "doesn't define this family." Glancing over at Rex and Mordoc, they nod, agreeing with Michael.

The sound of plastic hitting plastic catches my attention for a moment before I head into the bathroom. I stare at the stick of doom and curse the fact I'm being subjected to this bullshit. I've railed against everything since day one. Is it wrong that I hope this godforsaken stick comes up positive? Peeing on this stupid thing is much harder than I would have thought. Now I'm questioning if I pee'd enough on the blasted thing. Snapping the cap on it, I step out of the bathroom and touch the tattoo for Aunt Sigrun.

Within moments, Sigrun is beside me, and I mention what's happening. For solidarity's sake, she takes a test from my mom and enters the bathroom. She skips out of the bathroom and drops hers with ours already in the box. Mom sets the timer on her phone and sits it on the counter.

Shaking my head, I sit back down and have Aunt Sigrun do the braids on my temples, giving me a mock mohawk. Carefully, she places the Valkyrie beads in my hair. Starting at the top of my head, she starts the dragon braid and weaves beads and chains into the intricate pattern.

The tone of the rooster rings out, and the entire room freezes. Casually glancing up, I look at my mother and sister. "Seriously? This isn't that big of a deal." Thankfully, Sigrun is done with my braid, so I grab the box and shake it around, ensuring it's mixed up.

Instead of going to the women with the sticks, I go to the men in the room. May as well get a good laugh out of it. I head over to Raphael first, and he refuses to take one. Instead, my father reaches in and grabs a stick, holding it with the window to his chest. "Chicken," he says to Raphael, and I snort a laugh. Leave it to my father to say exactly what's on his mind.

I head directly to Sandalphon and shake the box in his direction. "Come on, Uncle, take one." My canines descend, and my eyes blaze with the fire of the phoenix in my chest. Deep down, I am still furious at Raphael and the others for the damage they did to my and Michael's bond. So every chance I get to rub in, I do. It's beyond me that my sister is okay sleeping with the man we called uncle our entire life. He hesitates, draws out a stick, and holds it close to his chest.

Turning next to Mordoc, I offer him his choice next. Dramatically, he waves his hand around before plunging it into the box and drawing out a stick. Just like the others before him, he holds it to his chest and laughs. "The tension is so thick, my chaotic heart sings with joy." Arching a brow at him, I briefly smile at him before heading to Sigrun to take the last stick.

She looks at me questioningly. "It's only fair one from each family, leaving you to take the last one."

"Makes sense. I'll go first." Sigrun looks down at the stick in her hand, then up at the others before laying it screen-up. The words, *not pregnant* clear on the screen. Looking around, I wait to see who is going to go next.

"For fuck's sake, people!" Cyrus exclaims before looking down at the screen. A small twitch of his eyebrow screams the results. Slyly, he looks around the room before humming the tune for a funeral march as he sets the positive stick on the table.

Davina bounces around excitedly, and I show no reaction one way or the other to the positive result. Rolling my eyes, I glance over at Mordoc, and he steps forward. He slaps the stick down onto the table with his hand covering the window. His blood-red eyes search the room before lifting his hand. A negative test sits on the table. Davina and Mom huddle together, looking at Sandalphon. He, too, steps forward and sets his test window up. A third negative test appears, and now Mom and Raphael are looking around curiously.

"I wonder who it is?" Raphael moves to his daughter first and beams. "Well, that was easy," he says, smiling as he draws his daughter into his arms.

"Okay, now that bullshit is over. Let's get ready to go." I snap at the others as Satan walks in the door with the dry cleaning.

"What did I miss?" He sees the tests on the table, and his eyes dart back to me.

"Not it! They knocked Princess Perfect up." My venomous tone rolls off my tongue like silk.

"Nikita!" my mother shouts at me.

Spinning to face her, my wings explode into existence and ignite immediately. "What?" I stare at her, waiting to see what favoritism bullshit is going to come out of her mouth.

"Aren't you going to congratulate your sister?" Mom's stance changes radically. It's amazing how the power dynamic in the family has changed since I died.

"No, she's gotten enough participation trophies in her life. I refuse to add to the list."

I'm angry, and if I'm being honest with myself, I'm hurt and disappointed. Raphael didn't even bother checking anyone else to ensure the test wasn't wrong. I turn around and head into my room, leaving everyone to their own devices.

There's a knock at the door, and I stretch my senses out and feel my father on the other side. "Come in, Dad."

Laughing, he closes and locks the door behind him. "Still amazes me you can do that." He comes and sits next to me on my bed and bumps his shoulder against mine. "What's actually wrong?" Only my dad would see through the false bravado and sense the heart of the problem.

"Is it wrong? I kind of wished it was me?" I raise my eyes to look at him, and he shakes his head no. "What actually pissed me off is that Arc-dumbass didn't even bother to check me or Mom in case the test was wrong. Those things aren't perfect. There's been mistakes made before." Shrugging my shoulders, I try to allow the pain to roll off me. Unlike all the other bullshit in our short lives, this is the one thing that hurts the most. Fucking Raph has always treated me like I have the plague.

"Not at all. I never thought I wanted children until you came along. Then your brother came, and I finally felt complete between the two of you." Dad leans in and kisses my temple.

"There are so many dangerous things I need to face, and I worry about the guys dying, leaving me with the children." Glancing down and away, I get to the crux of my problem. Now that my shift is a phoenix, I will resurrect over and over again. Even though the guys are immortal in their own rights, they can still be killed.

"Then that's a conversation you need to have with your nest." Dad kisses my temple, then stands up and heads towards the door. "I'll see you at the ball tonight. I left you a little something in the closet." Dad winks, then steps out into the hallway closing my door behind him, leaving me to my thoughts.

Moving to the closet, I fling open the door and stare at the piece of art that my father left in my closet. The dress is incredible, and I cannot wait to wear it tonight.

CHAPTER 38

MAELESTOR REX

OF ALL THE ARCHAIC NONSENSE THESE POOR NEPHILIM HAVE TO ENDURE, this is the most barbaric. The Mated Ball has been going on since long before I was born and still carries on for years un-numbered. Nikita's gown her father supplied seems to change color based on temperature. The bottom of the gown is black. As the material gets closer to her body, it fades into shades of red.

There's a war waging within Nikita tonight. I watch her schooled stoic features and see little things that bleed tension. The tightness in her jaw, the way she holds her hands flexing their grip on her clutch. Then there's the movement of the bird under her skin. It's barely able to be perceived if you're not looking for it. When Michael steps away from her, I take her clutch from her hand and offer it to Satan, then drag her to the dance floor. I know we're supposed to remain in line. Fuck it, my mate needs to relax. If I have to, I will burn this place to the ground to give her the comfort she needs.

Laughing, Nikita holds onto me tighter as I spin us for the first time. "You realize we are breaking about a dozen or so rules right now?" Her voice is almost musical, with amusement lacing her sultry tone.

"Ask me if I care." Holding my head up high, I glare at those staring at us.

Arching a brow, Nikita just smiles. "No need to. I already know you don't give a shit what they think. It's one of your more redeeming qualities. You place me and the nest above all else. Society be damned."

Nodding with her assessment, I smirk slightly. "We should probably rejoin the others before the Archangels in your mother's nest lose their minds." As much as it kills me, I really don't want to present her and our bond to these antiquated fools.

"Fine, let's get this over with." She motions with her head back to where the others are. For appearances' sake, she allows me to take control and lead her back to the others.

Arriving back in line, two nests are ahead of us, and the guys check Nikita over. If I have to guess, Nikita has a plan up her sleeves. I watch her move between the four of us, adjusting our hair and outfits. There's no rhyme or reason why she would bother. She's so anti-establishment it's not funny.

When it's our turn, Nikita motions, and Michael steps forward. "Uriel, as head of this nest, allow me to present my family." He names each of us in turn, and Uriel's golden gaze lands on each of us.

"Per tradition, I need to judge the nest based on your female." He tilts his head to the side and stares at Nikita, expecting her to obey.

Off to the side, we can hear Cyrus say, *'Oh shit, that was a mistake.'*

Smirking, Nikita steps forward, her head lowered slightly with her eyes locked on Uriel. "I shall not be judged!" Her voice booms as her wings explode into existence. Black flames blaze to life over her feathers. Feeling the power radiating from my mate is such a turn-on; a confident female is always sexy.

The minute her wings become visible, the rest of ours rip free from our bodies. Michael alone stands tall without wings, staring at his old brethren.

"You will submit to be judged like your mother and sister before you." Uriel raises his tone, and the other Archangels flank his sides.

Laughing, Nikita shakes her head. "No, I won't. You cannot judge me any longer." Nikita notes Raphael, Metatron, and her sister's mates standing beside Uriel. Nikita looks over at Thana and joins her, standing in solidarity with her daughter. Turning her head to Davina, and she joins her as well. "The days of being treated as a commodity and as breeders are over. I am Death Eternal, and I will end this ancient rite."

Her head slowly turns, and she looks at Michael. He draws in a fortifying breath and assumes the form of War. The heavy gothic armor covers his massive frame. As soon as he shifts, his body mass doubles in size. She motions with her hands, and her mother and sister leave her side. She shifts to Death. The Pale Rider stands before the Choir of Angels and tilts its robe-covered head. "Death and War existed before your kind. We will exist long after your light is extinguished." Nikita raises her hand, and her bone index finger points at Uriel. He pales and steps back, looking between her and Michael in their new forms. I am enjoying watching the Archangels panic before my mate. Uriel and Raphael's colors have paled, Metatron looks resigned, and the rest of their choir steps back.

"What is the meaning of this? I thought you were Death Eternal." He looks over at Azrael.

"Only one creature walks the earth and controls life and death, creates and destroys life as they see fit. Death Eternal was never my mantle to assume. I merely carried the genetics to make it happen; Samael carried the other half," Azrael says as he moves to stand next to Nikita.

Hearing the words fall from her grandfather's lips, she turns her gaze to him and nods before shifting back. "The judgment of bonds no longer falls to you." The tone she hits almost drives me and the others to our knees. Uriel isn't so lucky, it forces him down before her, and she tilts her head, looking at him. "How many bonds have been destroyed by you over the millennia?" Nikita calms down and touches Michael, making him return to normal.

Stepping forward, I fold my wings behind me, flexing the claws on the tips. Gently, I rest my hands on my mate's shoulders. "It's amazing that Angels called dragons barbaric all these years. Yet here you are, curating bonds like a huge breeding program." Satan and Mordoc step forward with us and stare at Uriel as he stands up.

"Even vampires don't do this to our nests. Unless there is a safety problem in the nest, there is no reason to interfere." Mordoc's words cause the Archangels to look between each other and pull back and away from everyone.

I turn Nikita in my arms and kiss her lips softly. "You did good," I whisper just for her. Her eyes blaze to life for a moment, then back to normal.

"What do you think is going to happen?" Davina says as she steps closer to our group.

"If they are smart. Nothing," Nikita says boldly before reaching out to Satan and Michael. "I have changes at home I need to make when I get there." Her eyes blacken for a second, then go back to normal.

The home she means is the castle, and I am pretty sure she is going to revoke the Archangels' right to enter it and her part of the Shadow Realm. Tension bleeds from Nikita. She reminds me of a predator ready to strike. I feel her fingertips digging into my side as she flexes her hand, trying not to lose what's left of her cool.

Eventually, Uriel turns and stands before everyone again. "Considering the changing times, we shall no longer judge bonds." He turns his gaze to Nikita. "Does that please you?"

"No..." Shocked, I look at my mate as she pulls away from me.

"The ban on flight and females using their wings needs to end!" she yells so the entire gathering hears her. "Thousands of females have died since the dawn of time because we can't show or use our wings before we have mates. Let nature take its course. Nephilim grow slightly faster than a human, bar the taking of a mate until after the eighteenth birthday. But allow mothers and fathers to teach their daughters to fly." Nikita's impassioned speech has all the women in the room up in arms with her.

"Dragons teach their daughters to fly and fight for their safety. You claim to revere females, yet you treat them like livestock. They are more valuable than mere livestock and far stronger than you give them credit for." Flexing my wings, I stare at the one named Uriel. How this group of closed-minded males is in charge blows my mind.

Many of the men in the room side with Nikita. They don't want their daughters as defenseless as their mates and sisters. The tide slowly changes in the room, and I watch the brilliant smile creep across my mate's lips.

"Uriel, you should have known my mother and the Valkyrie would not raise a weak, easily manipulated daughter. Change starts with you. Realistically, Angels and Nephilim outnumber Archangels twenty to one. Throw in the Dark Nephilim, Demons, and Fallen the number rises to over several thousand to one." I watch my mate spit facts at Uriel as Michael flanks her side.

"If we raise the dead and command the ghosts of the past..." Michael leaves the sentence hanging, raising his eyebrows to accent the point. Once upon a time, he was shackled by the old ways of doing things. Now that he sees how much damage was done, he's making moves to help his mate bring about change.

"That won't be needed, old friend. No more Mate Trials, no more females hiding their wings. We have lost far too many women and young girls because they couldn't fly and save themselves," Gabriel says as he steps forward and rests his hands palms up in front of Nikita. The minute she rests her hands on his, he smiles. "We will do better. You and your mother have imparted wisdom that we have been too blind to see. We," he motions to the Archangels with him, "have been stuck in the past for so long we became blind to the changes in the world."

"Maybe listen to Davina. She's as close to an Archangel as she's going to get," I offer and gently nudge my sister-in-law forward.

"I will be more than happy to gather information and present it to the Choir." She bounces in place, excited to help.

My gaze turns to my mate, and she's shaking her head. "You are too one-sided, and two of your mates are in the Choir. Three females should represent the population. A dark one, a mid, and a light. My mother, sister, and I cover all three on the spectrum."

Davina glares at Nikita. "You know your powers can't hurt me, so glare all you want."

The way Nikita calls her sister out on her bullshit is comical. "I believe this concludes this year's ball. I'm taking my bond mates and wife home to enjoy the evening." Nikita and the guys turn on their heels and head back down the aisle. Between my mate and our bond, we single-handedly destroyed an institution that has existed for thousands of years in less than an hour.

"Well, that was fun..." Nikita says with a slightly sarcastic undertone. The roll of her eyes tells me she was expecting the bullshit that happened.

"Are you not pleased it's going in the direction you wanted?" Mordoc looks puzzled as he stares at Nikita.

"I'm very pleased. Just sucks. I had to die to get it to come to pass." Shrugging her shoulders, she looks over at Michael. "Took you falling and my birth to allow Demons to walk on earth to find their mates."

"I'm all for toppling empires, but we have bigger fish to fry, don't we?" I stop walking just before we exit the building.

"We do, and that's what we are going to go plan next." Nikita motions to a door to our right and opens the door for us to enter.

"Nikita!" Metatron's voice carries, and she pauses at the door.

"Either enter or leave. There is no middle." She's turned cold towards her father, and it almost hurts my soul. Metatron enters, and I move to block the door after them.

"You basically started a war, dropped a bomb, then walked away," he says, frazzled. His hands rake through his long hair as he gives it a tug before he frees his fingers.

"I know I did. Don't be daft. The only way some of the Choir sees anything is after they get smacked in the face by it. It's no worse than the human government where the left doesn't know what the right is doing, and the only people hurt are the citizens they represent." Nikita stands firm. Her analogy is accurate and a fair assessment.

"I get that. When do you plan to schedule the first meeting?" His phone is blowing up in his pocket. Pulling it out, he stares at it, puzzled. "How come my nest can't sense me?"

A semi-feral grin crosses my lips. "That's my fault. Wyrm Skull Dragons don't like being found. It's a gift of ours that comes with age." I allow my dragon to bulk my frame, making me larger than Metatron, then I cross my arms over my chest, staring at him.

He turns and glances at me, and the color drains from his features. "Oh…"

"As for the meeting, we have other things that take precedence before it. Good luck solving your own problems." I give him a two-finger salute as Nikita rips open a portal to her castle, and the guys start to walk in.

"I'll come with you and help with strategies." Metatron tries to walk in before me and hits an invisible wall.

Pushing past him, I step into the portal and look back at him. "Sorry, nest members only. Let Thana know we will call when we are ready." Nikita closes the rift behind me and leads us to the war room. No one will be getting any rest tonight.

CHAPTER 39
NIKITA

I cannot believe the level of bullshit the Choir has curated all these centuries. Females are basically breeders for who knows how many thousands of years. I simply can't wrap my head around all the crap that has been allowed to happen. *Why didn't my mother put a stop to it sooner?* She's strong enough, or so I thought.

Getting the family back to the castle was the simple part. Now the actual work begins. "We have to be precise when we go after Lucifer and Mephistopheles." I keep walking down the hallway as the torches ignite just before I get to them. The sliding of stones and creaks of boards moving make my mates look around warily.

"Is there something you're not telling us?" Michael asks as he tries to catch up with me.

"No, just being extra cautious." Glancing over my shoulder, I stop short and touch the wall, which opens. Within is a grand war room, maps and 3d representations of key structures all over the rings rest on pedestals.

Once everyone is inside, I turn and look at Rex. "I gift you this room. Make it yours." By gifting the room to my Wyrm Dragon mate, it falls under his ancient power of cloaking. No one will be able to see or detect the room without his permission.

Rex half shifts and drags his talons over each of the four walls, marking it as his. "Done. That was a clever move, my love." His eyes shine with the power of his dragon as he moves around the room, dragging his talons over every item marking it as his.

"You know they will be waiting for us," Satan states as he looks over the maps, and I see a glow flicker in his eyes.

"Ah, that's what I was looking for. Rex, mark Satan as yours. I just saw his eyes flicker for a second for no reason." Satan looks at me, panicked.

"What do you mean?" Mordoc moves forward and sees the same flicker in Satan's eyes. "Ah, now I see."

Rex comes up behind Satan and gets him in a headlock. "Sorry old friend, your connection to your other half makes you a liability." Rex sinks his teeth into Satan's shoulder, making him scream.

I move to stand before Satan as I watch his eyes change colors several times as his face contorts. "Lucifer has been using you this entire time. I don't know why I didn't see it earlier." It explains how he knew where I was, when to grab me, and how to kill me. Satan had been present for all the discussions. It makes me wonder exactly how much information he really has on my family. How many years' worth of intel has he gathered? For all we know, they resurrected him much earlier than we initially thought.

The gears turn in my head a million miles a minute as I try to process the information. I am torn emotionally at the moment.

Part of me feels betrayed because he has always used my mate as a puppet. He has been unintentionally spying on me for years. My thoughts drift to all the meetings and discussions he has been privy to since the beginning.

I watch Satan closely, and he comes from being bitten from behind. When Rex releases him, I step closer and look him over, watching for any hints of him still being used. "I'm sorry your other half has been using you like this. I didn't know it was possible." Guilt chews me up inside as I stare at him. Maybe I should have known or had it as a concern in my head.

"Nikki, you have to believe me. I didn't know he could use me. I thought it was over once your mom killed him, and I was finally free." He reaches up and rubs where Rex bit him.

Looking down for a moment, I make one of the toughest decisions of my life. "I need you to step out of the war room and wait for us in the living room. Maybe start dinner for us?"

Reluctantly, he nods and heads for the door, pausing as his hand reaches for the handle. He looks over his shoulder at us, and my chest constricts. I know he can't help it, but we can't risk the lives of others on the off chance he may still be being used. Once he steps outside, Mordoc closes and locks the door behind him. Exhaling loudly, I head back to the map of the ninth ring, remembering exactly where Lucifer killed me.

"If I have to venture a guess, he's still hanging out here." Moving my hands over the map, it becomes three-dimensional before us. It's the ninth ring of Hell and the cavern they murdered me in.

Concentrating on the 3d rendering before me, it moves and changes shape, showing exactly what I remember from the interior of the cavern. The sword is still embedded in the wall where I was impaled, and I fully intend to shove one of those bastards upon it.

"Are you okay with this? I mean, going back will be difficult." Michael slides up alongside me and looks at the rendering.

Glancing over at Rex, I lower my eyes. "Most of it is honestly a blur. The blade through my chest and the night of the living dead looking mother fucker is still taunting me." Shaking my head, I turn my gaze to the door, looking in the general direction Satan had gone. "Then, for him to be using my mate as a spy, I can't wait until I can sink my talons into his flesh." A deep growl escapes my lips as I flex my fingers, watching the talons extend. "I want vengeance!" My voice booms, shaking things free from the shelves. Glassware falls and shatters upon impact.

Mordoc moves forward and takes hold of my hands, not concerned about the talons. "Vengeance is a dish best served cold. We cannot sense you the way you used to be. At this very moment, you have the tactical advantage over everyone else." He leans forward and kisses my lips, warming me from the inside and making my greedy core clench.

"Let Rex send his people into the abyss to do recon for you. I'll send mine to search the other rings, making sure they aren't hiding anywhere else." He nips my bottom lip, drawing blood.

His lips ghost over mine as he suggests the strategic moves. His tongue darts out, licking the fresh blood from my lip. "Let your mates take care of your needs tonight." Mordoc pulls away and stares deep into my eyes. The crimson in his orbs pulses slightly as he stares at me. It's not a purposeful thing. Compulsion often happens when a vampire is aroused.

Smiling, I allow my upper and lower canines to descend. "Let's go then. Someone grab Satan and meet me in the bedroom. We'll skip dinner and head straight to dessert." I step away from my mates, open the door, and leave the war room. The steps leading to the bedroom are not far down the hallway. Taking the stairs two at a time, I race to the bedroom. After tonight, the war will be upon us. If I know Rex and Mordoc, they are already communicating with their people.

I make it to the bedroom ahead of the guys, or so I think. When I step into my room, Satan walks around the room in a thong barely containing his length. "Hmmm, what have I found here?"

He spins, and his wings explode and spread wide before curling in close to his back. "Apparently, I've been bad and need to be punished." Satan drops a chain from his hand and clips a collar around his neck.

Arching my brow, I stare at him curiously. The collar thing isn't my kink; the chase and hunt are mine. "I think you're confusing mates, love. That's not my thing."

The sound of the handle turning catches my attention, and a gasp escapes behind me. Turning my head, Mordoc stands there with his mouth wide open, and I suddenly understand. Mordoc will be rough with him and make him feel punished. Mordoc is on him like a mosquito on a kid in the summer heat. They put the collar to immediate use. Mordoc drives Satan to his knees and thumps him on the nose with his dick. Greedily, Satan sucks Mordoc's cock into his mouth and starts working his length.

"What do we have here?" Rex comes up behind me as Michael circles around the front. Within moments, they have me sandwiched between them, and their hands grip my flesh.

"Satan wanted to be punished. So Mordoc has put him to work." Leaning my head back, I rest it against Rex's shoulder as I feel Michael's hand slide lower.

The thickening length of Rex's cock presses against my ass as his hands slide up to cup my breasts. "I see. It's nice that you are allowing someone else to handle that for you." His voice becomes rough as he leans down and nips at my ear. Michael slowly drops to his knees and lifts the layers of my gown, hiking them up before throwing my legs one at a time over his shoulders. The way Rex is cupping my breasts, his biceps support me under my arms.

"Sneaky males." Rex pinches my nipples hard as Michael rips my throng free from my body.

"Someone enjoys watching. You're soaked." The slight growl in his voice reverberates over my sex, making me clench.

"Of course I do. They are my mates. What pleases them pleases me." Michael takes that as an invitation and sucks my clit into his mouth as his index finger slowly slips into my depths. He works my core like he owns it. Slow, purposeful strokes make my muscles flutter around his finger.

Rex inhales deeply and lifts me up slightly, changing the angle Michael has. "Someone is close and ready to be bred." Soon as the words leave his lips, Michael's finger leaves my pussy, and I can feel him working on pulling down Rex's pants. Once free, they spin me, ripping my gown off of me. Once free, I wrap my legs tightly around Rex's waist and my arms around his neck. In a single maneuver, he lines himself up and rams his cock deep within me. Crying out, I grip his shoulders harder as he thrusts into me several times before I hear the popping of a top behind me. Glancing over my shoulder, I see Michael working the lube along his length.

He moves and presses his back against the wall, and Rex moves us to join him. They press my back to Michael's front, again sandwiching me between them. Rex strokes his length slowly within me as Michael slowly eases his cock past my rosette. So full, so much pressure feeling both of their dicks within me. Several moments pass as they allow me to adjust before alternating between who is thrusting up and who is pulling out.

"I'm going to breed you, Nikita, fill you with my seed and my young." Rex's tone is all dragon as he leans forward, whispering in my ear. Part of being a primal is the need to have a dominant mate, to fight, fuck and eventually breed. His words send me over the deep end, screaming my release as I try to move against them. Rex picks up the pace and slams his cock deep within me, harder and faster. Michael's grip on me changes as he takes control of my thighs, spreading them wider for Rex to rut into me as hard as he can. Every thrust of Rex's moves toward Michael, increasing the sensations I'm feeling. The two of them are playing my body like expert musicians, hitting every note and cord, stretching out the symphony that is my orgasm.

Both males bite me over their mating marks at the same time. Their cocks pulse and throb deep within me, filling me with their essence. Every throb causes my greedy core to pulse and milk their lengths for every single drop of seed.

They slow down, their thrusts dragging their slowly softening lengths free. Michael turns me in his arms and cradles me to his chest. Rex, however, has other plans and takes Mordoc from behind, driving his cock into his ass hard and deep. A rutting alpha is no joke, and apparently, it's dragon breeding season. Michael walks us into the bathroom and fills the tub with hot water. He sits me down on a bench nearby as he goes for the essential oils and adds lavender and chamomile to the mix. Watching him prepare our bath puts him in a whole new light from what I railed against.

War is being kind and gentle, protective and nurturing. There's a duality to War; there's the demon lurking under the surface. The demon craves destruction and death and will stop at nothing to achieve it. I head over to the tub and slip into the hot water's soothing embrace, allowing it to relax my muscles. Michael soon joins me and slips himself under me to hold me to his chest. I drift off to sleep in his arms. It's funny to think that Death has fallen in love with War.

CHAPTER 40

MICHAEL

The war is upon us, and the creature in my chest is out for blood. He wants vengeance for the murder of our mate. He is spitting fact after fact in my head as he goes over potential scenarios that can happen on the battlefield. I feel like Dr. Strange seeing the millions of possibilities flashing before my eyes.

Nikita moves to stand before me, and the voices silence immediately. Her eyes narrow and her brows furrow as she searches my face for answers. "What did he tell you?" Her question catches me off guard as if she could hear him too.

"There are too many viable options for what can go wrong on the battlefield." I step closer to the maps, looking over the largest map that displays the full nine rings.

"My team has seen both targets in the ninth ring," Rex states as he walks into the war room in full armor. "Eight swarms are at your command, Nikita. The total count is nine hundred dragons of all different ages, ready to battle." Rex pounds his fist over his heart.

"Cut that number down. The young who still have families or have not had a family need not fight. They are the future of your clan and species. I will not be responsible for the genocide of the younger population." Nikita stands firm with her request, and we watch Rex's eyes glow.

"That cut leaves us with three hundred total over eight swarms. Are you sure that's wise?" He tilts his head, looking at her, and I want to growl because he is questioning her judgment.

"Wise as in saving your species, yes. Tactically, maybe not." Shrugging her shoulders, Nikita moves back to the maps to look them over.

There's a knock at the door, and we turn to look at it. Slowly, the door opens, and Satan pokes his head in. "Nikki, your mom is here, and she doesn't look happy."

With a wave of her hand, Nikita flings the door open, and Thana stands there, looking beyond pissed off. Her chrome eyes bore into each of us as she stomps towards her daughter. "You barred the Archangels from being able to enter your section of the Shadow Realm."

The statement barely registers with Nikita as she moves things around on the map in front of her. "Yup." She doesn't even bother to raise her eyes to look at her mother.

"Michael, what is the meaning of this level of disrespect?" Thana turns her rage on me.

Laughing, I look from my mate to her mother. "I hate to say it, Destroyer, but you're being met with the same respect you are showing her." Stepping around the back side of the map to stand side by side with Nikita. "You storm her castle, invade her private space, and start yelling at her like she's five all over again."

Resting a hand on my mate's shoulder, I can feel the tension slowly bleed out of her.

"I barred the Archangels from my castle because they have no respect for us, or for females in general. The war I am about to wage is going to have a high mortality rate." The coldness in Nikita's stare as her eyes shift from gray to amber, then pitch black, tells me she is ready to scorch the underworld just to make sure the dastardly duo doesn't escape.

"Your fathers are different." Thana slams her hands down on the table.

"My dad is not an Archangel. Your other mates besides Daddy Gage were all very hands-off with me. I am as close to a natural-born Fallen Angel as you can come. Raphael has always feared me. Metatron has always accepted me. Christian doesn't want to rock the boat with the other two, so he does the safest thing possible. He stays quiet." Laughing to herself, she steps out from behind the map. "Until Seraphina was born, Metatron was just as bad as Raphael. Now he thinks before he takes sides." Stepping forward, I rest a hand on Nikita's lower back, offering my silent support.

Thana steps back and starts pacing the outer edge of the room before she stops and faces Nikita. "I didn't realize it was that bad." She runs her hands down her face and sighs. "Taking your stance at the Ball started a war within the house. Your sisters are proud of you, and your brothers hope they will meet their mates soon. The Dads are not thrilled at all." A forced laugh escapes her lips.

"Holding our wings hostage has killed off most of the female population. My wings, my choice. Men should not hold jurisdiction over what I can and cannot do with my wings." Crossing her arms under her chest, she stares at her mother. The slow nod Thana gives hints at the fact she agrees with her. I'm honestly shocked that she hasn't stood up to the patriarchy sooner.

"So, what's the plan?" She approaches the massive table with the nine rings on it.

Stepping forward, I touch the maps and zoom in on the ninth ring, allowing Nikita to move about to the other tables, setting them where she needs them. "We have lined up all the extra forces we need to make this attack effective," I state, looking down at the map before me.

"My people have checked the other rings and gathered additional demons to be ready to run when we call," Mordoc mentions as he steps into the room and heads to the flat map, adding the additional creatures to the assembled troops.

Thana turns and looks at what he has done, then back at the four of us. "Why isn't mate number four in here?"

Nikita's face contorts, and she looks at me, almost begging me to answer for her. "We discovered Lucifer may have been using Satan all this time. As much as it pains us, as a family, we left him out of the planning phase." Thana's head whips towards the door, then back to us.

"Shit..." Thana's face morphs at least a dozen times as she remembers how many meetings Satan had been privy to.

"Exactly what we thought." My eyes search Nikita's, and I can see the hurt in how pinched her eyes are. The physical pain the thought causes by how she's biting her bottom lip and gripping her shirt. I can read my mate like a well-written novel. "We are hoping we can put him and Satan back together by weakening Lucifer. The only concern with that is which personality will be dominant." If I am honest with myself, I don't think it will work out the way Nikita wants it to, but we have to try, for both their sakes.

Nikita turns and buries her face under Rex's beard. "We will be ready to head out in a few hours. We figure a mid-day attack would throw him off since he would likely expect dusk or in the middle of the night." Rex mentions as he wraps his arms tightly around Nikita, holding her flush to his chest. His eyebrow arches as he looks down at Nikita before looking over at Mordoc. He tilts his head, staring at our mate, before looking at me.

"I'll head back to my nest. I will meet you at the edge of the eighth ring and will join in the attack. It wouldn't hurt to have a basilisk on your side." Thana smiles before stepping out of the room and closing the door behind her. Thankfully Nikita has imbued the castle to not allow outside the nest portaling or shadow walking.

The minute I feel Thana leave the castle, I turn to look at Rex and Mordoc. "What are you two not telling me?" My question makes Nikita pull away from Rex and look between her other two mates.

A slow, soft smile creeps across Mordoc's lips, and seeing that look on his face is disturbing. "I hear five heartbeats." He looks away from me and over at Nikita.

"Five? There are only four of us here." Rolling her eyes, she heads back to the map on the table to look over the terrain for the millionth time.

"I hear the fifth heartbeat as well, Nikki." Rex moves alongside her, takes her hand away from the map, and places it on her stomach.

It makes sense to me, in that moment, when the guys first sensed it. They heard two additional heartbeats, and Raphael assumed Davina was carrying twins. When in fact, both sisters are pregnant. "Wow, shit... how are we going to keep her safe?" Motioning to the map, I look between my two bond mates.

"That's easy. She can command the armies from on top of my dragon's head. When she is needed, we do not leave her side," Rex states.

Nikita laughs a little. "Taking a play out of Aunt Aurora's play book I see."

Thinking back, I remember the stories Aurora told about the several years-long war she fought across two continents and at least a dozen nations. The stories of her attacking not only from on top of her father's dragon's head but her mate's dragon's head must have stuck with Rex. "Tactically, it's brilliant." I decide to throw my two cents in.

"Exactly why I suggested it. It's been proven twice over to work." Rex's confidence cracks me up sometimes.

"So, how are we handling the elephant in the room?" Mordoc motions to Nikita, and she rubs her stomach lightly.

"Not sure yet. Mom's basilisk will come in handy to help keep me safe. I can easily raise the army of the dead from on top of Rex's dragon. So that's not a concern." Nikki walks around the map and stares at the three of us. "Keeping the baby safe is my priority, so I will not jump into the fray unless absolutely needed." We nod, hearing her decision. As analytical as she's being about this, I know something else is below the surface.

"It's been almost a month since we heard the heartbeat, so if you carry like your mother, we have time before you deliver," I mention trying to ease some of the concern from her.

"So if you guys are correct and you heard the heartbeat a month ago, that means, more than likely, I am around two months along." She paces as she looks at us and then at the map. "The phoenix will still be a safe shift. Death may not be."

Sometimes we forget she's a nurse at her human job and knows far more about the biology of it all than we do. "We will be your sword and shield. Your weapons to wield how you see fit." I rest my fist over my heart and give it a thump like Rex did.

Shaking her head, the emotions that seem to move through her are contradictory to what she's showing us. On the outside, she appears to be cold and calculating. On the inside, for the first time, I feel fear. Glancing at the others, they nod, deciding I am the best person to handle her right now. One by one, they kiss her temple, then leave the war room, citing that they need to prepare their people for the strike later today.

"Talk to me, Nikki." Moving closer, I draw her away from the maps and into my arms.

"What's there to talk about? I fucked up. My body decided now was the best time to give me a child." The tears dancing at the edge of her eyelids tell a different story than what is falling from her lips.

"Nikki, I know when they tested everyone the last time, it disappointed you that your test wasn't positive and that Raphael didn't check you." Pressing my lips to her temple, I feel the first shudder of emotion move through her. "Tell me what's really wrong." I have not tried begging her for answers before; perhaps the change in tactics may work.

"I'm scared for the baby." Her head whips up, and her eyes ignite with the power of her phoenix. "I can die a thousand times, and a thousand times I will resurrect. I'm not sure the baby will be so lucky." Sighing, she pulls away as her hand rests on her lower abdomen.

Nikita was always the soft one when it came to baby animals and other defenseless creatures. Her twin was the polar opposite and usually said if it was strong enough to live, it would. Dozens of times, Nikita hid animals in the guest room where I stayed in her mother's home. Her soft heart behind the death persona only made me fall in love with her more as the years went on. She has the heart of an Angel and the temper of a Demon. Out of the twins, I believed she received the wrong wing color until recently. In the last six months, she's boldly taken stances even her mother has been scared to. The amount of change my dark Angel has brought about is mind-blowing.

"You will not die on the battlefield. I will be within shouting distance of you at all times. Rex plans on laying a ring of acid around himself to protect you. We will not allow anything to happen to you as long as we live." The tenseness that Nikita has been holding in her shoulders slowly relaxes as she processes what I had said.

"This little one is a miracle. I am Death Eternal, from what everyone has said..." She leaves the words hanging. Raphael telling her she may never have children hurt her more than she let on.

Laughing, I shake my head. "You always had a unique ability to prove Raphael wrong. It's almost as if it's your life mission to do it." Smiling as I say it to her.

She nods slowly, then falls silent. In the deepest reaches of my mind War starts talking again. His voice echoes along with Nikita's as she starts mentally issuing orders to her troops. "I have someone I need to see before the war begins. Lead the family to the war zone, and I will meet you there." No sooner do the words fall from her lips is she is gone from the castle and the realm. I have no clue where my mate had gone, but I do know whatever she's off doing is of the utmost importance.

CHAPTER 41

NIKITA

THE WINTER PALACE- SIBERIA

Aunt Aurora always said if I ever needed anything to come to her. Opening a rift in the courtyard of the mountain castle of her mate Alaric is quite risky but necessary. The first thing that hits me is the blistering cold of the arctic air and the powerful winds that move across the mountainside. No sooner do I move towards the castle than the dragons are on me like kids chasing the ice cream truck.

Unlike my mother's other daughters, I have something the others do not. Turning, I raise my white hair, revealing a single white scale Aurora gave me. "I am your Queen's god-daughter Nikita Dawnstrider, daughter of the Destroyer, Thana Dawnstrider." Several of the male's eyes glow briefly before they turn to lead me into the castle.

"Nikita!" Alaric shouts as he steps out of his office close to the front door.

"Hi, Uncle Alaric. How have you been?" He scoops me up in a hug, then stiffens and pulls back suddenly.

"You have a dragon mate?" He looks me over, then up to the top of the stairs where Aurora is standing.

"Yes, I do, Maelestor Rex, Marco's ancestor." Aurora practically runs down the stairs and hugs me tightly.

I hear Aurora breathe in deeply, then squeal. "How far along?"

"About two months, maybe less. It's why I'm here." She nods and ushers us into Alaric's office, dragging him along with us. "We are going after Lucifer and Mephistopheles in the ninth ring of Hell, and I need to borrow your mythril battle gown." I rest my hand over my stomach to emphasize the importance of acquiring the gown.

"It's yours." Aurora smiles, comes closer to me, and hesitantly extends her hand to my stomach. I reach out and take her hand, pressing it to my lower abdomen, letting her feel the small protrusion. "I remember carrying the twins. As much as it was a magical experience, it was terrifying as well. Unlike me, you have a large support system outside of your mates. Auntie Rory will be there every step of the way with you."

From what my mother tells me, Aurora took to the motherhood thing like a duck to water. She went from isolated, lost princess to battle phenom. Then from warrior to mother and queen seamlessly.

Aurora leads us out of the office, leaving Alaric to do whatever I had interrupted earlier. We walk to the curved staircase, head upstairs to the second floor, and down the hall to the right. Aurora stops us at the third door on the right. "You remember Klaus's grandmother, right?"

"How can I forget? She makes the best cookies ever." I feel like a little kid speaking about Elsa.

The door opens, and Elsa's face lights up, seeing me. Immediately, she hugs me tightly, then stiffens and jumps back. "You're with pup. This is fantastic. Let's check you out and make sure you and the little one are doing okay." Her grip is surprisingly strong, given her age. Then again, Aurora had stolen the essence from a Siberian Tiger alpha and pushed it into her, rejuvenating her.

"It's not a pup, GG. My baby is either Angelic, Demonic, or Dragonic. I don't have a wolf for a mate." She moves me to an examination table, lays me down, and starts palpating my stomach.

GG pulls out an ultrasound machine from the closet, and covers the wand with gel, then puts that evil cold thing on my lower stomach. "I can see a very healthy little peanut." She turns the monitor, and I can watch the tiny life move around in its own little bubble.

"Wow..." I can't verbalize the level of amazement I am feeling. My heart is full as I look at the little one the resident healer in the family said I would never have.

"Do you want to know what the baby's gender is?" Elsa gets a sneaky little smile as she glances over at Aurora.

"Of course she does, Grams. Don't tease the poor girl." Aurora rolls her eyes as she stares at the monitor.

"It would be nice to know instead of saying the baby." I giggle, a little excited and scared to know who I am carrying.

"You are carrying a boy." She smiles and prints the image out, and offers it to me. "Do you know which mate is the father?" She cleans my stomach up and helps me to sit up.

"Not a clue. They all will be fantastic fathers." I stare at the image in my hand and see the future so clearly. My son, I am carrying a son. Until the day we did the pregnancy tests, I never thought I wanted children. Now my only focus is finishing this off as quickly as possible so I can tend to the little miracle in my stomach. The war we are about to wage will help secure a safe future for everyone.

"I'm sure they will be once they get over the fact you are giving birth to a son." Aurora laughs slightly.

Shaking my head, I huff out a laugh. "Rex will lose his mind when he finds out my first child is a boy. Michael will be happy that it's healthy." Furrowing my brows, I try to parse the other males' reactions. "We aren't sure if a vampire demon can have children. Satan is a redeemed Fallen one and yet another mystery as to whether he can have children. No Fallen ones have ever survived being cleansed." Shrugging my shoulders, I follow Aurora down the hallway and into her grand suite. Dimitri sits on the hope chest, putting his boots on.

"Uncle Dimitri." His head whips up, and he stands as soon as his laces are tied.

"How's my favorite god-daughter?" He nuzzles my cheek, and his bear rumbles to me. "I can smell you have a stowaway on board." He kisses my cheek and backs up slowly. "Congratulations."

"Thanks! I'm carrying a son." Beaming, I caress my stomach, holding it proud of the little bean.

"A son, that's grand news! Deliver my congratulations to the father. When I return to the bear camp, I'll send your nest a barrel of my finest ale." He reaches into his pocket and fires away a message to his brewmaster. I use my phone and text him Michael's address since we never got around to moving.

"You have a war to get to. No more distractions," Aurora calls from the door of her massive walk-in closet.

Dimitri bows his head slightly, then leaves the room, and I take that as my hint to follow Aurora into the closet. Aurora has the mythril gown constructed specifically for her to go to war during pregnancy. "Try it on, Nikita. I want to see if it fits you properly."

Without hesitation, I strip down to my bra and underwear and start putting on the three layers that comprise the gown. The first layer is a spider silk gown that is damn near indestructible. The gown hugs my body as if they made it for me. Other than being tight over my breasts, it fits perfectly. The second layer is a very fine layer of small loop mythril to keep arrows and other projectiles from penetrating my flesh. The last layer is the thick mythril and ornate in construction. "This gown has stopped swords, dragon claws, arrows, and dirks. If there's going to be a need for armor, this is the armor to wear if you want to live," Aurora says, beaming with pride as she adjusts how the gown sits.

Reaching into a box on a shelf, she pulls out what looks to be a Valkyrie helm that has the same mythril armor hanging down to protect my neck. The helm itself has large feathered wings pointing up off the sides of the head and a guard down over the bridge of my nose, protecting over half my face. "I feel like a warrior queen in this," I say as I turn slowly in the mirror. Shockingly, the armor and all three layers with the helmet weigh next to nothing on me.

"The only problem with the armor is you will not be able to use your wings." Aurora looks at me, then at the armor, as she adjusts the dress again, making sure it lays right.

"Sacrifices must be made. I have mates with wings that can fly me places. Besides, our safety takes precedence over my ability to fly." Moving forward, I hug my aunt tightly. She fought not once but twice pregnant and lived to tell the tale. I can only hope this is my first and last war for me. "Thank you, Auntie. I love you." I kiss her cheek and smile fondly at her, trying to keep my emotions at bay.

"Love you too, sweetpea." She laughs a little, grabs a tissue, and dabs my eye. "Pregnancy hormones are the worst. Eat plenty and rest when you can. Above all else, blood is life." Her eyes glow with the power of her beast as she stares at me, and I know what she's saying. I will heal faster and regain my strength quicker by drinking blood.

"I'll come visit once it's all over." I rip open a rift in my castle and step back into it.

"You better!" Aurora yells as the rift closes in front of me.

"Has everyone been gathered?" Rex is glued to my hip like a freckle after I tell the guys that the baby I am carrying is a boy. Michael was disappointed. I honestly think he wants to be a girl dad badly. Rex and Mordoc fist pumped, and Satan stared at me, not sure how to react.

"Yes, everyone is ready to move on your command," Rex says close to my ear as my mother paces, looking down into the ring.

"I'm not thrilled with you fighting in your condition." The grating tone of Mom's condescending voice sets my phoenix on edge.

"She will be fine, Thana. Relax." My dad slaps Mom on her ass and elicits a growl from her.

"Shift if you need to. Unfurl your wings and prepare to ride into battle!" I call out across the army. I watch dozens of creatures assume their true horrific forms as their lethality increases tenfold.

Mom becomes the basilisk beside me, and Dad becomes a Reaper. Rex's dragon stands tall behind me before he lowers his head and brings his tail around to lift me up. Carefully I step onto his tail and get brought up to his large spiral boney horns on the top of his head. As ancient as his dragon is, it looks more dead than alive. Bone protrusions stick out all over his skull, and the shape of his scales gives the appearance of rotting flesh. I take my place, settled in between his bone plates. Michael climbs up onto Rex's back for the ride to the ninth ring, holding onto two of the bone spikes along Rex's spine.

Tilting my head back, I let the cry of my phoenix carry across the land, sending my troops into the ninth ring of Hell. The shrill tone sets the entire operation into motion. With several flaps of Rex's powerful wings, we are diving into the unknown. The wind whips past me, drowning out all the other available sounds. The click of his ignitor fires as other winged Demons rise from the abyss to meet us head-on. A huge jet of flaming acid shoots from his mouth, bathing the Demons, melting the flesh from their bones, and sending the corpses to the ground with a wet thud.

Several more masses of Demons rise to greet us as we descend. The deeper we dive, the more horrific the bestiary becomes. Creatures that would give most nightmares rise from the depths, roaring and using their breath weapons. Rex banks hard to avoid a direct hit, and Michael is knocked free from his back. "Michael!" I scream, and something snaps within me.

I lock my senses on every living creature I can sense. A Skull Dragon from Rex's flight is closest to where Michael is plummeting to his doom. As much as I don't enjoy doing it, I take control of the dragon and send him on an intercept course with Michael. The dragon barrel rolls, catching Michael in its taloned hand and holding him close to its body. Releasing my hold on the dragon, I refocus on the task at hand, storming the Bowels of Hell.

CHAPTER 42

NIKITA

A VAST ARMY OF DEMONS AND RANDOM OTHER UNDEAD CREATURES GREETS us outside the cavern I died in. Rex roars, and the other dragons line up on our flanks, lowering their heads, prepared to unleash their acid breath upon the enemy. Rex raises his head high, ensuring nothing can reach me.

The next volley is lackluster, and I honestly think something is going on that we are not yet privy to. I look around, trying to figure out what Lucifer and his minions are doing. A screech comes from behind us, and as I turn, hundreds of Armanites thunder across the dead expanse of the abyss. They are a Demon Centaur species, more Demon than horse, and definitely more brawn than brains.

Mordoc and Michael lead the charge with several hundred of our troops to cut them off. Swords and spears clash on the battlefield, and dozens of these new arrivals fall by my mates' swords. Something still doesn't feel right. Turning slowly, I try to keep an eye on the horizon to prevent a sneak attack.

Noise emanates from the cavern, and we turn to face it. Something in my gut yells at me to turn, but I'm too slow. Mephistopheles blindsides me, knocking me off of Rex's head. His arms tighten around my ribs like a vise as he flies up higher and higher. "I wonder how many times I can kill you before you stay dead?" His scratchy voice grates on my nerves.

I know I can't unleash my wings in this armor, and I risk destroying the armor if I shift to my phoenix. "Haven't you heard? I can't die." Reaching up, I shift my fingertips and sink my talons into his flesh. Mephistopheles tries to drop me, and I feel his flesh ripping as he yells, trying to shake me free.

Without warning, I let go of his arms and freefall. His high pitch cackle catches my attention, and it makes me laugh. My phoenix bursts free from my human form, and I soar up into the air. My shift screeches loudly as I turn to pursue Mephistopheles. For an elder demon, he is quite adept at banking on a dime and evading each volley of fire I shoot at him. We dive down and fly just over the top of the war waging below us. Mephistopheles makes one fatal mistake. He flies close to where Satan and Michael are battling, close to Mordoc. Time seems to slow down as I see Satan turn to face a screaming Mephistopheles. His sword comes up as his speckled wings propel him into the air. His sword impacts Mephistopheles' right wing, severing it at the joint. He spins out of control, spraying blood everywhere before crashing into the black sand.

Touching down the heat from my shift turns the sand to glass before resuming my human form. I am pleased to find Aurora's gown is still in one piece. "I never could understand how an all-powerful Demon like yourself can allow yourself to fall for the pitfall of pride." Satan flanks my side and offers me his sword.

"Some Nephilim you are, getting ready to strike me down while I'm wounded." He sneers, trying to taunt me.

Taking the sword from Satan, I look the blade over as I turn my wrist, examining both sides of the tang. A soft laugh escapes my lips as they curve up in a cruel smile. "There's your mistake. I'm not a Nephilim. I am the Pale Rider, created by the very sword you and Lucifer plunged deep into my chest. You created the weapon of your own destruction." Taking Satan's sword, I raise it high, then bring it down as hard as I can, driving the blade deep into his chest to the hilt.

Mephistopheles tries clawing at my arms, but the armor keeps me safe. "Your time here is over. Oblivion calls." Diving forward, I spread my fingers wide as he screams, terrified, seeing the mass of blackened flames in the palm of my hand coming for him. Gripping his skull, I funnel the flames of my phoenix, turning his body to ash. I cover what's left of his body with my fire until there's nothing left of him. I have utterly destroyed his soul and body in the purifying flames of my phoenix.

I stare at the ashes for far too long before turning to look at Satan. Several emotions flicker over his visage before he settles on me again. "That was... Harsh..." He kicks at the sand, then looks back over at me.

"Sometimes drastic measures have to happen. We don't always have a choice. In this instance, it's kill or be killed." Instinctually, I rub my sternum, thinking about how the sword was driven through my chest.

Satan lays a hand on me, rubbing my shoulder. "I'm sorry. Since your mother saved me, I have issues with violence."

I can understand that, and it's more the battling the humanoids in the battle than the actual demons. "Keep your nest mates safe.

I'll handle the dirty work." I return to Rex, who assists me in getting back on top of his dragon's head.

The battle rages on around me as Rex occasionally fires his acid breath at the demons approaching us. My mother's basilisk is attacking and occasionally turning creatures to stone. My father has become my personal bodyguard remaining close to Rex and me, watching my back. Gage has joined the fray and seems to live his best life. From what he told me of his younger days, he had a thirst for battle and the way he's hacking through the enemy, I truly believe it.

It feels like forever before Michael gives me the signal, and I focus on the powers of Death Eternal. Reaching my senses out, I feel every single corpse on the field. Reanimation is a difficult power to use. Raising the dead is like a huge puppet show. You have to be able to multitask on a whole new level to make it work well. I look at the bodies picking out the more lethal species to raise and use to attack their own people. As the Dragonkin and various other species rise, the frightened looks of the enemy bring a smile to my face.

Rex lumbers forward as the masses rise and enter battle with the single purpose of destroying those on Lucifer's side. My mother and father move from the battlefield to take to the air, following us closely. The hunt for Lucifer is on, and I will not stop until I find him.

Dozens of voices rise, and we search for the source of the commotion. Over the ridge, the first glints of light reflect off our new opponents' helms. The minute they crest the ridge, I know we are in for a battle. Driders with their swords and shields defy gravity and walk down the cliff face. Half drow and half spider, they are the Fallen of their community. They turned the ones that failed the Spider Queen Lolith into these abominations and set loose to do her bidding, sometimes being sold to the highest bidder as mercenaries. Lucifer is desperate, and it shows by hiring Lolith's children to battle.

The battle intensifies as the Children of Lolith enter the fray. Some are even so bold as to climb onto Rex to get to me. It's almost laughable as they approach, and I ignite them with my phoenix flames. Exhaustion slowly creeps up on me as the battle continues. I need to feed sooner than later. If I am not careful, I can harm myself and my baby. Daddy Gage sees me waver slightly and lands next to me.

"Are you all right? You seem a little pale, even for you." Hearing Gage's words, Rex makes an odd sound at the back of his throat.

"I need to feed. I've spent too much energy without feeding." I glance around and see another dragon lumbering towards Rex. If my instincts serve me, he summoned a single male to be my food source. The dragon shifts back to being human and waves at us. Gage takes me in his arms and flies us down to meet the man.

"I'm Caladar. Rex summoned me to serve you however you need me." He bows slightly to me as Rex moves and stands over us, keeping watch.

"I need your blood, I'm starving, and I don't wish to risk my child's health." I look at the thick veins running along the striations of his forearm. Part of me feels weird asking someone for their blood from outside of my nest. But I understand why Rex sent him to me. For the rest of the battle, I would be worried if I drank too much and put my mate at risk.

His copper eyebrows rise almost in shock as he glances from me, then back to the battlefield. "It would honor me to serve you. Rex told me I can depart from battle once I am done so as to not risk my life." He rolls up his sleeve up the rest of the way and offers me his wrist.

Looking at his wrist, I smile and gently take his arm in my hands. "To bite the wrist is to risk nerve and tendon damage. If it is okay with you, I will bite mid-forearm so I don't hurt anything important." My stomach chooses now to grumble, and we share in a laugh over it.

His amber eyes drop to look over his wrist, then raise it to meet mine. "Thank you for being so considerate. Please allow me to feed you." He lifts his arm slightly, encouraging me to bite him.

My gums burn as my upper and lower canines break through my flesh. The rich copper tang of blood awakens my more primal side. Lowering my head, I raise his arm to my mouth. His scent reminds me of a day at the beach, salty and fresh. I open my mouth and sink my teeth into his flesh, feeling it bend, then break under my canines. The muscles bend, then finally yield to me, releasing the rich blood within. He has almost a sweet taste to him that is the precursor to the metallic taste left behind from the iron in his inchor. The blood explodes on my taste buds, eliciting a rumble of appreciation from me.

Caladar's scent changes, and male musk floods my senses as a moan escapes his lips. Feeding, if done right, can be a rather intimate thing. For me, it's food. For him, it's a once-in-a-lifetime experience to have a Wyrm dragon's mate feed from him. When I have drank my fill and feel renewed, I release his arm and lick the tip of my finger, pressing it to the holes I created in his arm.

"Thank you, Caladar, for your sacrifice. I will remember your name when we return home." Behind him, I rip open a portal and motion for him to return to the mountain kingdom of his people. He bows graciously, then walks through, disappearing from sight.

"Feeling better, pumpkin?" Daddy Gage asks as we step out from under Rex.

"Yes, it's time to finish it." I pat Rex's leg, his massive head lowers, and he stares at me. "Call back our troops, then have your people wipe the playing field. It's time to cut the head off the snake." Rex slightly nods his head, then stands up tall. The roar that escapes his maw shakes the ground under our feet and causes several landslides.

My people retreat quickly, and you can hear the demonic cheers of Lucifer's army. They did exactly what I was counting on; they let down their guard. "Now, Rex!" I yell as loud as I can, and I hear the clicks of the dragon's ignitors. The roar of the acid breath being released is deafening as Gage grabs me, getting back onto Rex's head and away from the acid's deadly gases. Horrified screams fill the air as we sit back and watch the flesh melt off the bodies of Lucifer's army.

"That was tactically brilliant." I hear my mother's voice come from behind me.

"I remember the stories you shared from Great Grandfather's memories with me. The dragons and knights and the taming of the Shadow Realm. My mate's people have been instrumental in most of the major war campaigns." I didn't think it was possible to be any more proud of Rex, but here he is, making it happen.

"We just have to wait for the acid to clear, then onto the cave and Lucifer," Mom says as she looks back at Satan standing on Rex's back with Michael and Mordoc. "You know you may lose him forever if you try this." Mom rests a hand on my shoulder and looks me deep into my eyes.

Biting my bottom lip, I stare at my mate's scales under my feet. "We need to try," Satan says as he passes my mother. "I'm the reason Lucifer lives. Who knows how long he's been using me to spy on everyone and everything?" He sniffles and wipes his eyes with his sleeve. "I feel so guilty. Please let me make amends. Let me try." He stares openly at my mother, and he never does that. I can feel his guilt and pain through the bond, making my heart hurt.

"If that's what you want…" My mom lets the sentence hang as she looks from him to me. "I hope you have a plan."

"We do…" Mordoc manifests out of nowhere and then looks back to the cave. "It's show time.

CHAPTER 43
MORDOC

ALL HOPE ABANDON, YE WHO ENTER HERE... IS CARVED INTO MY forearm. It's a line from the divine comedy Inferno. Rolling my sleeve up to look at the scarification of my favorite quote. I gave up on hope shortly after I was turned. I had a wife and family before the demon came calling to get payment for their services.

Shaking my head, I clear the memory from my mind before I transform into a bat and head towards the cavern. The bond I share with my mate is unique. Because of who she is to me, we can see through each other's eyes when needed. As I approach the cavern, I can already hear Lucifer complaining and losing his temper with whoever is in there with him.

Landing on the rock face of the cavern, I slowly crawl my way inside, sticking to the shadows to hide myself. The closer I get, the more blood I can smell. It seems like Luci has killed off some beings tasked with keeping him safe. Rounding the corner, a severed head rolls towards the cave entrance. It seems like he has definitely become unhinged.

"What do you mean she has hundreds of Skull Dragons, and they wiped the battlefield clear?" Lucifer screams as another head flies past me.

He's up another two kills just in the time I have been here. "My lord, we don't know how she lives. We watched you kill her." What sounds like a Balor speaks to him.

Creeping slowly along the ceiling is taking far longer than I would like. But for this plan to work, stealth is key. I use a stalactite as a shield as I finally enter the chamber Lucifer and his minions are in. It's clear to me now that he has three Balor and several Infrit in the room and a half dozen spiny devils. It's an interesting mix of creatures at his disposal, but most of them do not seem as loyal as they were in the beginning. Slaughtering half of your inner circle probably didn't help solidify any loyalty bonds with his troops.

The soft hum of my mate makes my blood vibrate in my veins as I feel her approaching. It's amazing how her blood sings to me when she gets closer to my location. I just need to wait for her to get into position and do my thing when the time is right.

"Oh Luci! I'm home..." Nikita sings as she walks into the cavern, unafraid. She's purposely making excessive noise as she moves through the cavern.

"Impossible..." He runs across the room, and there on the wall is what's left of the Matsumora sword that killed Nikita.

"I believe you mean inconceivable." Nikita stands there wearing Aurora's gown, her hands shifting to blackened talons. Satan is the only person from our nest besides me in the room with her.

"Ah, so I see you brought my weaker other half with you. How droll..." Lucifer fakes a yawn as he leans against the stone wall.

"This is not at all how I expected this to go down," Satan remarks as he stares at his other self.

"Luci here has a bad habit of running his mouth." Nikita's eyes watch Lucifer and occasionally dart over to his minions.

"I've killed you once before. I can do it again." No sooner do the words leave his lips, than the hot-headed Balors charge forward.

I have to give it to Nikita; she stands her ground and does not flinch. Raising her hand, black flames erupt and engulf the Balor, reducing them to ash and bone. "Who's next?" The Infrit is the next to lob balls of fire at Nikita, and she simply fills her hands with flames and absorbs the Infrit's fire. When they realize their fire is useless against her, they flee out the back of the cavern.

"Where are you going?" Lucifer shouts as he turns to watch the Infrits leave. He turns to face the spiny devils, and they shake their heads and step back into the shadows, disappearing from sight.

"I guess you never learned about team building, did you?" Nikita taunts as I make my move. Her eyes blacken with gold flecks in them as she stares at Lucifer. No one knows what Nikita can see like this, but she needs it, whatever it is.

"You should be dead. I drove the sword through your chest. I watched the color fade from your cheeks." He thrusts his hand toward what's left of the sword that's sticking out of the stone like Excalibur.

"I did die." Nikita reaches for the mythril gown and pulls the majority off, leaving the underdress. With a slow roll of her head, her obsidian wings break free and spread wide, igniting in phoenix fire. "Thanks to you. I ascended to Death Eternal and chose my ultimate Reaper form, the dark phoenix." She steps closer to what's left of the blade that killed her and touches it, melting it into a pile of molten Damascus steel.

"Being the Phoenix, I can never die. I will be reborn repeatedly until the end of time and even beyond that." Tilting her head, she watches me get into position as I shift and drop down silently behind Lucifer.

"Fables all of it. Death Eternal doesn't exist." He crosses his arms over his chest, staring defiantly at Nikita.

"I'm sorry, Luci, it's time for you to get a grip on yourself and come to terms with your duality." Soon as Nikita looks down and closes her eyes, I strike.

Swiftly, I overpower Lucifer, press his lean body against the wall, sink my teeth into his throat, and start drinking deeply. His blood tastes like liquid sin, warm and silky on my tongue. Nikita comes and leans against the wall next to us, and she watches with sadistic glee as my wings rip free of my body and I use the claws to hold us to the wall.

"A little more, Mordoc. His heart is slowing down." Nikita kicks off the wall and slowly strolls over to Satan. "Your turn, my love." Nikita sinks her teeth into his neck and drinks deeply from him.

Thana walks in while we are feeding, picks up Aurora's armored dress, and waits for us to weaken the two halves. "That should be enough. Bring them here." We spin our halves to face Thana, and she smiles as she takes on the form of the Destroyer. "The one that is layered on top will be the dominant half." She takes Satan from Nikita and brings him towards me. "No matter what happens, do not let go." The command in her voice makes my knees buckle slightly, and I can only nod at her.

Thana places Satan's back to Lucifer's front and places her hand in the center of his chest. "I call upon the Dark Ones. Hecate, Lilith, and Nyx, I beseech you. Lend me your dark gift, and allow me to fix what was shattered. A child of darkness and light was torn asunder, and we need to set it right. What they broke to be whole again. Dark Ones hear my plea. Return this man to whom he used to be." A chill fills the cavern, and a wind rises up from out of nowhere. "They heard me..." Thana says as she pushes Satan and Lucifer back together again.

We weakened Lucifer enough that he doesn't fight the process. Satan, on the other hand, still tries to fight Thana. Nikita acts quickly, taking her mother's place, knowing full well that Satan will not hurt her. He would never endanger the life of an innocent, and to hurt Nikita now might kill the babe in her womb.

"Mom, I'm not strong enough alone," Nikita cries as she keeps trying to force their bodies to meld. Michael and Rex must have sensed Nikita's sadness and come to assist.

"What can we do?" Michael looks at Thana, then at Nikita.

"Each of you, take a side and help push. It will take the love of the nest to do it," Thana says as she moves off to the side, giving us more room.

Rex comes up behind me to stabilize me and grabs hold of Lucifer's shoulders. Michael moves behind Nikita, running his arms under hers to press against Satan's chest. With the combined strength and love of the family, the edges between them blur. Little by little, Satan slips within Lucifer's body until we can't see him anymore.

The newly reformed Lucifer drops like a ton of bricks, and I catch him before he hits the ground. "Let's take him home so he can recover. Hopefully, everything went according to plan."

Thana steps into view, opens a rift into her castle, and motions for us to walk through. "If there's an issue, I would rather it happen where there's backup than where most cannot tread." Thana give's Nikita a look that even makes my blood run cold. Nikita rolls her eyes as she walks into her mother's home ahead of us. Michael grabs Lucifer, or is it Satan's feet so we can carry him in easier.

Nikita walks through the castle, and the torches light for her, making her mother pause. "I am your daughter, and your heir doesn't act so shocked." She heads to a room on the lower level and pushes the oak door open. A grand gothic bedroom opens up before us, and Nikita moves to throw a blanket over the duvet before we lay Luci-Satan down.

She begins stripping his clothing off and leaving him in just his underwear. Mixed emotions flicker over her features as she stares at the face of the man that killed her. Michael seems the tensest out of him and Rex as they stand near her. Thana motions for me to follow her out into the hallway.

"How are you adapting to being in a nest like my daughters?" Thana seems genuinely interested in my well-being, which is odd. They taught us from the moment they turned us that the Destroyer lives up to their name and destroys everything.

"With a nest like this, it's not a far leap. My mate made the surface accommodations suitable for me. Since we both drink blood, a food source is readily available, so hunting isn't needed. It's paradise in a nutshell." I smile the best I can without showing my fangs, and she nods, taking in what I said.

Motioning back to the room, she sighs. "This may not end well. For one, he looks like Lucifer. Second, this is the first time this has been attempted in recorded history." Thana appears torn as she glances from me to the door.

"We will do whatever is needed to keep Nikita safe. Even if it means killing Lucifer all over again." I must have said what she wanted to hear because she smiles briefly, then turns and leaves.

Re-entering the room is probably one of the more difficult sights I have had to deal with in all of my centuries of life. Nikita is sitting there in her nightgown, the small bell of her stomach becoming visible as she stares at the face of the man that killed her, knowing her mate is in there somewhere.

Rex and Michael stand back, watching, offering their silent support, waiting to see what needs to be done. Was all the damage repaired when they put him back together, or is he lost in his mindscape, unable to return?

CHAPTER 44
SATAN

I thought I knew what Hell was like. Boy, was I wrong. Lucifer and I are locked in a perpetual battle for control of the body we both inhabit, and there doesn't seem to be an end in sight.

"Give up, weakling! This body is mine, and when I wake up, I will kill that bitch all over again!" he roars in my face as our swords clash repeatedly.

"Never! I won't let you hurt her!" Something flickers in my chest, an unknown foreign power I don't remember ever feeling.

"Face it! You have always been in my shadow, and a shadow is where you will remain." He charges again, except this time I sidestep him and bring my sword down in time to knock his free from his hand. I've never been this good. What's happening to me?

"I am not a shadow!" I scream back at him and glide forward with a grace I have never experienced. My sword strikes true and plunges straight through his heart. With a flick of my wrist, he falls to the ground, staring up at me in abject horror. Hell has frozen over. I have defeated my greatest demon—myself.

There's so much pain, and I feel like I can't wake up. I'm struggling against an unseen force, restraining me, shoving me down into the clouds.

"Satan, open your eyes. It's me..." The sweetest, most angelic voice calls to me from the darkness, and I run towards the sound.

When I first gain control of my body, it takes me several moments to get my eyes to open. The world around me is blurred and has a haze around it. Nothing is coming into focus, no matter how I struggle. Putting us back together came at the cost of my sight. "Nikki?" I flinch at the sound of my voice. It's Lucifer's tone, not mine.

"I'm here..." I turn my head to face her, and I hear her gasp.

I feel the bed shift and then the warmth of her lips as they press against my forehead. "Everything will be alright. Rex is going to get Raphael. If he can fix your eyes, he will. He's the best healer that's ever existed." Her tone wavers, and she sniffles, trying to hold back her tears.

My heart breaks for my mate as she helps me stand beside the bed. I know what Raphael needs from me. He needs to see my wing color to know if he can even attempt to help me. "I got here as fast as I could. Holy crap..." The shock in Raphael's tone causes me to laugh.

"I know I've gotten a bit uglier, but unfortunately, it's what I have to work with." Forcing a smile, I grip Nikita's hand tightly.

"It's going to take a bit to get used to. That's all, old friend." Raphael gives my shoulder a squeeze. I can make out a hazy outline of him in front of me, but that's about it.

"I need to see your wings." His tone is as unsure as I feel. My stomach is in knots as I mentally prepare to expose my wings. I don't even know what color they would be. Lucifer's were black; mine were mottled. Who knows what I have now?

"Here goes nothing." Flexing my back, I hear my wings rip through the material of my clothes. The thud of a body hitting the floor and losing Nikita's hand tells me it was her. "Is she okay? Can someone please tell me if she's all right?"

"She's okay. She passed out seeing your wings. They are like mine." Raphael's words hit me like a ton of bricks. "Like pre-fall white... Archangel white?" I hyperventilate, thinking of the ramifications of this news. I've been forgiven and punished at the same time.

"I can be a guardian again?" I look in the direction I last heard Raphael.

"Maybe, but not in the same sense as you once were. Try shifting your eyes. Use your Angelic sight." Raphael instructs. As he does, I feel Metatron enter the room. It's odd how his vibration alerts me to his presence.

For the sake of what's left of my sanity, I close my eyes, then shift them to what should be the golden orbs of an Archangel. When I open my eyes, it restores my eyesight. Raphael gets close and looks deep into my eyes. I hear the shuffling and then see Nikita stand beside Raphael staring into my eyes.

"Nikita, shift your eyes for me." When Nikita does, we see the gold flecks in her abyssal orbs. "Interesting. Your eyes are the inverse of the others. You are meant to guard, Nikita." Raphael turns his gaze to me and smiles. "You have divine purpose again. Welcome back."

Raphael claps me on the back and moves out of the way for Metatron, then Christian. The light side of Thana's bond seems extremely excited about this revelation. Nikita turns and leaves the room, and I watch her walk away. "It will take time. The visage you possess now was the last she saw before she died." Metatron smiles sadly before hugging me.

Returning his hug, I retract my wings and return my eyes back to being blind. I can only assume it's the punishment for this body that I now control. At least this way, Nikita doesn't have to stare into the eyes of her killer. My heart breaks thinking about how I look to my mate, and I am now the man she has despised for months since her death.

"Shift your eyes back, Satan. Let's get you home and cleaned up." Michael's tone doesn't leave any room for argument.

I do as Michael instructed and use my angelic sight to walk through the castle and to the front door. Rex walks out ahead of us, shifts to his dragon, and lays down. "It's faster to travel this way since Michael can't fly," Mordoc states as he walks past us and climbs up onto Rex's back, taking a seat between his wings against a spine.

"Does it bother you?" Turning to Michael, I try to watch for any flicker of emotion from him, and I see none.

"It did. But I got over it just like you will get over this." The backs of his knuckles brush along my jaw before he walks away, leaving me behind with his words.

I stare at his back for several beats too long before joining the guys and taking my place on Rex's back. He launches up into the sky and we soar across the Shadow Realm in moments rather than the hours it would have taken us on foot. So many thoughts fly through my head as I watch the scenery pass by. *Why do I look like him? How will Nikita get over this and be able to look at me again? Are we still mates even though this body isn't mine?*

I feel like I'm ripping myself apart over all the what ifs. "Don't be so hard on yourself. No one could have predicted what happened. Nikita is tearing herself apart as well. Mostly guilt..." Mordoc says as he looks down, parsing out Nikita's feelings through the bond.

"But what if we aren't mates now?" As soon as the words fall from my lips, it's as if time stops. All eyes are on me. Even Rex turns his dragon's head to glance at me briefly.

"Fuck." Michael paces along Rex's spine, running his hand down his face.

"We didn't even think of that possibility." Mordoc's resigned tone tells me this is the first they are considering the ramifications.

"Yeah... add in this..." I motion to my face and sigh as I leap off of Rex's back, allowing myself to plummet before unfurling my wings and taking flight. I need time to think, and being around everyone feeling bad for me will not help.

I circle Nikita's castle at least a dozen times, trying to find the words I want to say to her. Then I remember; she barred Archangels from entering her castle. Landing in the front yard, I slowly approach the gates that lead to the castle and rest my hand upon them. Nothing happens. Pushing the gates open, I half expect to be smited on the spot, but nothing happens. The journey across the courtyard feels like the part in the book where the guys have to walk towards the execution chamber past all of their friends. I feel judged and doomed all in the same breath.

The front door has an ominous feel to it. As I raise my hand to grip the doorknob, it opens of its own volition. Stepping into the place I once called home doesn't exactly feel like a homecoming. It feels more like a death sentence. As I walk through the halls, I'm expecting some sort of castle self-defense protocol to kick in and obliterate my ass on sight.

"It's an adjustment…" Nikita's voice comes from the stairwell that leads to the second floor.

"I understand that. I can't stand to look at myself in the mirror. This…" I circle my face with my index finger. "Isn't me." Nikita looks over my face slowly, and the twitch in her right eye says it all. She's fighting her instincts.

"I can't say this is going to be easy for either of us. The body you're in killed me." Her hand raises up, pulling the collar of her shirt down to show the keloid scar just to the left of her sternum. Blood tears well up, and she uses her sleeve to wipe them away as quickly as they appear.

"We will work through this, Satan. I'm not giving up on you." She closes her eyes and leans forward to kiss my lips softly. When she pulls away, she unfurls her wings and stands before me. She flexes them several times, then ignites them. No reaction from me. Slowly she nods her head and turns, walking away. Rex happened to be coming down the stair and saw the whole thing.

"What do I do?" Turning to him, he looks down for a moment, knowing exactly what happened and what it means for us.

"Fight for what's yours. You know she's yours. She knows she's yours. It's the body, not the soul." He grips my shoulder to follow Nikita.

There are exactly three months before Nikita gives birth, and I will fight every step of the way to win my place back at her side.

CHAPTER 45

MAELESTOR REX

Screams fill the castle as we run in the direction of Nikita's voice. The tones she's hitting have set the castle's defenses on high alert. It sense's its owner is in pain and has gone into lockdown mode. Nikita, before the labor intensified, removed the blockade of the Archangels from entering the castle so that Raphael could be on hand if needed. The majority of the family is here as the rest of us pace in the sitting room outside of the main bedroom.

"The wait is killing me," I growl out as my hands roughly drag through my hair.

"Why aren't we allowed in?" Mordoc looks at us, obviously not understanding what happens during birth.

"Thana and Raphael feared the blood involved would be too much for you to maintain control." As soon as the words sink in, he nods and returns to his perch by the window.

What seems like hours pass, and the screaming finally stops. We turn and stare at the door expectedly, and eventually, Raphael

336

appears smiling. "Time to meet your son." He opens the door wide and we head in as quickly as possible.

They propped Nikita up in bed with the baby already latched to her breast, with her mother sitting beside her, brushing Nikita's hair. She looks up at the four of us, and that radiant smile remains as she looks down at the babe in her arms. "Little one time to meet your daddies." She kisses the boy in her arms and pulls him free from her breast.

Brilliant blue eyes stare at us, and instantly we know without question who's son he is. Michael rushes to the edge of the bed and takes the bundle of joy from his mother's arms. Oddly, he unwraps the blanket, and two little wings with black fluff pop out. "Just like your momma." Michael leans forward and kisses his son's forehead. Thana makes room for Michael and drags Raphael out just as Cyrus and Azrael arrive.

Glancing over at Satan, I can see the mixed emotions on his face, and I move closer to him. "You okay?" Bumping his shoulder, I attempt the squishy shit the other mates are much better at. The whole guys talking about feelings thing still creeps me out.

"Is it wrong I hoped he was mine?" I watch him wring his hands before him as he shifts uneasily.

"Not at all. We all had an equal shot at it. There's always next time when Nikita is ready." I return my gaze to the boy in Michael's arms. "Do you have a name for him yet?" The child's name holds power in my people's belief, and it's the same with the vampires.

Nikita looks up at Michael, and he nods and bows before stepping away. "I've been toying around with names for weeks. Michael, oddly enough, has sat through all of my insanity with it. And I can't think of a finer name than the one I came up with." She slowly scoots herself out of the bed, takes her son back from

Michael, and hands him off to Cyrus. "Cyrus Azrael Dawnstrider. After my father and my grandfather, the two most influential men in my life. Through Death and War, your names shall carry on for as long as he lives." Nikita motions to herself and Michael before stepping away to see the rest of us.

"How's my terror doing?" Bending down, I kiss her forehead, pull her to me, and hug her tightly.

"Surprisingly good. Mom told me to concentrate my phoenix fire where I needed to heal, and boom, all better." Shrugging, Nikita laughs. "Fire crotch…" We share a good laugh with her, thinking of flames shooting out of her hoo-ha.

She moves away from me to hug Mordoc, and he tells her how delicious she smells. The soft scent of blood lingers on her skin. Shaking her head, she slaps him softly before pulling away to walk over to Satan.

"I think I know what's wrong. I had a revelation while pushing out the watermelon over there." She hikes her thumb over her shoulder in the direction of her son.

"Oh? I would love to hear it." It's the most hopeful he's appeared in a long time.

"I need you to trust me. I learned something while I mediated the other day, and I want to try it." She looks over at me and jerks her head towards Satan. "Be prepared to catch him."

There's no telling what Nikita is up to at this point, but that look in her eyes tells me it's a Hail Mary play to end all plays. She grabs Mordoc's arm and sinks her teeth in, feeding quickly, and I watch her eyes flicker between black and amber fire of her phoenix. When she has drunk enough, she releases his arm and turns her fiery gaze on Satan.

"Close your eyes and think of the way you were before the melding." Her voice is hypnotic and has me under her sway. Double blinking, I watch her reach out and run her fingers over Satan's temples. "Listen to the sound of my voice. Get lost in its tone and feel its weight upon you." She slowly speaks the words as she rocks her head from left to right, then back again.

Satan wavers in my arms, then I feel all the fight drain out of him as she speaks. "I am Death Eternal, the keeper of the Dark Realm and the River Styx. I call upon the power of the Dark River and the souls contained within." Almost violently, Nikita's wings rip free from her back and ignite immediately. "I call upon the dark mother Nyx, Hecate, and Lilith, hear me, sisters of the night. Return my mate to the man he was; return to him his sight and visage bind him no longer." When the final words leave her lips, the castle starts to rumble and shake as if an earthquake is hitting. Nikita leans forward, leaning her head against his forehead and exhales roughly before moving back and striking Satan square in the chest.

It's the strangest thing to watch. Layers of skin fall from his body like sand hitting the ground at his feet. Nikita looks like someone had stepped out of a horror movie. Her canines are bared as her eyes glow almost the same fiery crimson that Mordoc's do.

Satan staggers one last time, then stands up straight. His wings burst from his back and spread wide. Mottled black and white feathers adorn his wings, and Cyrus gasps because of what he sees. Nikita flexes her wings and smiles. "Satan, look at me." The command in her voice makes my knees want to buckle.

Hesitantly, he raises his head and looks at Nikita. His wings open wide and vibrate as he looks at her. "There you are. Welcome back baby..." Tears break free from Nikita's eyes as she lunges forward and wraps Satan up in the tightest hug ever.

"Wow, that was impressive," I say to Cyrus, who is still holding his grandson.

Cyrus passes the baby off to me and smiles. "Through her, all things are possible. We are merely the vessels to help them achieve greatness. Be the man she needs, not the one she wants. That's the secret of dealing with a powerhouse of a mate." He claps me on the shoulder as I cradle the baby to my chest.

I watch the others reunite with Satan, and I have to say I am damn impressed Nikita pulled it off. He looks almost exactly like he did before we rejoined him with his other half. I can only hope we hit some clear sailing from here on out.

Five years later…

"Cyrus, Ambrose, and Celeste get back here!" I yell as the three children play tag in the air, completely ignoring their mother's summons.

"But Dad!" Ambrose lands in front of me, flexing his leather wings behind him.

"You know your mother. She wants dinner on time and everyone clean and seated before she places the food on the table." Patting my son on his shoulder, he nods, then reluctantly complies, heading into the house.

Celeste is the next to land, and her little mottled wings look so much like her father's. She comes over, wraps her little chunky toddler arms around my leg, and hugs it. "Din din, Daddy?" Her little gray eyes look up at me and twinkle like her mother's.

"Yes, little one, din din. Go find momma and get ready." Bending down, I kiss the crown of her head and watch her head into the house.

Cyrus is always the last and the most difficult of the children to wrangle. He darts around in the air for a few moments before landing. When he lands, he fist bumps with me and starts towards the house. All I can do is shake my head, watching him head inside. The house is in literal chaos, and Nikita is standing there shaking her head, watching the children running amok. Nikki raises her hands, and the children stop immediately, then rush to their seats at the table.

"All right, everyone, time to eat!" Nikita says as she has Michael help her bring the food to the table.

Looking down at Mordoc, I feel a sadness for him. Unlike the rest of us, he can never father his own children. According to Mordoc, it is against Vampire law to turn a child because their impulse control is non-existent. He is elbow deep in helping raise the children and literally takes the night shift when the babies wake up in the middle of the night.

Nikita walks around the table to rest on Mordoc's shoulders and smiles. "We have an announcement." Nikita waits until everyone looks her way before she starts speaking again. "There is a Nephilim baby born at the hospital that the mother wants to put up for adoption." She bites her bottom lip and draws in a deep breath.

Mordoc reaches up and places his hand over hers. "We want to ask the family if it's okay for Nikita and me to adopt the baby to give it a better life. She's a Dark Nephilim, and her mother didn't want to raise her because of her wings." Nikita looks at each of us anxiously.

"If the baby needs a home, she has one here with us," I say and lock eyes with the other two mates driving my point home.

A chorus of yeses flood the air, and even the children get involved. "That's settled then. Mordoc, congratulations on becoming a father again!" We start to celebrate the impending arrival of the newest baby to the family. It's moments like this that make me proud to be a part of this nest. It reminds me of the days of yore when nests fought for each other and took care of each other.

I definitely got lucky getting a second chance with my inamorata.

EPILOGUE

Draven

The Underverse itself is a dark and foreboding place, filled with tunnels and caverns. It's completely subterranean. The only light is provided by glowing crystals in the blackened stone of the caverns. Massive nightmare creatures are attacking not only our forces but the Drow as well. Tia chooses now to shift back to her human form. Her taloned gauntlets glow with the power of her force weapon. Just as a giant flying eyeball with tentacles changes course and veers towards me, she spins just in time to blast it with her weapon. "Damn Beholder..." she mutters before taking off to join her mother's beast in battle.

Knox and I shift back and chase after our wayward mate and mother-in-law. The Drow are master mages powerful in the dark arts. Thankfully for us, their hand-to-hand is weak for the most part. Knox and I slice through Underdark creatures and Drow with our taloned gauntlets. Tia and Aurora seem to enjoy the battle immensely as they dance back and forth, taking turns battling creatures.

"Draven? Why doesn't Tia just decimate the Drow and these horrid creatures?" Tilting my head to the side, I ponder my brother's question.

My gaze lifts, and I inspect the Underverse at all the Underdark creatures that live here. Besides the Drow, thousands of creatures of different sizes and strengths are in the mix. "She's conserving her strength for the battle ahead. I have a feeling we will be battling for days on end at this rate before we reach the Drow city." I say in a huff as I look at the expansive battle before us.

"This is insane!" Knox says, exasperated, as he motions towards the battlefield. "I have total faith in Tia and Aurora, but even they will get tired at some point, then what?" The concern in Knox's voice pulls at the tightness in my chest. My thirst for vengeance must be sated, but not at the cost of possibly losing my mate.

"We will rest and feed as we need to. Several of these Underdark creatures are edible, so we will be fine." Tia says with a confidence that's awe-inspiring. Tia moves towards me and kisses me firmly on my lips. I can feel her love for my brother, and I flood the bond as she caresses my cheeks.

"I will not fail your father even if I have to burn this entire place to ash." The tones of her dragon take over her normally sultry voice. The raw emotion and power radiating off of my mate make the scales on my arms stand on edge. Tia moves over to Knox and kisses him just as passionately.

After she breaks away from my brother, her eyes blacken, and she focuses on the gathered forces. Through the dragon bond, she calls all the dragons back to her and motions to the cavern nearby. "We'll rest here for tonight. Tomorrow we'll head west towards the mountain range in the distance." She raises a taloned hand and points at the range she's talking about.

Halfway up the mountainside, you can see what looks like buildings and a castle. "I believe what we are looking for is there." Tia pulls out a small dagger that I remember my father gave her. "I feel the pull from what we lost in that direction. Extinction is high on my list of things to do." All I can do is nod as the rest of our dragon forces enter the cavern behind Tia. There's safety in numbers, and tonight we sleep as a clutch. I assign sleep rotations to make sure we are safe through the night. My mate, brother, and mother-in-law will sleep first. Tia has opted to wake up early in what should be morning on fourth watch. For now, I'll watch over my family and keep us safe for as long as I can.

TIAMAT

Morning comes far too early, and just our luck, a massive army has amassed outside of this very cavern. My mother comes up alongside me and looks out across the expanse before us. "What do you plan to do?" She rests her hand on my shoulder as we study the creatures as they move.

"Nikita and her mother rule the underworld. So summoning Nikita would probably be the best and easiest solution." Looking over at my mother, she smiles and backs away from the cavern entrance.

I start a small fire on the cavern floor, drawing my mates' attention. "What are you doing, Tia?" Draven looks briefly from the cavern entrance, then at me.

"Calling for reinforcements." Cutting my hand, I let my blood fall into the fire.

"I call upon Death Eternal on *khlōros* she rides."
"I beseech the Pale Rider to manifest and wipe the field clean."
"I offer in sacrifice my blood as payment for this boon."

The fire pulses several times, then dies but emits no smoke.

"Did it work?" Knox asks as he paces back and forth near the entrance.

"Yes, now we defend this position until Nikita gets here." I can only hope my sister from another mister isn't too busy with her nest to assist. I would hate to burn out this far from our target.

A thunderous roar shakes the very earth under our feet, and it feels like we have waited forever for it. It's the call of a Wyrm Dragon, but that's not what I summoned. We race to the mouth of the cavern, and the largest Skull Dragon I have ever seen is laying waste to the dark forces that threaten us.

Once the majority of the demons and demon spawn are destroyed, the dragon lands, and two figures step down. One looks like a white specter with a horse made of rotted flesh and bone that rides up beside it. The second doubles in size and mounts a much larger red horse, and they thunder across the land. The specter raises its hands, and the dead begin to rise and follow behind it.

Between the dead and the large man on the red horse, they destroy the rest of the demons on the battlefield. They ride up to the cavern as the dragon lumbers closer to us. I don't know if we should prepare to fight or run for our lives. Now, the skeleton horse vanishes from under its rider, and the rider shifts. Nikita stands before me with her mate Michael as well as the legendary Maelestor Rex.

"You summoned me, and I have come. Let's finish this." Nikita gets a wicked glimmer in her eye, and from here on out, I know we will be all right.

Finish the fight!
Hybrid Royals Fire and Ice - World at War.
Coming 2024

DARK ANGEL HOLIDAY

BONUS STORY

THANA

The last eight Christmases have been all about the children. This year is different; I want to make it the most memorable holiday to date.

I never thought I would have the life that I'm living and I'm grateful. To start, I have five mates that love me unconditionally. My angelic side keeps me honest, and my dark side balances the good with whom I truly am. I have friends and family that love and accept me, even the darker parts, with no hesitation.

Leaning over the balcony from the third floor, I watch my mates struggle to get the Christmas tree just right. Christian makes us buy trees we can plant on the mountainside after the holiday is over; it's a lovely tradition that I look forward to every year. My eyes run over them fondly until I'm distracted by moans and the thumping of a headboard against the wall. The darker side of my bonds is having their own party.

Smiling to myself, I leap over the rail and glide down it to land behind Metatron. I wrap my arms around his thick waist and rest my head between his shoulder blades, sighing in satisfaction.

"Oh no, The Destroyer captured me!" He feigns fear, but I know he's trying not to laugh.

I use my wings to land on his back and band an arm around his neck. "I have, so you will do my bidding."

"You want to go to the nest?" he asks with a grin. He prepares to take off immediately, which makes me smile.

Nuzzling his cheek first, I slide my mouth back to nip his earlobe. "Later, handsome. Right now, we have a different mission." Dropping off his back, I turn on my heel and head towards the front door.

"Where are we going?"

"I'll explain in the car," I call over my shoulder. I turn to look at him as he shivers in anticipation; he loves riding in my Hellcat. Clicking the remote, the beast fires up and her rumble fills me with joy. Metatron climbs in and puts on his seatbelt, settling his large body in the sleek vehicle. Flipping through my playlist, I settle on *Anarchy by Lilith Czar*.

We take off like a bullet from a gun, rocketing down the road at top speed. It's a good time while he's belted in, so I go ahead and drop my bombshell. "So I found Gage's dream board on social media when I was poking around one night. He's been pinning all the pieces for his dream wedding with Cyrus."

"What does this mean for us?"

I can see his arched brow out of the corner of my eye. "I called Klaus and Jayce for help. They told the rest of their family my plans to make his dream happen."

After making several turns and driving for over three hours, I arrive at the venue I booked for the wedding.

"Wow, this place looks like a Gothic castle." Metatron's awed tone makes my heart squeeze.

"It is a Gothic castle—Wernigerode Castle, to be exact. It has lots of fun things to do and I rented it for a week. Aurora and her family should arrive later today. I used the 'family vacation' premise as an excuse to get everyone here." I get out of the car and head towards the staff waiting for us.

After introductions, they take us on a brief tour of the castle so we can pinpoint the rooms that will suit our needs. They set lunch up in the eastern garden. As we look over the menu for the wedding, I finally ask, "What do you think?"

"It's a beautiful venue. I feel bad that we never did anything like this for you." Sadness clouds his stoic visage, and I shake my head.

Moving to climb into his lap, I wrap an arm around his neck and place my forehead against his. A soft sigh escapes my lips as we look at one another. "I didn't think I was worthy of you. A ceremony like this wasn't needed. You gave me a life and children—that's all I ever wanted." Pulling away, I duck down to press a kiss to his lips.

Metatron hums into the kiss before releasing me. "As long as you're happy, that's all that matters to me." He presses his lips to mine one last time before my phone chimes.

Aurora: Ana, are we still good for tomorrow?

Thana: Yes! We just took the tour, and it's perfect. Of course, it's nothing like your castle in Siberia, but it's still exceptional.

Aurora: If you think it will work, we are good to go. Alaric got ordained online because, apparently, the title of Dragon King doesn't count in human courts. LOL.

Thana: Those bastards! I'm furious they treat us like we don't matter.

Aurora: I know, right?

Thana: See you tomorrow, Rory.

Aurora: :heart emoji: Bye.

Laughing, I turn my phone so Metatron can read our conversation. He shakes his head, then runs his hand down his face. "You two concern me."

"I concern me sometimes." Shaking my head as he lifts me and stands me on the ground, I let Metatron us lead back into the castle to make the final preparations.

Jayce and Klaus are bringing the cake.

Aurora's children are providing the music.

We planned the venue and dinner for the reception.

Alaric is performing the wedding.

All that's left is to have the tailor drop off the tuxes I had made for the guys.

With any luck, this is going to be an exciting vacation.

CYRUS

My dark angel is up to something; I can feel it in my bones. She's flittered through the house like she has a secret for days. After that, she announces a surprise family vacation, and it has the hairs on my neck standing on end.

Today, Metatron and Thana did not return for several hours. I ponder how I'm going to get the secret out of someone. It would be virtually impossible to get answers out of him, but Thana will be a piece of cake. I know exactly what to do.

Spreading my wings wide, I glide to the ground floor and land behind her. My midnight wings wrap around her, engulfing her in darkness the way I know she loves.

"What are you up to, Cy?"

Her throaty whisper makes my cock harden almost instantly. Taking her earlobe between my teeth, I bite down with enough pressure to make her squirm. "I could ask you the same thing, Kitten."

"What could I possibly be up to?" She spins to face me when I release her ear, looking at me with chrome orbs that glow faintly in the darkness.

I tilt my head to the side as I tick off the things that stand out. Thana shivers slightly, and I know I've got her. "A surprise vacation, you and golden boy vanishing sneakily in your car... The method of transportation tells me you're dealing with humans. But why?"

Without warning, she rips us through the shadows. When I open my wings, we're in her castle in the shadow realm.

"Sorry for the abrupt shift." Pouting, she crosses her arms under her chest, looking frustrated at my questions. "I secretly planned Gage's dream wedding. It's supposed to be a surprise."

"I see." Flexing my wings, I lean against the wall and watch her.

"Please don't be mad, Cy. I wanted to do it for him."

Tears well up in her eyes and my black heart damn near breaks. "Shhh, Kitten. I didn't mean to make you cry." Closing the distance between us, I wipe away her tears. "Thank you for being so thoughtful."

"Do you want to see the venue?" She bounces on the balls of her feet, her grin playful.

"Of course."

Before I get another word out, Thana grips my biceps and drags me through the shadows. At the rate I'm being hauled around today, I'll develop whiplash.

We manifest in the tree line outside of a castle. I blink when I realize where we are. "This is the castle Gage fell in love with after the Hundred Years War." I'm amazed Kitten remembered that offhand story he told years ago.

"I knew how much it meant to him, so I booked it." Taking my hand, Thana leads me towards the castle grounds. It's past visitor hours, so the staff are gone for the night and we don't have to hide.

Spreading her wings wide, Thana launches up to the sky and flies to the wall, landing on it gracefully. I join her before we drop to the other side of the wall together. As we stroll, Thana points out the royal gardens, outlining how it will be prepped for the wedding.

"What day is the wedding?" I wait for her response, studying the lush garden appreciatively.

A sigh escapes her lips as she murmurs, "The anniversary of Gage falling to save us."

I turn to her, noticing her bottom lip quivering from the powerful emotions invoked by the memory. Closing the distance between us, I pull her to my chest. "Kitten, that's a powerful statement. You're turning one of the worst days in our lives into a happy memory. I love it." I place a kiss on her forehead and rest my cheek on top of her head as my wings wrap around her.

Thana nuzzles against my throat. "I wanted to give him something he's always wanted but was afraid to ask for."

She pulls away from me to look at me with huge doe eyes, and I'd give her the entire world if she asked. "Did you pick a dress for the wedding? I'll walk you down the aisle."

My dark angel's face lights up and she kisses me passionately. I want to take her here and now, but Thana has different plans. She drags me through the rest of the castle to show me the reception hall and where the ceremony will take place.

I've never seen my girl so excited about little details, and it makes me smile broadly.

When she pulls me to the groom's dressing quarters, I can tell why she's so excited. Hanging on the rack is the most incredible peacock-inspired tux I have ever seen. She must have had it made for Gage, and it's perfect. "He's gonna love it, Kitten."

I'm at a loss for words. Our mate is incredibly thoughtful; she planned out every detail to the letter.

"You're the epitome of fashion, Cy, so that means a lot coming from you." Beaming happily, she tugs me out of the room to another. A lacy, pitch-black wedding gown with a mermaid tail and plunging neckline is hanging there. It has a familiar Goth feeling about it, and I wink at her.

"Kitten, that dress is sexy as hell."

Thana gives the gown a once over, then shrugs as she looks at me. Taking the gown off the rack, she races into the changing room, calling over her shoulder. "I was going for a sexy, spooky kind of vibe."

I'm not a patient man, especially when I know my beautiful mate is putting her a sexy dress on for me. My heart damn near wants to explode as I try to keep myself from barging in on her. I distract myself by looking out the window, gritting my teeth.

The click of the latch catches my attention and I turn to see Thana looking like an absolute vision. The gown looks a lot like the dress a certain Gothic wife on TV wears. A wolf whistle escapes my lips and she blushes. "Damn, Kitten."

Her hands go to her stomach, and she smooths them over the fabric. I know what's bothering her, and I drop to my knees to kiss her stomach. "Get those thoughts out of your head, Kitten. This womb carried our children. You created life and carried it with in your body." I kiss her stomach several more times before standing up and hugging her.

"I know, Cy. But I still feel like my body isn't mine anymore." She buries her nose under my chin and sighs.

"You shared your body with ten children. You performed ten miracles, and if it wasn't blasphemous, I'd say you were in line for being a goddess."

My statement elicits a giggle, and she pulls back to look up at me. "I'm banned from the Silver City. Let's not add to it, shall we?" That little wicked minx of mine boops me on the nose, then walks into the dressing room to change.

I use the bond to let the guys know we're out for date night, so they won't wait up. Gage can't know what Thana has planned for him, but I don't want them to worry.

When my angel returns, we finish touring the castle. The amount of thought she put into this moment amazes me; I almost fall in love with her all over again. Neither of us had the easiest childhood, so we're frequently drawn to one another. We understand each other's pain more than our other mates can.

Archangels and angels simply exist. Nephilim like Gage, Thana, and I grow up with parents and problems.

She reaches out to hold my hand as we stroll the rest of the gardens. We get to the area where the wedding ceremony will take place. They covered the archway in climbing roses with an overarching trellis. The satisfied smile that spreads across her crimson lips warms my black heart.

"What do you think, Cy?" She must have called me several times because she looks quite irritated.

"It's stunning, Kitten—absolutely fucking stunning. I have to admit something, though." I lean against the wall and smirk at her playfully.

"What?" She moves closer, resting her hand on my chest.

"It pales compared to you." My mate is the most beautiful woman in existence. If it takes a million years, I will tell her every day until she believes me.

"This sweet talk is why you are my Dark Knight." She kisses me as I feel the familiar dip and pull of the shadows. When she releases me, we're at our house and she's smiling up at me. "Go get packed, Cy. We're leaving in the morning to meet Aurora and her family."

With a wink, she steps back through the shadows, vanishing to lord knows where.

GAGE

Thana and Gage are buzzing around like a pair of bees hopped up on energy drinks. Watching them run around is hysterical. The luggage is stacked in a pile in the center of the downstairs by the front door. Even though the children are almost adults now—angels have extremely rapid growth rates—Thana is still hovering over them as we prepare to leave.

"What car are we driving to get to this place?" Raphael shouts from the landing.

"I'm portaling us there!" Thana yells from the third story.

Shaking my head, I drop the last our bags onto the pile in the center of the foyer. Thana seems really excited about this trip. She's been on the phone with Aurora constantly since she and Cyrus got home yesterday.

"Time to go!" Thana yells before launching herself over the railing and gliding to the ground.

Children and mates pour out of every room to gather in the foyer. With ten children and six adults, I feel sorry for whoever has to deal with us. Add to that, Aurora has six mates and eleven children. It's like relocating Pompeii to get all of us to a destination.

"Children, grab the hand of your buddy and an adult." Thana looks at the one bare wall in the foyer intently.

My two children grab my hands, and I can't help but smile.

Thana and Nikita rip open a portal to what appears to be a throne room. On the other side, Aurora and her family are gathered, waiting for this moment. Aurora ushers her children and mates into our house, all dragging their luggage with them.

"Damn, Ana. That's an impressive trick!" Aurora kisses her cheek as she passes by, her eyes dancing with merriment.

"Not everyone is a queen; we have to make do," Thana teases as she closes the portal.

"True—but at least you can fly." Aurora's tone is somber, and Alaric pulls her to his side.

Thana's eyes drop, knowing flight is a sensitive subject. Drawing in a slow breath, she rips another portal open and holds it open. The other side leads to a huge, ornate garden that looks familiar. Thana watches me as I pass through with my children in tow. Once I'm standing in the grass, awe comes over me as I realize where I am.

"Is this?" I can't bring myself to finish the sentence.

"Yes. Welcome, everyone, to Wernigerode Castle."

I scoop Thana up as she finishes her sentence, and she squeals when I spin her in a circle.

After I set her down, she kisses my lips gently. "I'm glad you like it."

"This is incredible!" I barely contain my excitement as I look around at the castle I'd dreamed of visiting.

"If I remember correctly, this was your human mother's family land." Raphael's words are somber because he knows my mother's family is long dead. It doesn't bother me like it used to, but I appreciate his caution.

"There are more happy memories here than bad ones."

I look at Thana as she speaks and all I can think is how much she loves us. It amazes me that she remembers the little details from our pasts. We are blessed to have such a wonderful mate.

A man in a suit clears his throat while Thana looks at the last rays of the sun. "This is Orpheus, the castle's keeper. He's also the ruler of the castle's Gargoyle clan."

Alaric almost has to pick Aurora's jaw up when she hears Orpheus is a real Gargoyle. Aurora looks from me to Orpheus. "The kids can shift at will, then?"

I unfurl my wings and flex them behind me several times. "Yup. Be comfortable, everyone!"

"Master Gage." Orpheus's voice calls to me, and I turn to smile at him.

"Good to see you, old friend." We exchange a quick bro-hug, and he laughs.

"Looks like your feathers have changed. If I remember correctly, they were white." Orpheus arches an eyebrow at me.

"The things we do for love, old friend." I have zero regrets about falling to save Thana, Nikita, and Cyrus. I love them to the end of the world. I would die for them a thousand times so they could live.

Either Orpheus doesn't know who Thana is or she never told him. She hates titles and designations, because of how she was treated. I didn't notice how others treat me differently because my wings are black now until recently. I'm still me, but the color change altered people's perceptions of me.

Standing back under the old cypress tree, I watch Aurora and her children play. Our children join in the games, making it an interesting experience. Aurora passes off her newest baby to Thana, and she's instantly smitten.

The quickest way to lose Thana is with a baby, especially one of Aurora's.

"Are you okay being here?" Cyrus steps in front of me and spreads his wings wide, blocking me from everyone else's view.

"As well as can be expected. It's surreal, you know?" Shrugging my shoulders, I try to come to terms with some of the old feelings surfacing.

"Thana and I should know if you are not okay. I love you, Gage."

Leaning forward, I close the distance between Cyrus and me. His kisses always make me swoon. He slowly sips from my lips, being more tender than usual, knowing it's exactly what I need at the moment from him. The clashing of swords catches our attention and kills the moment in an instant.

We turn around to find Nikita and Tiamat training. The two moms are shoulder to shoulder, pointing out what their daughters are doing. Unfortunately, Nikita disarms Tiamat, and she loses her temper. Frost flames manifest in her hands. Nikita smirks and engulfs herself in hellfire. Blood red and black flames surround her; it's like hell on earth.

This is the first time that Nikita has taken this form, so Thana jumps into action. She passes off the baby and goes full Destroyer in front of Nikita. The frigid chill of death fills the palace grounds and everyone freezes in place, watching the titans stand off.

Alaric and Raphael take it upon themselves to back the rest of the family away from ground zero. The two most powerful daughters would eventually have a fight. After all, it's in a dragon and a wolfs instincts to establish dominance in the pack. Since Tiamat takes after the dragon's side, it's more imperative, especially since she can sense the power within Nikita.

"Okay! That's handled." Metatron booms, knocking Thana and Nikita free from their standoff.

"That was close." Jayce, the omega from Aurora's family, approaches and smiles.

"It was expected." Klaus says flatly as he kisses Jayce's forehead.

"I still don't like it." Jayce pouts then looks at Cyrus and me. "How are you two doing?"

"Good, and you?" Cyrus says before I have the chance to finish opening my mouth.

"Very well, thank you." Klaus answers and extends his hand out to shake.

Cyrus shakes his hand first, then I do. "I love your pastries. Thana brings them home as treats all the time."

"See, Klaus! I told you Thana shared with her family." Jayce chuckles.

Rolling his eyes, Klaus finally smiles. "Yeah, but she would buy the same amount for herself before the trials happened."

"This is also true." Jayce's tone is soft and reminiscent of the old days.

With no warning, Thana and Nikita take off. Once they're flying in the clouds, I realize they're probably going to see Sigrun and the girls.

"I wonder what that's all about?" Cyrus muses.

"Nikita wanted to see her aunt." Christian says as he comes forward. "Her shift was a shock to us. Thana needs the Valkyrie to help temper her rage." He stares at the sky as if the answers to the universe are written there.

"Stranger things have happened." Dimitri laments as he joins our group.

Laughing, Jayce and I speak at the same time. "Stranger things have happened?" We immediately crack up, barely able to contain the laughter.

Aurora looks between us and then over at Nikita. "I see my niece took after some of my worst character traits."

"It appears so. Your 'eff 'em if they can't take a joke' mantra is the one she's lived by since day one." Davina looks down at her nails, then back up at Aurora.

"You can say 'fuck', sweetheart. You're an adult." Aurora says as she grins at Davina.

Smirking, Davina unfurls her opalescent wings and flexes them several times. The typical archangel glow encompasses her feathers. "Hard pass, Aunt Aurora." Her eyes travel to Metatron and Raphael, and they nod their approval at her response.

Arching a brow, I study Davina. It's the first time I've seen her wings like that. "When did this happen?"

Davina flexes her wings several times, then puts them away. "My last trip to the Silver City. I would like to announce that I have ascended to Speaker. I am the recorder and divine intervention, the hammer and shield, the equalizer." Davina's voice does the reverberation thing that we know Metatron for before she puts her wings away.

The wave of power that comes off of her is incredible. Cyrus rubs my side and smiles. "Let's go get everyone settled for the evening and reconvene at dinnertime."

Cyrus and Aurora herd the family inside what was my home hundreds of years ago. It's strange to be here after so many years. The halls still have that oppressive feeling from when my grandfather lived here. Scooting ahead of everyone, I give the tour of the castle, but some small part of me wishes I wasn't here. However, another part wants closure from this homecoming.

There's two wings on the second floor. Both have large main bedrooms and a dozen guest rooms. I send Aurora and her family to the east wing while I lead my family to the west wing. The kids pick their rooms and roommates for the stay. Once the rooms are settled, I open the door to our bedroom. My bond mates and I start unpacking, making sure everything is in place for Thana's arrival.

Thana lands on the balcony and pushes the doors open right as we get settled. "That was an adventure," she says.

"What happened?" Cyrus rushes forward, worried about his daughter.

"Not much. Sigrun gave her an amulet to help her cool her jets." Shaking her head, she laughs. "It's all hormonally related." She raises her eyebrows, subtly hinting at a feminine issue.

Cyrus's eyes widen as he stares at Thana. "No…. you can't be serious." He glances at us, then back again. "That explains a lot."

"What does that explain?" Glancing between Thana and Cyrus, I swear I missed something.

Thana steps forward and whispers in my ear what's going on, and my heart damn near stops. "That's horrible timing."

"Tell me about it." Thana shakes her head and exits the suite.

Cyrus fills the other dads in on the code red situation through our bond. We look at each other, remembering the last time someone had pissed Nikita off during her cycle. We all know we'll need someone to save us if she goes nuclear.

CYRUS

Everyone else has gone to bed, but I'm seated deep inside Gage, sliding out until I make him moan. I reach around, gripping his length tightly. With every thrust, I stroke him, tightening my grip as I get closer to the tip. I pull back and withdraw, then stroke forward. It's a well-choreographed dance and we fit together as we move perfectly.

The love between us makes it even more satisfying.

When I feel him twitch, my hand works him faster while I push deeper inside of him. His orgasm hits him hard—he screams and practically rips the arm off the chair he's holding onto. I continue sliding my palm over him, wanting to extend his pleasure.

"Cy, please. I'm so sensitive," Gage gasps as he shudders with every stroke.

"Then it's my turn." Standing up, I ram my length into him in a punishing rhythm. The slapping of skin is music to my ears, especially paired with his whimpering moans. My balls draw up and the tingles start in my abdomen as my release builds.

I grab Gage and yank him to a standing position. The change is almost enough to make me blow my load early. My hand slides to his neck, where I grip tightly as my fangs descend. I bite the meaty part of his shoulder and he comes when my fangs pierce his skin. Hot, liquid iron flows into my mouth when I take a healthy gulp of his blood. With one final upward thrust, I bury my cock deep in him and finally allow my orgasm to flow over me.

Every pulse is pure euphoria.

I slowly withdraw, only to violently thrust into him as I ride the crest of my pleasure. My hand loosens around his throat when I'm completely spent. Once I can manage, I navigate Gage to the bed, then wobble to the bathroom for towels to clean up with.

Gage's smile warms something deep within me when I return with the clothes and clean us up. I kiss his cheek before I throw on some sleep pants and walk out of the room.

Hushed whispers echo up from downstairs when I enter the hallway. My curiosity is piqued, so I move through the shadows to see where the noise is coming from. I move from shadow to shadow until I end up in a ballroom. Thana is directing a team of gargoyles as they decorate the room. "What do we have here, Kitten?"

She almost jumps out of her skin when I speak. Turning to face me, she smacks her head. "Crap on a cracker! I'm busted."

"What do you mean, busted?" I tilt my head as I look at her questioningly.

"We're setting up for the wedding." She pouts as she looks down at the carpet beneath her feet.

"Do you desire my help, Kitten?"

"Your input would be incredible." She bounces up and kisses my lips softly. Her nostrils flair as she catches Gage's cologne. She looks up at the ceiling and over toward his room. I swear sometimes she can see through walls and shit. "Am I interrupting?"

"No, Kitten. He's sleeping by now." Smiling, I kiss her temple. I love how accepting she is of Gage and me having a relationship. Our love is different because if any of the archangels or angels were to have sex with a man, they would fall, and it would cause the nest to be off balance.

"What do you think of the flowers?" she asks abruptly.

My eyes drift around the room. It's a Goth's dream wedding brought to life—black orchids and lilies are mixed in with blood-red roses all everywhere. Next to the altar is a stone slab held up by bones and bound by a matching ribbon. I chuckle and motion to the altar. "Aurora's creation?"

"Yes! I'm so happy you recognized her work. Is it too much?" Arching a brow, she grins playfully.

Fuck, I don't want to say the wrong thing; she's trying so hard. "Its stunning, love. I'm sure Gage will love it."

"Do you love it, too?" Thana leans in close and wraps her arms around my waist.

Laughing, I kiss the crown of her head. "Of course, I do. You designed this beautiful wedding set-up. I'm honestly a little jealous that it's you and Gage up there."

"Will you walk me down the aisle?" She bounces up and down, looking up at me expectantly.

"If that's what you want, of course I will." Squealing, Thana breaks away from me and spreads her wings wide as she returns to decorating the hall.

Agreeing to walk my angel down the aisle apparently made her night.

I watch her for a few more moments, then head back upstairs. Returning to Gage's side was the easiest decision I've made today. I curl around him, holding him tightly as I drift off.

The night gives way to morning, and the next day is busy with a flurry of activity. Thana and Aurora have activities planned for the children. The fathers are gathered under the willow tree, watching the kids and our mates.

"Such an odd couple, aren't they?" Klaus leans against the wall nearby, motioning to the girls.

"They are actually similar, if you think about it. Both spent their lives without their mothers; they're strong, independent women. And they have the power to destroy the world if they want to." My words make all the males pause their chatter to consider the conversation Klaus and I are having.

"Thana and Aurora are world-ending weapons engineered by a higher power," Raphael adds as Alaric nods his agreement.

"They scare the shit out of me," Jayce admits sheepishly. "Especially when they're together."

We dine outside as a family so we can enjoy the peace that togetherness brings.

I understand why Thana loves Aurora and her mates. For each mate of Aurora's, there's a counterpart in our family. Arnulf is the only outlier—he's a mystic—and we don't have one of those. Aurora spends dinner telling us how he summons her mother for her, and I marvel at his skill again.

Thana stands up suddenly, her eyes on the setting sun. I hear the sounds of cracking stone, and I know the gargoyles are awakening. She turns and grins. "Aurora, it's time!"

Within seconds, Aurora has her family gathered up and heading into the castle.

"Did I miss something?" Gage asks, looking perplexed.

"Yes. Christian, help Gage prepare for phase two. The rest of you: it's up to you to start phase three."

Thana's riddles are killing me. "What the actual fuck is going on?" I growl in frustration.

Her eyes glow so brightly that the chrome is almost white. "You know what's going on. Don't be daft. Remember last night?" she asks, huffing indignantly.

The pieces click into place, and I grab her hand to hurry inside. We race through the castle to her suite. I help her into her dress, fix her hair, and place the veil on top of her head. Slipping into the suit she has set aside for me, I wait as she ties my tie perfectly.

A knock sounds at the door. When I open it, Jayce gives me two thumbs up before he heads down the hallway. Confused, I look over at Thana.

"It's show time!" she snarks in her best Beetlegeuse impersonation.

I roll my eyes but follow as Thana leads the way through the castle. She navigates a maze of hallways while staff pops out, making adjustments or handing her handfuls of flowers. By the time we get to our destination, Thana has crafted a bouquet that would make a queen jealous.

We reach a large oak door and Thana raps on it in an odd pattern. Eventually, Dimitri opens the door and Thana takes hold of my arm. The scene that greets us is like walking into a fairytale. Flowers line the aisle and hang from the ceiling.

Aurora and Tiamat stand on either side of the stage. With a raising of their hands, the temperature in the room drops and snow falls from the ceiling. The music changes, and Thana starts us down the aisle.

My heart is in my chest, watching us get closer to Gage. He looks so fucking handsome in his custom tuxedo. With how nervous I am, you would think I was the one getting married today. Alaric emerges with an ancient tome in his hands, his crown sitting proudly on top of his head.

We climb the last few stairs, and I prepare to hand Thana off to Gage. She stops, placing my hand on Gage's.

"I love you both so very much," she says passionately. "Five years ago today, Gage fell from grace to save the lives of Cyrus, our daughter, Nikita, and myself."

Thana unfurls her wings, exposing them to the masses before she turns her chrome orbs on us. "Their love allowed Nikita and me to live. I wish to honor their love by hosting their wedding."

With a single movement, the dress burns away from Thana's body and the armor and helm of the Destroyer manifest. "With the power granted to me by Samael, I bless this union now and forever." Raising her sword, she taps mine and Gage's shoulders.

I feel the power move through me like a wave.

Alaric clears his throat and reads the rites of marriage from the ancient dragon text. Gage and I perform each of the tasks without fail. Arnulf moves forward and plucks a single hair from each of us and tosses it in with some herbs and sets them on fire.

From the ashes, two figures rise.

I'll be fucking damned. My mother's ghost and what I guess is Gage's mother's ghost rise. Both moms tell us how proud of us they are and offer us their blessing. Nikita moves forward and stares defiantly at my mother.

"She's just like you, Cy," my mother says lovingly.

Nikita merely arches a brow, then moves to stand next to her mother.

My mom laughs. "I see she got her good looks from her mother."

Thana holds her helm in her hands and offers my mother a slight dip of her head.

Gage and I pluck a feather from our wings and exchange them. As the feathers touch our spouse's hands, they turn into rings. Alaric motions for Thana to move forward again. She slits her palm and bleeds over our joined hands. "From now until forever."

An odd warmth moves through our hands and up our arms into our chests.

We repeat Thana's vow, staring into each other's blackened eyes. Usually our orbs are fathomless, but today I see myself reflected in Gage's eyes. Thana moves in closer and kisses Gage on the cheek, her eyes locked with mine.

In an instant, he's gone. I look around frantically, but he's nowhere to be seen. My eyes find Thana and the minute her lips touch mine; I vanish as well.

GAGE

The minute I vanished, I knew where Thana was sending us.

We are at the castle in the Shadow Realm—specifically, in her suite. Her personal room is as ornate as it is deadly. Black and blood red silk hangs from the light in the center to the walls. At first glance, you can't see where the exit—or anything else—is from here.

Soft twinkle lights frame the ceiling, adding an almost magical feel to the room. Through the silk, Cyrus emerges and smiles. "I guess I we know now what Thana was up to." Cyrus laughs as he takes in the sights in the room.

"She pulled a fast one on us. But I'm thankful for her." A fond smile crosses my lips as I think about how thoughtful our mate is.

"It's amazing what she pulled off in such a short time." Cyrus muses as he looks under the silken wall hangings.

"I'm sure Aurora and the daughters all had a hand in the decorating the hall. They did a phenomenal job." Smiling, I close the distance between us. Gliding my hand over his chest, I stretch up and kiss his lips.

"How is my new husband feeling?" Cyrus nips my lip, hardening my cock almost instantly.

Moaning softly, I close my eyes, reveling in the feel of his teeth on my flesh. "Feeling like I need you..." Breathy, I exhale the words, sounding needy.

"Hmmm... good boy... Why don't you strip for me? Climb on the bed." Cyrus dropped his tone and took that alpha stance, looking down at me. His eyes blacken as he stares at me, and I can see the thick, hardened mass in his pants.

Without hesitation, I rip the shirt from my body and head towards the bed. Facing the bed, I draw my slacks down my body. Inching the slacks over my ass, I can feel Cyrus approaching.

"Stay like that. Don't move a muscle." Cyrus palms my ass cheeks, then slaps them hard before rubbing away the sting. He smacks my ass again, and this time I feel my cock pulse in time with the rubbing.

The pop of the top of the lube is my only warning that Cy is getting ready to have his way with me. The cold, slick feeling of the lube on the tips of his fingers as he massages my anus loosening me up. Slowly, he slips a finger in as his other hand slides around my hip to grip my length, giving it a good squeeze.

"There's my good boy..." Cyrus's tone and grip on my length makes me squirm in his grip.

"Please Cy, I want to feel you..." Practically whining, I push back, forcing his finger in deeper.

His hand drops free of my length and he spanks my ass, then rubs the area again. "Naughty husband... Be a good boy and I'll give you what you desire." He hits that TV Lucifer tone that has sparked many a night of role play. It became even more interesting when Thana played the part of the detective and brought handcuffs into the bedroom.

Distracted by my memories, Cyrus presses the head of his cock into my ass. The slide of his long, thick length fills me to the point my back arches and a gasp escapes my lips. "yessssss...." I hiss out as he pulls back before driving forward, burying himself deep inside me again. His strokes are deep, and purposeful as he drives me forward onto the mattress.

Each stroke makes my cock leak, and I can't help but reach down and stroke myself in time with his thrusts. The harder I grip myself, the more it intensifies Cyrus fucking me. A cool soothing feeling of Thana reaching through the bond to us, the calm caress of her for a moment, is all the blessing I need. She loves us and accepts our love in a very open and honest way.

Doubling down on his efforts, Cyrus thrusts into me harder. "Feel that, Gage? Feel our angel showing us love." He grunts into my ear as his grip on my hips tightens.

"Yesss.. I do..." Moaning, I come hard, shooting my load all over the bottom of the comforter.

His movements become jerky, harsh, and erratic. He pulls me flush to his chest and wraps his arms around me, hugging tightly. "I love you..." He whispers in my ear as he drives up one last time and pulses deep within me. He roars his release as he buries his face between my shoulder blades.

Stroking his arms, I soothe him. "I love you, too, Cy." Smiling, I lean my head back and sigh. What was a dark moment in our family, the day I fell to save Cy, Thana and Nikita. Today has turned into a beautiful day. Thana took a stand in the angelic community, fighting for marriage and mating equality for everyone. Same sex matings have just started being acknowledged last Sunday.

Cyrus withdraws from me and walks to the bathroom and comes back with towels to clean us both up. Once we're clean, we climb up onto the bed and he rests his head on my chest. My fingers glide through his hair, trying to soothe him as we lay here in the afterglow.

"We got lucky with Thana." Cyrus muses.

Kissing the crown of his head, I smile against his hair. "Yeah, we did. Definitely."

Laughing, Cyrus kisses my chest. "Our family is amazing. I never thought that I would be a father, husband, and mate. Hell, I thought I would have been killed by now." His laughter almost makes my heart hurt.

"That's not funny, Cy. Joking about your death isn't funny." Pouting, I turn my head away.

I can feel the loss of Cyrus's warmth beside and I prepare to roll over and pout more. His hands come to frame my face as he sits on my hips, trying to get my undivided attention. "I'm sorry Gage… Dark Nephilim didn't have a long life expectancy before Thana became the Destroyer."

Lifting my gaze to meet his, I see the regret etched over his features. The slight downturn of his lips tugs at my heartstrings. Reaching up, I press my thumb to his lips, trying to rub away the sadness I see there. "Thana's changed in the last ten years. I'm sorry you had to live with that fear throughout your existence."

Reaching up, I pull him down and press a kiss to his pillow soft lips. "Thank you for opening up to me. I know it's outside of your wheelhouse to deal with your emotions." I can't help but beam at the resident bad boy in the family.

He presses a finger to my lips and shakes his head. "Shhhhh... you'll ruin my rep."

Cyrus makes me laugh at his statement. Shaking my head, I raise an eyebrow, looking at him. "No one would believe me even if I said something." Scrunching my nose, I reach out and touch the tip of his as I grin, looking at him, trying to start trouble.

"True." He gets that haughty look to him that makes me hard all over again.

"Hmmm, someone is hard again so soon. I'm such a bad husband if I didn't do my job." Cyrus has that look in his eyes and I know I'm in trouble.

His grip on my length is tight, almost strangling my cock. A whine escapes my lips as he strokes me from root to the tip. "I love it when you whine. It's the same delicious tone Klaus rips from Jayce's lips. The tone that says I have your submission." His eyes blacken as he stares down at me. A thrill runs up my spine as a pulse of desire goes straight to my groin.

Dropping to my knees before him, I stare up as his cock comes back to life. My tongue slips from between my lips, wetting them as I stare at the thickening shaft bobs to life. The thick vein runs up from the base and coils its way up his length, vanishing into the iron shaft.

"Lick me..." Cyrus's low tone makes me leap into action.

Sticking my tongue out, I flatten it to encompass as much of his girth as I can. Root to tip, I drag my tongue up to his phallus. Sweet sticky pre-cum escapes his slit and rolls down his shaft. Hungrily, I lap at my reward. A soft rumble of appreciation escapes Cyrus's lips as I wrap my lips around his engorged head.

Thrusting my head forward, I suck his cock into the back of my throat. The soft head of his phallus hits the back of my throat. Relaxing, I press his cock past the pharynx and down my throat. As Cyrus starts to throat fuck me, his fingers thread through my hair. He withdraws enough to allow me to breathe, then thrusts back harder and deeper, filling my mouth and throat.

Cyrus's movements falter. I reach up and grip his balls, rolling them in my hand, squeezing them. When I realize he's about to come, I draw in a deep breath and shove him deep down, feeling his pulsing cock spilling his seed. Gently, I stroke his thighs as he draws back, allowing his softening cock from my mouth. He beds down and kisses me.

Today has become a day that will live in my memory for the rest of my existence. I pet his face, feeling the stubble under my fingers, and smile as we kiss. We have the best of both worlds, the love of the man in our lives and the love of our beautiful Thana. We climb into each other arms and crawl into bed, curling up together, allowing sleep to overtake us. Tomorrow is another day, and I can only imagine what Thana has planned for us.

CYRUS

The sun breaks over the horizon, creeping past the curtains into the room. Gage looks as beautiful asleep as he awakes. The sheet rests on his hip, leaving his chest bare to me. My eyes wander over his toned physique and I appreciate the Adonis before me. It's as if the Goddess of sin sculpted him to embody every wet dream I've ever had. From his broad chest to his strong thick ass, I love groping.

I think about all the changes that have happened in the last seven years. Finding our mate in Thana, and all of our children. The bonus in all of this is the love I have found with Gage. He was the wild card pops up at the most clutch time. His love and affection and unconditional nonjudgmental way he is with me. Kissing his cheek, I decide to wake him up. His smile is radiant as he stretches his body out as he turns to face me.

"Morning handsome." Gage caresses my cheek.

"How's my husband this morning?" Leaning forward, I kiss his pillow soft lips. My heart swells with love and happiness. It almost ranks up there with the day that I realized Thana was mine and we had our children.

Laughing softly, he scoots himself up off the bed and sighs. "Fantastic. We have the best family anyone could ever hope for."

"I know a bastard like me never felt I deserved to have a mate. But to have a mate and a husband. Mind blowing. Children? It was never an option on the plate." I try to use my, as Gage calls it, my bad boy swagger. I turned the smolder on and watch Gage melt before me and he sighs.

"You deserve everything, Cy." Gage's tone is filled with love as he slides off the bed and kisses me before slipping into the closet.

I leave the bedroom and wander as I think about the grand life that I have. Gage and Thana make me question everything every single day. I was an asshole most of my life, then I was a coffee and cookie thief with Thana at work. Call it my way of expressing I had a crush on the pretty nurse. As much as Raphael was a thorn in my side, he ended up being one of my biggest allies.

Musing over my life with Thana and the guys is easy. Metatron has a rather dickish side to him when he wants. He likes to use the last of whatever your favorite thing is when he's mad at you. Christian is a master at pressure points and when he's upset, he hits that point, sending you to your knees. Raphael is a whole different animal. When he's upset, he consumes Thana's time being an attention whore.

Shaking my head, musing over how our family deals with things almost cracks me up. Take Thana, for instance. When she's mad at Gage and me, she heads to the angelic realm where we can't sense here. When she's mad at the angelic side, she heads into hell and hangs out in the ring. When everyone has calmed down, we sit together as a family and hear out what bothered the person who's upset.

Finishing my musing, I had wandered out of the suite and downstairs to the main part of the castle. Nikita and Tiamat have come to an accord and are sitting gossiping thick as thieves at a table alone. The rest of the children disperse throughout the room in little groups, talking and playing. The other fathers gather around the island at the edge of the kitchen, watching Klaus and Jayce cook in the kitchen.

"Good morning, gentlemen!" I announce as I approach the group.

Jayce comes squealing around the counter and wraps me up in a hug. "We hope you enjoyed the wedding. Thana and everyone worked so hard on it!"

Laughing, I return the hug before he scampers off back around the counter. "That was surprising," Raphael states with an amused smirk on his face.

"Why's that, oh fearless leader?" I wink at him before grabbing the offered cup of coffee from Christian.

"Usually you're not the hugging type." Christian's statement is spot on, and I arch a brow in response.

"Yeah?" I'm not even sure how factual that statement is.

With a solid backslap, Metatron rocks me forward from the impact. "Besides Thana and Gage, you are distant."

"Don't forget the children! He's very good with them." Gage's dreamy tone makes me turn to face him as he arrives.

"Always the children. The rest of you fuckers need to earn the hugs." The shadows wrap around me for a mere moment before vanishing as I hug Gage.

Thana manifests before us and smiles, her tricolored wings on display. "How's the newlyweds?" She swoops in for a quick kiss and nuzzles both of us.

"Wonderful Kitten. Where are you off to?" Glancing around, I can only assume she and Aurora are about to head out on an adventure.

Shaking her head and rolling her eyes, Thana laughs. "Aurora and I are off to visit her father and stepmom for a little bit. He believes there's a demon in the winter castle, so I'm gonna investigate."

The mere thought of battling a demon has Thana excited to the point the air feels electrified. Hell, both females are legends in battle, and to have them teamed up is terrifying. It's then that I look over at Nikita and Tiamat as they approach.

"Mom…" the girls say at the same time. Nikita with shadows in her snow-white hair and Tiamat with frost coating hers.

Thana and Aurora look at each other for a moment, then back to the girls. "Get your shit together wheels up in ten minutes." Aurora barks at the girls and they take off to get their things together.

"Wheels up? You realize they can fly?"

"Cyrus… I like you. Don't be such an asshole." Aurora narrows her eyes at me and points a taloned finger in my direction.

"Noted. Have a safe trip. Summon us if you need anything." Honestly, I'm not sure which female is more terrifying? The one that can rip your soul from your body or the one that can turn you into nothing.

"I know that look well, Cyrus." Alaric rests a hand on my shoulder, watching our mates move with precision through the hall to the exit. "Best bet is to not piss either off. I don't know about you, but

I like my balls right where they are." Alaric's words ring true, and all I can do is nod along. I've got nothing.

Tiamat and Nikita return to the hall to say their goodbyes.

"Daddy..." Nikita is taking that commanding tone her mother uses, and it's frightening.

"Yes, Angel?"

"Can I go full strength, or do I still need to hold back?"

"If there's danger... Do whatever you and your mother have to do to come back in one piece. Keep Aurora and Tiamat safe and their family there."

A slow curl of Nikita's lips sends a chill up my spine. The minute her eyes blacken I feel as if death itself stands before me. Her presence is stronger than her mother's in some senses. Lunging forward, Nikita hugs me and kisses my cheek before departing.

The minute she's next to Tiamat, she takes her hand and they vanish in a wisp of smoke. Stretching my senses out, I can feel that she's hot on her mother's tail, heading towards the Winter Palace. Those two will be a force to be reckoned with. Deep down, I know that when push comes to shove, they will back each other one hundred percent, just like their mothers do.

A bellowing laugh draws me out of my thoughts and I see Dimitri shaking his head, looking at me. "What's on your mind, big guy?"

"There goes Aurora and Thana. Take two."

"Except they exceed their mother's powers tenfold." Arnulf states as if its common knowledge.

"What do you mean, they exceed their mother's powers? Thana is the Destroyer, Aurora is the last Marelup," Raphael states, clearly confused.

Laughing, Arnulf waves and dismisses Raphael. I'm liking the Eagle more each time I get to be around him. Raphael's rank doesn't mean jack shit to him. "You cannot see their auras like I can. Trust me when I say they are stronger than their mothers." Without a backward glance, the fucker shifts into his golden eagle and flies out into the yard through the open door.

"Well, shit boys... I guess we have our hands full now, don't we?"

AUTHOR SOCIALS

About the Author

Serenity Rayne spends most of her time either howling at the moon or creating cheeky crafts in her lair. Since she published the first book in the bestselling Aurora Marelup series, she's released sixteen more books while surviving being a nurse during the COVID-19 pandemic.

Serenity writes strong women who find their way in the world through blood and fire, learning to love and trust the men who adore them. Her books also feature positive LGBTQ representation, loss, and all the emotions that transcend species. Though her catalog has been focused on paranormal why choose and horror, she is now branching out to write contemporary why choose as well. She lives on a farm with dogs, chickens, peacocks, a one-eyed horse, and her son, who is way more like her than he wants to admit.

FOLLOW SERENITY EVERYWHERE:

Facebook: Serenity Rayne

Readers Group

Twitter: Author Serenity Rayne

Instagram: Author Serenity Rayne

Goodreads: Serenity Rayne

BookBub: Serenity Rayne

Amazon: Serenity Rayne

Website: https://www.serenityrayne.com

JOIN MY PACK UPDATES!

Bi-weekly updates on new releases, snippets from works in progress and contests. Click the link and join in on the pack fun!

https://www.subscribepage.com/o0b9s4

Also by Serenity Rayne

Pre-orders:

Claimed by the Alpha Pack

Luna Found

Shifters:

Children of the Moon: New Moon Rising

Her Elemental Mates

The Aurora Marelup Saga

Ascend

Hunt

Fight

Attack

Welcome Home

Klaus Christmas

Princess Lost

Destiny Found

Tiamat

The Dark Angel Chronicles:

Discovered

Innate

Balance

Destroyer

Nikita

Stand alones:

Heart Shaped Box

Blood Moon Pack

Once Upon the a Raven